catal

Chapter 121

The sun blazed a fiery red, embedded amidst the clouds woven from crimson leaves. The azure sky was trimmed into ribbons by branches, winding between the sun and the clouds.

Within this enchanting scenery, Zhou Yi swiftly dashed across the fields and entered the Yuan family estate. Although it was daytime, Zhou Yi's speed was unimaginable. Even if someone caught a glimpse, they would only perceive a flicker, unaware that a person had passed right under their noses.

This was the result of Zhou Yi's recent epiphany atop the mountain, where he fused the natural drizzle and mist with the innate light-footwork techniques of the Xiao family's two brothers, creating a brand-new art of nimble movement. Zhou Yi named it the "Cloud and Rain Soaring Technique." Although this was his first official technique creation, its power far surpassed the brothers' innate technique.

However, this was because the Xiao brothers were merely at the acquired realm and couldn't truly master the innate technique. If a true innate expert acquired their light-footwork technique and cultivated it to its peak, the comparison between these two techniques would depend on the cultivator's specific accomplishments.

Yet, in the absence of innate experts, when Zhou Yi displayed this technique, he became like a ghostly phantom, traversing without anyone's knowledge.

Upon returning to his room, Zhou Yi's heart surged with emotions. If he were still atop the mountain peak, he would undoubtedly let out another resounding howl to release the excitement within him.

The cultivation of the innate realm evoked an entirely different sensation compared to the acquired realm.

In the acquired realm, internal energy is cultivated step by step. Even with Zhou Yi's remarkable talent and physique, it would take about half a year to reach the pinnacle of a certain stage.

However, the innate realm was entirely different.

This morning's enlightenment at the mountain peak was not merely about comprehending a set of light-footwork techniques. His innate true qi reached an astonishing state of abundance. It seemed that during that moment of enlightenment, his body ascended to a new level, capable of accommodating several times more innate true qi than before.

At this moment, his innate true qi was at least twice as profound as yesterday. This transformation naturally filled him with ecstatic joy.

His eyes scanned the room and immediately realized that someone had been here. However, that person hadn't touched anything; they entered and left immediately, not even disturbing the Great guan dao he had placed in his bedding.

His eyebrows furrowed slightly but quickly relaxed. Only his Uncle and Elder Brother would dare to enter without his permission. As for the servants of the Yuan family, they probably didn't have the audacity.

Zhou Yi's face broke into a smile as his eyes shifted. Although his clothes had dried under the heat of his true qi, they had developed some wrinkles. He changed into a fresh set of clothes, placed the worn ones in a basket in his room, and positioned the basket by the window.

This was a rule of the Yuan family: if one placed their clothes in this designated spot, dedicated servants would come and retrieve them, sparing guests any unnecessary effort.

Evidently, Yuan Chengzhi and the others had gone to great lengths to ensure their comfort during their stay at the Yuan family.

Zhou Yi left his room and swiftly arrived outside his elder brother's door in the courtyard. His ears twitched slightly, and he immediately heard the long and powerful breaths emanating from inside.

As Zhou Yi listened to the sound of breathing, it gradually gave him a sensation as if he were standing in boundless plains. He silently admired it, knowing that his elder brother was diligently cultivating his internal energy, which made his breaths become so long and forceful. Through his innate realm perception, Zhou Yi also knew that Zhou Yitian had made significant progress in the Earth-element cultivation techniques and had deeply grasped their essence.

This was perfectly aligned with his natural disposition that harmonized well with Earth-element techniques. It was estimated that in a few more years, even without the Energy-Boosting Golden Pill,he could reach the pinnacle of the seventh layer. However, when he would be able to break through to the eighth layer and advance his internal energy, no one could guarantee.

After listening outside the door for a while, until he noticed his brother's breath suddenly thinning and becoming rapid, Zhou Yi lightly knocked on the door. He had already discerned from the sound of breathing that his brother had completed his practice.

This place was not the Zhou family's main residence, and it wasn't possible to engage in long periods of cultivation here. Zhou Yitian was surprised to hear the knocking on the door right after he finished his practice. He got up and opened the door, a hint of joy flashing across his face, followed by a complaint. "Little brother, where did you go last night? Did you go to track that masked person?"

Zhou Yi scratched his head with a sheepish smile, chuckled twice, and then walked into the room.

Zhou Yitian shook his head slightly as he looked at Zhou Yi's mischievous smile, feeling a sense of helplessness. But then he was taken aback and scrutinized Zhou Yi with a bewildered gaze.

Zhou Yi was taken aback and asked, "Elder brother, what's wrong?"

Zhou Yitian furrowed his brows and said, "It's strange. It seems something has happened to you. There seems to be a change compared to yesterday."

Zhou Yi was astonished in his heart. His emotions had fluctuated greatly yesterday, and this morning he had gained insights from observing the clouds and rain. Although his appearance hadn't changed much, his mental state had indeed undergone a transformation, and his innate true energy had become nearly twice as abundant.

However, his elder brother's perceptiveness was remarkable. He could even notice such subtle changes.

Zhou Yi chuckled and said, "Elder brother, you're overthinking. I am still me. Am I not?"

Zhou Yitian was momentarily puzzled by his words but quickly understood. However, the feeling he had before had completely disappeared. He teasingly scolded, "You little rascal, always talking nonsense." Then his expression slightly darkened as he continued, "That person yesterday was a master at the tenth level of internal energy, and a practitioner of the Fire element. Yet you dared to secretly follow and spy on them. You have such audacity. When we return, I will have to report this to grandfather and the others."

Zhou Yi smiled bitterly and quickly interjected, "Elder brother,I have returned unharmed, and there was absolutely no danger."

Zhou Yitian snorted lightly, still seemingly dissatisfied.

He reached out and wiped his body, and as he withdrew his hand, it seemed as if he had performed magic, revealing a jade bottle in his hand. Zhou Yi looked at his elder brother with a smug expression on his face.

Zhou Yitian exclaimed in surprise,He couldn't believe his eyes as he failed to see how zhouyi achieved it. He felt a momentary blur, and suddenly there was an object in his hand. The skill and speed displayed were beyond his reach.

In fact, it was due to Zhou Yi's mastery of the innate imprint technique that his actions became so agile, far surpassing his previous abilities. Without grasping this extraordinary innate seal technique, he could never have performed such exaggerated movements.

"Big brother, do you know what this is?" Zhou Yi asked.

Zhou Yitian glanced at it with a hint of disdain on his face and replied, "What, you want to bribe me? I'm not interested."

With a smirk, Zhou Yi opened the bottle and poured out a golden pill.

The pill was pale yellow and as soon as it poured out, it began spinning rapidly in Zhou Yi's palm, filling the entire room with a peculiar fragrance.

Zhou Yitian's expression gradually turned serious. Although he had never seen a golden pill before, the invigorating aroma immediately informed him of its considerable value.

"What is this?" he asked.

"This is a golden pill," Zhou Yi replied.

"A golden pill?" Zhou Yitian stood up suddenly, his gaze filled with astonishment. After hesitating for a moment, he whispered, "Little brother, is this the kind of golden pill that can break through the limits of one's cultivation?"

Zhou Yi shook his head slightly and said, "No, big brother. That kind of golden pill is called the Limit-Breaking Golden Pill. What I have here is a Energy-Boosting Golden Pill."

A tinge of disappointment flashed across Zhou Yitian's face as he asked, "What is its use then?"

"The Energy-Boosting Golden Pill is a kind of elixir that enhances one's vitality. Once consumed, it instantly boosts one's energy. If you cultivate diligently during this period, it can greatly enhance your inner strength, even reaching the pinnacle of your current level," Zhou Yi explained solemnly.

He was not wrong in his explanation. This kind of golden pill had a significant effect on cultivators at the ninth level of inner strength. If Zhou Yitian, who possessed only the seventh level of inner strength, were to consume it, he would undoubtedly reach the peak of the seventh level in a short period of time.

A flicker of excitement appeared on Zhou Yitian's face. Although this golden pill didn't possess the exaggerated effects of the Limit-Breaking Golden Pill, it was still a precious and rare item for cultivators. It would be deceiving to claim that he was not moved by it.

Zhou Yi handed the golden pill over and said, "This item is extremely valuable. Even a ninth-level cultivator can only consume one every ten days. I estimate that if you consume one per year, it should be sufficient."

Zhou Yitian carefully accepted the item, hesitated for a moment, and asked, "Where did you get this? Did you encounter that masked person?"

Zhou Yi shook his head slightly and said, "Big brother, don't worry about that. We only have a few days left before the ten-day agreement with the Fan family. You should take it quickly and elevate your inner strength to the peak of your current level."

Zhou Yitian looked at the golden pill in his hand and finally couldn't resist the temptation that was almost fatal for a cultivator. He sat back down, consumed the pill, and his expression immediately changed. He began circulating his inner strength.

After taking a few steps back, Zhou Yi left his elder brother's room and gently closed the door. He released a subtle strand of true energy, and the hidden mechanism on the door automatically locked, as if controlled by invisible hands.

Next, Zhou Yi found the steward of the Yuan family, who was in charge of this courtyard, and instructed him to inform everyone that his elder brother was diligently cultivating his inner strength and should not be disturbed by anyone.

The steward naturally nodded and dared not show the slightest hint of negligence.

Zhou Yi was quite satisfied with his attitude and turned to his uncle's residence. From a distance, he could hear the voices of two people in the room, accompanied by the sound of something peculiar, as if small stones were being struck.

An image instantly appeared in his mind.

Zhou Quanxin and Yuan Chengzhi, sitting in the room, sipping tea and playing chess.

He smiled faintly, feeling increasingly free in controlling and comprehending true energy. It seemed that the quantity of his true energy was also constantly increasing. However, he didn't know when it would reach its full capacity.

The door to his uncle's room was not closed, and Zhou Yi softly called out from the doorway. Zhou Quanxin replied loudly, "Yi, come in."

After receiving news of Zhou Yi's disappearance, Zhou Quanxin appeared indifferent on the surface, but in reality, he was somewhat worried. It was not until Zhou Yi returned that he finally felt relieved.

Zhou Yi approached the two of them, briefly scanning the chessboard before looking away.

He didn't have time to delve into the arts of music, chess, calligraphy, and painting. He recognized the chess pieces, but to him, their primary purpose was as hidden weapons.

"Uncle, my elder brother asked me to inform you that he intends to seclude himself for a few days," Zhou Yi said.

Zhou Quanxin placed the chess piece he was holding down and asked in surprise, "Why would he suddenly have this idea? It's not the time for seclusion."

In front of Yuan Chengzhi, Zhou Yi didn't want to reveal the matter of the golden pill, so he forced a bitter smile and said, "Perhaps my elder brother had a sudden inspiration."

Zhou Quanxin gave him a sharp look, clearly disapproving of his explanation. However, because of Yuan Chengzhi's presence, he didn't want to delve into it at that moment.

Zhou Yi quickly changed the topic and said, "Uncle Yuan, I have a question to ask you."

Yuan Chengzhi laughed heartily, "Yi, don't be polite. If you have any questions, please go ahead. I won't hide anything from my nephew."

"I wanted to ask if you know a person named Lv Xinwen," Zhou Yi asked solemnly.

"Lv Xinwen?" Yuan Chengzhi took a deep breath, a trace of astonishment appearing on his face. He said, "Why do you want to inquire about this person, nephew?"

Seeing his expression, Zhou Yi's heart tightened, but he didn't show any flaws on his face. Instead, he smiled and said, "During our last visit to the county city with my elder brother, I overheard someone mentioning him. It seems that he is a formidable individual."

Yuan Chengzhi finally understood, he sighed lightly and said, "Nephew, what you said is true. This person is indeed an extraordinary individual."

Curiosity sparked within Zhou Quanxin, as he asked, "Brother Yuan, who exactly is this extraordinary person? Could he be the patriarch of some prestigious family?"

Yuan Chengzhi smiled wryly and replied, "If this person were the patriarch of a renowned family, I wouldn't hold him in such high regard. Let me tell you about Lv Xinwen. He is said to be an orphan who wandered the rivers and lakes from a young age. However, he possessed exceptional intelligence and was diligent in his martial arts training. Over time, his fame grew, and he became a renowned master in the region. Countless noble families sought to recruit him, but he always dismissed their advances. Eventually, his disdainful attitude ignited the fury of a thousand-year-old influential family. He was ambushed by three peers of the same level as him, but he fought his way out, leaving a trail of bloodshed before disappearing."

Zhou Quanxin's expression subtly changed, for he knew the implications of facing three peers at the same level, which undoubtedly meant they were experts at the tenth level of internal strength. Otherwise, Yuan Chengzhi wouldn't have spoken with such caution.

"What happened afterward?" Zhou Yi inquired, eager for more information. "He couldn't have disappeared forever, right?"

Yuan Chengzhi nodded slightly and continued, "You're right. Lv Xinwen reemerged after a complete disappearance of ten years. Twenty-five years ago, his first act was to enter the stronghold of that thousand-year-old family and slaughter every member, earning him the nickname 'Butcher of Blood.' He left no one alive, annihilating the entire family."

Yuan Chengzhi's face displayed a hint of terror as he added gravely, "Their entire lineage, men, women, and even the pets were not spared."

Zhou Quanxin's face turned pale, a look of sheer astonishment in his eyes. "A innate expert?" he asked.

"Yes," Yuan Chengzhi nodded, his voice heavy with weight. "That family had a thousand-year-old heritage and possessed four experts at the tenth level of internal strength. Only a innate expert could have slain them all on the spot, leaving no chance for escape."

Zhou Quanxin pondered for a moment and asked, "How did he become a innate expert?"

Yuan Chengzhi sighed helplessly and said, "There are many legends surrounding this, but the most credible one suggests that he discovered the cave of an ancient innate cultivator and obtained a innate (innate) Golden Pill, which enabled him to break through."

Zhou Quanxin clicked his tongue, his eyes filled with envy. Such good fortune could only be encountered once in many lifetimes.

Suddenly, Zhou Yi raised his head and calmly asked, "Uncle Yuan, how many people are in that family?"

"From top to bottom, including servants, there are at least a thousand," Yuan Chengzhi replied.

"A thousand?" Zhou Yi murmured, pondering for a moment before asking, "Uncle Yuan, if over a thousand people scattered and fled, how could one possibly kill them all?"

Yuan Chengzhi shook his head, believing it to be obvious. "I don't know, but a innate expert should be capable, shouldn't they?"

Zhou Yi rolled his eyes, realizing that Yuan Chengzhi was overly superstitious about innate experts. While innate experts were formidable, possessing an inexhaustible supply of innate Qi, they were still individuals. If a thousand people dispersed, it would be impossible to slaughter them all. Achieving such a feat would transcend being a innate powerhouse; it would require god-like powers.

Yuan Chengzhi sighed deeply, a solemn expression on his face. "An eye for an eye, uprooting the grass, that is the true nature of a man."

Zhou Yi was taken aback, his gaze towards Yuan Chengzhi carrying a trace of curiosity. Killing over a thousand people, including the elderly, weak, and innocent, was described by Yuan Chengzhi as the true nature of a man. This mentality...

He understood it, but at his current stage, he couldn't fully accept it. However, upon hearing this news, his expression subtly changed as well. He hadn't expected this person's thirst for revenge to reach such extreme levels. It could be foreseen that once this person learned that his three disciples had been killed by Zhou Yi's hands, he wouldn't stop until he had sought vengeance, possibly even involving Zhou Yi's family.

But upon further thought, the Xiao family brothers had already made it clear that they would seek Lv Xinwen's assistance to completely annihilate the Zhou family. Even if Zhou Yi hadn't acted and killed their three disciples, they wouldn't spare the Zhou family. In that sense, whether he acted or not didn't make much difference.

With this thought, his determination grew within him. Although he had heard that Lv Xinwen was a powerful figure who had entered the innate realm over twenty years earlier than him, Zhou Yi's heart remained calm and resolute.

Before stepping into the innate realm, he had yearned for it and held various fantastical speculations. But after attaining it, he realized that while time played a role in cultivating the innate realm, the most important factor was the process of enlightenment.

A moment of enlightenment could lead to a tremendous increase in strength.

His fists tightened slightly, and if Lv Xinwen were to come, he would let him experience the power of the Great Guandao's Thirty-Six Forms of Mountain-Crushing

Chapter 122

After leaving Uncle's room, Zhou Yi returned to his own chamber, taking out the great guan dao and heading once again towards the depths of the mountains.

Knowing that Lv Xinwen was a cultivator of innate strength, Zhou Yi didn't feel any fear, but he also dared not be careless. When facing an innate powerhouse, any negligence or deception would be no different from seeking death.

Zhou Yi's most powerful martial technique at the moment was undoubtedly the " Thirty-Six Forms of Mountain-Crushing." This innate technique could not only be used as a palm technique but also integrated into his blade techniques.

Of course, only by employing the great guan dao could the full power of this innate technique be unleashed. Zhou Yi didn't understand why he had this feeling, but using the great guan dao to perform the Thirty-Six Forms of Mountain-Crushing gave him an unparalleled sense of exhilaration.

Given the upcoming confrontation with a formidable enemy, Zhou Yi naturally wouldn't give up his most potent weapon and technique. With the great guan dao strapped to his back, his movements were swift as lightning, even faster than before, as he ran towards the mountains.

He seemed to transform into a wisp of light smoke, carried away by the gentle breeze, swiftly vanishing from the vicinity without anyone noticing, leaving the Yuan family estate behind.

This speed showcased the utmost mastery of the Cloud and Rain Soaring Technique, with a sense of increasing proficiency the more he utilized it.

Before long, Zhou Yi arrived at the location where the great guan dao was being re-forged. The scenery remained in disarray, and he knew that he wouldn't be able to completely restore the area to its original state in such a short time.

He reached out and unfastened his backpack, then Zhou Yi gently lifted one corner and gave it a flick in the wind. The three sections of the great guan dao instantly soared into the sky.

The seemingly heavy great guan dao floated in the air as if weightless. In that moment, Zhou Yi's body trembled, but it was just a slight sway. He felt as though he was about to vaporize, as if standing in place not as a person but as an illusion, a mist.

Then, his footsteps moved, and it was no longer just one person. In an instant, he took countless steps, as if simultaneously stepping out dozens, hundreds, or even thousands of steps around him.

These footsteps were not mere illusions but solidly landed on the ground. It was like an endless mountain rain, shrouding the entire mountain.

In a trance, Zhou Yi's figure transformed into this mist, into this storm of rapid winds.

Suddenly, his figure paused, and he alternated his feet, consecutively tapping the air multiple times. At the same time, his arms extended, catching the three sections of the great guan dao as they fell from the air.

His hands shook with incredible speed, leaving a trail of afterimages in the sky, and in an instant, he assembled the great guan dao directly in mid-air.

With the display of the blade technique, suspended in mid-air, the Thirty-Six Forms of Mountain-Crushing were unleashed, as if the weight of Mount Tai was pressing down.

With a loud bang, Zhou Yi thumped onto the ground, though not completely falling flat on his backside. He was in quite a disheveled state, but fortunately, the handle of the great guan dao was firmly embedded in the ground, preventing him from falling.

Taking a slight breath, a faint blush appeared on his face as the awe-inspiring momentum from before vanished in an instant.

Looking at the great guan dao in his hand, he secretly breathed a sigh of relief in his heart.

What he had just attempted was to integrate the Thirty-Six Forms of Mountain-Crushing from the great guan dao into his own body movement technique. If he could combine these two innate combat techniques, Zhou Yi was certain that he would unleash unparalleled immense power.

Two innate techniques, if they could truly overlap, the effect would be not just additive but terrifyingly multiplicative.

If he could truly achieve this, then he would have an extra level of confidence when facing the impending innate experts.

However, the Thirty-Six Forms of Mountain-Crushing belonged to the metal element innate technique, while the body movement technique he created, the Cloud and Rain Soaring Technique, was clearly a type of elusive and ethereal technique, resembling a graceful dragon. It had significant differences from the indestructible Thirty-Six Forms of Mountain-Crushing. It wouldn't be easy to successfully merge these two techniques into one.

With a soft sigh, Zhou Yi's brow furrowed once again.

In fact, he had long considered this issue and knew that resolving the conflict between these two techniques wasn't very difficult. After all, it was a matter of coordination between combat techniques, far less challenging than reconciling conflicts between primary cultivation techniques.

As long as he had sufficient time, say one or two decades of dedicated practice, he could essentially resolve this problem.

At that time, it wouldn't be a difficult task to use the body movement of the Cloud and Rain Soaring Technique to wield the great guan dao and unleash the Thirty-Six Forms of Mountain-Crushing.

However, what Zhou Yi currently lacked the most was time. He was certain that Lv Xinwen would never allow him to delay for ten or twenty years before dueling with him.

If possible, Lv Xinwen would undoubtedly eradicate the Zhou family, killing them all, and Zhou Yi would undoubtedly be the first on that list.

After hesitating for a moment, Zhou Yi looked up, his gaze fixed on the sky, as if something remarkable up there had captured his attention.

Suddenly, his figure moved again, this time climbing towards the tall mountains, until he reached the spot where he had gained enlightenment earlier that morning.

He gazed into the distance, where the mountains stretched endlessly, appearing boundless. In comparison, he felt like a mere speck of dust, so insignificant in this vast expanse.

He slowly extended the great guan dao, the formidable weapon that had drawn the attention of countless people, yet even it couldn't surpass a fraction of this grand mountain.

Zhou Yi closed his eyes slowly, and it seemed as though his consciousness returned to that moment of enlightenment.

At this moment, in this place, he seemed to once again enter that wondrous state he experienced during his initial realization.

In his mind, the silhouette composed of clouds, rain, and mist appeared once more.

As the figure executed the Cloud and Rain Soaring Technique, it seemed to possess a more graceful and carefree aura than Zhou Yi himself. Gradually, the mist churned and coalesced into a great guan dao in the hands of the figure.

However, after obtaining the great guan dao, the transformation of the figure seemed to encounter some obstacles.

But this situation didn't last long. The great guan dao in the figure's hand gradually became weightless and skillfully wielded.

A series of sharp blade techniques were unleashed by the figure, but it wasn't the Thirty-Six Forms of Mountain-Crushing. Instead, it was a spontaneous blade technique that harmonized with the body movement.

Within these techniques, there were no fixed patterns but constantly shifting movements in tandem with the body technique.

As Zhou Yi focused all his energy, the images that appeared in his mind were not of monsters or demons, but rather an ability he had discovered after his enlightenment.

After observing the mountain rain and morning mist, his inner Qi spread boundlessly. As he exchanged Qi with the world's natural energy, a profound sensation arose in his mind. It seemed that after exploring the mysteries of the origin of clouds and mist, the essence of clouds and mist merged with his subconscious, allowing him to fully grasp the transformative abilities of clouds and rain.

Reflecting this subconscious in his mind was an additional presence—a silhouette that was proficient in all the variations of clouds and rain. It was this subconscious entity, imbued with the power of the cloud and rain origin, that consolidated all the techniques into one and ultimately created the Cloud and Rain Soaring Technique.

At this moment, what Zhou Yi was attempting to do was to integrate the great guan dao and the Thirty-Six Forms of Mountain-Crushing into this subconscious entity. He hoped that his subconscious silhouette would fuse these two extraordinary techniques together within a short period of time.

This was not a mere legend but a unique training method. Just as some avid readers, despite tirelessly studying and memorizing the previous night, couldn't retain everything, their memories often became clearer after a good night's sleep. With continuous recitation, these memories would become more ingrained until they became unforgettable.

Zhou Yi found himself in a similar situation. However, he was once again in an enlightened state. After mastering the power of the cloud and rain origin, it seemed to trigger a mysterious force within his body, manifesting this ability more tangibly in his mind.

Through the practice of the subconscious silhouette, Zhou Yi was able to compress the time required to integrate these two incompatible innate combat techniques to a terrifying extent.

After a long time, Zhou Yi, standing at the mountaintop, suddenly moved. His footsteps were as swift as the wind and rain, treading vigorously in all directions. Despite being on the mountaintop and closing his eyes, it seemed as if his feet had invisible eyes. No matter how exaggerated his movements were, he never stepped beyond the edge and faced the tragic fate of falling off the cliff.

When his feet reached a critical point, his body suddenly leaped high, gliding in mid-air as if he had grown wings like a bird. If an ordinary person witnessed this scene, they would surely bow and call him a deity. But if a practitioner witnessed it, their eyes would widen in astonishment.

To attain such mastery in lightness techniques was almost beyond the limits of what the human body could achieve. Indeed, the bodies of every innate expert had been cleansed by the Qi of heaven and earth and continued to undergo transformations from the Qi. Their physical strength far surpassed that of postnatal cultivators, which was the greatest advantage innate experts possessed.

It was not an exaggeration to say that they exceeded the limits attainable by postnatal cultivators.

Hovering in mid-air, Zhou Yi flipped his wrist, and the great guan dao once again cut through the air. A massive blade light surged forth from the first section of the blade, resembling a lightning bolt as it shot out with immense power.

This blade light, despite being ethereal in nature, possessed the strength of a peerless divine weapon forged from refined steel. Any place touched even slightly by the blade light would instantly be severed into two halves. Even the weathered rock walls that had withstood countless years of wind and rain could not escape being cleaved open by a single strike.

Zhou Yi's feet touched the ground, and a powerful surge of true Qi erupted beneath him, resembling the forceful jet stream of a jet engine.

A booming sound, like the beating of a drum, echoed from the ground, inexplicably creating two large craters.

At the same time, Zhou Yi's body leaped high into the air, lifting the great guan dao high above his head like a demonic deity. A tremendous aura surged from his body, and the towering great guan dao finally came crashing down with great force.

A gleaming blade light separated from the blade, swiftly traversing the space before it, and in an instant, it appeared on a massive tree tens of meters away. Then, in a flash, it vanished without a trace.

Zhou Yi opened his eyes, his mouth agape in astonishment. The movements he had just performed seamlessly fused the Thirty-Six Forms of Mountain-Crushing with the Cloud and Rain Soaring Technique. Not only did he encounter no obstacles, but it seemed as if the two techniques complemented each other perfectly, like a fish in water.

And his final strike was unimaginably powerful, to the extent that it even triggered the release of the blade light from the great guan dao. This was something he had never imagined before. Even he was overwhelmed by the astonishing outcome. The combination of these two combat techniques seemed to have elevated their respective powers to a whole new level.

However, all the credit belonged to that ethereal silhouette that appeared in his mind after his enlightenment. It seemed to possess a miraculous ability to unify fragmented and incomplete techniques into one, creating something entirely unique to Zhou Yi himself.

This connection had a great deal to do with his unique physical attributes.

Zhou Yi's body contains all the techniques of the Five Elements, but the internal force and true Qi condensed from these techniques become a chaotic mass once they pass through his meridians and return to his dantian. It seems that no matter what technique he cultivates, the total amount of his true Qi always increases. And when he uses a particular set of techniques, his true Qi automatically acquires all the characteristics of that set.

It is precisely because of this strange and miraculous constitution that Zhou Yi was able to break through his limits and reach his current state in such a short period of time. Previously, only his internal force and true Qi exhibited this characteristic, but now, after a mysterious enlightenment, it seems that even his combat techniques have undergone a similar transformation.

Letting out a soft sigh, Zhou Yi's mind was filled with endless questions. He knew that all these changes ultimately stemmed from the extraordinary encounter he had at the bottom of the lake that day. However, what baffled him was what exactly that mass of light was and how it possessed such incredible abilities.

"Whoosh... Crash..."

A loud noise echoed from ahead, startling Zhou Yi from his contemplation. He raised his head in astonishment and his gaze froze in an instant. Before his eyes, the tree that had been struck by the blade light had collapsed. In the middle of the tree, smooth as silk, it had been cleanly severed by the blade without any resistance.

Following the tree's roots, he noticed a not-so-thick, elongated scar on the ground. This scar started from the tree's roots and extended in a straight line towards the distance.

Zhou Yi couldn't hide his expression of shock anymore as he witnessed all the trees and flowers along the way being severed by that long scar. He finally understood that the power of the blade light after it detached from the Guan Dao was immense, far surpassing the impact of his own fierce strikes with the great guan dao. If he were to encounter a similar blade light, would he truly be able to withstand it barehanded?

He withdrew his gaze and looked at the great guan dao in his hand. This enormous and terrifying weapon had become oddly endearing in his heart. However, a question emerged in his mind: Was the great guan dao really just an ordinary iron weapon?

After a while, he put away the great guan dao. Upon attempting to enter the state of enlightenment again on the mountaintop, he realized that no matter what he did, he couldn't enter that state anymore. He let out a sigh and turned to leave. Within a short day, he had entered the state of enlightenment twice in succession, which was truly remarkable. If he wasn't satisfied with that, it would be like a snake trying to swallow an elephant due to insatiable greed...

Inside the Zhengtong County City, at the residence of the Fan family, all the servants were extremely cautious and dared not make any loud noises. Their master, Fan Shu He, the current head of the Fan family, appeared unusually irritable and uneasy today. In the memories of the elder members of the household, it had been decades since they last saw him with such an expression. Therefore, everyone understood that something major had happened, something that even the master found troublesome and distressing.

Fan Haori hurriedly rushed into Fan Shu He's room, his face also filled with seriousness. He said, "Father, I have searched everywhere, but there is no trace of the two uncles."

A glint flashed in Fan Shu He's eyes as he asked, "Did they leave behind any letters?"

Fan Haori shook his head affirmatively, saying, "No, I personally searched the rooms where the two uncles stayed. There wasn't even a scrap of paper."

Fan Shu He fell into silence, seemingly deep in thought. After a moment, Fan Haori spoke softly, "Father, could it be that the two uncles left without a word because of their defeat that day?"

"Hmph." Fan Shu He snorted in anger and said, "I have known the Xiao family brothers for decades. Do you think I don't know what kind of people they are? They would never abandon their friends and flee before a battle."

Fan Haori took a step back, not daring to speak further, but he said, "But, Father, the two uncles have been missing for more than a day, and there are no signs of a struggle in their rooms..."

Even in his vexed mood, Fan Shu He couldn't help but chuckle and said, "Don't let your imagination run wild. Based on the abilities of your two uncles, it's impossible for someone to capture them without alerting us."

Fan Haori recalled the scene where the Xiao brothers joined forces to fight Zhou Quanxin that day and had to agree with his father's point.

With their combined strength, even as experts with ten layers of internal energy, it would be impossible for them to be subdued without alerting anyone. Fan Shu He furrowed his brow, pondering incessantly.

Suddenly, he felt that the surrounding air seemed different. He swiftly turned around, his face pale with shock. He exerted a slight force with his feet, leaping backward like a spring. In that instant, he instinctively and without hesitation reached out, grabbing Fan Haori's arm and pulling him gently behind him.

Chapter 123

In a spacious room, a warm fireplace radiated with vibrant charcoal fire, creating a stark contrast to the outside world. However, at this moment, Fan Shuhe felt a bone-chilling coldness enveloping his body.

In his room, at an unknown moment, there appeared an additional person.

This individual's temples showed hints of gray hair, yet his gaze was clear and slightly stern. His face, tinged with a purplish-brown hue, displayed a remarkable fullness on the forehead, cheeks, eye sockets, and ears, exuding an oddly lively and animated aura. Accentuating his rectangular face were well-defined thin lips, stubbornly downturned and slightly recessed.

With an icy stare, he fixed his gaze upon Fan Shuhe, as if in his eyes, this expert at the tenth level of internal strength was no different from a beggar on the street, incapable of stirring even the slightest ripple within his heart.

It was precisely this calm gaze that filled Fan Shuhe with shock and an indescribable sense of fear. As the current head of the Fan family, he was undoubtedly a well-traveled individual, having achieved the peak of the tenth level of internal strength before the age of sixty. His talent and efforts surpassed the imagination of ordinary people.

Similarly, in order to revive the Fan family, he had cultivated friendships with many highly skilled individuals. For instance, the Xiao brothers from the Xiao family were friends he had spared no effort to win over. However, among all his acquaintances, he had never encountered someone as profound and inscrutable as this person, and he had no clue as to when this person had entered his room.

After pulling his son, Fan Haori, behind him, Fan Shuhe took a step forward and a step back, assuming a stance that was both offensive and defensive. With composure, he asked, "May I know who you are, and what brings you to my humble abode?"

Fan Haori stole a glance from behind his father, and the shock in his heart was no less than that of his father's. It was the first time he had seen his father's slightly panicked expression moments ago.

He had always believed that his father was an indomitable man, a ten-level internal strength expert who could remain unperturbed even if Mount Tai collapsed before him. Therefore, when his father showed signs of fear, it stirred up a tumultuous storm within his own heart.

The peculiar figure, with slightly grayed hair yet brimming with vitality, did not respond nor acknowledge them. Instead, he turned around and seated himself on the grand chair in the middle of the room. His movements were not swift, but they evoked an unparalleled sense of gravity in Fan Shuhe and his son.

"You said it correctly," the man spoke slowly. His voice wasn't loud, yet it carried a daunting power.

Fan Shuhe was taken aback. How did this statement relate to his previous question? Cautiously, he respectfully asked, "Sir, are you referring to..."

"My disciples, indeed, are not the kind to flee at the critical moment," the man interrupted.

Fan Shuhe gasped, his eyes widening. "You... You are the master of the Xiao brothers?"

The man replied coldly, "What? Those two rascals didn't tell you?"

Fan Shuhe hesitated briefly, drawing back his feet and standing upright, he respectfully spoke, "Esteemed senior figure, the Xiao brothers have never mentioned their mentorship to me. They claim that only when their internal strength reaches the tenth level are they qualified to reveal the identity of their master."

Though his words seemed peculiar, they were undeniably true. Prior to this, Fan Shuhe had subtly inquired about the Xiao brothers on multiple occasions, but their responses had always been evasive, with the same statement.

If an ordinary nine-level internal strength expert had said such things, Fan Shuhe might not have believed them. Reaching the tenth level of internal strength was the limit that a postnatal cultivator could achieve. While there were many experts at the ninth level, who could guarantee that they would break through the final barrier and reach the tenth level?

However, the Xiao brothers were different. Not only did they possess two incredibly precious armguards, but they also clearly mastered a unique innate combat technique.

Words spoken by such individuals naturally carried little room for doubt.

Fan Shuhe had speculated countless times in secret, even entertaining the thought that their master might be an expert at the innate level. But it was merely speculation, for the gap between him and an innate expert was insurmountable, leaving him with an overwhelming sense of unattainability.

However, at this moment, upon seeing this extraordinary figure, his heart raced intensely. Perhaps his previous conjecture was not far from the truth...

Finally, a hint of a smile crept onto the man's lips, evidently pleased with the statement.

Fan Shuhe observed that confident smile and felt his heart sink slightly.

His demeanor grew even more respectful. "I am Fan Shuhe, and I have had a close relationship with the Xiao brothers for many years, treating each other as brothers. May I ask for the esteemed elder's name? If you are willing to reside in my humble abode, I am willing to serve as a representative of the Xiao brothers and attend to your needs."

The man paused for a moment, then chuckled arrogantly. "I am Lv Xinwen."

Both Fan Shuhe and his son trembled slightly.

Zhou Yi didn't recognize the name, but as members of the Fan family, born and raised in the Kingdom of Jinlin, how could they not know the name that represented terror?

Especially considering this person's notorious reputation for slaughtering thousands in a single day, it was enough to send shivers down the spine of any force.

In front of innate-level experts, unless they fought to the death without retreating, postnatal cultivators, no matter how numerous, would never be able to kill them. Before innate-level experts, postnatal cultivators posed no threat unless they amassed an overwhelming number.

In other words, innate experts regarded human lives as insignificant, relying solely on their individual strength.

The muscles on Fan Shuhe's face twitched slightly, and he hurriedly said, "So it is senior figure Lü's esteemed visit. I was unaware, please forgive me."

Lv Xinwen waved his sleeve and said, "Forget it. Since you have a connection with my two disciples, I won't make things difficult for you." Then, his gaze shifted to Fan Haori's face, and he suddenly asked, "Are you afraid of me?"

Fan Shuhe's heart tightened. The temperament of these innate-level experts was unpredictable. If Haori didn't handle the situation well, it would be extremely problematic.

However, despite being extremely nervous, Fan Haori remained remarkably composed. He took a step forward, walked out from behind his father, and knelt in front of Lv Xinwen, bowing deeply. He said, "senior figure Uncle, I was indeed afraid just now, but now I am not."

Lv Xinwen looked at him with interest and didn't stop him from kneeling. Instead, he asked, "Why is that?"

"I was afraid before because I had heard of your reputation, but as soon as I thought of you being the master of the two Xiao uncles, I wasn't afraid anymore," Fan Haori replied. While he spoke, there was still a hint of trembling, but he quickly became fluent, indicating that his words were sincere and not deceitful.

A hint of satisfaction appeared in Lv Xinwen's eyes, and he said, "Indeed, you are clever and have a decent level of courage. Being in your twenties and already at the seventh level of inner strength, more importantly, without having swallowed any Golden Pills, this aptitude is truly rare."

Fan Haori's heart trembled, and he suddenly felt an inexplicable joy. He immediately kowtowed again, his forehead touching the ground with a clear sound, as he did not use his inner strength to protect himself.

Lv Xinwen smiled faintly and asked, "Why do you kowtow to me?"

Fan Haori said solemnly, "senior figure, I admire you and only wish to serve you day and night in the future, accompanying you to fulfill my filial duty. I do not seek to become your direct disciple."

Fan Shuhe, standing behind his son, was both shocked and delighted. He knew that if they could gain the favor of the elderly man before them, it would be an incredible stroke of good luck for Fan Haori and the entire Fan family.

However, when facing Lv Xinwen, Fan Haori remained silent and dared not make any requests. He could only look at him with hopeful eyes and bend his waist respectfully.

Lv Xinwen, with an unchanged expression, said, "You want to serve by my side. Aren't you afraid of my notorious reputation?"

Fan Shuhe thought to himself, So you know about your own infamous reputation as well. However, he didn't dare show any signs of agreement and silently worried about how Haori would respond.

Fan Haori raised his head and said loudly, "senior figure, your reputation is renowned throughout the Kingdom of Jinlin. How can it be considered a notorious name?"

Lv Xinwen laughed heartily and said, "For over twenty years, it has been widely rumored in the Kingdom of Jinlin that I slaughtered over a thousand members of the Zhu family. Isn't that considered a notorious name?"

Fan Haori confidently replied, "senior figure, if I remember correctly, it was the Zhu family who provoked you first. It was only after you achieved your cultivation that you openly sought revenge. If we worry about this and that, how can we call ourselves men?"

Lv Xinwen finally burst into laughter, and his laughter was filled with indescribable satisfaction.

Both Fan Shuhe and his son felt relieved. The pressure they felt when they first heard of Lv Xinwen's name disappeared completely.

Both of them marveled at the situation because even they didn't understand why they had such a strange feeling. At that moment, their admiration for the old man before them grew even stronger.

Lv Xinwen put away his smile and said, "Alright, you child, you suit my taste. I'll keep you by my side."

Fan Haori was overjoyed and quickly prostrated himself. However, before his head could touch the ground, Lv Xinwen waved his sleeve, causing him to involuntarily rise.

"Now that I'm keeping you by my side, there are some things I can tell you. Over the years, the rumors circulating among outsiders are not entirely true. Although the Zhu family was despicable, I didn't completely annihilate them. I only killed around a hundred stubborn core members who refused to give up. As for the others, they had long scattered and fled." He smiled and continued, "Even if I had the intention to slaughter them all, it would have been impossible for me to do so. The rumors circulating outside are full of falsehoods and should not be entirely believed."

The Fan father and son widened their eyes and took a while to react. However, their hearts were not filled with disdain; instead, genuine gratitude appeared on their faces.

For someone of Lv Xinwen's status to explain this to them was a great honor they could never have imagined before.

Lv Xinwen glanced at them and asked, "Do you know why I told you about this?"

"Your junior doesn't know," Fan Shuhe respectfully replied, their tone more reverent than ever.

Lv Xinwen calmly said, "The Xiao Yi Fan brothers always speak highly of you after each expedition, calling you their sworn brother. Besides, I also find this young child pleasing to the eye. Otherwise..."

Slowly rising to his feet, Lv Xinwen declared, "Arrange a room for me to rest for half a day. As for the Xiao brothers, you need not worry. They should be off to pick up my esteemed disciple. It's just strange that no news has reached us."

Fan Shuhe felt a stir in his heart and gathered his courage to ask, "senior figure, has my big Uncle also arrived?"

Lv Xinwen smiled faintly, appreciating the child's obedience.

"Indeed, my esteemed disciple is named Zhuang Yuan. Have you heard of him?"

Fan Shuhe's expression changed slightly as he replied, "I have heard of him. My Uncle is a renowned practitioner in our kingdom of Jinlin. It is said that he has reached the tenth level in the Fire Elemental Art." Pausing for a moment, he added, "However, to my knowledge, my Uncle has yet to join any prominent family, a trait he seems to have inherited from you, senior figure."

Lv Xinwen nodded enigmatically, and then Fan Shuhe personally arranged accommodation for him. As for Fan Haori, he truly set aside his status as the young master of the Fan family and began to personally serve his senior figure.

However, this good mood lasted only two days. On the third day, there was still no news from Zhuang Yuan or the xiao Yi Fan brothers.

At this point, even Lv Xinwen, who had great confidence in them, began to feel restless. He summoned Fan Shuhe and started asking detailed questions, with the process of the xiao Yi Fan brothers' confrontation with Zhou Quanxin being the most concerning to him.

After hearing this news, Lv Xinwen pondered for a long time. He had Fan Haori get into a small carriage and headed towards the Yuan family estate. They left the city and traveled west until they reached a small forest outside the Yuan family estate.

The land in this area belonged to the Yuan family estate, but at this moment, Lv Xinwen suddenly called for a stop. Fan Haori, who was driving the carriage, quickly complied. He then saw Lv Xinwen's serious expression as he got out of the carriage and walked several rounds in that inconspicuous little forest.

Although Fan Haori was filled with doubt and unease, he didn't dare to speak out. Since Lv Xinwen arrived at their home, he had always exuded confidence, as if he were an invincible deity, as if nothing in this world could pose a challenge to them.

Indeed, with the combat power of an Innate expert, if there were things they couldn't accomplish, it would be difficult for others to do so as well.

However, in this small forest, Lv Xinwen's expression was one of disbelief, anger, sadness, and other intense negative emotions that made Fan Haori find it hard to believe. It seemed as if that expression contained a profound shock.

At this moment, the old man before him no longer seemed like the lofty Innate expert but had suddenly transformed into an ordinary elderly person.

After a long time, Lv Xinwen silently returned to the side of the carriage, seemingly lost in thought.

Fan Haori asked cautiously, "What happened, Uncle Grandfather?"

Lv Xinwen glanced at him and replied in a slow voice, "When I passed through this small forest, I suddenly felt extremely uncomfortable."

Fan Haori's face turned pale, and he said, "Uncle Grandfather, please take care of yourself."

Lv Xinwen forced a smile, waved his hand, and said, "It's nothing. It's just some uneasiness. But just now, I suddenly remembered Zhuang Yuan and the xiao Yi Fan brothers. That's why..." He sighed heavily and continued, "I am somewhat worried that they may be in great danger."

Fan Haori's heart turned as cold as ice, but he still said, "Uncle Grandfather, Uncle and the two brothers possess unparalleled martial skills. They will definitely be fine."

Lv Xinwen nodded slightly and said in a solemn tone, "I am well aware of their combined strength, more so than you. If there is anyone capable of posing a threat to them, it would only be an Innate expert."

With that, he strode forward, abandoning the carriage and heading directly towards the Yuan family estate. His pace became slower and slower, and his expression grew increasingly grave. Fan Haori, who followed behind him, became more and more anxious.

Finally, at a distance of over a hundred meters from the entrance of the Yuan family estate, Lv Xinwen came to a complete stop. He looked up, fixedly gazing at the vast manor, his eyes shimmering with an unparalleled brilliance.

Their movements had already alerted the guards stationed at the gate of the estate, but at this moment, those guards didn't even dare to take a breath. Although they couldn't possibly know who this old man was, they keenly felt the pressure emanating from him, rendering them motionless, like frogs being stared at by a venomous snake.

Suddenly, Fan Haori trembled all over. He couldn't explain why, but he felt an immense and unimaginable pressure. Although he didn't know where this pressure came from, that terrifying feeling, like the weight of Mount Tai pressing down on him, was undoubtedly real.

Fortunately, that pressure disappeared in just an instant.

However, at that moment, Lv Xinwen turned around and headed back without even looking back. Startled, Fan Haori immediately turned around and followed closely.

Lv Xinwen returned to the carriage and coldly asked, "How many days are left until our agreement with the Yuan family?"

"Uncle Grandfather, there are five days remaining," Fan Haori replied, still trembling from the lingering fear.

"Good, return immediately," Lv Xinwen's voice was eerily calm, devoid of any human emotion. "After returning, I will seclude myself and cultivate in peace. In five days, I will have a battle with that person to avenge the death of my disciple."

Fan Haori's face turned deathly pale, devoid of any trace of blood.

Chapter 124

At the summit of the mountain, Zhou Yi merged and comprehended the two profound ancestral combat techniques, then returned to the Yuan family, quietly awaiting what was to come.

Unexplainably, he had a certain feeling that Iv Xinwen would definitely come.

On this day, he rose early in the morning and silently practiced his cultivation in his room. Occasionally, a peculiar radiance would emanate from his body. This was a method he used to absorb the innate energy and refine his own acupoints. Although this method wasn't very efficient, it continuously stimulated his acupoints and gradually enhanced the resilience of his acupoints trained in the Five Elements Technique.

Unaware of it, Zhou Yi, who was engrossed in his training, couldn't possibly know that immediately after stepping into the innate realm, he could sense all his acupoints throughout his body and find ways to refine them. Although he wasn't the first to achieve this, he was definitely an extremely rare existence, like a phoenix feather horn.

This, in fact, was due to his unique constitution.

Suddenly, a powerful aura swept from outside the estate.

Within this aura, there was an immense and unimaginably oppressive force.

This force far surpassed the acquired realm and couldn't be sensed by ordinary acquired experts.

At this moment, a realization dawned upon Zhou Yi. That person had arrived, and he was openly issuing his most powerful provocation towards this place.

If it were a few days ago, before Zhou Yi successfully achieved enlightenment at the mountain summit, before his innate true qi had substantially increased, and before he merged and comprehended the two different ancestral combat techniques, he would have undoubtedly felt uneasy upon sensing this intense provocation.

But now, his eyebrows arched, and a similarly imposing pressure surged from his body, matching the magnitude of the other party's without falling short in the slightest.

However, unlike the other party, Zhou Yi didn't recklessly release his imposing aura. Instead, he soared his true qi into the sky, condensing it into a sphere suspended in mid-air. Then, he directed it towards the source of the tremendous pressure outside the estate.

This method, while avoiding detection by the people within the estate, presented a greater challenge in terms of release.

Outside the estate, lv Xinwen naturally didn't show any weakness either. The majestic aura released by the two innate experts clashed fiercely in this moment.

In the presence of an equally mysterious expert at the same level, both of them held back to some extent. However, even so, when the immense intangible forces of true qi collided unpretentiously outside the estate, it still resulted in a massive and terrifying outcome.

At the epicenter of the collision, all living creatures within a radius of several hundred meters felt a surge of unease. It was as if suddenly someone had stealthily infiltrated their surroundings and let out a resounding roar right next to their ears.

Although this method wasn't a direct killing technique, it could cause a person's heart to beat several times faster. For individuals with weak hearts, there was even the danger of their hearts being tightly gripped and succumbing to a sudden demise.

In that instant, the entire area fell into silence. A complete and utter silence. Not only did all voices cease to exist, but even the sounds of insects and birds instantly ceased. The fierce guard dogs in the estate, one by one, cowered with their tails tucked between their legs, their limbs weakened, as if they had encountered a natural predator, devoid of any strength.

Eerily, this space seemed dead, devoid of any signs of life.

Then, lv Xinwen swiftly turned around and departed.

However, Zhou Yi was slightly taken aback because from the intensity of the other party's true qi, he sensed the immense power of lv Xinwen. He could even conclude that if it came down to the strength of their true qi alone, despite his recent substantial increase, he might not necessarily be able to surpass this person.

However, for some reason, as soon as the other party made contact with his own true qi, after just one touch, it immediately retreated on the spot. This seemed to contradict the personality traits he had gathered about the Butcher.

Rubbing the large guan dao on the bed, Zhou Yi furrowed his brows. He had been prepared for these past few days, conserving his energy and sharpening his spirit to the utmost. That's why he was able to launch the most fierce counterattack upon initial contact and challenge with an even stronger momentum.

However, the other party's reaction was far beyond his expectations. Instead of continuing the engagement, they withdrew.

This was extremely unpleasant for Zhou Yi, as if he had thrown a full-force punch that was effortlessly deflected by the other party, or as if he had struck into a bundle of cotton, exerting no force at all.

Even he felt exceptionally uncomfortable with this sensation.

In a moment of clarity, he suddenly understood why lv Xinwen had retreated so easily.

Releasing his grip on the large guan dao, Zhou Yi's lips curled into a bitter smile. Innate experts, none of them were easy opponents after all!

Just then, a familiar set of footsteps came from outside the door. Zhou Yitian, his elder brother, had somehow emerged from his seclusion and found him, calling out, "Little brother, come out quickly. My father is looking for you."

In the county town, the Fan family, father and son, wore solemn expressions. If one were to judge solely based on their current demeanor, they appeared even more tense than the previous day.

In these past few days, although the disappearance of the Xiao brothers from the Xiao family had made them feel a sense of unease, they did not believe that there were individuals among the Yuan family who had the capability to detain the two of them.

However, after lv Xinwen had visited the Yuan family and made his rounds, their hearts were completely stirred. This was because Fan Hao had received verified information.

To their astonishment, there were experts at the innate realm within the Yuan family, and based on lv Xinwen's behavior, it seemed that this innate expert's strength was not to be underestimated. Not only were lv Xinwen's three disciples in great danger, but even lv Xinwen himself inexplicably retreated after circling the Yuan family estate.

All these signs deeply unsettled the Fan family, to the point where they regretted not knowing earlier that the Yuan family had the ability to invite an innate expert. If they had known, they would never have actively provoked them.

Fan Shuhe let out a long sigh and said, "Haori, you should go down first. Regardless of the circumstances, you must stay by the senior figure's side these few days. The Fan family has no way out now, and whether we can survive this disaster depends on senior figure Lv."

Fan Haori acknowledged with a nod, understanding the gravity of the situation. After reporting the details of his journey to his father, he promptly left.

The accommodations arranged for lv Xinwen were naturally the best private courtyard within the Fan family. Every detail inside was meticulously arranged, surpassing even the room where Fan Shuhe resided.

lv Xinwen was personally waiting before entering the courtyard. At this critical moment, Fan Haori didn't dare to disturb lv Xinwen's meditation easily.

However, a gentle voice came from inside, saying, "Come in."

Fan Haori was taken aback, then immediately respectfully walked in. When he saw lv Xinwen, his face couldn't help but change slightly.

At this moment, lv Xinwen's face showed a touch of sadness that hadn't been there before. Even though he had verbally stated that his three disciples were in great danger before entering the Yuan family estate, he had been as steady as a mountain, showing no signs of wavering. However, upon returning to this place, he couldn't conceal this expression.

Fan Haori's lips twitched, unsure of how to speak.

lv Xinwen suddenly asked, "Fan Haori, do you think that I am too cold-hearted and weak? Knowing that my three disciples are in great danger, with the culprit within the Yuan family estate, yet I dare not seek revenge for them immediately?"

Fan Haori quickly knelt down and respectfully said, "senior figure, your humble nephew absolutely does not have such thoughts."

"Oh, then how do you think?" lv Xinwen questioned.

Fan Haori hesitated for a moment, still kneeling, and continued, "Your humble nephew believes that the sudden appearance of an innate expert in the Yuan family is a matter of great significance. And at this moment, I can see that the enemy is in the dark while we are in the light. If we rashly challenge them, we might fall into a trap set by the enemy in advance. Therefore, it might be better to step back for now, gather information about the enemy's background, and then make a decision."

lv Xinwen looked at him quietly and finally showed a hint of relief. He said, "Rise."

Fan Haori slowly stood up, but his heart still felt as if walking on thin ice. Even his breathing was suppressed to the point of being barely noticeable.

"Although what you said is not entirely correct, it's not far off," lv Xinwen sighed softly. "I once had a brief exchange of true qi with the person from the Yuan family."

Fan Haori remembered the sudden overwhelming pressure at that time and instantly understood. He couldn't help but feel even more awe towards the innate expert because he didn't even understand how those two experts had tested each other.

Iv Xinwen's voice was gentle and ethereal. Fan Haori looked up and suddenly felt that the old man's figure seemed elusive. The words he spoke were not meant to explain anything to a nameless junior like him, but rather as if the old man was explaining it to himself.

"The person from the Yuan family has been preparing diligently, reaching the peak in terms of momentum, physical strength, and true qi. Meanwhile, I just sensed that my three disciples had suffered a tragic fate, causing my mind to waver. If we were to fight at that moment, even if I have a higher cultivation level, it would be difficult to win. Do you understand?"

Fan Haori respectfully replied, "Yes, I understand."

Iv Xinwen nodded slightly, waved his hand, and said, "Since you understand, you may leave. I will come out to meet you all in five days."

Fan Haori kowtowed once more, then slowly left.

The courtyard gate closed slowly, and there was no more movement inside. Not even the slightest sound could be heard. It was as if the inside and outside had suddenly become two different worlds, completely isolated by the closed door.

Fan Haori inexplicably stared at the closed door, casting aside all his worries in that moment. For some reason, he had a feeling that five days later, when the old man emerged, it would be the peak moment for him.

"Uncle, you called for me," Zhou Yi smiled as he entered his uncle's room. He knew very well what had happened. With his uncle's level of internal energy cultivation, he could undoubtedly sense that overwhelming pressure reaching its peak. That's why his uncle must have called for him.

In the room, besides Zhou Quanxin, there were Yuan Zeyu and Yuan Chengzhi, father and son.

Yuan Zeyu seemed to have made up his mind to pass on the leadership of the Yuan family. He had secluded himself during this period, not leaving his retreat. However, at this moment, he couldn't hold back any longer.

"Yi, did you sense it?" Zhou Quanxin asked with a solemn expression.

Zhou Yi nodded slightly and said, "Yes, I sensed it."

Zhou Quanxin spoke with a deep voice, "Brother Yuan, it's your turn to speak now."

Yuan Chengzhi nodded solemnly and said, "Uncle Zhou, nephew Yi, a message came from the servants who were guarding the main gate. A strange person arrived at the estate and lingered for a moment before immediately leaving. However, during that time, we all felt an immense pressure. Some of the servants still can't stand up because of it." He paused for a moment and continued, "If I'm not mistaken, all of this is the doing of that person."

In fact, Fan Haori was accompanying lv Xinwen, but the imposing aura of the innate powerhouse was too magnificent, attracting everyone's attention. Fan Haori was like a firefly in the sunlight, completely unnoticed. If Zhou Yitian were present, perhaps he would have noticed Fan Haori, but expecting the gatekeepers and servants to have such keen perception would be too demanding.

Zhou Quanxin spoke with a deep voice, "Brother Yuan, do you know who that person is?"

Yuan Chengzhi sighed repeatedly and said, "If I knew, I would have told Brother Zhou long ago. There's no need to keep it a secret."

Zhou Yitian glanced at his father and said, "Father, is this person related to the person from that night, the one who helped the Fan family?"

Zhou Quanxin shook his head expressionlessly and said, "I don't know, but since this person has come here, they are likely connected to the Fan family."

Yuan Zeyu suddenly let out a soft sigh and said, "Quanxin, I have a question to ask."

"Please go ahead," Zhou Quanxin slightly bowed.

"If this person truly assists the Fan family, do you have any confidence in being able to contend with them?" Yuan Zeyu stared at

Zhou Quanxin without blinking, as if he wanted to obtain some assurance from him.

Zhou Quanxin frowned slightly, and after a long while, he finally said, "Uncle Yuan, although I haven't seen this person, under the pressure of their aura just now, I couldn't even muster the thought of resistance."

The faces of Yuan Zeyu and Yuan Chengzhi turned pale. Zhou Quanxin was their strongest asset, but now the Fan family's experts kept emerging one after another. First, the Xia family brothers who possessed the innate light-footwork technique and armguards, and then someone infiltrated the Yuan family at night to test Zhou Quanxin's strength. Now, an inexplicable old man had appeared, and without even showing himself, he had already made Zhou Quanxin utter words of surrender.

These individuals were like rising tidal waves, one wave higher than the other, leaving the Yuan family overwhelmed and unable to cope.

Gradually, Yuan Zeyu's complexion changed several times, and he said, "Quanxin, what do you think about this person's strength? If Brother Zhou Wude personally takes action, can he win the fight?"

Although Zhou Quanxin was a powerhouse at the tenth level of internal energy, compared to Zhou Wude, who had already reached the pinnacle of the tenth level, he fell short. That's why he asked with a hint of hope.

Without hesitation, Zhou Quanxin shook his head and said, "Uncle Yuan, if my guess is correct, I'm afraid that person has already broken through the innate realm."

Although he spoke hesitantly, his tone was firm and unwavering.

The faces of Yuan Zeyu, Yuan Chengzhi, and Zhou Yitian instantly turned grim, while Zhou Yi maintained an unchanged expression.

All of this was observed by Zhou Quanxin, who couldn't help but sigh inwardly.

Yuan Zeyu pondered for a moment and suddenly said, "In that case, we don't need to prepare anything. Chengzhi, issue the order for our entire family to immediately withdraw from the estate. From now on, we will leave this estate

Yuan Chengzhi's expression changed, and he exclaimed, "Father..."

In fact, Yuan Zeyu and his group had long prepared for contingencies. They had already moved valuable items elsewhere beforehand, and they could leave at any time if they wished. However, until it came to the final moment, how many people could easily give up everything?

Yuan Zeyu waved his hand and said, "No need to say more. Since the other side has even hired innate experts, we have no chance of winning at all. Instead of dying at their hands, it's better for us to retreat first." He sighed deeply and helplessly added, "It's better to live in peace than to die gloriously. Being able to save our lives is the greatest fortune amidst misfortune."

Yuan Chengzhi and Zhou Quanxin exchanged glances, both wearing grim expressions. But as they recalled the oppressive pressure they had felt earlier, each person's heart felt as heavy as a boulder.

Yuan Zeyu forced a bitter smile and tried to console them. "We should actually consider ourselves fortunate. If that person had rushed in without reason, it would have been difficult for us to leave."

Everyone was startled by his words, and even Yuan Chengzhi seemed to waver.

Seeing the expressions of the group, Zhou Yi suddenly burst into laughter and said, "Uncle Yuan, I have a question I'd like to ask."

Yuan Zeyu was taken aback. "Go ahead."

"I want to ask, you all keep saying that this person is related to the Fan family. But do they really have a connection?"

Everyone was taken aback, and then a glimmer of hope appeared in their eyes.

Yuan Chengzhi slapped his thigh and said, "That's right! Who knows if this person simply took the wrong path..." As he said that, he shook his head, obviously not believing his own words. But he continued, "Regardless, we should investigate. Even if we have to retreat, we need to confirm the information.

Yuan Zeyu hesitated for a while but eventually agreed to his son's suggestion.

However, in the following days, they couldn't gather any information about that mysterious person. And amidst their anxiety and uncertainty, the ten-day deadline finally arrived.

Chapter 125

The mountains trembled with cold, the rivers stiffened, and the air seemed to solidify.

However, in front of the Yuan family estate, a fiery atmosphere prevailed. Led by Yuan Zewei, the members of the Fan family arrived at the Yuan's estate carrying a large sedan chair for eight people.

Although there were regulations in Jinlin Kingdom that ordinary people were not allowed to ride in an eight-person sedan chair, such rules were completely disregarded by these powerful families. Even the royal family of Jinlin Kingdom turned a blind eye to it.

The gates of the Yuan family estate had long been opened. When they arrived, Yuan Chengzhi personally came forward and led them to the martial arts training ground behind the estate.

Yuan Zewei was well-prepared for this. For him, everything in the Yuan family estate was already familiar, and the training ground in the backyard was the best place for today's competition.

Yuan Chengzhi's gaze occasionally swept over these people, with a hint of strangeness and satisfaction in his eyes. However, when his gaze fell on the mysterious sedan chair, he couldn't help but feel a sense of unease.

On the training ground, led by Yuan Zeyu, Zhou Quanxin and others had been waiting for a long time. However, just like Yuan Chengzhi, when they saw an eight-person sedan chair being carried directly into the backyard, everyone's eyes couldn't help but show a hint of peculiarity.

Even the composed and dignified Zhou Quanxin couldn't help but speculate on what might be hidden inside the sedan chair.

If it was just one person, then their arrogance would be a bit excessive.

Vaguely, those who had some knowledge of the recent changes couldn't help but associate the sedan chair with the enigmatic figure that appeared at the entrance of the estate a few days ago. However, without confirming the truth, they would rather deceive themselves and pretend not to know.

Naturally, the two sides formed their own factions. Yuan Zeyu withdrew his gaze from the sedan chair and spoke loudly, "Master Fan, although the Yuan family may not be a prominent household, we don't turn away friends at our door. I wonder who is in this sedan, and why they are reluctant to reveal their true identity until now?"

Fan Shuhe sighed inwardly. To be honest, he had no idea what Lv Xinwen was thinking when he made such a request. Not only did he want to sit in the sedan chair, but he also refused to get out of it.

However, even if he had the courage, Fan Shuhe wouldn't dare to ask.

At this moment, he wore an inscrutable smile and said, "Lord Yuan, the person in the sedan is a senior whom I respect. He enjoys sitting in the sedan. However, I wonder if anyone from your side is worthy enough for him to reveal himself."

Yuan Zeyu's heart sank. Could the person in the sedan really be the mysterious figure from that day at the estate?

However, even within the Fan family, only Fan Shuhe and his son knew about Lv Xinwen's visit. The other servants had no knowledge of such a powerful expert. As for the Yuan family, it was even more impossible for them to have heard any rumors. So, although they were suspicious, they would not show any signs of weakness in this situation.

Yuan Zewei took a step forward and exclaimed, "Second brother, now that we're here, I urge you, for the sake of our sibling relationship, to tidy up and leave. If the two sides really engage in a bloody battle, it will be difficult for you to escape."

Yuan Zeyu smiled faintly and said, "Big brother, it seems a bit too early to say that now."

Yuan Chengzhi spoke loudly, "Indeed, the victor is still unknown."

At this moment, Fan Haori, who was closely following beside the sedan, tilted his ear slightly and clearly heard the voice from inside the sedan, "Who is the man with the long cloth strip on his back?"

The voice was not loud, but it was unmistakably Lv Xinwen's voice.

Fan Haori didn't dare to neglect and quickly lowered his head, whispering, "Great-uncle, that is Zhou Yi, a junior from the Zhou family invited by the Yuan family to assist them."

"Zhou family junior?" The voice from inside the sedan suddenly carried a strange tone. After a moment, it continued, "Who else among them is related to him by blood?"

"There is also Zhou Quanxin, who has reached the tenth level of inner energy, and his son Zhou Yitian. They are said to have close blood ties with Zhou Yi," Fan Haori respectfully replied.

"Good." The voice from inside the sedan suddenly became calm, "If you and your father can take care of them and kill the two, I will accept you as my disciple and pass on my teachings to you. Perhaps one day, you can also advance to the innate realm."

Fan Haori looked at him in astonishment, his eyes filled with shock.

Fan Haori's eyes sparkled with determination. He had made up his mind. This was something worth risking his life for, no matter what.

He decisively turned around and approached Fan Shuhe, whispering a few words in a low voice. The same expression appeared on Fan Shuhe's face, and his fists clenched tightly.

Zhou Quanxin was a master at the tenth level of inner energy. According to the information from the Xiao brothers, he was also a master of the earth element, which countered Fan Haori's water-based martial arts.

However, when Fan Haori glanced at the tightly covered sedan, his heart suddenly became ablaze with determination.

Lv Xinwen had actually agreed. As long as they could kill the father and son from the Zhou family, he would help Fan Haori advance to the innate realm. This promise alone was enough to make the entire Fan family throw themselves into it.

For a family, a master at the tenth level of inner energy was already an incredibly important figure. But when compared to a innate expert, the difference was like heaven and earth.

If the Fan family could truly produce a innate master, the family might one day become a prestigious lineage spanning thousands of years.

He took a deep breath, ready to go out, but was stopped by Fan Haori.

"Haori, what are you planning to do?" Fan Shuhe said discontentedly.

"Father, let me make the first move," Fan Haori replied.

"You?"

"Yes, Uncle Xiao once mentioned that Zhou Yitian, the son of Zhou Quanxin, inherited the same earth-based inner energy as his father.

In that case, allow me to strike first and kill him on the spot. Zhou Quanxin will undoubtedly be thrown into disarray. At that moment, you can take advantage and surely kill him on the spot," Fan Haori said, a hint of sinister intent flashing in his eyes.

Fan Shuhe's eyes brightened, but then he shook his head and said, "No, it won't work. The martial arts you practice, like mine, are water-based, and you're only at the seventh level of inner energy. You might not be a match for him."

Fan Haori was confident and said, "Father, Uncle Xiao said that even though his inner energy is at the seventh level, it hasn't reached the peak. At best, it's in the middle stage. My inner energy has already reached the peak of the seventh level, surpassing him. As long as I stay steady and methodical, I will surely win."

Fan Shuhe hesitated for a moment but eventually nodded slowly. He knew that even though the Xiao brothers were one level lower in inner energy cultivation, their insight and perception were exceptional. Their ability to observe others was incredibly precise. Otherwise, he wouldn't have asked them to pose as guests of the Fan family and gather information.

Fan Haori strode out confidently and quickly arrived at the center of the training ground. His sudden interruption silenced the argument between Yuan Zeyu and others, who were engaged in a verbal dispute.

Fan Haori clasped his hands together and bowed deeply, saying, "Everyone, we have reached this point where verbal disputes are futile. I, Fan Haori, am merely an insignificant junior. I have come forward today not to show off but to set an example and lead the way. I wonder who will come up first?"

At this moment, both sides felt a sense of surprise. They all knew that today's matter wouldn't be resolved through mere words but required a real battle. However, no one expected that the first one to step forward would be Fan Haori.

Yuan Zeyu frowned. He was aware of Fan Haori's strength, but among their younger generation, there was no genius with the seventh level of inner energy.

Fan Haori laughed and suddenly said, "Brother Zhou Yitian, your father's battle with our two Uncle Xiaos in the past has left a lasting impression on me. I know my abilities are far inferior to your father's, and I dare not challenge him. But I would like to have a match with you, if you're willing."

Zhou Yitian paused for a moment, then a confident smile appeared on his face as he replied, "Since Brother Fan is interested, I will gladly oblige."

With a wave of his sleeve, Zhou Yitian walked out without hesitation. When he emerged, Yuan Zeyu and others felt relieved. Among the many people present, perhaps only Zhou Yitian and Fan Haori were the best candidates to deal with each other.

The two of them stood in the center of the field, without drawing their weapons. They simply bowed to each other as a gesture of respect before facing off.

However, it was only a momentary standoff. Fan Haori's figure moved like flowing water in an instant. He practiced water-based martial arts, while Zhou Yitian practiced earth-based martial arts. If they were to remain motionless, Fan Haori would be at a disadvantage in terms of momentum.

So, after a brief standoff, he immediately made the first move. As he moved, his entire body glided forward like he was riding on a pulley, and the ground beneath him seemed incredibly smooth.

Almost simultaneously, his palm shot up, gathering his water-based inner energy to its peak in an instant. Although he was not yet thirty years old, his inner energy had reached the peak of the seventh level, and he was on the verge of breaking through to the eighth level. This strike represented the culmination of all his inner energy, coming fiercely and aiming to finish the battle in one fell swoop.

Fan Haori had planned everything before making his move. As long as Zhou Yitian took a step back, Fan Haori's martial skills would flow relentlessly like a mighty river, with every move aimed at killing his opponent. He was willing to risk severe injuries to ensure Zhou Yitian's demise.

"If Zhou Yitian were to die, Zhou Quanxin would undoubtedly be thrown into disarray due to the loss of his son, and Fan Haori estimated that he would be able to achieve at most 80% of his full potential in such a chaotic situation."

The successful completion of the mission entrusted to him by lv Xinwen relied on the death of Zhou Quanxin and his son at their hands.

The thought of being taken as a disciple by a innate expert and having the opportunity to become a innate expert himself filled Fan Haori's heart with intense excitement.

However, at this moment, Zhou Yitian raised his palm. His palms were as steady as a rock, and amidst the onslaught of Fan Haori's fierce attacks, he found the exact position to intercept them. The palms of the two individuals collided heavily.

Suddenly, an immense and unimaginable force surged out from Zhou Yitian's palm. This force was incredibly powerful and unyielding.

Fan Haori let out a cry and was sent flying backward. He spun in the air before landing steadily. However, when he looked at Zhou Yitian, his eyes were filled with astonishment and incomprehension.

The force behind Zhou Yitian's palm, although not yet at the peak of the seventh level, was not far from it. It was merely a hair's breadth away.

His expression turned extremely ugly. It turned out that Xiaoyi Fan had underestimated Zhou Yitian's inner energy. It wasn't at the mid-stage of the seventh level, but rather close to the pinnacle.

Due to the limited difference in their inner energy strength and their opposing nature, Fan Haori's palm was unable to move Zhou Yitian. Since he couldn't even achieve the first step, all his plans were rendered futile.

However, the fight couldn't simply end there. Fan Haori gritted his teeth and charged forward once again. He moved around Zhou Yitian like a slippery mudfish, constantly engaging him in palm-to-palm combat.

In that moment of retreat, Fan Haori had changed his strategy. Although Zhou Yitian was formidable, his inner energy was still inferior. As long as Fan Haori circled around him and continuously engaged in palm-to-palm combat to drain his inner energy, victory would ultimately be his.

However, after dozens of palm clashes, Fan Haori became increasingly alarmed. He suddenly realized that Zhou Yitian's inner energy seemed to be progressing at a terrifying and unimaginable speed.

Every time their palms clashed, Fan Haori felt that the force emanating from Zhou Yitian's palms grew stronger. Zhou Yitian was like an inhuman monster with limitless potential, or a spring that bounced back with greater force when compressed.

This unprecedented situation left Fan Haori in utter despair. After fighting for a while longer, he became even more despondent. When their palms met, he discovered that Zhou Yitian, who was initially weaker than him, now possessed strength that could fully contend with him.

He finally confirmed that Zhou Yitian had reached the pinnacle of the seventh level of inner energy during their battle. It was a bitter realization, as he had never expected such an incredible breakthrough from his opponent during their confrontation.

Moreover, Zhou Yitian seemed to possess boundless energy. While Fan Haori was feeling somewhat exhausted after countless palm clashes, Zhou Yitian remained lively and even grew more excited with each exchange.

At this moment, the only thought in Fan Haori's mind was whether this guy was a freak...

Inside the large carriage, Lü Xinwen's eyes sparkled with intensity. He was now certain that his three disciples had all perished, and everything they possessed had been lost completely.

This person named Zhou Yitian must have recently taken a Energy-Boosting Golden Pill

Only the immensely powerful properties of the Energy-Boosting Golden Pill could produce such incredible effects. Each strike from Fan Haori was like a massage and pounding that helped Zhou Yitian assimilate the medicinal power of the pill into his body.

Without this battle, it might have taken Zhou Yitian several months to fully unleash the effects of the Energy-Boosting Golden Pill. However, with such a formidable opponent intentionally engaging in an inner energy clash, the vaporization of the pill's effects would accelerate, enabling him to reach the pinnacle of the seventh level of inner energy ahead of schedule.

Not only that, because the Energy-Boosting Golden Pill enhanced the body's energy, when Zhou Yitian's inner energy reached the peak of the seventh level, the residual medicinal power continuously replenished the energy he consumed during the fight.

Fan Haori's plan to wear down Zhou Yitian using the Water Grinding Technique was simply impossible.

The elderly man slowly closed his eyes. He took a deep breath as the true energy in his entire body began to flow. The flow rate was not particularly fast, but it appeared incredibly natural, as if his entire being had merged with nature, becoming a clear stream.

As Zhou Yi watched the battle, he turned his head and looked at the mysterious carriage. He listened to the sounds coming from inside, and his expression grew solemn. In his perception, the stream inside seemed to be growing bigger and larger. Perhaps when the small stream turned into a vast ocean, it would signify that the person inside had gathered their true energy to its peak.

Zhou Yi took a step back, but his true energy converged entirely within his body. At this moment, he gathered all his essence and strength, like a beast with all its energy coiled, ready to release an earth-shattering arrow when unleashed.

If someone were to focus their attention on him at this moment, they would notice that Zhou Yi appeared like a stone carving, inconspicuous and unremarkable.

However, the others present failed to notice these abnormalities as their gazes remained locked on the intense fight between the two.

Zhou Yitian suddenly moved, raising his foot and taking a step forward. With clenched fists, he launched a punch that broke through the air. Even the sound of the fist cutting through the air seemed particularly piercing.

This was the first time Zhou Yitian had left the ground in today's battle, and it was his first active attack. But with this punch, he had already brought forth his optimal state.

Fan Haori's expression changed slightly. He wanted to dodge, but at this moment, his inner energy faltered slightly, making him realize he couldn't hold on any longer in their energy clash.

In that momentary pause, Zhou Yitian exhaled and his punch became even more powerful.

With a thunderous boom, their fists collided.

Zhou Yitian's feet moved slightly, but he stood firm, exuding an aura of self-confidence and indomitable spirit.

Fan Haori staggered back several steps, finally stabilizing his stance. A faint trace of blood trickled down from the corner of his mouth. Looking at Zhou Yitian's expression, he felt immense anger welling up within him. Unable to hold back any longer, he forcefully spewed a mouthful of blood, staining the ground with scattered red spots.

Chapter 126

Zhou Yitian took a deep breath, no longer glancing at Fan Haori in front of him. He turned around and returned to his original position, proclaiming loudly, "Father, your son has returned victorious."

Zhou Quanxin burst into laughter and said, "Well done! Truly worthy of being a descendant of our Zhou family."

While praising his son without reservation, deep astonishment filled his heart. He couldn't believe how fast Yitian had advanced.

Moreover, witnessing the scene of internal energy consumption just moments ago left him even more amazed. Zhou Yitian's endurance seemed endless. If they had switched places or engaged in an internal energy confrontation at the seventh level, he feared he would have been overwhelmed by this seemingly boundless internal energy.

Of course, now was not the right time to inquire. He could only keep his wonderment in his heart and address it later.

Zhou Yitian, however, knew it well. He gratefully looked toward his sixth brother but was slightly taken aback. His brother stood there with a countenance that seemed detached, as if his thoughts were not confined to his physical body. What's more, Zhou Yi's presence seemed absent, as if he were not alive, if not for his visible form.

Zhou Yitian harbored doubts, contemplating whether he should approach and observe carefully. But at that moment, he heard a commotion behind him, involuntarily diverting his attention.

A figure flickered, and Fan Shuhe appeared behind his son, gently patting him on the back. A profound internal energy flowed into him.

Just like the father-son relationship between the Zhou family, they too were inheritors of a long-standing lineage.

With their shared water-based martial arts, they indeed possessed a unique advantage in the realm of healing. However, Fan Haori suddenly broke free and looked into Fan Shuhe's eyes. He shook his head slightly, his face tinged with a sense of shame, and said, "Father, I've lost."

Fan Shuhe silently gazed at his son, the self-mockery and sorrow evident on his face, weighing heavily on his heart. He knew that his son appeared versatile on the surface, even willing to humble himself before Lv Xinwen. But deep down, he possessed an immense pride. Today, losing to someone of his own age undoubtedly dealt a significant blow to him.

In this moment, Fan Shuhe clearly saw the disappointment and confusion in Fan Haori's eyes. He also knew that if Fan Haori couldn't see through all of this, it would be difficult for him to make any progress in the future.

This realization felt like a sharp needle piercing his heart.

Gradually, Fan Shuhe's expression calmed down, as if he had made a resolute decision in the face of a difficult dilemma. Patting his son's shoulder, his heart suddenly brimmed with an unprecedented sense of courage as he declared, "It's fine, I'll stand up for you."

Fan Haori was taken aback, watching as Fan Shuhe stepped forward with determined strides. In that moment, his father's figure appeared so solid and dependable! With each step, Fan Shuhe exuded an unwavering steadiness, as if a massive boulder were moving, reaching the epitome of composure.

The gazes of Yuan Zeyu and others froze, filled with astonishment and disbelief.

As widely known, Fan Shuhe is a master of the tenth level of water-based internal energy. However, in this moment, this tenth-level expert in water-based internal energy took such heavy steps, completely devoid of the gentle and ethereal feeling associated with water-based techniques.

Yet, the more this occurred, the heavier and more uneasy the hearts of the onlookers became. A master of water-based techniques exhibiting such incredible power—what did this signify?

Zhou Yi's eyes seemed to flicker, sensing an immense will to fight—a release of all his own aura, an unwavering resolve to battle with no reservations.

In his short sixteen years of life, Zhou Yi had encountered numerous experts, both acquired and innate. However, from anyone he had encountered, he had never felt such an intense will to fight.

When an ordinary man is furious, blood will be shed within five steps.

Zhou Yi unexpectedly experienced this terrifying sensation for no apparent reason.

He suddenly realized that this was a true expert who had entered the battlefield with a mindset of sacrificing their own life, approaching the fight with a reverent attitude.

"Brother Zhou, your son truly possesses remarkable skills, and I admire him. However, at this moment, it's time for you and me to face off, isn't it?"

Fan Shuhe smiled faintly, his expression calm and serene, as if he were casually discussing a trivial matter.

The smile completely vanished from Zhou Quanxin's face. He keenly sensed the intense danger emanating from this person. But at this moment, he couldn't afford to back down.

"Since Brother Fan wishes to test Zhou's techniques, Zhou dare not decline."

The spectators from both sides fell into silence as Zhou Quanxin stepped onto the field. Involuntarily, tension filled the air among the onlookers.

In the hearts of most people, Zhou Quanxin and Fan Shuhe were the ultimate trump cards of their respective families today. Once they determined the winner, today's contest would essentially come to an end, and the ownership of the Yuan family estate would be decided in this very battle.

When Fan Haori challenged Zhou Yitian earlier, everyone expected to witness many similar spectacles. However, it was unexpected that immediately after the conclusion of their fight, Fan Shuhe eagerly stepped forward to issue his challenge.

The final battle unfolded so swiftly and abruptly that most people felt caught off guard, lacking any sense of preparedness.

Just as Zhou Quanxin was about to step forward, Zhou Yi said, "Uncle, please wait a moment."

Everyone was taken aback, their gazes shifting towards him, wondering what he intended to do.

Zhou Yi took a few steps forward, turned around, and blocked the view of the crowd. He then swiftly moved his hands in a motion that exceeded the perception of ordinary human eyes, creating a blur of movement. Afterwards, no trace of his actions could be seen.

He had practiced the art of imprinting, and his hands were exceptionally dexterous. This display showcased his full skills, as fast as lightning, with his movements becoming a blur that vanished completely.

Then, he softly said, "Uncle, be cautious."

Having said that, Zhou Yi returned to his original position and once again entered the state where his entire being converged into a single point of focus.

Zhou Quanxin's expression became extremely peculiar. He clenched his fists, then relaxed them, as if experiencing some discomfort in his body. However, he did not linger or delay, but instead raised his head high and entered the center of the arena.

As Yuan Zeyu and his son exchanged a glance, their eyes were filled with deep concern. They couldn't fathom what had gotten into Zhou Yi, staging such a farce at such a critical moment. Judging from Zhou

Quanxin's expression and demeanor, it seemed that he was far from being in his peak state. The situation didn't appear to be too optimistic when he stepped forward.

"Please," Zhou Quanxin said, cupping his fists, signaling his readiness. Upon hearing those words, Fan Shuhe made his move.

At this moment, the distance between them was almost identical to the one between Zhou Yitian and Fan Haori when they engaged in combat earlier, as it was the standard distance for formal duels.

Fan Shuhe slightly raised his palm, lifting the heels of his feet, and then pushed off the ground with force, sliding forward. His movements were identical to Fan Haori's initial ones, but if there was any difference, it was that his speed was faster, more agile, and flowed like water.

The still waters of the ancient well instantly transformed into the agile and ever-changing currents of a great river. This sudden transformation gave everyone a contradictory feeling, as if Fan Shuhe had become a completely different person, or perhaps two distinct individuals taking turns to strike.

Zhou Quanxin showed no signs of relaxation, and his reaction mirrored Zhou Yitian's. He raised his palm, as if placing it there, calmly waiting for the impact from his opponent.

With a resounding clash, their palms collided in an instant, unleashing an unparalleled force from their powerful internal energy. Invisible waves of internal energy erupted from under their feet, causing cracks to appear on the ground due to the fierce confrontation between two tenth-level internal energy experts.

Zhou Quanxin's figure stood firm like a rock, withstanding the powerful onslaught. After a slight tremor, he steadied himself.

On the other hand, Fan Shuhe's body shook, and he took a step back. Although his water-based martial arts were formidable, his internal energy cultivation was on par with Zhou Quanxin's at best. Under the principle of martial arts counteracting each other, he was inevitably at a slight disadvantage.

However, Fan Shuhe's retreat was only a momentary touch of his toes on the ground before he surged forward once again, this time thrusting with his index finger like a knife.

A faint glimmer of light shimmered on the slightly protruding middle finger, resembling a droplet of water reflecting sunlight as it descended.

Zhou Quanxin adapted to the ever-changing situation with an unchanging stance, raising his palm once again to lightly collide with his opponent's fingertip.

Suddenly, Zhou Quanxin's expression changed slightly. He sensed a strange power, seemingly soft as cotton and not particularly strong. However, this power exuded an indomitable momentum, as if it could penetrate through anything it encountered.

A chill ran down Zhou Quanxin's spine. This feeling was eerily reminiscent of the characteristics of metal-based martial arts. Yet, the contact of their internal energies made it clear to him that Fan Shuhe was still using water-based internal energy without any alteration.

Fan Shuhe continued his half-step retreat and half-step advance, each time thrusting with his fingertip like a knife.

However, despite facing such a seemingly simplistic and almost lethargic fighting style, Zhou Quanxin's expression was filled with unimaginable seriousness. He slightly bent his legs, steadily blocking each of his opponent's attacks. However, he had yet to throw a single punch throughout the encounter, not even a token strike.

Zhou Yi's eyebrows twitched slightly. At this moment, he had focused all his mental and true energy, reaching a state of heightened concentration that surpassed his usual capabilities. In his perception, Fan Shuhe was no longer the torrential river but rather the slow descending droplets from a cliff.

Although these droplets seemed insignificant, their power was not to be underestimated. While the mighty river could span thousands of miles in an instant, when the floodwaters receded, the mountains remained mountains, and the land remained unchanged. The entire earth would not be destroyed by the river.

However, the water droplets falling from a height were different. They might never reach the water level capable of submerging the large rocks below, but their persistent efforts could create a new miracle.

That miracle was the erosion of stone by dripping water.

When the number of droplets reached an infinite amount, when they continuously dripped onto a specific spot on the large rock over months and years, even the hardest stone could be pierced by these seemingly powerless droplets, creating a small hole.

At this moment, Fan Shuhe compressed all his internal energy within his body, meticulously releasing it bit by bit, aiming to pierce through the large rock in front of him.

However, this technique of forcibly compressing internal energy undoubtedly had an impact on the human body itself. Doing so for a short period presented no issues, but if sustained for a long time, even the strongest of individuals would not be able to withstand it.

However, this self-damaging fighting style also possessed unimaginable power. Despite the opposing nature of their techniques, Fan Shuhe unquestionably held the absolute upper hand. Zhou Yi understood this, and anyone with a seventh-level internal energy cultivation present would have been able to see it as well.

The confusion and despair in Fan Haori's eyes had disappeared completely. In its place surged excitement and guilt. Suddenly, he understood the meaning behind his father's earlier words. He knew that his father's actions were akin to staking his own life for victory.

By doing so, he was declaring to everyone, "My son has been struck, and I will avenge him, even if it means gambling with my life."

In a daze, a gleam of brilliance flickered in Fan Haori's eyes. His fists unconsciously clenched tightly together, his heart surging with a desire to take his father's place on the battlefield. The negative impact of the humiliating defeat had completely vanished. He could feel the gradually emerging powerful internal energy within him. He even had an inexplicable feeling that given more time for cultivation, he could break through the seventh-level barrier and reach the realm of the eighth level.

In the arena, Zhou Quanxin finally couldn't bear it any longer. He stumbled backward, taking a step back. Just as water's power accumulates to its utmost limit, it becomes invincible. Fan Shuhe's eyes brightened, and his pupils sparkled with brilliance. At this moment, the faintly throbbing meridians in his body seemed to have no further impact on him.

Fan Shuhe let out a loud roar as his previously composed figure rapidly spun, resembling the flow of a river, wave after wave surging forward relentlessly.

A large stone, if it stands firm, cannot be washed away by the water. But if its foundation is loose, a wave crashing against it will inevitably carry it away.

After Fan Shuhe staked his life as a bet, he finally won. His fists circulated, and his entire being transformed into a raging storm, overwhelming Zhou Quanxin, as if intending to completely engulf him.

Zhou Quanxin lost his balance, knowing it was dire. But at this moment, there was simply no way to resist. He could only do his best to withstand the storm-like onslaught.

However, in a clash between masters, once one falls into a disadvantage, it becomes extremely difficult, if not impossible, to turn the tables again.

As he saw the fluttering palms swirling around him, Zhou Quanxin finally felt overwhelmed. Although he harbored countless unwillingness and helplessness, he let out a long sigh. Then, with a burst of energy, he extended his arms like an iron whip, lashing out.

The faces of Yuan Zeyu and Yuan ChengZhi finally changed. Although Zhou Quanxin was at a disadvantage, with the powerful defensive properties of his earth-based technique, if he remained purely defensive, there might still be a glimmer of hope.

However, at this critical moment, he chose to take the initiative to attack.

Wasn't this tantamount to seeking a death wish...

A trace of ferocity flashed in Fan Shuhe's eyes. His palm, seemingly boneless, pressed forward. He was absolutely confident that if he could neutralize the force on this arm, he could take advantage of the momentary gap to injure his opponent, even launching a series of continuous attacks, ultimately killing him on the spot.

Fan Shuhe's hands were already raised, one inward and one outward, revealing his murderous intent. The powerful and fierce aura pointed straight to the heart.

Zhou Yitian's eyes turned bloodshot, and he clearly saw the undisguised killing intent emanating from Fan Shuhe.

In an instant, the two 10th-level inner strength experts had reached a life-or-death moment.

However, when Fan Shuhe's palm made contact with Zhou Quanxin's arm, his face suddenly changed, and an expression of extreme shock appeared in his eyes.

A surging force transmitted from Zhou Quanxin's arm.

It was a formidable strength, far surpassing his imagination.

At this moment, he even began to doubt whether even a peak 10th-level inner strength expert in the Metal element could exert such tremendous power.

The pain in his meridians became more intense, but he no longer had time to worry about that. All of his inner strength surged out like a tide, trying to block the incoming strike.

Block it, block it, unable to block...

That arm, combined with an unparalleled power, broke through Fan Shuhe's palm defense and heavily struck his chest.

Fan Shuhe's body flew up as if he had grown wings, somersaulting in the air before falling down limp.

Fan Haori moved like lightning, ignoring his injuries, and pounced on his father, firmly holding him in his arms.

Fan Shuhe's eyes widened, staring intently at Zhou Quanxin.

At this moment, the clothing on Zhou Quanxin's arm had already been torn apart, revealing a golden armguard shining with brilliance.

A look of realization appeared in Fan Shuhe's eyes. His lips trembled twice, and finally, a trace of blood flowed from his mouth. He let out a long breath and ceased to show any signs of life.

Chapter 127

Fan Haori suddenly looked up, his eyes filled with an unmistakable gaze of hatred towards Zhou Quanxin. It was a deep-seated hatred that, at a single glance, made everyone feel a strange sensation— that this person's remaining years would likely be lived under the shadow of revenge.

Zhou Quanxin shivered involuntarily, despite his current cultivation at the peak of the tenth layer of inner strength. He couldn't help but feel a chill sweeping over him.

"This is the armguard of my uncle and second uncle, Xiao Yifan and Xiao Yilin," gritted Fan Haori through clenched teeth, his voice seething with anger. "Where did you get them?"

Zhou Quanxin furrowed his brow, his mind filled with questions. These armguards were skillfully placed on him by Zhou Yi with incredible dexterity before he went into battle. However, Zhou Yi's movements were so swift that not only others but even Zhou Quanxin himself barely noticed them being put on. By the time he realized, it was already impossible to inquire about the origin of these armguards.

However, he couldn't have imagined that today's battle would be so perilous. If it weren't for these armguards...

Zhou Quanxin's gaze shifted towards the lifeless body of Fan Shuhe. If it weren't for these armguards, the one lying on the ground at this moment would have been him.

Yuan Chengzhi's eyes lit up, and upon seeing Fan Shuhe's death, it felt as though a heavy burden had been lifted from his heart. He no longer had any reservations.

The Fan family was not a prestigious or influential clan. It was solely sustained by Fan Shuhe, a peak tenth-layer cultivator of acquired inner strength. Given a hundred years of development, perhaps they could have become a new aristocratic family. However, now that Fan Shuhe had already died, this small family would never have another day in the sun.

Not to mention the Yuan family, they will certainly settle the score with the Fan family in the future. Even the families that were previously swallowed up by the Fan family won't miss this golden opportunity.

Yuan Chengzhi seeing Zhou Quanxin frowning and remaining silent thought he was disdainful of answering the question. He immediately stepped forward, understanding the situation, and said, "Nonsense! You're just a young kid, what do you know? You think what's yours is really yours? I can say that everything belonging to your Fan family is mine as well."

His voice was loud, filled with a hint of undisguised delight, and his statement exposed his ambitions to swallow up the Fan family.

Yuan Chengzhi wore a disdainful smirk on his face and said, "Young Master Fan, you witnessed your father's actions just now. Every move was lethal, ruthlessly deadly. Unfortunately, your father's skills were inadequate and he was instantly killed by Brother Zhou. It was his own cruelty that led to his own humiliation." He raised his head and clasped his fists towards those around him, saying, "Everyone, think about it. Doesn't what I say make sense? Should Fan Shuhe be allowed to kill but not be killed by others?"

Fan Haori's face instantly turned extremely ugly. He turned around abruptly and saw the servants and guests in the house shrinking back, none of them daring to stand by his side. Many of them were half-bowing, nodding repeatedly, seemingly agreeing with Yuan Chengzhi's words.

In that moment, Fan Haori understood one thing: the Fan family was finished...

Suddenly, a clear voice rang out, "What if I say these armguards are mine?"

Although the voice was not loud, it was as clear as a whisper, and everyone present could hear it distinctly. A glimmer of hope appeared on Fan Haori's face, as if he had grasped the last straw while drowning. He knew that only this person was willing to lend a hand, providing the final opportunity for the rise of the Yuan family.

Yuan Chengzhi's gaze sharpened, but he dared not be disrespectful in the face of this sedan chair. After all, the immense inexplicable pressure they had experienced a few days ago had a profound impact on them.

He hesitated for a moment and asked, "May I ask who you are..."

The sedan curtain swayed gently without any wind, and a tall figure emerged slowly from within. As soon as he appeared, he captured the attention of everyone present. Although there were a few strands of white hair above his temples, his entire being exuded an immense vitality that anyone could sense. Because of this, no one could accurately guess his age.

The expressions of Yuan Chengzhi and the others changed dramatically. Although they didn't recognize this person, his appearance and attire were almost identical to those described by the servants guarding the mansion gate on that day. In this moment, their fleeting hope was completely shattered.

So, the Fan family indeed had a transcendent(innate) powerhouse.

However, what puzzled them was why, with this strong reinforcement, the Fan family wasted time initially, allowing the father and son from the Fan family to take action, which ultimately led to the unexpected death of Fan Shuhe.

After stepping out, the person slowly opened his mouth and said in a leisurely manner under the gaze of everyone, "I am Lv Xinwen. Have you ever heard of me?"

As soon as these words were spoken, the silence in the scene became absolute. After a moment, a faint sound of "thud..." broke the stillness. Startled, everyone turned their heads in the direction of the sound. They saw a weapon falling to the ground from the hands of a middle-aged man in the Yuan family's camp, and his face had lost all color.

Moreover, the people in that direction wore nearly identical expressions on their faces, as if shrouded in a cloud of darkness, appearing lifeless.

On the other hand, Yuan Zewei and the others were overjoyed, especially the servants and guests belonging to the Fan family. They completely shook off their previously lifeless expressions. However, some of those who had been nodding and bowing earlier now resembled individuals who had just swallowed a fly, unable to utter a word.

Lv Xinwen's gaze immediately fell upon the golden armguards worn by Zhou Quanxin.

He whispered, "Your young one consumed the Energy-Boosting Golden Pill, and the armguards were used by you. My three disciples were most likely killed by all of you, right?"

Zhou Quanxin forcefully suppressed the urge to turn around. At this moment, he understood that this matter was definitely the doing of Zhou Yi. But what was the Energy-Boosting Golden Pill all about?

However, he had no time to ponder over it now. Taking a deep breath, he said, "Yes, I alone am responsible for this matter. I am willing to bear all the blame."

"Your doing?" Lv Xinwen's face revealed a hint of ridicule. He continued, "With your level of strength, can you really kill my three disciples?"

Zhou Quanxin was instantly rendered speechless. At this moment, anyone with a bit of intelligence would know that the Xiao Family brothers and the Inner Energy expert who came to provoke them that night were Lv Xinwen's disciples. However, from Lv Xinwen's tone, it seemed that these three individuals had all perished.

He couldn't fathom the identity of such a powerful figure.

Zhou Quanxin's lips moved, about to speak, when suddenly, his vision darkened. He was taken aback and, upon careful observation, noticed a rectangular cloth strip blocking his view.

His heart skipped a beat, and he quickly said, "Yi..."

"Uncle, leave it to me."

Zhou Yi's voice, tinged with a hint of a smile, resounded. It seemed to possess a certain enchantment, rekindling a flicker of hope within Zhou Quanxin's despairing heart.

Zhou Yi smiled faintly and said, "Junior Zhou Yi, I've seen the senior."

Lv Xinwen chuckled and said, "Since you have already stepped into the Innate realm, there is no longer a distinction between seniors and juniors."

Zhou Quanxin's mouth fell open, his eyes widened. He looked at his nephew, his expression bordering on stupefaction.

What did Lv Xinwen say?

Perplexed, Zhou Quanxin glanced around, only to see everyone wearing the same incredulous expression.

At this moment, almost everyone thought they were experiencing auditory hallucinations!

Zhou Yi chuckled lightly, his voice carrying far and waking everyone from their stupor. However, the gazes directed at him had changed significantly. Especially Zhou Quanxin and his son, as well as Yuan Chengzhi and others who had spent more time with him, wore expressions of disbelief. The despair in their eyes had vanished, replaced by a glimmer of hope.

Zhou Yi spoke loudly, "May I ask, Brother Lv, are you so certain that your disciples have perished?"

Lv Xinwen lowered his eyelids and said, "Brother Zhou, are you recently advanced to the Innate realm? Why are you not clear about this basic principle?"

Zhou Yi's expression became serious as he said, "Indeed, I am not aware. Please enlighten me."

Lv Xinwen sneered and said, "As individuals in the Innate realm, we have a deep impression of the aura of those close to us. We cannot be deceived by the places they have recently stayed in. In the dense woods in front of the Yuan family's estate, there is a strong aura emanating from my three miscreants. This aura is both intense and concentrated, only released upon their violent demise."

Zhou Yi's face showed a look of realization. Although he had advanced to the Innate realm, he had not fully comprehended the special abilities possessed by some Innate experts.

Lv Xinwen suddenly said, "Initially, I thought Brother Zhou had left these auras as a challenge to me. But now I understand that it was your momentary negligence. If Brother Zhou wishes to cover your tracks in the future, simply perform a set of Innate fist techniques in that area to completely disrupt the aura and render it undetectable."

Zhou Yi forced a bitter smile and cursed inwardly. If only I had known this method earlier, would I still be facing you now?

Lv Xinwen asked leisurely, "Brother Zhou, I'm curious. My three disciples were not reckless individuals. They would not provoke an Innate powerhouse. And Brother Zhou, who has advanced to the Innate realm at such a young age, surely wouldn't covet a mere pair of armguards and a few Energy-Refining Pills. So, I want to know, why did you take their lives?"

Zhou Yi looked at him in astonishment. Lv Xinwen seemed genuinely puzzled, as if he truly didn't understand this matter.

Nodding slightly, Zhou Yi said seriously, "On that day, after Zhuang Yuan infiltrated the Yuan family's residence and retreated, I followed closely behind. I encountered the three disciples in front of the dense woods. I initially didn't intend to intervene, but the three disciples said they had requested your assistance to annihilate my entire Zhou family, leaving no one alive, not even chickens or dogs."

At this point, Zhou Yi paused and continued, "Since they harbored such malicious intent, how could I spare their lives?"

Zhou Quanxin and the others listened, feeling a chill run down their spines. Now they understood the reason behind it. Their gaze toward Lv Xinwen was tinged with anger. Annihilate the entire Zhou family? If these people were not killed, then where was justice?

Lv Xinwen finally let out a long sigh and said, "I understand now. So, it was the wish of my three disciples to exterminate your entire family. Allow me to fulfill their wish."

A heavy, substantive aura of killing intent slowly but resolutely emanated from him.

Zhou Yi's face showed no surprise. He had long known that the enmity between him and this old man had become irreparable when Xiaoyi Fan proposed the annihilation of his family.

Now that everything had been laid bare, Zhou Yi naturally wouldn't hold back any longer.

He took a half-step back, steadying himself. Instead of removing the cloth bag from his back, he slowly raised both hands. A profound and unfathomable hand seal mysteriously appeared on his hands.

His ten fingers intertwined and concealed the palms within the fingers. In the hidden space between his hands, the center of his palm slightly bulged, as if something was cushioned inside.

This was the Hidden Needle Seal, a seal derived from the Cloud and Rain Seal. It was the first time Zhou Yi had used it in actual combat since creating it.

Zhou Yitian stared at his sixth brother in a daze. Among these people, only he had witnessed Lin Taoli's hand seal technique. Although he couldn't possibly know the specific variations of the technique, the overall structure of the hand seal seemed strikingly similar. Moreover, he knew that there was no special hand seal technique within the Zhou family.

Thus, he felt a sense of strangeness in his heart. Could it be that Lin Taoli had actually passed down the family's hand seal technique to his sixth brother? But that Lin Taoli didn't seem so foolish!

Since Zhou Yi assumed the posture of the Hidden Needle Seal, it was as if he had vanished completely. Although everyone could see him with their eyes, in their perception, Zhou Yi was no longer there.

Compared to the immense vitality emanating from Lv Xinwen, Zhou Yi seemed to have turned into an inert rock, devoid of any life force.

Everyone held their breath, their hearts filled with indescribable emotions.

Everyone knew that the duel between these two individuals would determine the final outcome of today. The victorious side would undoubtedly gain tremendous benefits, while the defeated side might even lose their life.

Although they hadn't made any moves yet, the worries and fears in their hearts far surpassed those of the two innate experts in the arena.

Suddenly, Lv Xinwen seemed to make a move. He took a step forward, and in a blur, he appeared three steps away from Zhou Yi.

No one could perceive how he had moved. It was as if he had suddenly disappeared and reappeared. People blinked their eyes, confirming that they hadn't seen it wrong. A few timid individuals even muttered to themselves, wondering if this person was a legendary demon or monster. Otherwise, how could he create such illusions?

However, at that moment, Zhou Yi also moved.

His hand twitched slightly, and everyone saw a flash of golden light in their eyes.

It happened in a blink of an eye, so fast that not even a single blink could catch it.

Lv Xinwen's figure trembled strangely, retreating towards the rear with an incredible speed.

If no one saw him move forward, then when he retreated, everyone clearly saw a series of residual images extending from three meters in front of Zhou Yi. The images continued until twenty meters away, where he finally raised his palm and placed it flat against his chest.

A flicker of golden light shimmered in his palm before dissipating into nothingness.

After catching this golden light, Lv Xinwen's figure seemed to pause for a moment before rotating once again. This time, his movements became even more rapid, and in an instant, he had circled around Zhou Yi several times.

In the eyes of the onlookers, the old man's figure had already disappeared. They seemed to see a misty and elusive fog swiftly swirling on the battlefield. Even Zhou Quanxin, a master at the tenth level of Internal Energy, was just as clueless as the ordinary people; he couldn't fathom what was happening.

His face instantly turned extremely unsightly. Although he had heard Zhou Wude mention before that the gap between a innate expert and a peak expert of the acquired Realm was enormous, reaching an inconceivable level, he still had some doubts in his heart.

But now, he finally believed it completely.

The two individuals fighting in the arena, whether it was Zhou Yi or Lv Xinwen, could take each other's lives at any moment if they wished to.

At this moment, his only consolation was that Yi had become a innate expert, and his only prayer was that Yi could emerge victorious from this battle. If his actual strength was indeed inadequate and he lost, then at least he would have a chance to escape with his life.

Yi was still young, and as long as he remained alive, there would always be a day for him to seek revenge.

The spectators outside the arena each had their own thoughts, but the two individuals inside the arena had focused all their attention on each other.

Lv Xinwen moved like the wind, his figure transforming into a gust of clouds, a mass of mist. This cloud of mist kept revolving around Zhou Yi, and with each rotation, the surrounding air seemed to condense, increasing the pressure within.

Zhou Yi could clearly sense a whirlpool-like energy gradually forming, continuously compressing and exerting pressure on him.

It was a water-based technique, and not just any water-based technique but a innate water-based technique.

At this moment, Zhou Yi had already understood the nature of Lv Xinwen's innate technique.

Facing the constantly compressing force from all directions, Zhou Yi stood firm like a mountain. His ten fingers moved swiftly, and strands of innate qi alternately surged out from the palms of his hands.

Every time the needle imprint from the Hidden Needle Seal was activated, it was like poking a big hole in the surrounding clouds, instantly providing an outlet for the seemingly celestial pressure, rendering it unable to exert any force on him.

The speed at which Zhou Yi activated the Hidden needle imprints was clearly beyond Lv Xinwen's expectations and exceeded what he could endure. The old man let out a long roar and soared into the air, instantly retreating dozens of meters away.

It was only at this moment that everyone could see clearly that he had somehow acquired a white garment on his hands. It turned out that he had used his extremely fast body movement to wave this garment, creating the illusion of clouds and mist.

However, the garment was now riddled with holes, completely tattered...

Chapter 128

Lv Xinwen looked at the tattered clothes in his hands, a trace of regret flickering across his face. He said, "What a pity. If this garment were made from the combination of the Northern Ice Mountain's Heavenly Silkworm Silk and the Southern Wasteland's Human-Faced Spider Silk, it could have withstood your innate needle strike today."

Zhou Yi's heart skipped a beat as he asked, "Does that mean, Brother Lyu, your martial arts must rely on such specially crafted weapons to unleash their full potential?"

Lv Xinwen smiled bitterly and tossed aside the tattered clothes in his hand, saying, "Even without such specially crafted weapons, I can still annihilate your entire clan."

With that, he took a step forward, his palms interchanged. This time, his speed was far from the imperceptible swiftness he displayed earlier; instead, it seemed somewhat slow.

However, it was merely an illusion. With just three steps, he had already crossed a distance of tens of meters and forcefully struck out with a resounding palm.

Water-based martial arts were not suited for direct confrontation, yet this old man chose the path of aggressive assault.

Having had their initial conversation, he already understood that Zhou Yi was a newcomer to the realm of innate strength. Though he couldn't comprehend why Zhou Yi possessed such formidable innate martial arts like the Hidden Needle Imprint, since Zhou Yi had only recently advanced to the innate realm, his innate true energy was undoubtedly far inferior to that of Lv Xinwen, who had been at the innate level for over twenty years. Therefore, after failing with the Mist Compression Technique, he immediately opted for the most reliable approach.

"One force can subdue ten techniques" was a simple principle, but often the most practical one.

As if emerging from the void, a palm suddenly thrust toward Zhou Yi's chest. If this palm strike landed solidly, even as an innate expert, Zhou Yi would find it difficult to bear the consequences.

However, in the face of this sudden palm strike, Zhou Yi's hands swiftly flipped, and the previously hidden Needle Imprint instantly transformed into a steady and solid Earth Seal.

This seal technique was also learned from Lin Taoli, but it was the most perfect one he had mastered. Although it had some differences compared to when Lin Taoli used it, those variances were modified to suit Zhou Yi's own characteristics, making it the most suitable technique for him.

The elusive hand in the void wavered for a few moments, seemingly trying to find a flaw in Zhou Yi's defense. However, its owner suddenly realized that once Zhou Yi changed his hand seal, there were no longer any vulnerabilities on his body. It seemed that his entire being was protected by this peculiar seal.

After countless swaying motions, both real and illusory, in various directions, the hand finally collided heavily with Zhou Yi's Earth Seal.

It was as if his hand seal had been waiting there, specifically anticipating this hand's arrival.

Lv Xinwen felt an extreme sense of frustration. The strike he just executed was his full strength, yet he still couldn't gain the slightest advantage in terms of martial arts.

His insight was keen, and with just one glance, he could see that these two hand seals had a common lineage but also had distinct paths. However, there was no doubt that both hand seals were innate martial arts.

He was astonished in his heart, wondering about the origins of this young man. How could he have mastered two innate hand seal techniques?

If it were merely learning them, it wouldn't be so surprising. However, Zhou Yi not only learned them but also grasped their essence, which was truly unbelievable.

At this moment, he began to doubt Zhou Yi's age.

The advancement of internal energy could be achieved through consuming Golden Pills and stepping into the innate realm, even possessing the rare Innate Golden Pill. However, mastering a martial art had no shortcuts. Aside from the exceedingly rare enlightenment that occurs once in a hundred years, the only way was through continuous practice, practice, and more practice. Only by ingraining the techniques into one's marrow could they achieve familiarity and skill through repetition.

Yet, Zhou Yi's performance completely defied this rule. The two innate hand seal techniques he demonstrated had reached a level of fluidity and mastery that surpassed his over twenty years of arduous cultivation. Confronted with such an anomaly, even the bloodthirsty butcher Lv Xinwen couldn't help but feel a wave of helplessness.

The moment Zhou Yi's palm made contact with Lv Xinwen's hand , his feet pressed into the ground, his knees slightly bent. With this movement alone, he transferred half of Lv Xinwen's innate water-based true energy to the ground. Then, with a powerful push from his feet, an overwhelming force surged from his feet to his knees. His knees trembled and straightened in an instant, releasing an immense elastic energy that simultaneously emanated from over three hundred acupuncture points within his body. In an instant, it condensed into a rope-like force, propelled by the Earth Seal.

"Bang..."

A not-so-loud sound reverberated, but it carried a heavy and muffled tone, like an explosion within an iron box, causing a sense of oppression in people's hearts. Lv Xinwen's eyes widened abruptly as his palm fiercely collided with the Earth Seal. The tremendous true energy from both sides met without any fancy tricks.

However, the outcome of the clash between their true energies left Lv Xinwen incredulous. A powerful force, far beyond his imagination, emanated from the Earth Seal. Moreover, this force was purely of the Earth attribute, completely restraining him even in terms of innate attributes.

In a state of shock, Lv Xinwen was sent flying backward like lightning. During his retreat, his feet continuously made small, stomping steps on the ground. Each footstep left behind a distinct and clear footprint. In the span of a few breaths, he had left a total of 360 footprints on the ground.

The force that burst forth from Zhou Yi's over three hundred acupuncture points had been completely dissipated by Lv Xinwen in this peculiar manner.

Lv Xinwen raised his head in astonishment, unable to comprehend how a young man who had just stepped into the innate realm could possess such powerful innate true energy. The strength of this true energy was not the slightest bit inferior to his own over twenty years of diligent cultivation and practice.

At this point, a hint of doubt finally emerged in his mind, and his belief in being able to defeat and kill Zhou Yi wavered.

Zhou Yi's eyes suddenly widened. At this moment, he keenly sensed that the opponent's momentum seemed to have suddenly diminished. The intense focus and concentration of spirit that was present before had disappeared entirely.

As Lv Xinwen's aura waned, Zhou Yi's own aura involuntarily surged.

Without hesitation, Zhou Yi let out a long roar and lifted his foot, transforming into a streak of lightning. With a speed no less impressive than Lv Xinwen's earlier speed, he charged straight ahead.

Zhou Yi's footsteps on the ground were incredibly fast, reaching an extreme frequency at this moment. The sound of his footsteps echoed in the ears of the onlookers, giving them a sensation as if they were caught in an endless drizzle in the mountains.

In an instant, Zhou Yi became a torrential rain, stepping out countless small and rapid steps, sealing off all possible paths of evasion for Lv Xinwen with his lightning-fast body technique.

At the same time, Zhou Yi raised his hand, and the Earth Seal appeared before him once again. However, this time, the Earth Seal was not used for defense but transformed into a formidable offensive move that came crashing down like Mount Tai.

In Lin Taoli's hands, the Earth Seal was merely a pure defensive seal. However, when it fell into Zhou Yi's hands, he made slight adjustments to the internal energy flow, giving this technique an unexpected variation, which became the sole attacking method within this form.

Powerful true energy emanated from the Earth Seal, tightly locking onto Lv Xinwen. It was as if countless invisible ropes bound him tightly, leaving no room for mistakes.

Lv Xinwen's eyes flickered with fear, and he was filled with disbelief. With the previous strike, he had already determined that Zhou Yi was a cultivator of the Earth attribute. Yet, at this moment, Zhou Yi displayed a light-footed technique that undoubtedly belonged to the Water attribute.

The heaviness of Earth and the gentleness of Water were both simultaneously exhibited in him, and they were executed with such perfection. At this moment, Lv Xinwen couldn't help but feel a heartfelt admiration.

However, Lv Xinwen was an innate powerhouse nearing a hundred years old, having experienced numerous battles throughout his life. In this crucial moment, he took a deep breath and regained his composure.

Since he knew he couldn't evade, Lv Xinwen immediately abandoned everything and unleashed his innate true energy to the extreme, striking three consecutive palms in rapid succession.

With each palm, a powerful force surged forth. The first palm made contact with the Earth Seal, causing Lv Xinwen's body to slightly recoil. The second palm created some distance between him and

Zhou Yi, and when the third palm met the Earth Seal, he shot forward like an arrow, swiftly retreating.

Zhou Yi's footsteps came to a halt, not because he didn't want to pursue, but because each of Lv Xinwen's three palms surpassed the previous one, culminating in an immensely powerful strike with the third palm. Even though Zhou Yi had the upper hand, he was forced to stop and rely on the solid and steady ground beneath him to neutralize this tremendous force.

Raising his head, Zhou Yi watched as Lv Xinwen flew backward. A strong sense of emotion surged within him. Initially, he had chosen a defensive stance rather than launching a strong attack. When Lv Xinwen failed to break through his defense and his momentum weakened, Zhou Yi suddenly counterattacked using the Cloud and Rain Soaring Technique and the Earth Seal, akin to Mount Tai pressing down. However, in the end, Lv Xinwen effortlessly broke free from this seemingly fatal situation with his consecutive three strikes.

Innate powerhouses were indeed not to be underestimated. Killing this man was definitely not something Zhou Yi could achieve with bare hands.

However, Zhou Yi was unaware of the profound shock that Lv Xinwen experienced in his heart. Those three strikes were not just ordinary consecutive attacks; they were the true essence of Lv Xinwen's skills, something he had never used in combat since reaching the innate realm.

The consecutive three strikes were originally a marvelous technique of stacking true energy, something that Lv Xinwen was unable to master at his current level. However, he had a fortuitous encounter in the past where he gained some understanding in this area. After much exploration, he could barely execute the three-fold attack with true energy. However, once used, it would inevitably cause some damage to his body, and he absolutely couldn't use it continuously.

Even though it had its flaws, this was already the limit he had reached after countless attempts over the past twenty years. He originally believed that with this skill, he would be able to dominate the world. But in today's battle against Zhou Yi, he was forced to use this technique as a last resort for self-preservation. The fear in his heart was indescribable.

Although Zhou Yi's counterattack had not achieved any significant results, his spiritual perception was remarkable. In his perception, Lv Xinwen's momentum seemed to be increasingly weakened. As they say, as one side diminishes, the other side grows stronger. If such an opportunity was missed, who knows if there would be a second chance.

His shoulder shook suddenly, and the muscles on his back instantly bulged. The vine tightly coiled around his shoulders snapped inch by inch, and a piece of cloth measuring over a meter in length flew up abruptly.

With skillful manipulation of true energy, the three sections of the giant guandao flew over his head as if they had sprouted wings. Zhou Yi's footsteps didn't stop, and he raised his hands high. With a strange movement in mid-air, he swiftly assembled the terrifying giant guandao.

Taking a step forward, he pounced fiercely behind Lv Xinwen, while the giant guandao emitted a peculiar and resounding roar, striking at Lv Xinwen aimlessly.

This seemingly casual strike actually contained a mysterious and unimaginable power.

The first technique of the "Thirty-Six Forms of Mountain-Crushing" was perfectly displayed through the giant guandao. Lv Xinwen's eyes narrowed, and a hint of fear finally surfaced in his heart. From this nearly four-meter-long weapon, he sensed the scent of death, a feeling he hadn't experienced since reaching the realm of the innate.

He instantly realized that the giant guandao wielded by Zhou Yi had the ability to bring him to his demise. In this moment, he no longer harbored the thought of annihilating Zhou Yi and his companions. To him, Zhou Yi was like a nightmare, bringing him an overwhelming sense of terror.

With a forceful stomp of his feet, Lv Xinwen's figure trembled, abruptly changing direction and rushing toward Zhou Quanxin and the others. This sudden turn of events caught everyone off guard, not just Zhou Yi.

For someone of Lv Xinwen's status to choose to flee instead of fighting a battle against a innate expert, and to go towards the opponent's family, it was clearly an attempt to take hostages. Such an action was beyond anyone's expectations, even Zhou Quanxin couldn't react in time.

Zhou Yi grew anxious, letting out a loud shout as he swung his blade like a thunderbolt. Meanwhile, with a strong push of his legs, his entire body turned into a streak of light, swiftly covering the shortest distance and arriving at Zhou Quanxin's side.

However, as soon as he reached Zhou Quanxin's side, Zhou Yi knew something was wrong. Because after Lv Xinwen agilely evaded his strike in mid-air, he immediately escaped the range of his blade, darting away like a nimble cat.

Zhou Yi immediately understood that Lv Xinwen had no intention of taking hostages. He merely wanted to break free from the entanglement of Zhou Yi's Thirty-Six Forms of Mountain-Crushing. In an instant, Zhou Yi realized that Lv Xinwen had already entertained the thought of retreat; otherwise, he would never have sacrificed his dignity and made this choice.

With this realization, a tremendous and almost all-encompassing confidence filled Zhou Yi's heart.

This fact acted as a stimulant, pushing Zhou Yi's spirit to its peak. His hands trembled as a massive surge of true qi instantly flowed into the giant guandao. In that moment, he held nothing back.

Under the intense stimulation of overwhelming self-confidence, the Five Elements technique was activated. The powers of the Five Elements complemented each other, igniting an immense force.

A sudden blade radiance appeared on the giant guandao, its pale golden light expanding and contracting like the core of a venomous snake, making it too dangerous to look at directly.

Zhou Yi shouted loudly, swinging the giant guandao. The blade radiance shot out like a comet chasing the moon.

Time seemed to come to a halt, not because time had truly stopped, but because the speed of the blade radiance was too fast, reaching a point where it could tear through space and disregard distance.

After evading the range of the giant guandao, Lv Xinwen moved like lightning and arrived beside Fan Haori. With a swift grab, he caught Fan Haori and immediately fled into the distance.

Fan Shuhe had already died, and if Fan Haori were to be left behind, it would be tantamount to entrusting his life to the conscience of Yuan Chengzhi and the others. Lv Xinwen's intentions were unclear, as he unexpectedly pulled Fan Haori with him before leaving, seemingly wanting to take him far away.

With his speed, no one could stop him. However, as soon as he arrived beside Fan Haori, he felt something amiss behind him. An unprecedented sense of danger instantly enveloped him.

Almost without hesitation, he extended his right hand and swung it backward. He seemed to sense a strange power, a power that was sharp, formidable, and seemed invincible, capable of shattering anything.

He felt a lightness in his wrist and turned his head to look. His right hand had been severed from the middle and dropped to the ground. The golden blade radiance did not stop and instantly struck him.

A strange blue color flashed across Lv Xinwen's face as the blade radiance swept across his body and disappeared.

Just as everyone was dumbfounded, Lv Xinwen leaped up as if nothing had happened. He held Fan Haori in his left hand and, like a shooting star, leaped over the wall, instantly disappearing without a trace.

On the ground where he departed, there was a severed hand, but strangely, apart from the blood left on the severed hand, there was no blood on the ground. It was as if there was not a drop of blood on Lv Xinwen's body, making it impossible to leave any traces behind.

Chapter 129

Zhou Yi's face changed slightly, as he had repeatedly unleashed the powerful blade aura of the great guandao during his recent cultivation. He was well aware of the devastating power of this blade aura. He considered it his last resort。

However, when this blade aura landed on Lv Xinwen, he casually escaped as if nothing had happened. This perplexed Zhou Yi immensely, and he quickly made up his mind, saying, "Uncle, I'll be right back."

With those words, he swiftly disappeared, even though he held the weighty great guandao in his hand. But in his grasp, it seemed as light as a feather, devoid of any burden.

After the two formidable experts departed, there was a moment of silence in the field, followed by a sudden and intense transformation on both sides.

The servants and guests of the Fan family behind Yuan Zewei let out a cry and scattered like frightened birds and beasts, leaving only a few pale-faced individuals who continued to gaze at Yuan Zewei. They had followed him, not being members of the Fan family, and though they understood that the Fan family was now utterly defeated and they would never have a chance to claim power in the Yuan family, they were unwilling to abandon Yuan Zewei in this critical moment.

However, at this point, Yuan Zewei had lost all fighting spirit. His facial muscles trembled for a few moments, and finally, he let out a long sigh.

With that sigh, he seemed to have found complete liberation as his body slowly collapsed to the ground, devoid of any vitality in his eyes.

He had fought ruthlessly throughout his life for the position of the head of the Yuan family. Just as he believed he was about to achieve great success, he discovered that this dream had been utterly shattered.

The old man couldn't bear such a heavy blow and finally sought his own demise.

Yuan Zeyu's eyes also carried a sense of bewilderment. He took a few steps forward and approached the lifeless body of Yuan Zewei.

Yuan Chengzhi took a step forward, seemingly wanting to say something, but hesitated for a moment. In the end, he chose silence. However, the hatred in his eyes towards Yuan Zewei made it clear that he had no sympathy for his deceased uncle.

Yuan Zeyu stood up and spoke calmly, "Chengzhi, go to the county town and bring back all of our eldest brother's descendants."

Yuan Chengzhi was taken aback and hurriedly said, "Father..."

Yuan Zeyu waved his hand, saying, "Say no more. I've already made up my mind. You can manage the shops in the town, but the lands and properties under the main branch will all be returned to them."

The old man's words were firm, leaving no room for negotiation.

Although Yuan Chengzhi was reluctant in his heart, he didn't dare to defy his father's stubbornness. He let out a long sigh and reluctantly agreed.

Yuan Zeyu turned around and clasped his fists towards Zhou Quanxin, saying, "Nephew Quanxin, our Yuan family's survival today is all thanks to the support of your Zhou family. I am truly grateful..."

He bent his knees, about to kneel down.

Zhou Quanxin's face changed drastically, and he quickly stepped forward, swiftly supporting Yuan Zeyu before he could kneel.

Yuan Zeyu struggled for a moment, but Zhou Quanxin's arm remained as steady as a rock, unmoved.

Zhou Quanxin spoke with a serious expression, "Uncle Yuan, with the decades-long friendship between you and my father, if I were to accept this bow from you, how could I face my father when I return?"

Yuan Zeyu let out a long sigh, stood up, and suddenly said, "Quanxin, there is something I'd like to ask you to witness."

Zhou Quanxin quickly responded, "Uncle, if you have any matter, I am at your service."

Yuan Zeyu pointed to the lifeless body of Yuan Zewei and said, "As the saying goes, once a person dies, it's as if a light goes out.

Regardless of what he did in his lifetime, now that he's passed away, it's all in the past."

Zhou Quanxin hesitated for a moment and said, "Uncle, you're right."

"Good, since you also agree, I would like you to witness something. I want to officially include the descendants left behind by my eldest brother into the Yuan family lineage and return their lands and houses," Yuan Zeyu said with a serious tone. "I request your presence as a witness, so that if anyone covets their land and wealth in the future, you can ensure justice for them."

Zhou Quanxin's gaze fell on Yuan Chengzhi's face, showing a hint of dilemma.

Yuan Chengzhi's face turned grim as he asked, "Father, what do you mean by this?"

"You should understand my intention," Yuan Zeyu sighed lightly. "I simply don't want my eldest brother's bloodline to be extinguished a hundred years from now."

Yuan Chengzhi let out a disdainful snort and said, "Father, both Yuan...Uncle treated you this way, and yet you still want to do this? Do you really think they will appreciate it?"

Yuan Zeyu spoke calmly, "Whether they appreciate it or not is not important. I just hope to preserve their lineage."

"What if they turn against us again in the future?"

Yuan Zeyu calmly said, "What I want to preserve are simply honest and peaceful individuals."

Yuan Chengzhi's expression eased, and he replied, "Yes, I understand, Father."

Yuan Zeyu turned his head and asked, "Quanxin, what do you think?"

Zhou Quanxin finally nodded and said, "Since it is entrusted by Uncle, I dare not refuse."

Although he agreed, he also knew deep down that this was merely an act of goodwill from the old man. Even if Yuan Zewei's descendants could return to the Yuan family, at most, they would live a comfortable life without worries. It was impossible for them to become decision-makers in the Yuan family as they did in the past.

After being marginalized for decades, it was uncertain whether this branch could even survive. If Yuan Zeyu were still alive, perhaps no one would dare to oppress them, but once the old master passed away, everything became uncertain.

All Zhou Quanxin could do was to give this branch a glimmer of hope and prevent the rest of the Yuan family from openly targeting them.

As the old master left, the heavy atmosphere gradually dissipated. Yuan Chengzhi let out a sigh of relief and efficiently directed the servants to tidy up everything.

※※※※

In the vast forest, a figure swiftly passed through the ground like a bird.

In the hands of this figure, there was another person being carried, but it seemed weightless, as if it had no weight at all.

Finally, after passing through a mountain pass, the figure stumbled and came to a halt.

As soon as he stopped, he immediately collapsed to the ground, as if all his strength had been depleted in that moment.

"Grandmaster."

A cry of surprise sounded from beside him, and Fan Haori quickly stood up and supported the old man.

This person was Lv Xinwen, who had just been defeated in a battle against an Innate expert. At this moment, there was no longer a trace of the powerful life force he had once possessed.

In the short span of time, Lv Xinwen's hair had turned completely white, resembling an ordinary old man. Even his forehead was covered in dense wrinkles, as if decades had passed for him in that instant.

Fan Haori, although not an Innate expert, understood something when he saw the old man's transformation. His complexion also turned incredibly pale.

Lv Xinwen cleared his throat, his voice becoming hoarse. "I've checked, there's no one following us."

Fan Haori was taken aback and quickly replied, "Yes, Grandmaster."

"Do you know why I brought you away from there?" Lv Xinwen asked in a deep voice. Despite the dire situation, he showed no signs of impatience.

Fan Haori's lips moved, and he finally said, "grandmaster, you wanted me to avenge you and the two deceased uncles."

A bitter smile appeared on Lv Xinwen's face. He shook his head slightly and said, "Actually, when I first saw you in the Fan family, I knew about your nature and physique, which happened to be suitable for cultivating my techniques." He raised his head, sighed deeply, and continued, "I had intended to wait for the three of them to arrive and then accept you as a closed-door disciple. But unfortunately, they can never come back."

Fan Haori's eyes widened in shock, and his voice trembled as he exclaimed, "grandmaster, you..."

"I was struck by Zhou Yi's blade aura. Unexpectedly, at such a young age, he has not only reached the Innate realm but can also unleash blade aura through the air. Hehe..." Lv Xinwen chuckled self-deprecatingly and said, "I underestimated him."

Fan Haori opened his mouth to speak, but Lv Xinwen waved his hand and said, "Listen to me, don't interrupt me randomly. I don't have much time."

Fan Haori felt an even stronger sense of foreboding in his heart and immediately closed his mouth tightly.

"Zhou Yi is an exceptional talent with limitless potential in the future. Even if you were to cultivate diligently your whole life, you wouldn't stand a chance against him. I saved you not with the expectation of seeking revenge because that would be no different from seeking death," Lv Xinwen took a long breath and continued, "I saved you in the hope that you can inherit my techniques and pass them down, so that our lineage of techniques won't perish."

Fan Haori's expression changed rapidly. Today, he was defeated, his father died, and the Fan family's downfall seemed inevitable. In such a situation, even if Lv Xinwen could let go of his enmity with Zhou Yi and his three disciples, it was not something he could easily let go of.

Lv Xinwen took a few deep breaths and said, "There's a rumor in the martial world that I found the legacy cave of a senior expert and obtained treasures from it, allowing me to reach the Innate realm."

Upon hearing these words, even Fan Haori, at this moment, couldn't help but focus his attention and listen carefully.

"Hehe, I really don't know how these people came up with such speculations. They actually stumbled upon the truth," Lv Xinwen said helplessly.

Fan Haori inwardly thought, it's not that they stumbled upon the truth, but rather, every person who suddenly experiences a significant increase in martial skills will have similar rumors circulating. When someone like you, who has reached the Innate realm in a short period, emerges, if such rumors don't spread, it would be strange.

Lv Xinwen let out a long sigh and said, "In fact, thirty years ago, I was ambushed by the Zhu family. Although I managed to escape by a stroke of luck, I was seriously injured and almost lost my life. Later, by a stroke of fate, I did find a cave left behind by a senior expert. Inside that cave, there were not only miraculous inner energy and martial arts techniques but also two Innate Golden Pills."

Fan Haori's eyes widened instantly. In the small place like Zhou Family Village, perhaps not many people knew what an Innate Golden Pill was, but living in the county city, he was well aware that an Innate Golden Pill was a pill refined from the inner core of a spiritual beast with a lifespan of over 500 years. Once consumed by a peak-level Houtian expert, there would be a chance to step into the Innate realm.

Although Limit-Breaking Golden Pill and Energy-Boosting Golden Pill were precious, compared to the Innate Golden Pill, they were nothing. The Innate Golden Pill, which had the potential to cultivate Innate experts, could be described as invaluable.

"I had swallowed one of the two Golden Pills, allowing me to advance to the Innate realm. I had originally planned to give the remaining one to one of the two brothers from the Xie family. But now that all three of them are dead, I'll pass it on to you," Lv Xinwen said.

Fan Haori knelt heavily on the ground and said, "Thank you, grandmaster."

Lv Xinwen waved his hand slightly and said, "No need to be polite, but remember, not everyone is qualified to consume an Innate Golden Pill. The Golden Pill I obtained was derived from the inner core of a water attribute spiritual beast. So only practitioners with a water attribute can have a chance to step into the Innate realm after consuming it. Otherwise, the medicinal power produced by the Golden Pill will not assist them but instead cause a conflict of energies, ultimately becoming a poisonous pill that could claim their lives."

Fan Haori's expression changed slightly, and he quickly said, "Yes, Disciple understands." However, in his heart, he thought, such a good thing should be kept for himself to consume.

Lv Xinwen seemed to see through his thoughts and, struggling, took another breath and said, "I know you are also tempted, but you must remember, if you cannot reach the peak state of the tenth level of inner energy before you turn eighty, then never touch this Golden Pill."

Fan Haori quickly asked, "Why?"

"A person's physique has limitations. If you cannot reach that standard before turning eighty, your body will slowly age and will no longer be able to withstand the impact of the Golden Pill's medicinal power. Even if you achieve the peak later on, that aged body will still be unable to withstand the impact of the medicinal power," Lv Xinwen said solemnly. "Remember this very well, do not forget."

Fan Haori lowered his head and respectfully said, "Yes."

A tinge of disappointment flashed through his heart. Eighty years old was not considered a very old age for an Innate expert, but for ordinary people and ordinary cultivators, it was a day when one foot had already stepped into the coffin.

In fact, in this world, the majority of ordinary people did not live to be eighty years old.

However, even with his talent, it was not certain that he could reach the peak state of the tenth level by the time he reached eighty.

Lv Xinwen took out a sheepskin scroll from his bosom and handed it over, saying, "This sheepskin scroll contains the specific location of that cave. You can take it. As long as you are careful, you will surely be able to find it."

Fan Haori carefully received the scroll, looked at it cautiously, and put it into his bosom.

Lv Xinwen sighed, "The cave I stumbled upon back then was built by an unknown predecessor. It was filled with traps and mechanisms that were beyond my ability to decipher. Luckily, there was a quiet chamber inside that seemed to be the place where the predecessor resided on a daily basis, so there were no traps. I found the Golden Pill and the manuals in that quiet chamber."

Fan Haori was taken aback and instinctively asked, "Why did the predecessor leave these things in the quiet chamber?"

Lv Xinwen shook his head slightly, his mouth filled with bitterness. "I don't know about that either, but based on the situation in the quiet chamber, it seems that something important happened at that time, so the predecessor left in a hurry. However, for some reason, the predecessor never returned. Ah... perhaps that predecessor ended up in a fate similar to mine."

Fan Haori's expression tightened, and he quickly asked, "Senior, how is your body?"

Lv Xinwen smiled bitterly and said, "The cross-space blade aura from Zhou Yi has completely severed the vitality within my body. I suppressed my injuries and brought you here, but I have already done everything I could. As for my life... there is no way to reverse it anymore."

Fan Haori's face darkened, and tears welled up in his eyes. From a certain perspective, they were now in the same boat. Seeing this elderly man about to pass away, he couldn't help but feel a strong sense of sorrow.

Lv Xinwen's voice grew weaker and weaker as he said, "The Golden Pill and my insights on cultivation are all in the cave. Go find them and continue our lineage. Don't let it be severed."

Fan Haori knelt heavily, kowtowing three times, and solemnly said, "Yes."

Lv Xinwen nodded in satisfaction. His eyes slowly closed, and he murmured, "How could his innate qi be so strong? Could it be that he was born as an innate powerhouse? Is he the legendary naturally-born innate expert?"

His voice grew softer and softer, eventually becoming inaudible.

Fan Haori remained kneeling without moving. After a long while, he reached out to feel Lv Xinwen's breath. Then, his face gradually twisted.

He once again knocked his head heavily, as if he was speaking to Lv Xinwen and to himself, "Senior, rest assured, I will definitely avenge you and the Fan family for this deep enmity." His teeth gritted together, making a grinding sound. "Perhaps I will never be a match for Zhou Yi, but the Yuan and Zhou families have only one Zhou Yi. If I achieve success in my cultivation, I will first kill every member of the Yuan and Zhou families, leaving none alive. I will make them live in eternal regret."

His voice resounded thunderously, resolute and unwavering, as if each word was a nail firmly embedded in the wall, impossible to erase...

Chapter 130

Ever since severing one of Lv Xinwen's hands, it appeared as if he had escaped unscathed. While others might not have noticed anything unusual, Zhou Yi keenly sensed that within Lv Xinwen's body, the once immense and nearly overflowing life force had been completely severed by his strike. The power of the sword exceeded even Zhou Yi's expectations.

Of course, if Lv Xinwen hadn't fought Zhou Yi beforehand and had no idea of the horrifying trump card he possessed, it would have been impossible for Zhou Yi to assassinate him in such a nearly covert manner.

Deep down, Zhou Yi held a deep admiration for the old man. Setting aside everything else, the fact that he could maintain such a high level of vitality and escape to such a distance despite his bodily functions having been completely extinguished was beyond the imagination of an ordinary person. Perhaps it was only with such perseverance and strength of will that he had the qualifications to ascend to the realm of the innate.

After a moment, Zhou Yi's eyes opened slightly. Through the residual essence, he sensed the direction in which Lv Xinwen had departed. Moreover, he realized that the sensation was growing stronger, indicating that he was gradually closing in.

However, the air was also permeated with an increasingly intense aura of death, suggesting that Lv Xinwen couldn't hold on for much longer.

With a slight thought, the innate energy within Zhou Yi's body surged like mighty waves.

The strands of true qi flowed through Zhou Yi's meridians like flowing water. With the surging of this true qi, Zhou Yi's physical form underwent an incredible transformation.

The muscles on his face quickly withered, and his limbs became as rigid as wooden stakes. At first glance, he seemed like an entirely different person.

The Xu family's Withered Wood Technique became even more unimaginable after reaching the innate realm. When the innate true qi operated in this technique, Zhou Yi's body truly resembled a wooden stake.

A vast amount of aura emanated from him, but this aura seemed entirely different from the aura of a human body. It harmonized with the surrounding mountains and forests.

If a blind innate expert were to arrive in front of him at this moment, ninety percent of them would mistake him for an ancient tree, dense and having lived for thousands of years.

When Lv Xinwen stopped, he once utilized a powerful true qi sensitivity in a last-ditch effort, akin to a dying glow, to explore his surroundings.

He entrusted his origins and the parchment to Fan Haori with confidence because in this place, he had no one to rely on. More importantly, he was certain that Zhou Yi had not pursued him.

Zhou Yi's cultivation in the Earth and Water techniques alone was already remarkable. Therefore, Lv Xinwen's true qi exploration focused on the perspectives of the Earth and Water techniques. If Zhou Yi had been close, the aura of the Water and Earth elements around him would have been a hundred times stronger than elsewhere.

When Zhou Yi gathered the power of the Withered Wood Technique, the aura of the Wood element around him was intense like a beam of light. However, no matter how Lv Xinwen speculated, he could never have guessed that it was Zhou Yi.

As he approached death, Lv Xinwen found it inconceivable that Zhou Yi could cultivate multiple different elemental techniques simultaneously. However, precisely because of this, he believed that Zhou Yi wouldn't have the ability to cultivate the Wood technique alongside the others.

Since he couldn't sense any changes in the auras of these elemental techniques, Lv Xinwen concluded that Zhou Yi must have given up the pursuit. Little did he know that Zhou Yi possessed not only the true qi of Earth, Metal, and Water but also the complete set of Five Elements.

So, when Zhou Yi slowly and steadily closed in, Lv Xinwen remained oblivious, along with his companion. Unbeknownst to them, Zhou Yi's understanding extended beyond just the true qi of Earth, Metal, and Water—he possessed the true qi of all five elements.

After activating the Withered Wood Technique, Zhou Yi's breath even ceased, and the human-like aura of life within him was suppressed to its extreme. This level of suppression was difficult to achieve, even with the Breath-Holding Art.

Quietly concealed a hundred meters away from them, Zhou Yi's true qi spread through the energy of the surrounding trees. In this densely forested area, even if the Wood element's energy was slightly stronger, it wouldn't arouse suspicion.

As he focused his attention, Zhou Yi caught every word of their conversation in his ears. At first, he remained calm, especially when he heard Lv Xinwen's words trying to dissuade Fan Haori from seeking revenge. Zhou Yi had already decided to spare the two of them. However, he never anticipated that when Lv Xinwen died, leaving only Fan Haori behind, he would make such a ruthless vow.

He vowed to annihilate the Yuan and Zhou families, ensuring that Zhou yi lived in eternal torment.

If he truly accomplished this, Zhou Yi knew that the latter half of his life would be exactly as Fan Haori desired—eternally living in pain.

The thought triggered an overwhelming sense of murderous intent within Zhou Yi.

Even when Zhou Yi had heard earlier about the Xiao borther's desire to eliminate the Zhou family, his intent to kill was not as resolute as it was at this moment. Especially after hearing Fan Haori's resounding words, he understood that only one between the Zhou family and Fan Haori could survive—this animosity was irreconcilable.

With a slight movement of his body, he leaped like a wooden stake. In mid-air, the Withered Wood Technique within him transformed into the Ripple Technique, resembling a meandering stream with a gentle murmur.

His muscles quickly swelled and, within a few movements, returned to their original state. If he were to change his outer appearance at this moment, no one would ever associate the previously emaciated figure with him.

Although his technique had changed, Zhou Yi landed silently.

After confirming Lv Xinwen's demise, Zhou Yi naturally relaxed his movements and was no longer as cautious.

Fan Haori, a mere peak-level Inner Strength cultivator at the seventh layer, wasn't worthy of such wariness.

As he turned around a corner, Zhou Yi arrived outside the mountain hollow. Fan Haori was digging a hole, seemingly intending to bury Lv Xinwen on the spot.

Zhou Yi let out a soft sigh, his power surging through his arms.

Although his sigh didn't produce any sound, Fan Haori, who was digging the hole, seemed to sense something. His actions suddenly froze, and he slowly turned his body.

When he saw Zhou Yi in front of the mountain hollow, the flush of excitement on his face instantly vanished. In its place, his eyes filled with a fierce and chilling resentment.

Under Fan Haori's scrutinizing gaze, Zhou Yi furrowed his brows slightly, clearly displeased with that look.

"So, you've come. I never expected you to deceive even grandmaster" a voice emerged as if it had leapt out from between clenched teeth, bearing evident resentment.

Since Zhou Yi had tracked him here, he must have heard Fan Haori's final words. Knowing his intentions, Fan Haori realized that Zhou Yi would not spare him.

"Yes, I've come," Zhou Yi looked at the now-closed eyes of Lv Xinwen and spoke slowly, "Actually, he didn't need to die. If your Fan family didn't covet the Yuan family's wealth, he, his three disciples, your father, and you... none of you would have needed to die."

For some reason, an infinite wave of emotion surged within Zhou Yi's heart. If certain words weren't spoken, it seemed to bring about a suffocating sensation.

Perhaps it was related to the fact that a Innate cultivator died by his hands.

The formerly prestigious Fan family, due to their greed for things that didn't belong to them, ultimately couldn't escape the fate of annihilation, even with the assistance of a Innate cultivator.

Although Zhou Yi was young, during his time spent with Yuan Chengzhi, he had come to understand certain things. If Yuan Chengzhi spared the Fan family, it would be as if the sun rose from the west and set in the east.

Knowing Yuan Chengzhi's character, not only would he absorb all of the Fan family's assets, but he probably wouldn't even spare any remnants of the Fan family.

However, all of this was their own doing, and even Zhou Yi couldn't intervene.

All they could do was naturally obtain their share in this feast.

A slightly abnormal redness appeared on Fan Haori's face as he sneered, "Our Fan family is powerful, while the Yuan family is weak, and someone even provided us with evidence and an excuse. Why shouldn't we seize their assets? What we didn't expect was that the Yuan family would invite you..."

Upon hearing his blatant and undisguised explanation, Zhou Yi's heart suddenly chilled.

Could the Yuan family of today not become the Zhou family of the future?

Despite the prosperous appearance of the Zhou family today, if there comes a day when the Zhou family weakens, there will surely be other clans vying to replace them.

At this moment, a vague goal took shape in Zhou Yi's heart. He must make the Zhou family a long-standing noble family, like the Linlang Lin family and the Fire crow Xie family.

Only such a complex network of connections, with intertwined influences in various regions and deep-rooted foundations, can deter and cope with the challenges posed by emerging clans, wave after wave.

Although Fan Haori mocked with his words, his body didn't dare to make a move.

Even in a life-or-death situation, he didn't want to die immediately. Therefore, he dared not move at all, as any movement might lead Zhou Yi to misunderstand, and he wouldn't even have a chance to defend himself.

Fan Haori's gaze lowered slightly, falling upon a parchment scroll on his chest. It was a sheepskin scroll given to him by Lv Xinwen before his death. The old man's wish was for him to inherit the unique martial arts technique.

However, Fan Haori's only thought at this moment was how to destroy the map without leaving a trace.

He accepted his imminent death, but even in death, he couldn't leave the map to Zhou Yi, let alone let him find the secret cave and obtain Lv Xinwen's legacy.

His eyes darted quickly, and a bead of sweat even formed on his forehead. Suddenly, his eyes brightened, and he said, "Master Zhou, I know I'm destined to die today, and I dare not ask for your forgiveness. But please allow me to finish digging this pit and bury Master Lv Xinwen first before I take my own life."

Zhou Yi pondered for a moment and said, "Very well."

Fan Haori clenched his fist, turned around, picked up a rough stone slab, and jumped into the half-dug pit, continuing to dig. He pretended to inadvertently steal a glance in Zhou Yi's direction, only to see that his gaze was still fixed on Lv Xinwen, as if there were something incomprehensible in his eyes.

Fan Haori felt secretly delighted and blocked Zhou Yi's line of sight as he stealthily reached into his chest. With his seventh-level internal energy, a simple squeeze would completely destroy the map. Even if it fell into Zhou Yi's hands, it would be useless.

However, just as his fingers touched the sheepskin scroll, a look of satisfaction, ferocity, and smugness froze on his face. He suddenly realized that he couldn't move. Not only was his internal energy unable to circulate, but his body also couldn't make the slightest movement.

Zhou Yi walked out from behind him, his gaze open and honest as he looked at Fan Haori and said, "Since Brother Fan knows that death is inevitable, then the map that Lv Xinwen gifted you should be of no use to you. So..." He sighed softly and continued, "I will take charge of preserving this map. I will fulfill Lv Xinwen's wish and ensure that his lineage's teachings do not come to an end."

Fan Haori's face turned pale, and his body went limp, collapsing to the ground. Only his mouth could still move. His eyes were filled with rage, and his face contorted like a heated iron block. He stubbornly bit his lower lip, which had turned red from the pressure. If gaze could ignite, Zhou Yi's body would likely be engulfed in raging flames.

"You dare to snatch even the belongings of the grandmaster? You deserve to die!" Fan Haori exclaimed with his mouth still able to articulate.

Zhou Yi smiled and replied, "Fan Haori, didn't you just say that the Yuan family is weak and the Fan family is strong, so it's only natural for you to take their place? Now that you are weak and I am strong, why can't I do the same?"

Fan Haori was stunned. His lips trembled, and his eyes widened, splitting at the corners and oozing two streaks of red liquid. Then, he burst into loud laughter that echoed in the distance. His laughter continued until his voice became hoarse and unpleasant, like the sound of grinding stones.

Eventually, his laughter subsided, and he murmured, "Retribution, retribution. We have our retribution, and you will surely have yours in the future."

His voice grew faint, and he suddenly spat out half of his tongue, as a large amount of fresh blood gushed from his mouth.

Zhou Yi didn't intervene but showed a trace of pity in his eyes as he silently watched Fan Haori.

After a short while, Fan Haori's body twitched a few times and never moved again.

Zhou Yi shook his head slightly, reached out his hand, and picked up the crude stone slab that Fan Haori had discarded. He jumped into the pit and continued Fan Haori's work. Within a few moments, he had dug a deep hole.

Zhou Yi continued to dig the deep hole, knowing that burying the bodies in the forest leading to the Endless Mountains required a deep enough pit. Otherwise, wild beasts would drag the buried corpses out and leave nothing behind, not even bones.

Although Lv Xinwen had already passed away, he was still a top-notch innate powerhouse and should not be left exposed in the wilderness. No matter the circumstances, he deserved a proper burial.

As for Fan Haori, while the downfall of the Fan family was deserved, after this incident, Zhou Yi had come to understand a truth. The strong survive, and the weak perish. It was the only truth in this world.

The Fan family's actions were also an attempt to establish their lasting legacy. Only through absolute strength could they avoid being replaced by other families. In a way, what they were doing was not entirely wrong.

However, in Zhou Yi's heart, there was still a forbidden zone that he dared not inquire about or think too much about. Forty years ago, Old Master Zhou Wude, along with Zhou Laibao, had established Zhou Family Village with a large Guan Dao in hand. How much blood was shed during that process? How many small clans were obliterated?

Or perhaps, they had the ability to build Zhou Family Village without harming others...

Although Zhou Yi held great respect for his grandfather and he knew their power was formidable within Taicang County, he believed that achieving such a feat might surpass their capabilities.

Zhou Yi carefully collected the belongings of Lv Xinwen and Fan Haori before burying them deep in the pit he had dug. The depth of the hole was approximately two meters, making it unlikely for ordinary wild beasts to drag the bodies out. Before burying them, Zhou Yi searched their bodies and took anything that could be useful.

After all, these items had no value to the deceased, and he might find some use for them.

There wasn't much on Lv Xinwen, but Zhou Yi found some valuable items on Fan Haori. Apart from the specially made parchment scroll, he discovered several gold ingots and a bottle of elixirs. When he opened the bottle and sniffed its contents, Zhou Yi's expression changed slightly. Inside were Energy-Boosting Golden Pill,a total of five of them.

Zhou Yi suddenly realized that these golden pills were likely not originally owned by Fan Haori but were obtained from Lv Xinwen. No wonder there was nothing on the body of an innate powerhouse. However, Fan Haori couldn't have anticipated that although he gained the golden pills and the map, he would immediately follow in Lv Xinwen's footsteps without even getting a chance to enhance his own strength.

After collecting everything he obtained, Zhou Yi spread out the parchment scroll.

Chapter 131

By the touch alone, one could tell that this was no ordinary parchment scroll. It seemed to have undergone some sort of special treatment, rendering it remarkably resistant to damage. Gently unfurling the scroll revealed a series of intricate patterns, not merely painted on but meticulously stitched with resilient threads of varying colors. The entire design resembled a gigantic apple, so lifelike that it created an illusion of wanting to take a bite.

In an instant, Zhou Yi felt a stirring in his heart. He held the parchment scroll above his head, studying it intently. Within the lush green exterior of the apple-shaped pattern lay a round white flesh, and at the core of that flesh, a peach-shaped red heart. Under the sunlight, this red heart displayed a peculiar transparency.

His palm grazed the surface of the parchment scroll, and he sensed an aura of profound antiquity, as if it had weathered a thousand years. Deep down, he knew that this creation was not crafted by Lv xinwen but rather discovered from some distant place. The history of this parchment scroll must be extensive, yet there was no sign of wear on the sheepskin, and the colors of the stitched lines remained vibrant, as if they had been freshly embroidered.

A peculiar notion suddenly arose in his mind, and after a brief hesitation, he lightly clasped the corner of the map, applying a bit more force as he gently pulled.

However, the result of his pull was far beyond his expectations. It simply would not budge. He applied a bit more force, but the outcome remained unchanged. Eventually, Zhou Yi dared not exert any further strength. Nevertheless, the experience he just had made him realize that the durability of this object far surpassed his imagination. If it had fallen into the hands of an ordinary person, it would likely be indestructible.

At this point, one thing was certain—the origin of this map was extraordinary. He then recalled the words spoken by Lv xinwen before his death, mentioning the numerous mechanisms in that underground cavern that even himself couldn't decipher. This only deepened his curiosity.

Lv xinwen was a formidable innate expert. Could there be mechanisms capable of trapping or hindering someone of such caliber? It was truly peculiar.

In his heart, a strong desire surged, as if urging him to immediately seek out that underground cavern and explore what mechanisms lay within that even innate experts feared.

His gaze swept over the map once again, and his brows furrowed tightly.

The embroidered terrain on the map was unfamiliar to him. This did not surprise him, for the continent was vast and diverse. Not even he could claim to be familiar with every location.

Several key places on the map were accompanied by stitched words, indicating the names of those locations. However, the problem was that while others might recognize those characters, Zhou Yi himself did not. These peculiar script styles were something he had never encountered before.

After considering for a moment, Zhou Yi carefully tucked away the map. It was not something suitable for others to see, and as for the directions within, he would search for them slowly.

Although these characters were difficult to understand, in the vastness of the world, surely there would be someone who could recognize them. Otherwise, Lv xinwen wouldn't have entrusted it so confidently to Fan Haori, as he believed that Fan Haori could easily decipher it.

If that were the case, even if these characters were not widely known, there must be some who were familiar with them. Adjusting his emotions, Zhou Yi turned and left.

When he came, he was cautious and discreet, tracing Lv xinwen's steps. But now, on his way back, he had fewer worries. Once he unleashed his speed, his body became like flowing clouds, propelled by the power of the wind, swiftly heading towards the Yuan Family Manor at a speed far surpassing that of an ordinary person.

※※※※

In the blink of an eye, seven days had passed.

During these seven days, Zhou Yi enjoyed treatment within the Yuan family's manor that was almost equivalent to that of an emperor. Without his command, not a single person dared to enter the courtyard where the Zhou family resided. Even the previous owner of the estate, Yuan Chengzhi, had to seek permission from the servants in charge of serving them before venturing inside.

In the earlier days, although the Yuan family treated them politely, it was far from the level of awe and reverence they showed now.

However, after learning of Zhou Yi's true strength, the entire Yuan family underwent a tremendous transformation in their attitude towards them once again.

A long, drawn-out breath could be heard emanating from Zhou Yi's room. Whether inhaling or exhaling, each breath seemed endless, as if it would never cease.

From this, it was evident that Zhou Yi had a much larger lung capacity than an ordinary person. Even Zhou Quanxin, who had reached the tenth level of internal energy, was probably not even half as capable as him.

Suddenly, the sound of footsteps ceased, and Zhou Yi opened his eyes with a smile. "Big Brother, if you have something to say, just come in."

The door immediately swung open, and Zhou Yitian awkwardly walked in, his face full of embarrassment.

"Little brother, how did you know I was coming to find you?"

Zhou Yi rolled his eyes and replied, "You were pacing back and forth outside my room. It made my head spin. If I still didn't know, wouldn't that be too foolish?"

Zhou Yitian saw that Yixing's attitude towards him hadn't changed at all, just like before, and he felt a sense of relief. He forced a wry smile and said, "Little brother, you actually advanced to the Innate Realm without a sound. It's truly unbelievable."

Zhou Yi smiled faintly, realizing that any explanations now would seem inappropriate, so it was better not to say anything.

"Actually, when I found out that you had advanced to the Innate Realm, I was worried," Zhou Yitian sighed heavily.

"What are you worried about, big brother?"

"I was worried about your attitude, whether it would suddenly change," Zhou Yitian said earnestly.

Zhou Yi was slightly taken aback, inwardly sighing. The truth was, his attitude towards his brothers had indeed undergone slight changes, but not to a great extent. After all, he had just recently entered the Innate Realm, while his relationship with his family members spanned over a decade. Such deep-rooted emotions couldn't be erased in a short period for no reason.

"Now, I am relieved," Zhou Yitian said with satisfaction. "You are still my little brother, still the most outstanding and diligent youth of our Zhou family."

Zhou Yi accompanied him with a hearty smile and said, "Big brother, I won't change."

Zhou Yitian nodded heavily and then wore a hint of distress on his face.

Zhou Yi was curious. He had a faint feeling that his older brother must have encountered some trouble, which was why he had specifically come to find him.

"Big brother, what's the matter?" Zhou Yi asked.

Zhou Yitian hesitated for a moment and said, "Sixth brother, yesterday I had a meeting with Elder Yuan Zeyu."

"What did he say to you?" Zhou Yi asked curiously. His older brother wouldn't mention this matter without reason.

"Elder Yuan Zeyu wanted to give me a concubine," Zhou Yitian said, his face slightly reddening.

Zhou Yi was taken aback, and a strange look appeared in his eyes as he looked at his brother.

"Big brother, you just got married last year," Zhou Yi tentatively asked, "Is your relationship with sister-in-law not good?"

Zhou Yitian shook his head repeatedly and said, "No, my relationship with your sister-in-law is very good."

"In that case, why didn't you refuse Elder Yuan?" Zhou Yi asked in confusion. "Grandfather and Uncle have both mentioned that for those of us who practice martial arts, although we don't abstain from romantic relationships, indulging in them for a long time may greatly compromise our strength and even hinder progress for a lifetime."

Zhou Yitian's expression slightly changed, and he finally said, "I understand. I understand everything. But... I like that person."

Zhou Yi opened his mouth, ready to say something, but as soon as he heard Zhou Yitian confess, "I like that person," he found himself unable to utter a word.

While it was true that Big Brother and Big Sister-in-law had a good relationship, their marriage was ultimately a result of the union between the two prominent families. Although Big Sister-in-law possessed a stunning appearance, she was not personally chosen by Big Brother as a lifelong partner.

Suddenly, a sense of unease washed over Zhou Yi, and he asked, "Big Brother, what do you intend to do?"

Zhou Yitian cleared his throat and said, "Little brother, there's something I need to ask of you."

Though Zhou Yi felt an inexplicable tingling sensation on his scalp, he didn't hesitate and replied, "What is it, Big Brother? Just give me your orders."

"Little brother, this time, there are two women by Yuan's patriarch's side, and I've taken a liking to one of them," Zhou Yitian said with some uneasiness.

Zhou Yi's eyes widened abruptly, and he asked, "Big Brother, what do you mean?"

Zhou Yitian sighed, "Dear brother, I have no other choice. You are now the true representative of our Zhou family. If you are willing to accept one of these two women, even if I accept the other, it wouldn't be considered a big deal."

Zhou Yi's expression became extremely comical.

Although he devoted himself entirely to martial arts, given his age, it was absurd to claim that he had no curiosity about women. However, his main focus was still on how to improve his own strength. Each training session brought him great joy, so he didn't feel a strong longing for romantic entanglements.

But now, with Big Brother suddenly bringing it up, he found himself struggling to make a decision.

After pondering for a moment, Zhou Yi shook his head and said, "Big Brother, do you think Grandfather and Big Uncle would agree to me marrying at this point?"

Zhou Yitian smiled wryly and replied, "Little brother, you've misunderstood. I don't intend for you to marry that girl." He paused for a moment and continued, "That girl is the legitimate daughter of Yuan Chengzhi, but she was born out of wedlock, and her mother passed away early. However, she carries herself with grace and propriety. Even if she becomes your concubine, it won't tarnish your reputation."

Zhou Yi looked skeptical and asked, "Concubine?"

"Yes," Zhou Yitian said proudly: Even if she were the legitimate daughter of Yuan Chengzhi, she would still only be worthy of being your concubine."

Zhou Yi's heart suddenly stirred, and he asked, "Big Brother, who is the person you have taken a liking to?"

Zhou Yitian's face blushed slightly as he spoke, "The one I have my eye on is Yuan Zewei's own granddaughter, a woman who knows when to advance and retreat and shouldn't compete with Yanli."

Zhou Yi's eyebrows suddenly raised as he exclaimed, "Yuan Zewei's granddaughter? Big Brother, are you mistaken? Yuan Zewei has already been expelled from the Yuan family, and he and Yuan's patriarch are like water and fire. If you were to marry his granddaughter, it would lead to a conflict between our families... Wait, how could Yuan's patriarch possibly introduce Yuan Zewei's granddaughter to you?"

Zhou Yitian let out a soft sigh and recounted the events that unfolded after Zhou Yi's departure. He mentioned how Yuan Zewei had met a tragic end, but out of consideration for brotherly affection, Yuan Zeyu not only readmitted members of Yuan's branch but also shared the details that Zhou Quanxin had vouched for.

This matter was undoubtedly a significant event for the Yuan family, but for Zhou Yi, it was a trivial affair, and naturally, there was no one who would gossip in front of him.

Therefore, after three days of his return, he was completely unaware of the events that had transpired that day.

After listening to his brother's words, Zhou Yi couldn't help but sigh. However, he was uncertain whether Yuan's patriarch's actions were truly justified.

Zhou Yitian continued, "Although Yuan Zewei's branch has been readmitted to the family, they no longer hold any power. Their decline and marginalization are predictable. To prevent their lineage from being completely extinguished in the future, Yuan's patriarch deliberately selected a direct granddaughter from their branch and a daughter born to Yuan Chengzhi's illegitimate relationship." He paused for a moment and said, "Do you understand what I mean?"

Zhou Yi nodded slightly. The conversation had reached this point, and if he still didn't understand, it would truly be foolish and ignorant.

Zhou Yitian said, "In reality, Yuan's patriarch still values the descendants of main branch. That's why he is sending Yuan Chengzhi's daughter to you and Yuan Zewei's granddaughter to me.

Women from prestigious families, despite their comfortable lifestyles, sometimes couldn't avoid making sacrifices in their marriages for the sake of their family's development.

With the Yuan family being weaker and the Zhou family stronger, such an outcome was only natural. However, all of this was also because Zhou Yi had reached the realm of Innate.

Seeing that Zhou Yi seemed somewhat intrigued, Zhou Yitian quickly seized the opportunity and said, "Little brother, since you're not actually marrying, but merely accepting a concubine, the commotion won't be as great. Besides, Yuan's patriarch also mentioned that even if there is no formal marriage at the moment, Yuan Miss can serve in our Zhou household until you marry, and then we can proceed with the marriage."

Zhou Yi was truly taken aback this time and said, "Big Brother, Yuan Miss is still a daughter of the Yuan family. Is it really acceptable to do this?"

Zhou Yitian chuckled and replied, "If it were anyone else, of course not. But now you are an Innate powerhouse. As long as you nod and let the rumors circulate, I guarantee that not only the Yuan family but even the legitimate daughters of the Lin family would willingly agree to such an arrangement."

Zhou Yi was stunned for a moment. He finally realized the immense power that came with his status as an Innate powerhouse. In reality, he had severely underestimated himself. A sixteen-year-old who had already reached the Innate realm—what heights would he reach in his future growth?

To please such a young powerhouse, it would be worthwhile to pay any price.

"Little brother, don't rush to make a decision. Perhaps you can come with me to meet Yuan's patriarch and see for yourself," Zhou Yitian advised. "As long as you make the decision and agree to it, Father will definitely not blame you." He paused, as if filled with boundless emotions, and said, "In the current Zhou Manor, there will never be anyone who blames you anymore, not even Grandfather."

Chapter 132

In the midst of the Yuan family, within a tranquil courtyard, resided the venerable patriarch, Yuan. Though the courtyard was secluded, it was bathed in abundant sunlight. Even in the depths of winter, rays of sunlight effortlessly streamed into the courtyard, casting a gentle warmth upon the chilly season.

As Zhou Yitian and Zhou Yi stepped into the courtyard, he could clearly see the joyous smile on Yuan patriarch's face. For him, being able to present his granddaughter, before such a young and formidable cultivator was already enough to bring satisfaction to both him and the Yuan family.

Welcoming the two warmly, Yuan's patriarch did not put on any airs of seniority. If strangers were to witness their interactions, they would surely mistake the three of them as close friends with a deep bond. However, the age gap between these three friends was indeed quite substantial.

Once the guests and hosts were seated, Yuan Ze Yu exchanged a glance with a clever servant who grasped the old patriarch's intention. Moments later, two women entered from the hall. One of them appeared to be in her early twenties, tall and slender. Her hair was sleekly pulled back into a large bun, accentuating her beautiful face. Above her eyes arched delicate eyebrows, and in the space between her well-defined brows and slightly elevated nose, a pair of large, bright eyes sparkled. Not only did these eyes enhance her smiling face, but they also seemed to illuminate the entire room as she walked in.

As the woman entered the room, Zhou Yitian's eyes instantly lit up. A gentle smile naturally formed on his face, with laughter evident in the corners of his eyes and brows.

The woman first glanced up at Yuan's patriarch, then discreetly surveyed the room. When her gaze met Zhou Yitian's, her eyes shimmered like autumn water, as if conveying a myriad of emotions. Although she quickly averted her eyes, a faint blush graced her cheeks.

Zhou Yitian stole a glance at Yi, his eyes filled with a pleading expression. Seeing the ambiguous exchange between this woman and his eldest brother, Yi instantly understood that she was the woman who had captured his brother's interest. However, while the woman possessed a captivating beauty, she was not necessarily an unrivaled beauty like Zhou's sister-in-law, Cheng Yanli. Yi wondered what exactly had captivated his brother's heart to such an extent.

This unabashed expression of affection undoubtedly revealed Zhou Yitian's determination. Yi, feeling somewhat troubled, turned his gaze backward and noticed a woman of similar age following closely behind the aforementioned woman.

Compared to the previous woman, this one's appearance was not inferior, but she exuded an air of innocence. However, within her demeanor, there was an elegant and gentle aura that could be distinctly felt. Her small mouth revealed a childlike innocence, and especially her eyes—so clear, so deep, always shining with brilliance.

Yet, in Yi's perception, this young girl didn't seem as pure as her outward appearance suggested. Within the depths of those eyes, it felt as though she harbored hidden thoughts unknown to others.

Her complexion was fair and delicate, meeting the standards of a refined young lady. However, someone as observant as Yi noticed a few calluses on her hands. Though these calluses were not prominent and would go unnoticed by most people, they couldn't escape Yi's keen eyes.

To be honest, when Yi first laid eyes on this woman, he couldn't quite grasp his own feelings. It was as if he was looking at a stranger, and she hadn't truly entered his heart. However, he already knew the purpose of coming here and the woman's identity, so naturally, there was a peculiar sensation within him.

The expressions of the two Zhou brothers were under the observation of Yuan's patriarch. Zhou Yitian naturally did not conceal his affection, but what truly caught the old patriarch's attention was Zhou Yi.

It can be said that if it weren't for Yi's identity, even as Yuan Zewei's granddaughter, she would not be considered as a concubine for Zhou Yitian. However, Yuan Grandfather felt somewhat disappointed because he couldn't discern any clues from Yi's gaze. But upon further thought, he suddenly felt relieved.

Although Zhou Yi was young, he was, after all, an innate powerhouse. How could he be easily seen through? As long as Zhou Yi didn't object and was willing to accept his granddaughter, it would be enough.

"Yi, let me introduce them to you," the patriarch said with a beaming smile. "These are my two granddaughters, Yuan Liwen and Yuan Lixun."

With each introduction, the two women slightly curtsied in acknowledgment.

When introducing Yuan Liwen, the patriarch did not explicitly mention that she was Yuan Zeyu's granddaughter, and the same was true for the introduction of Yuan Lixun as Yuan Chengzhi's eldest daughter. In light of this, Zhou Yi was content to remain oblivious, smiling and returning the greetings.

Although the patriarch addressed Zhou Yi by his name directly, his respectful tone didn't carry the air of an elder speaking. However, this approach perfectly conveyed a sense of closeness, goodwill, and respect toward Zhou Yi. When it came to dealing with people, this nearly eighty-year-old man indeed had his own set of skills.

They exchanged a few words in the hall, with the patriarch maintaining a cheerful and benevolent expression throughout. After a while, the patriarch stood up and said, "This old man is tired and needs to rest for a while. You two will represent me and entertain them properly."

After the patriarch left, Zhou Yitian cleared his throat and said, "Brother, there's something I need to discuss with Miss Liwen, so I'll step out first."

Yuan Liwen's face immediately turned red, and there seemed to be a hint of unease and constraint in her expression. Yet, the rosy hue at the corners of her eyes and brows exuded a captivating charm.

Zhou Yi felt a moment of confusion. His elder brother had always been steady in his actions, but today's behavior gave him an unfamiliar sensation. He cleared his throat and said, "Elder Brother, there's something I would like to ask you. May I?"

Zhou Yitian hesitated for a moment and replied, "Sure." He turned around and said, "Ladies, please have a seat for a moment. We'll be back shortly."

The two of them walked side by side out of the room, engaging in conversation in front of Yuan's patriarch's courtyard.

Although this was not their own home, the numerous servants of the Yuan family knew their identities. After seeing them, the servants respectfully saluted from a distance and did not dare to approach and inquire.

"Brother, you seem to have changed," Zhou Yi said earnestly, "You're not acting like yourself."

Zhou Yitian's expression slightly changed, and he replied, " I know I've been reckless, and I've caused you trouble."

Zhou Yi shook his head with a headache and said, "Brother, we're brothers. Why talk about these things? Besides, for me, it might not necessarily be trouble. But your state of mind seems off, and that's not a good thing."

Zhou Yitian pondered for a moment and then smiled bitterly, "Brother , you're still young, and there are things you don't understand."

"What don't I understand?" Zhou Yi said, displeased.

Zhou Yitian's smile became even more bitter as he said, "Brother Yi, if one day you see a woman and suddenly find that all your gaze involuntarily falls upon her, her image fills your mind, and her name lingers in your heart, then you will understand my feelings."

Zhou Yi stared at his elder brother, dumbfounded. He knew that his elder brother seemed to have developed a strong infatuation for that woman, but to be so captivated to this extent was truly extraordinary.

Almost involuntarily, Zhou Yi glanced towards the hall, where the two women sat, seemingly engaged in a whispered conversation. With his keen eyesight, he could clearly observe every movement they made. However, no matter how he looked at it, Yuan Liwen was merely a woman slightly above average. It was almost unimaginable how someone like her could captivate his elder brother to such an extent in such a short time.

He let out a bitter laugh, perhaps the only way to explain this emotion was through the concept of a karmic bond. However, deep down, he had serious doubts about whether he would ever encounter such a woman...

Most likely, it was an impossibility. Because what he truly pursued was the supreme and boundless path of martial arts. Yet, even though he didn't understand this feeling, since his elder brother had opened up his heart and revealed his innermost thoughts, Zhou Yi knew what decision he should make.

"Brother, even if you marry Yuan Liwen, don't neglect your wife," Zhou Yi sighed softly. "You've told me before that after your wife entered the family, she has been virtuous, and both you and Yiling have grown fond of her."

Zhou Yitian's eyes instantly brightened. He knew that since his younger brother had agreed, the matter was surely settled. Although Zhou Quanxin could be strict, considering Zhou Yi's current status, as long as he didn't propose something as outrageous as setting the Zhou family estate on fire, their father would probably not oppose it.

Bowing deeply to Zhou Yi, Zhou Yitian softly uttered two words, "Thank you."

Although those two words were spoken lightly, they conveyed his heartfelt gratitude.

Zhou Yi's body trembled. He knew that the deeper his elder brother's gratitude, the more he valued Yuan Liwen.

However, it had come to this point. If he opposed it now, he feared that the brothers would immediately turn against each other.

Letting out a soft sigh, Zhou Yi would rather engage in a battle of three hundred rounds with Lv Xinwen than get involved in this matter any further. Their conversation concluded, and naturally, they walked into the main hall.

With a beaming smile on Zhou Yitian's face, he disregarded everything and grabbed Yuan Liwen's hand in front of them. Though Yuan Liwen's face was flushed, she didn't struggle, allowing him to lead her out of the hall.

Zhou Yitian and Yuan Liwen exited the hall and arrived in the backyard. Many plum blossoms were planted here, as it was the old patriarch's spot for enjoying them during winter. In the center, there was a pavilion and some artificial rockeries, creating an ethereal ambiance reminiscent of an immortal realm.

"Liwen, our matter has been settled," Zhou Yitian whispered.

Yuan Liwen remained silent for a moment, then her gentle voice gradually sounded, "Young Master Zhou, you said yesterday that it would be difficult to pass your father's test. Why are you so certain today?"

Zhou Yitian laughed heartily and said, "If I were to plead alone, of course, I wouldn't be able to pass my father's test. But with Yi speaking for me, even if my father is unwilling deep down, he would never contradict Yi's face."

Yuan Liwen's eyes shimmered slightly as she asked, "Is Yi the Zhou family's innate powerhouse who defeated the butcher Lv Xinwen?"

"That's right, it's Yi," Zhou Yitian replied proudly.

Yuan Liwen let out a sigh of relief and said, "Since Sixth Young Master is willing to guarantee it, what more could I ask for? From now on, I will wholeheartedly serve the Young Master. I only ask that the Young Master considers my status and does not let my eldest branch of the family be subjected to humiliation."

Zhou Yitian stood firm and declared loudly, "Rest assured, as long as I, Zhou Yitian, am alive, I will fulfill today's promise."

Yuan Liwen lowered her head, and a hint of sadness, helplessness, and resentment flashed across her beautiful face. Yet, within her mind, she immediately recalled the events from five days ago when her parents brought her trembling before her second grandfather.

The words her second grandfather spoke to her were chilling and horrifying.

"Liwen, although my elder brother conspired with outsiders and failed in his attempt to seize the position of family head, he is still a member of the Yuan family. We used to climb mountains and search for bird nests together, playfully splash water in the river, and hide each other's flaws in front of our parents. We once had close and intimate days," the old man sighed, his wrinkled face seemingly gaining a few more lines. "However, after we grew up, due to the pursuit of the family head position, a rift was formed, leading to conflict within the family. Now that your elder brother has passed away, it is natural for me to ensure the continuation of his bloodline. While I am alive, no one in our main branch will dare to humiliate you.

"But if I were to pass away, knowing Yuan Chengzhi's temperament, he would undoubtedly go to great lengths to make things difficult for you. That would be the demise of your branch..."

"If you wish for your parents, siblings, and relatives to live a life as it was before, then you must find ways to stay by Zhou Yitian's side. As long as you can win his favor. I can assure you that with Yuan Chengzhi's character, he will not harm your main branch. Though he may not delegate any power, at the very least, he will ensure your branch's financial needs are met, and you can live as a wealthy family. In fact, not being involved in family matters may be a blessing in disguise..."

"I see Zhou Yitian as someone who may not possess the extraordinary talent of Zhou Yi, but he is a steady person. If you can earn his approval, it can be considered a good outcome..."

"I am already advanced in years, and I won't be able to hold on for many more years. You must think carefully..."

Recalling the pleasant words of her second grandfather, Yuan Liwen couldn't help but feel the bone-chilling coldness hidden behind his gentle demeanor. It was enough for her to forever remember that night's conversation.

Even in the helpless gazes of her parents, siblings, and relatives, she couldn't find sorrow or anger. All she saw was their uneasy and apprehensive expressions. It seemed that when Yuan Zewei passed away, the spirit of the branch had already crumbled and completely dissipated.

Her head drooped even lower, the sadness fading gradually and sinking deep into her eyes. Perhaps, in this lifetime, there would be no one who could truly understand her emotions.

"Liwen, what's wrong? Are you not happy?" Zhou Yitian asked.

"No, I'm happy, really, I'm, hap-py..."

※※※※

In the main hall, Zhou Yi furrowed his brow, seemingly troubled by something unresolved. After Zhou Yitian walked out, a heavy atmosphere settled in the hall. Before Zhou Yi could speak, Yuan Lixun dared not say a word.

She certainly understood the status of the person across from her, far beyond the comparison of ordinary aristocratic scions. At their first meeting, she couldn't afford to leave a bad impression on him, no matter what.

After a long silence, Zhou Yi still couldn't find any topics to discuss. He absentmindedly picked up the teacup on the table and drank it all in one gulp.

He was indeed an innate cultivator, but when it came to interacting with women, his experience was close to zero. Since the age of five, he had been focused on cultivating his inner energy, and until today, apart from being with his mother and his two sisters, Yi Ling and Yi Long, he had never been alone in a room with another woman.

Yuan Lixun stood up and picked up the teapot from the table, gently refilling his teacup. Zhou Yi looked at her in surprise; this was the first time he had received such treatment.

In Zhou's Manor, if he wanted tea, he had to prepare it himself. No one else would do it for him. As for Zhou Wude and the others who visited his residence, they were always served with cold water to steep the tea leaves.

After hesitating for a moment, Zhou Yi picked up the teacup and drank it all again. He didn't know what kind of tea it was, and he didn't feel anything after drinking it. Good tea or bad tea, it was all the same to him. He never paid attention to these details, but the feeling at this moment seemed... not bad.

A perpetual smile seemed to be etched on Yuan Lixun's face, and Zhou Yi found her initial impression as an innocent girl somewhat acceptable.

Yuan Lixun poured water from the pot into the teacup once again, which puzzled Zhou Yi. Was he supposed to keep drinking?

Just then, a faint commotion could be heard from outside. The sound seemed to come from the entrance of the estate, even though it was quite distant. Normally, Zhou Yi wouldn't pay attention to it, but in this environment, his senses were more focused, and his ears naturally started picking up the sounds from outside.

His ears twitched slightly, and amidst the commotion, he heard phrases like "Master is back" and a chorus of people eagerly greeting someone.

He immediately knew that Yuan Chengzhi and Zhou Quanxin, who had gone to handle the aftermath, had finally returned.

Chapter 133

On the second day, in the grand hall of the Yuan residence, Yuan Zeyu and his son sat with smiles on their faces, while Zhou Quanxin entered with Zhou Yi and Zhou Yitian. After exchanging greetings, they took their respective seats.

During these past few days, Zhou Quanxin and Yuan Chengzhi had worked together to handle the aftermath in the county town, and it was only today that they finally managed to complete the preliminary arrangements.

Upon entering the hall, Yuan Chengzhi waved his sleeves and dismissed all the servants. With a smile on his face, he said, "Yi, Yitian, our venture into the city has been quite fruitful."

Just by looking at his joyous expression, one could tell that his words held no exaggeration whatsoever. Seven days ago, when Zhou Yi had just returned to the Yuan residence, both Yuan Zeyu and Yuan Chengzhi addressed him as "Master Zhou" and never dared to call him by his name again. Although Zhou Yi remained silent at the time, Zhou Quanxin felt that it was inappropriate, so Zhou Yi continued to address Yuan Chengzhi as "Uncle" according to his uncle's wishes. However, although their relative positions remained unchanged, there was a subtle shift in the tone of their conversations.

Just like the current situation, although Yuan Chengzhi repeatedly called Zhou Yi "nephew," his expression and attitude were far from the way one would treat a younger relative. It was even more respectful than how he treated Yuan Zeyu.

Zhou Yi smiled faintly and said, "Uncle Chengzhi, congratulations then."

Yuan Chengzhi laughed heartily and proceeded to recount their experiences in the county town. Once news spread about the deaths of Fan Shuhe and Lv Xinwen, as well as the disappearance of Fan Haori, the entire Fan family fell into chaos. It was at that moment that Yuan Chengzhi and Zhou Quanxin, leading a group of experts from the Yuan family, entered the city and immediately seized control of the remaining Fan bloodline, Fan Haoyue.

In comparison to his father and brothers, Fan Haoyue was nothing but an insignificant figure. Once he learned of the news, it was as if the sky had come crashing down upon him. He had no time to gather the remnants of the Fan family's power. Instead, he rushed back home, packed up their belongings, and tried to escape. However, with Fan Shuhe and Lv Xinwen already dead, and no one to restrain the servants and guests of the Fan family, several audacious and cunning individuals set their sights on Fan Haoyue. They intercepted him halfway as he tried to flee.

Although Fan Haoyue had a good father and elder brother, his own strength was feeble, with only the cultivation level of the sixth layer of internal energy. When he was surrounded by several mediocre guests, his legs trembled, and he could hardly speak coherently.

At that moment, Yuan Chengzhi arrived with his men and promptly rescued Fan Haoyue. Subsequently, he took control of the entire Fan family, using his name to assume leadership in their absence.

During the turmoil within the Fan family, the Yuan family smoothly gained control of all their assets. Just yesterday, Fan Haoyue signed a contract with Yuan Chengzhi, selling the entire Fan family's assets to the Yuan family for a sum of one thousand two hundred silver taels.

For an ordinary person, one thousand two hundred silver taels would be an enormous sum, but for the entire Fan family, it was an incredibly low price. Fan Haoyue was well aware of this, but even his own life was in their hands.

As the saying goes, "When the butcher brandishes the knife, the fish has no choice but to surrender." The fact that he managed to preserve his life was already a great victory in itself. With the agreement signed, Fan Haoyue left Zhengtong County City in a disheveled state.

With these turn of events, the Yuan family not only safeguarded their existing assets but also acquired the entire wealth of the Fan family, a windfall beyond their expectations.

Naturally, the other prominent families in Zhengtong County City were envious of the Yuan family's gains. However, while they may have coveted what the Yuan family had obtained, they all sent representatives bearing substantial gifts, acknowledging that the Fan family deserved their fate and that its assets should rightfully belong to the Yuan family.

As Zhou Yi listened to this account, his gaze shifted towards his uncle. Zhou Quanxin nodded subtly, prompting Zhou Yi to force a bitter smile.

The other families showed their support because they had heard about Lv Xinwen's fate. This Butcher of Blood had once single-handedly exterminated a thousand-year-old prominent family within the Jinlin Kingdom. His brutal methods were unmatched, and all the families held a deep fear of him.

However, this time, the Butcher of Blood was defeated by the Yuan family, and it was rumored that he had met his demise. Under such circumstances, the other families no longer dared to harbor any intentions against the Yuan family.

After recounting these events in detail, Yuan Chengzhi's expression grew solemn. He said, "Yi, Brother Zhou, Yitian, over the past few days, we have made a rough assessment of the Fan family's assets." He paused and continued, "Although the Fan family is a newly rising clan, their rise to power involved ruthless methods, exterminating several smaller families and forcibly seizing their assets. Rough calculations indicate that the combined value of these assets amounts to around seventy thousand gold taels."

Zhou Yi's expression showed a slight change. Seventy thousand gold taels was a considerable sum, one that even the current Zhou family would find difficult to produce.

Yuan Chengzhi's tone turned serious as he said, "After discussing with my father, we have come to the conclusion that this remarkable achievement is all thanks to the three of you. Without the efforts of Brother Zhou and you two nephews, we wouldn't have been able to achieve such gains. If it weren't for you, the Fan family's assets would have been swallowed up entirely, leaving nothing for us."

Zhou Quanxin furrowed his brows slightly and said, "Brother Yuan, you're being too formal with your words. Our fathers have had decades of friendship, and our families, the Zhou family of Taicang and the Yuan family of Jinlin, have had a long history of business dealings. If the Yuan family faced any trouble, we would never sit idly by."

Yuan Chengzhi nodded deeply, expressing his heartfelt gratitude. He said, "Brother Zhou, I understand everything you've said. However, friendships are one thing, and transactions are another. We cannot confuse the two. No matter what, we cannot overlook the value of this transaction." He stood up and took out a document-like item from his pocket, handing it to Zhou Quanxin.

Zhou Quanxin glanced through it, and his expression subtly changed. He said, "Brother Yuan, this gift is too precious. We cannot accept it."

Zhou Yi and Zhou Yitian exchanged glances, both feeling immensely surprised. They couldn't fathom what Yuan Chengzhi had presented that would cause even the usually composed Zhou Quanxin to react this way.

Yuan Chengzhi smiled and said, "Brother Zhou, this is the result of discussions with my father. If you refuse to accept it, we would be too ashamed to face anyone."

Zhou Quanxin shook his head and firmly declined, not willing to change his mind under any circumstances.

Yuan Zeyu cleared his throat and said, "Nephew Quanxin, I have written a letter, and I entrust you to deliver it to Old Brother Zhou. These items are also gifts for Old Brother Zhou. Please pass them on."

Zhou Quanxin felt a brief moment of astonishment and couldn't help but wear a bitter smile. Since Mr. Yuan himself had spoken, he couldn't refuse. After all, he was not Zhou Wude himself and couldn't overstep his boundaries.

Zhou Yi, curious, reached out and the gift list on the table flew up, landing gently in his hand. This simple gesture may appear straightforward, but controlling Qi outside of one's body was a skill only attainable by a cultivator in the Innate Realm.

Even the former Lin TaoLi, despite being able to use the Innate Hand Seal to release internal energy, could only cause some damage. He couldn't perform such delicate manipulation of Qi through the air.

For a moment, Yuan Zeyu and the others fell silent and gazed at Zhou Yi with envy in their eyes.

In truth, Zhou Quanxin also knew deep down that receiving such an unexpected grand gift was not his own achievement. If it weren't for his nephew, , ,

Zhou Yi opened the gift list, and even with his composure, he couldn't help but feel a surge of excitement. Written on it were fifty thousand taels of gold, various precious items, a twenty percent share in the original Fan family shops within Jinlin County, and an annual profit concession of twenty percent in the transaction with the Zhou family. Furthermore, the original Fan family residence in Jinlin County was designated as the Zhou family's foothold in Jinlin County, now under Zhou Yi's name.

After a moment of dazedness, Zhou Yi looked at Yuan Chengzhi with a strange expression. Unbeknownst to him, he had unwittingly acquired a grand residence within Zhengtong County, and considering it was the former Fan family's residence, it was unlikely to be small.

In addition to the previous promise of ten thousand taels of gold and a ten percent annual profit concession in their private transaction with the Zhou family, now they were offering a staggering fifty thousand taels of gold and a twenty percent profit concession.

Although Zhou Yi was not a businessman and didn't fully grasp the value of these offerings, he, like his uncle Zhou Quanxin, understood that the gift was incredibly substantial. Leaving aside the other aspects, the twenty percent stake in the Fan family's assets alone was a hot potato.

On the surface, it seemed tempting, with the assurance of significant annual profits flowing into their pockets. However, obtaining that twenty percent stake was not as easy as it appeared. If they agreed to it, it meant that the Yuan family could openly approach them in the future whenever they needed assistance.

Thus, the decision of whether or not to accept this twenty percent stake was not one they could make lightly. However, since they had been offered a full fifty thousand taels of gold, even the most thick-skinned person would find it difficult to dismiss the opportunity.

Moreover, the annual profits from this twenty percent stake would undoubtedly be a substantial amount. If they accepted, it would render the smuggling business conducted by the Zhou family each year as insignificant. It would bring unparalleled benefits to the Zhou family's foothold in Taicang County.

Suddenly, Zhou Yi felt a sense of something unusual. He looked up and coincidentally met Zhou Quanxin's gaze, which was filled with inquisitiveness. Zhou Yi instantly understood his uncle's intention. It seemed that Zhou Quanxin was also hesitant and had sensed some hidden agenda. However, considering that the Zhou family was currently in a phase of rapid development and required substantial financial support, he couldn't make a decision. Hence, he wanted Zhou Yi to decide.

Immediately, Zhou Yi felt a headache coming on and silently complained in his heart. "Uncle, you are the elder here, yet you refuse to make a decision and instead signal me to decide. Isn't this putting me in a difficult position?"

He pondered for a moment and suddenly noticed his eldest brother, Zhou Yitian. Although Zhou Yitian sat calmly in his chair, seemingly unmoved and composed, Zhou Yi could sense his restlessness through his slightly accelerated heartbeat.

A sudden recollection of the promise he had made surged within Zhou Yi, and he reached a decisive moment in his heart. Once he made up his mind, he felt a sense of relief wash over him.

He understood that the Yuan family handing over the twenty percent stake to the Zhou family was merely an attempt to leverage the Zhou family's martial prowess to protect their acquired assets. In the past, the Zhou family wouldn't have had the capability, but now that he, a innate cultivator, had joined their ranks, the situation had changed.

Since everyone was already aware of his status as a innate cultivator, he no longer needed to hide or conceal it. In that case, why not accept the twenty percent stake?

With this thought, a surge of confidence filled his heart, and his entire demeanor seemed to undergo a subtle transformation.

"Uncle, since Uncle Yuan and grandfather Yuan have both expressed their wishes, let us respect their decision and comply," Zhou Yi said calmly, a faint smile appearing on his face.

Zhou Quanxin was taken aback. He hadn't expected Zhou Yi to agree so readily.

In the past, Zhou Quanxin might have refused or tried to persuade Zhou Yi, but ever since Zhou Yi defeated Lv Xinwen, there had been a subtle change in his mindset. Once Zhou Yi made a decision, Zhou Quanxin found himself devoid of any opposing thoughts.

With a bitter smile, Zhou Quanxin said, "Alright then, since it is the kind intention of Uncle and Mr. Yuan, I will graciously accept on behalf of my father."

Yuan Zeyu and Yuan Chengzhi exchanged smiles and breathed a sigh of relief. It had been a difficult task to present the gifts, and they felt a myriad of emotions. Finally, the gifts had been given, and they could now rest assured. Moreover, they knew that within the Zhengtong County of Jinlin, there were many noble families who had no means of establishing connections. They, too, wanted to establish a relationship with the Zhou family. As long as they could cultivate a good relationship with Zhou Yi, such a young innate cultivator, they would willingly offer even more precious gifts.

Clearing his throat, Yuan Zeyu looked at the three members of the Zhou family and said, "Zhou Quanxin nephew, since our two families have business cooperation and you now have properties and related industries in Zhengtong County, I have a proposal that I would like you to consider."

Zhou Quanxin quickly sat up straight and said, "Please enlighten me, Uncle."

Yuan Zeyu smiled and stroked his long beard. "I have two granddaughters. One of them, Yuan Liwen, is exceptionally intelligent and knowledgeable. If you don't mind, I would like her to accompany Zhou Yitian to Taicang."

Zhou Quanxin's eyes widened in surprise. He opened his mouth but couldn't help but laugh and cry. "Uncle, you may not be aware, but Zhou Yitian is already married. His wife is Cheng Yanli, the daughter of the prestigious Cheng family in Taicang County."

When Yuan Zeyu brought up this matter, Yuan Chengzhi's expression immediately changed. He was first taken aback, but soon understood his father's intention. His eyebrows furrowed, indicating his strong dissatisfaction with his father's arrangement. It wasn't just because Yuan Liwen was Yuan Zeyu's own granddaughter, but because Yuan Chengzhi had many concerns.

Fortunately, Zhou Quanxin's immediate refusal brought him some relief. Yuan Zeyu showed no signs of embarrassment on his face as he spoke in a deep voice, "That's fine. Since Yitian already has a legitimate wife, then let Liwen become a concubine."

Zhou Quanxin's expression tightened as he said, "Uncle, this matter goes against propriety and should not be considered."

Yuan Chengzhi also advised, "Yes, Father, since Zhou brother is unwilling, let's not force the issue."

Ignoring their words, Yuan Zeyu continued, "I have another suggestion. I have another granddaughter named Yuan Lixun. How do you feel about taking her as your concubine, Yi?"

This time, he bypassed Zhou Quanxin and directly asked Zhou Yi.

Zhou Quanxin and Yuan Chengzhi were both about to speak, but as their eyes fell upon Zhou Yi, they immediately fell silent and adopted an expression that conveyed their complete noninterference, allowing Zhou Yi to make his own decision.

Zhou Yi couldn't help but sigh inwardly. Not only did Yuan Chengzhi act this way, even his uncle did. It was evident that after he advanced to the innate cultivator realm, even someone as close as his uncle no longer dared to make decisions on his behalf.

Raising his head, Zhou Yi's gaze swept across the people in the room, and the one that touched his heart the most was the pleading look from his eldest brother, Zhou Yitian.

His heart warmed, realizing that his eldest brother's change was undoubtedly the smallest. Taking a deep breath, Zhou Yi's face even blushed slightly, and he said, "Uncle, I have met Miss Yuan Lixun. Please make the decision on my behalf."

Zhou Quanxin's expression was extremely strange. Although he claimed to be a martial arts fanatic in the Zhou family and didn't pay much attention to family affairs, being a martial arts fanatic didn't mean being a fool. As soon as he saw Zhou Yi's expression and actions, he understood his intentions. He shook his head slightly, intending to reprimand him, but when he thought that the nephew in front of him was already a powerhouse in the innate Realm, what right did he have to reprimand him? Could he even criticize him for indulging in women?

Letting out a sigh, Zhou Quanxin turned his head and suddenly noticed the surprised and mixed expression in Yuan Chengzhi's eyes. He couldn't help but feel a slight tremor in his heart. Could it be that

Yuan Chengzhi was unaware of this matter? Looking at the seemingly innocent Yuan Zeyu, everything suddenly became clear.

Yuan Chengzhi had been too busy these days to even have the thought for this matter. It seemed that everything was orchestrated by this old man behind the scenes. Although Zhou Quanxin felt somewhat dissatisfied, he still spoke, "In that case, thank you for your kind intentions, Uncle." Zhou Yi smiled faintly and said, "Thank you, Uncle. Since that's the case, when we return this time, we'll travel with Miss Yuan Liwen and Miss Yuan Lixun."

Zhou Quanxin was taken aback, his lips trembled a few times, but when he saw the smile on Zhou Yi's face and the resolute determination emanating from his upright posture, he couldn't help but feel a tremor in his heart. The words he wanted to say were swallowed back. At this moment, the only feeling in his heart was that Yi's momentum was becoming stronger and stronger, to the point where even he felt an inexplicable sense of obedience. This son of Zhou Quanming, he didn't know how he was born, but he was an irreplaceable treasure of the Zhou family...

Chapter 134

The sparrows darted past, their fleeting presence, as the ever-changing white clouds gracefully drifted across the cerulean sky, casting a verdant shadow upon the emerald plains below, painting the earth in hues of darkened green and shimmering jade.

It had been several days since their departure from the Yuan estate. When they arrived, it was the season of the Lunar New Year, and with utmost haste, the men rode their horses, galloping through the countryside. By the time they reached the Yuan household, seven of the eight horses were spent, their energy depleted.

Now, it was already the third month of spring, two whole months had passed since their arrival at the Yuan family's estate. As they prepared to depart, they were no longer a mere group of four people and eight horses.

The five wagon loads of gold, generously gifted by the Yuan family, were meticulously stacked on each carriage. Each vehicle carried a ton of weight, camouflaging a few scattered items to deceive onlookers.

In addition, the Yuan family dispatched over a hundred guards and escorts, blending in with the household servants and travelers. Of course, both the Zhou family and themselves knew the true purpose. This so-called escort was nothing more than a facade, their role merely to accompany and occasionally assist along the way.

If they were to encounter any audacious horse bandits on their journey, it would be an understatement to claim that even the skilled Zhou Yi, a master of the innate realm, or the father-son duo Zhou Quanxin, would easily vanquish them.

After all, there lay a grand official road from here into the Tianluo Kingdom, leading all the way to Taicang County. Even the invincible horse thieves within the boundaries of Tai'a County dare not casually dispatch large troops to this area. Doing so would only force the authorities of Tianluo Kingdom to take severe measures against them.

So long as the bandits did not arrive with a formidable army, these individuals would dismiss the petty thieves with disdain, for they were but inconsequential in their eyes.

The convoy consisted of ten large carriages. Apart from the five carriages carrying the gold, three carriages were filled with numerous chests, serving as dowry preparations for the two Yuan sisters. As for the last two carriages, they were specifically prepared for the two young Yuan ladies.

However, due to their shared loneliness and empathy for each other's plight, the two young ladies chose not to travel separately. Instead, they squeezed onto the same carriage, seeking solace in each other's company.

Within this convoy, Zhou Quanxin rode at the forefront, his face revealing a hint of subtle displeasure. Although he wasn't scowling, his unhappiness was evident. Zhou Yitian, despite his joy and excitement, refrained from expressing even a hint of it in front of his stern father. He didn't dare exchange any banter with the young lady inside the carriage. Feeling quite oppressed, he naturally wore a sullen expression.

To his surprise, this display actually alleviated Zhou Quanxin's suspicions. He no longer doubted his son's involvement. Otherwise, with his temperament, Zhou Yitian would have certainly faced either a physical reprimand or at least a verbal scolding.

The sun gradually veered towards the west, and the leading Yuan Lixuan glanced at the sky before turning back on his horse. He suggested, "Uncle Quanxin, it's getting late. There's a small town up ahead. Shall we rest there for the night?"

Although Yuan Lixuan was not Yuan Chengzhi's biological son, his gracious reception of the Zhou brothers had earned their favor.

Thus, he had risen in status within the Yuan family, becoming the lead figure responsible for escorting the convoy. He had meticulously organized all the arrangements, sparing the Zhou brothers any worry.

This newfound camaraderie, coupled with his astute demeanor, guaranteed a promising future for Yuan Lixuan. Once they returned, his prospects would undoubtedly be bright.

Glancing ahead at the distant horizon, Zhou Quanxin sighed inwardly. "Very well, let us find respite in that town."

After receiving Zhou Quanxin's permission, everyone entered the small town and secured the largest inn for themselves.

This time, Yuan Chengzhi spared no expense, providing enough silver for the entire group's expenses on the journey. Even if they were to reside in the most luxurious courtyard, it wouldn't pose any problem. However, in such a small town, even inferior to Taicang County, finding a decent courtyard was already a rarity.

Upon entering the rooms, they freshened up, and soon a meal was delivered. After the five of them finished their meal, Yuan Lixuan and Yuan Lixun, the two Yuan sisters, voluntarily cleaned up.

Yuan Lixun moved with grace and skill, appearing quite adept at the tasks, while Yuan Lixuan seemed less familiar. However, under Yuan Lixun's subtle guidance, it was difficult to notice unless one observed carefully.

Once they finished tidying up, they immediately bid farewell to Zhou Quanxin and exited the room. Their actions were swift and efficient, pleasing Zhou Quanxin.

Observing their departure, Zhou Yitian said, "Father, it's been over two months since we left home. Grandfather and the others must be extremely worried. But if Grandfather finds out that my little brother has already stepped into the Innate realm, I wonder how happy he would be."

A slight smile appeared on Zhou Quanxin's face, as the thought of his father's astonished expression filled him with anticipation.

However, as his gaze fell upon the opposite room, the smile in Zhou Quanxin's eyes faded significantly.

The Zhou brothers exchanged a glance, both wearing a bitter smile.

"Uncle, are you not pleased with my decision?" Zhou Yi asked cautiously.

Zhou Quanxin shook his head slightly and said, "Yi, now that you have become a powerhouse at the Innate realm, with your cultivation, I have no objection even if you take multiple concubines, let alone seven or eight. I have no qualms about it."

Zhou Yi coughed, feeling rather embarrassed.

A hint of a smile finally appeared on Zhou Quanxin's face as he continued, "Since you had the courage to bring it up, you should also have the courage to bear the consequences. You have met Miss Lixun and taken a liking to her. How is it that when the opportunity arises, you falter?"

Zhou Quanxin slowly retracted his smile and said, "Yi, although I don't oppose you taking concubines, you shouldn't be making choices for Yitian. He doesn't possess your innate talent and is far from being your equal. If he allows himself to be distracted by romantic pursuits, it's likely that he will achieve nothing in the end, unable even to break through the seventh layer's inner strength."

Zhou Yitian's expression changed slightly, and he quickly stood up, saying, "Father, please rest assured. I will diligently devote myself to practice and strive to break through the seventh layer's barrier as soon as possible."

Zhou Quanxin waved his hand dismissively and gruffly said, "Nonsense! Do you think breaking through the seventh layer's formidable barrier is so easily accomplished? Look at your second uncle and third uncle, both of whom remained at the pinnacle of the seventh layer for nearly ten years before being able to break through that ultimate barrier." Glancing at Zhou Yi before continuing, he said, "You think you're Yi? He..."

As Zhou Quanxin paused, he realized that he could no longer describe Zhou Yi's ability to break through the limits as easily as eating a meal. Shaking his head, he was about to speak when he heard Zhou Yi laugh and say, "Uncle, if you're worried about this issue, I can assure you that Big Brother will not disappoint you."

Zhou Quanxin's eyes brightened slightly, and he asked, "How do you know?"

Zhou Yi replied, "Uncle, you should remember that when Big Brother came from Zhou Family Village to the Yuan family, his inner power cultivation was only at the middle stage of the seventh layer."

"Correct," Zhou Quanxin nodded lightly. As Zhou Yitian's father, he was most concerned about his son's progress, so he naturally knew the details of his cultivation. Unlike Zhou Yi, who exhibited peculiar behavior, leading Zhou Wude to issue an order not to interfere with his training. This was also the main reason why no one could grasp Zhou Yi's true strength.

"Uncle, do you also remember the result of Big Brother's battle with Fan Haori at the Yuan family?" Zhou Yi continued.

Zhou Quanxin's heart immediately stirred with excitement. How could he forget that battle? However, through subsequent inquiries, he understood the reason behind it: Zhou Yitian had consumed an Energy-Boosting Golden Pill, and that pill came from Zhou Yi.

"Yi, do you still have Energy-Boosting Golden Pills?" Zhou Quanxin asked.

"Yes, not only do I have them, but Big Brother also has a few in his possession," Zhou Yi replied with a mischievous smile.

Zhou Quanxin immediately turned around, his expression displeased. "Yitian, why didn't you tell me?"

Zhou Yitian blushed slightly and said, "Father, at first, sixth brother gave me four Energy-Boosting Golden Pill, and my child just took one. But my child thought, since this golden pellet was obtained by the sixth brother, of course I should give it to the second uncle, so ......"

Zhou Tsuenxin then nodded his head in satisfaction and said, "Are you planning to give it directly to Quan Ming?"

Zhou Yitian maintained a serious expression and replied, "No."

Zhou Quanxin was taken aback, and his face darkened slightly. He asked, "Then how do you plan to handle this?"

"I intend to let Yixuan take one pill first and then give the remaining two pills to Second Uncle," Zhou Yitian's voice remained calm and unquestionable. It was evident that his words came from a sincere and genuine place. "If we were to give them directly to Second Uncle, I'm afraid Yixuan may not receive his fair share in the end."

Zhou Quanxin's face gradually softened, and he let out a snort, saying, "You little brats, you're becoming more and more disrespectful towards us elders, making decisions on your own without considering us. Hmph..."

Although his expression seemed fierce and menacing, the look in his eyes was actually very satisfied. Among the third generation of the Zhou family, they all thought of each other and refused to take advantage of one another. This truly brought him great comfort. Especially after witnessing the discord and conflict between Yuan Zeyu and Yuan Zewei, the brothers from the Yuan family, he attached even more importance to this point.

Zhou Yi's intuition was particularly sharp, and he immediately sensed his uncle's thoughts. He quickly said, "Uncle, do you believe me now? As long as we have the Vitality Golden Pills, even if Big Brother takes in not just one concubine but seven or eight, I believe there won't be any issues at all."

Having finished speaking, Zhou Yitian looked earnestly at his uncle, but the mischievous glint in his eyes was unmistakable.

Zhou Quanxin looked at him helplessly, surprised that the admonishment he had just given was swiftly turned back on him. Shaking his head, he said, "Yi, you..."

Suddenly, a commotion could be heard from outside. Though the noise wasn't particularly loud, it couldn't escape the attention of Zhou Yi and Zhou Quanxin.

After a moment, Zhou Yi furrowed his brow and said, "They're our people."

Almost simultaneously, Zhou Quanxin exclaimed, "It's from the Yuan family."

Though their words differed, their meanings were the same. There was an altercation happening outside, involving one of the Yuan family's attendants who had been traveling with them.

Zhou Yitian's expression changed slightly, and he looked up, meeting the gazes of his father and younger brother.

The three of them exchanged glances, equally surprised.

After all, this was the official road, and there were no bandits or marauders in sight. A convoy of over a hundred people walking along this road was already quite rare.

If they didn't possess a certain level of strength, how could they casually gather such a group?

Moreover, Yuan Chengzhi had put in great effort this time, carefully selecting the guests and attendants, all of whom were outstanding individuals. The family's century-long heritage was indeed far superior to the current Zhou family. Even the ordinary attendants of the family possessed a cultivation level of at least the fifth level of Inner Energy.

Though they couldn't be compared to the prestigious ancient families, this team, wherever they went, could be considered an elite force.

However, at this moment, there was someone in the inn who was arguing with them, which seemed rather abnormal.

Zhou Yitian abruptly stood up and said, "I'll go take a look."

According to seniority, it should have been Zhou Yi who intervened, but at this point, both Zhou Quanxin and Zhou Yitian no longer regarded him as an ordinary member of the third generation of the Zhou family. Therefore, it was only natural for Zhou Yitian to step forward.

Zhou Yi hesitated for a moment and said, "Elder Brother, Yuan Lixuan hasn't come out yet."

Zhou Quanxin nodded slightly and added, "That's right, let's wait a little longer."

This time, Yuan Lixuan had taken charge of the arrangements from top to bottom and had gained their trust and admiration. If they were to intervene before he appeared, it would likely undermine the reputation he had just built.

Zhou Yitian naturally had no objections. However, after a while, the commotion outside not only didn't subside, but it seemed to be growing louder. Zhou Yi's brows furrowed with dissatisfaction, and even Zhou Yitian could sense the powerful and intimidating aura emanating from his younger brother.

He knew, however, that this was the suppressed aura of his younger brother. If he were to unleash it completely, the immense power he had displayed in his battle with Lv Xinwen on that day would be enough to chill anyone's heart.

Zhou Quanxin let out a cold snort and said, "This is outrageous."

Zhou Yitian was slightly taken aback and asked, "Father, what's going on?"

Although he had reached the pinnacle of the seventh level of Inner Energy, he couldn't discern the specifics from the indistinct clamor outside the door.

Zhou Yi tugged at Zhou Yitian and said, "Elder Brother, a few newcomers have arrived outside. They want to stay in the best place in town and are asking us to vacate the courtyard." A cold smirk appeared on his lips as he continued, "They said they are willing to pay double the price."

Zhou Yitian let out a dissatisfied snort. No one would be pleased with such a situation while on the road.

"And Yuan Lixuan has already come out. He didn't get into a dispute with them. He just told them that the courtyard is already occupied, including women and family members, so he is willing to vacate the best room he was staying in," Zhou Yi continued.

Zhou Yitian was greatly surprised and said, "When did Lixuan become so easygoing? That seems somewhat unlikely."

Zhou Quanxin chuckled and said, "It's not that he became easygoing, but rather, we're here, and our belongings are relatively valuable, so he doesn't want to invite trouble. Besides, this isn't Zhengtong County in Jinlin. The Yuan family is relatively isolated here. If the other party is so assertive, they must have some background." Zhou Quanxin nodded and added, "This kid Lixuan is not bad.

If Yuan Lixuan knew that his act of giving up his room would win the favor of Zhou Quanxin, he would surely marvel at his good fortune.

Zhou Yi's face suddenly darkened, and he said, "They're fighting."

Zhou Quanxin and Zhou Yitian were both taken aback. Soon, they heard the noise outside growing louder, accompanied by exclamations.

Both of them were astonished. Zhou Yi had already determined that a fight had broken out even before the two sides engaged in combat. Moreover, what was more significant was that he was present at the scene but could still have such a clear understanding of what was happening in a distant place.

At that moment, Zhou Quanxin and Zhou Yitian gained a more direct understanding of the abilities of innate experts, deepening their awe for Zhou Yi. Zhou Quanxin stood up and said, "Let's go out and have a look."

Zhou Yi and Zhou Yitian responded simultaneously. If they were to hide like cowards due to the incident in the backyard, it would be unacceptable.

Before leaving the courtyard, Zhou Yi's footsteps faltered for a moment as his gaze glanced towards the other side of the wing room.

Through the gaps in the window, a pair of bright eyes were looking at them. As soon as those eyes met Zhou Yi's gaze, they briefly showed panic before quickly returning to normal and gradually disappearing.

Zhou Yi turned around with a smile, and his pace quickened slightly. He instantly caught up with his elder brother in complete silence. Zhou Quanxin and Zhou Yitian didn't notice anything amiss.

In the wing room separated by a wall, Yuan Lixun's eyes showed a hint of regret as she watched Yuan Liwen, who was diligently embroidering in front of the bed. She couldn't help feeling envious.

If she could also be as focused as her sister and not be curious, she wouldn't have been discovered by Zhou Yi in the end.

As if sensing her gaze, Yuan Liwen raised her head and, with a flick of her wrist, gently smoothed a strand of hair with her needle and thread. She asked, "What's the matter, little sister?"

Yuan Lixun hesitated for a moment and said, "Sister, why can you sit still on this journey?"

Yuan Liwen looked at her in surprise, seeming to consider something before finally saying, "Sister, it's because I have no way to retreat that I can sit still." After speaking, she lowered her head again and continued her embroidery with focus.

Yuan Lixun opened her mouth but didn't say anything. She only asked herself in her heart, "Do you still have a way to retreat?"

Chapter 135

Above the small town, there was only one exquisite inn, elegant and immaculate, exclusively designed for the affluent. Similarly, there was only one grand courtyard reserved for such wealthy patrons. When two wealthy individuals unexpectedly crossed paths and neither was willing to yield, a dispute naturally ensued.

At this moment, on the roadside in front of the inn, the two individuals confronted each other, empty-handed, engaged in a fierce clash. One of them was Zhong Pu Yuan, a customer from the Yuan family, whose cultivation had reached the eighth level. With his level of cultivation, he would receive excellent treatment in any prestigious household. However, due to the great favor he had received from the Yuan family during his youth, he willingly served the family and could be considered the most accomplished among the escorts in this particular group.

The other person was a middle-aged man dressed in a tight-fitting garment, remarkably lean and thin. His narrow shoulders, long arms, and legs seemed elongated, while his hands dangled outside his sleeves as if they had grown an extra length.

Surprisingly, his internal energy had also reached the eighth level. Moreover, his strikes were extremely vicious, with his long arms resembling spider legs. Each time they moved through the air, a strange whistling sound followed, as if his arms were his very weapons.

Zhong Pu Yuan felt a sense of caution towards the middle-aged man's arms, but when he made his moves, they were light and effortless. Every time, he could easily deflect the opponent's arms at crucial moments.

Although both parties had engaged in combat, they displayed considerable restraint and did not truly go for the kill. They had already sensed each other's significant backgrounds. In such circumstances, no fool would recklessly unleash a lethal attack.

Drawing a sword and killing someone at the slightest provocation upon encountering them on the road was not something that every cultivator could accomplish.

Perhaps those elusive horse bandits or exceptional innate experts like Zhou Yi could, but certainly not individuals like them who had a background and insufficient strength to surpass the law.

Beside them, Yuan Li Xuan and another person faced each other from a distance, both wearing unpleasant expressions. It seemed they didn't truly desire a conflict, but at this point, their swords were drawn and couldn't easily be sheathed.

Yuan Li Xuan possessed only a cultivation of the fourth level of internal energy. However, behind him stood at least five experts at the seventh level of internal energy, ready to serve him. Furthermore, the men continuously emerging from the inn, armed and displaying hostile expressions, exerted immense pressure on the opposing side.

Tension gradually built in the scene.

As more people gathered behind Yuan Li Xuan, the several individuals facing him grew increasingly uneasy. Especially the middle-aged man who was engaged in combat with Zhong Pu Yuan, his attacks were becoming more fierce.

Indeed, when anyone sees their enemies gradually increasing in number, they instinctively seek to eliminate the immediate opponents before dealing with the rest. Moreover, based on his recent observations, he had confirmed that Zhong Pu Yuan was the only expert among them at the eighth level of internal energy. Once he dealt with him, the others would be much easier to handle.

At the very least, even if they couldn't win, they could easily escape.

Sometimes, the restraining role played by a skilled expert far outweighed that of a large group of lower-level cultivators.

As the middle-aged man grew more serious, Zhong Pu Yuan suddenly felt tremendous pressure.

The middle-aged man clearly employed an extremely rare metal attribute technique, and at least half of his techniques were focused on his unusually elongated arms. With each swing of his arms, it was akin to wielding large blades, and the edges of his palms subtly shimmered with a metallic hue. This was undoubtedly a characteristic that emerged when one practiced a certain special level of mastery in a metal attribute technique.

In the midst of that person's increasingly frenzied activation, his palm grew even closer in resemblance to metal. The power of his strikes became stronger, and the ferocious whistling sound alone was enough to make one's heart skip a beat.

Yuan Li Xuan and the others wore worried expressions, and unconsciously, they gradually moved closer to the fray. After witnessing the opponent's formidable momentum, no one dared to take it lightly. They all planned that if things took a turn for the worse, they would immediately swarm him.

As formidable as the middle-aged man's martial skills were, he was still just an eighth-level cultivator of internal energy. If over a hundred people simultaneously attacked him, he would have no choice but to flee in desperation.

However, at that moment, a calm voice resounded from behind them, saying, "Everyone, come back and watch closely."

When that voice rang out, the anxious expressions on Yuan Li Xuan and the others disappeared instantly. They all breathed a sigh of relief and silently stepped back, distancing themselves from the battle between the two individuals.

Because they had recognized that voice. It belonged to Zhou Yi.

Although Zhou Yi was only sixteen years old, he was a legendary innate expert. The customers and attendants from the Yuan family had heard countless stories about this powerful individual during this period. In their hearts, Zhou Yi had become somewhat of a myth.

Since he was there, watching the battle, what else did they need to worry about?

Although those people retreated, the man who was fighting Zhong Pu Yuan and some others who were watching the battle from a short distance couldn't help but feel a sense of unease.

Earlier, when so many people surrounded them, although the imposing force was intimidating, these individuals were confident that even if they couldn't win, they could escape. However, just a single sentence that came from the inn caused these people to obediently lower their flags and cease their drums. What was even more terrifying was that there was not a trace of resentment on their faces. Instead, each person's eyes held a hint of anticipation and excitement.

These people were experienced and knowledgeable individuals, and they immediately understood the weight of the person who spoke. That person was undoubtedly someone who could suppress these over a hundred brawny men and make them acknowledge his authority.

At this moment, they were all shocked. If they provoked this hidden figure, it was likely that they wouldn't gain any benefits today.

The leader among them felt even more regret in his heart. Why did he have to snatch that courtyard? If he had known that these people would be so difficult to deal with, he would have agreed to stay in the upper rooms or simply leave.

Upon hearing Zhou Yi's voice, Zhong Pu Yuan's spirit was instantly revitalized. He let out a soft shout, and yet his palm techniques became increasingly gentle.

He was utilizing a water attribute technique, which might not be top-notch but certainly not considered weak either. His hands continued to trace peculiar circles within a certain range. After each circle was completed, a vortex formed in the center, resembling a spring that bounced the middle-aged man's arms away.

Although Zhong Pu Yuan hadn't directly clashed with the middle-aged man throughout the fight and seemed to be slightly at a disadvantage, it was like being stuck to a piece of taffy. Once you were stuck, it became highly unlikely to safely detach.

After a few more exchanges, a voice from the opposing side called out, "Li Fu Zhou, stop delaying and finish it quickly."

The middle-aged man, Li Fu Zhou, furrowed his brow but still responded.

Zhong Pu Yuan felt a hidden anger within him. They were both eighth-level cultivators of internal energy at the same level, and even though Li Fu Zhou's internal energy cultivation surpassed his own, it shouldn't be so easy for him to defeat me.

However, just as he felt irritated, Li Fu Zhou suddenly withdrew his arms and took several steps back. He had been on the offensive, having the upper hand, so naturally, he chose to retreat without any entanglement.

Zhong Pu Yuan was momentarily taken aback, unsure whether he should immediately chase after him.

However, in that brief moment of hesitation, Li Fu Zhou raised his arms. His unusually long arms converged together, and his hands spread open flat. The palms of his hands were much larger than an average person's.

At this moment, the ten fingers of his hands intertwined, forming an incredibly peculiar hand seal in the next instant. The hand seal appeared as if the fingers were clasped together, but the two thumbs strangely emerged from several gaps between the fingers, revealing two sections of snow-white long fingernails.

For some unknown reason, when Zhong Pu Yuan saw this hand seal, his complexion slightly changed. He inexplicably sensed that this hand seal contained a power he couldn't comprehend. Moreover, this power was extremely dangerous, giving him a feeling as if he were being targeted by a venomous snake.

At that moment, in a dark corner of the inn, Zhou Yi suddenly exclaimed, "I know who these people are!"

Zhou Quanxin and Zhou Yitian were taken aback, and the same thought emerged in their minds. Could these people be the ones Zhou Yi recognized during his previous outing?

Zhou Yi swept his gaze over them, smiling faintly, and said, "Uncle, elder brother, look at their attire."

Zhou Quanxin and Zhou Yitian carefully examined them and found their clothing somewhat familiar, but they couldn't recall it immediately.

Zhou Yi whispered, "Elder brother, your wedding day."

Zhou Yitian's eyes lit up as he finally remembered. "I recall now. These are the Lin family's people. This attire is exclusively worn by the Lin family's attendants. There's no doubt about it."

Zhou Quanxin nodded in agreement. In an attempt to win over Zhou Yi, Lin Taoli had personally visited Zhou Manor, but in the end, he left disappointed.

However, Zhou Yi had engaged in a battle with Lin Taoli and had a deep impression of their clothing. It was only natural that he recognized them.

However, what they didn't know was that Zhou Yi recognized them not from their clothing, but from the mark on Li Fu Zhou's hand. Although the mark was not the same as the Ground Seal or the Cloud and Rain Seal, Zhou Yi's keen eyesight allowed him to recognize that Li Fu Zhou's hand seal technique was of the same origin as the Lin family's innate imprint.

In comparison to Lin Taoli, Li Fu Zhou's display of the hand seal technique was undoubtedly much weaker in terms of power, almost on an entirely different level.

It was unclear whether Li Fu Zhou's mastery was lacking or if the inherent power of this hand seal technique was limited. In any case, the level of power displayed did not surprise Zhou Yi. However, while Zhou Yi could remain unfazed, the same couldn't be said for Zhong Pu Yuan.

Zhong Pu Yuan's eyes widened, displaying an unprecedented seriousness. His internal energy circulated throughout his body at the fastest speed, gathering all his strength to its utmost limit. The pressure exerted by the opponent's hand seal made him realize that this might be the strongest opponent he had encountered in his life.

Li Fu Zhou let out a sudden shout as he stepped forward, and the hand seal in his hand came crashing down toward Zhong Pu Yuan like a sledgehammer. Yes, he was using a smashing technique, descending with an imposing momentum, leaving no room for evasion.

Zhong Pu Yuan's legs smoothly retreated, but he quickly discovered that Li Fu Zhou's hand seal remained in the same position, seemingly ready to strike him no matter where he fled. He was greatly shocked. What kind of martial technique was this that could instill such a terrifying feeling without any apparent reason?

In reality, if he knew that this martial technique had evolved from an innate technique, he wouldn't be so disheartened. Innate techniques were incredibly powerful. Even if it was simplified and only retained 30% of its original power, it was still beyond what he could easily avoid as an ordinary postnatal expert.

His feet came to a halt. Since he couldn't avoid it, he had to give it his all. With a loud roar, he raised his hands, ready to confront Li Fu Zhou's hand seal head-on.

However, at this moment, he caught sight of the faintly mocking smile curling at the corner of Li Fuzhou's lips. It seemed to taunt his audacity and overestimation of his own abilities.

Zhong Puyuan felt a sudden chill run down his spine, drenching his back in cold sweat. Regret filled his heart, but it was too late to turn back. He had already unleashed his attack.

Gathering all his internal strength into a single point, he forcefully pushed forward.

In an instant, his vision blurred, and before him stood a figure that seemed to have materialized out of thin air.

His palms were already striking out, but faced with this sudden, close-range presence, Zhong Puyuan couldn't halt his motion. His hands landed heavily on the person's chest.

Shock coursed through him. How had this person appeared out of nowhere, like a ghostly apparition, catching him off guard?

"Pu..."

A soft sound reached his ears, and Zhong Puyuan was perplexed. It seemed that the sound didn't come from the person's chest but rather from their front.

He pondered, bewildered. What was happening?

However, in an instant, he realized the impossibility of such a notion.

As his body slightly shifted, he could see clearly now.

Standing between him and Li Fuzhou was none other than Zhou Yi.

Seeing Zhou Yi, he immediately understood that, despite his considerable palm strength, the idea of harming this person was nothing short of a fantasy.

With utmost deference, Zhong Puyuan stepped back several paces, allowing his hands to naturally hang at his sides. He appeared as obedient and submissive as could be.

In front of Zhou Yi, Li Fuzhou's palm imprint struck forcefully between Zhou Yi's chest and abdomen. This was a vital area of the human body, and Li Fuzhou, an eighth-level internal energy expert, combined his full strength with the power of top-tier combat skills to deliver a heavy blow to this spot.

According to Li Fuzhou's estimation, even if this person had nine lives, he would have lost eight and a half by now. Yet, looking at the young man before him with a smile on his face, there was not a trace of injury. Li Fuzhou staggered back several steps, his face turning pale, his gaze towards Zhou Yi filled with intense fear.

Although Zhou Yi displayed no trace of imposing aura, even with three times the courage, Li Fuzhou dared not provoke him any further.

The individuals behind them had their expressions slightly changed. They had witnessed the scene just now, causing each of them to silence their voices and restrain their breaths. No trace of arrogance could be seen on their faces anymore.

Zhou Yi extended his hand and lightly brushed it twice between his chest and abdomen, as if casually wiping away dirt from his clothes. He asked, "Are you all from the Linlanglin family?"

Li Fuzhou, relieved by his gentle tone, turned his head and the person leading behind him stepped forward quickly, clasping his fists and said, "Indeed, we are from the Linlanglin family. We were rushing on the road tonight and had a conflict with your side. It was all accidental, and we apologize for our mistake. We hope you can forgive us."

Zhou Yi sighed inwardly. These people had keen insight and quickly recognized that they were no match for him, which led them to lower their stance.

"No need to be polite. Since it was a misunderstanding, let's let it pass," Zhou Yi replied.

The man bowed deeply and said, "This humble one is Lin Wenkai, one of the stewards of the Lin family. May I ask... the esteemed surname of this gentleman?"

Upon seeing Zhou Yi's face clearly, Lin Wenkai couldn't help but be amazed. Such a young person possessed such unfathomable cultivation. He couldn't fathom how Zhou Yi achieved it.

Zhou Yi smiled and said, "I am Zhou Yi from Taicang County."

"Taicang County?" Lin Wenkai suddenly raised his head, his face filled with astonishment.

Not only him, but Li Fuzhou and the others behind him also showed the same expression.

The smile on Zhou Yi's face slightly faded. In his heart, an inexplicable strong sense of unease surged. He shivered, realizing that his intuition had rarely been wrong.

"Is there something wrong, everyone?" Zhou Yi asked in a deep voice.

Lin Wenkai hesitated for a moment, as if recalling something, and said, "Is the esteemed gentleman from Zhou family, one of the three major families of Taicang County, Zhou Yi?"

"Yes."

"Has you returned from outside and not yet arrived in Taicang County?" Lin Wenkai asked tentatively.

"That's correct," Zhou Yi's gaze became slightly sharp, and he said, "Could it be that something has happened to our Zhou family?"

Lin Wenkai sighed bitterly and said, "Master Zhou, to be frank, seven days ago, the four major bandit groups from Ta'a County joined forces and suddenly detoured to Taicang County, launching a swift attack and swiftly breaking through the defenses of Taicang County."

"What?!"

Two figures suddenly flashed by, and Zhou Quanxin and his son quickly appeared. Their faces turned extremely ugly.

"What happened afterward?" Zhou Yi asked.

Lin Wenkai shook his head slightly and said, "The last information we received was that the county had been breached, but what happened after that is unclear." He paused and added, "Our Lord sent us to Taicang County to gather information. However, these bandits are ruthless and disregard human life. This time in Taicang County, I'm afraid..."

Although he stopped there, everyone understood the implications.

Zhou Yi's face darkened, and his eyes were filled with an uncontainable bone-chilling coldness.

"Father, Mother," Zhou Yi looked up and whispered softly. Then, he took a deep breath and exclaimed, "Uncle, Brother, I'll go ahead."

As soon as Zhou Yi finished speaking, he vanished like a ghost.

Within moments, everyone heard the sound of rapidly approaching

horse hooves, resembling the beating of drums. Then, a red figure

disappeared from their sight...

Chapter 136

The stars had disappeared, hiding away in the depths of the unknown, while the dark veil of the night took on the visage of a menacing demon, revealing its sinister countenance. The entire town lay in a hushed silence, as if trapped within the clutches of desolate stillness.

Suddenly, a resounding sound of hoofbeats echoed from afar, a swift horse galloping with a rhythm that seemed faint at first, only to grow increasingly distinct within an instant.

Though shrouded in darkness, the mounted knight beheld the dilapidated gates of the town with startling clarity. These colossal iron doors, colossal to the average person, appeared as though they had been brutally battered by some weighty force.

The two massive doors cracked open, now irreparably damaged, revealing a pitch-black path leading into the heart of the town.

Zhou Yi's heart pounded with impatience. Yet, as his gaze fell upon the gate, his heart froze in an icy grip. Clenching his teeth, he urged his steed forward, and the crimson stallion, as if attuned to his innermost desires, quickened its pace.

Unimpeded, they breached the town's threshold, the thunderous sound of hooves resounding upon the stone pathways within, shattering the tranquility of the night.

Within the town, signs of devastation were omnipresent, visible remnants of a gruesome scene. Blackened bloodstains had solidified in large patches, and in the vicinity, Zhou Yi's gaze fell upon over a dozen lifeless bodies strewn across the ground.

Judging from their attire, they were undoubtedly ordinary townsfolk, unfortunate victims who hadn't escaped in time during the siege, mercilessly slain by the marauding bandits.

His ears perked up, mounted upon his steed, Zhou Yi even discerned the distant commotion, emanating from several sources nearby. Though uncertain whether these noises stemmed from surviving bandits or fortunate townsfolk, none of it piqued his interest to stay behind.

The speed of his crimson stallion surpassed that of any human reflexes, swiftly vanishing from sight when some people, hastily donning their garments and brandishing weapons, emerged from their hiding places.

As Zhou Yi passed by a grand mansion along the way, his gaze lingered momentarily upon it.

This place was not unfamiliar to him. He had ventured here numerous times before.

It was here that he, encountered Cheng master and discovered the Xu family's spy. He obtained the Fiery Flame Technique and engaged in a fierce battle with Lin Tao Li.

However, the resplendent and renowned Cheng Manor now lay in ruins, reduced to ashes by a raging inferno, its former glory relegated to fragments preserved solely within his memories.

His nostrils twitched slightly, detecting a faint lingering scent of charred remains in the air. Evidently, the mansion had not been razed for long.

Without pausing, Zhou Yi traversed the road, making his way towards the area within the town where the Zhou family resided.

Within the town, whether it was the once-mighty Cheng family or the innocent residents, his greatest concern lay solely with his parents.

For decades, his parents had dutifully managed a few shops within the town on behalf of the Zhou family. Although these establishments served as mere fronts to conceal their true operations, primarily smuggling goods, it was his father who orchestrated everything covertly.

When the town of Taicang fell, Zhou Yi's greatest fear was whether his parents had foreseen the impending danger and escaped in time. The thought of returning to the courtyards of the Zhou family only to discover the lifeless bodies of his parents haunted him.

If that were to be the case, even if he were to exterminate every last one of those bandits, it would be an irreparable failure to avenge the loss burning within his heart.

As Zhou Yi approached the grand mansion of the Zhou family, darkness enveloped the surroundings, devoid of even the slightest glimmer of light.

Without hesitation, Zhou Yi's figure moved, not waiting for his crimson stallion to steady itself. With a swift forward charge, he crossed the courtyard wall in an instant, landing firmly within the yard.

Prior to his arrival, he had worried that this place might suffer the same fate as the Cheng family, reduced to ashes by a single flame. Though the mansion still stood, his unease persisted, offering him no respite.

At that moment of entry, he feared nothing more than the sight of his parents' lifeless bodies within the estate.

Throughout his journey, though the town did not exhibit corpses strewn everywhere, he had encountered dozens of lifeless bodies, all visible along the streets he passed.

If one were to include those unseen and those who perished inside their homes, it would be impossible to determine how many more people had fallen victim to this calamity throughout the entire county.

Finally, Zhou Yi gained a clear understanding of the brutality of these bandits.

His gaze shifted, his figure moving like lightning as he traversed the various rooms. Only then did he breathe a sigh of relief when he found no corpses within the Zhou family's courtyards and houses. The interior remained undisturbed. It was apparent that when the bandits drew near, his parents had received some warning, allowing them to withdraw calmly.

Just as he was about to leave, a slight change in his expression prompted Zhou Yi to take a decisive step. He inclined his head, his mind focusing on listening intently for a moment.

His face shifted subtly, and with purposeful strides, Zhou Yi arrived before a miniature mountain within the courtyard. Extending his hand, he placed it flat upon the rock, circulating his inner energy. A tremendous force surged forth, as if an unstoppable avalanche, emanating from his palm.

The artificial mountain trembled and, astonishingly, rose abruptly from the ground, defying gravity under the force of Zhou Yi's palm. Dust billowed, revealing a gaping hole beneath the faux rock structure, leading to an underground chamber spanning over ten square meters.

Within this underground chamber, a bewildered figure looked up in astonishment, their gaze filled with terror as they locked eyes with Zhou Yi. To them, he appeared as a fearsome, otherworldly demon, causing even their body to tremble uncontrollably.

Zhou Yi's eyes gleamed, and he bellowed in a commanding tone, "Zhou Chen, what are you doing here?"

This Zhou Chen was a servant within the Zhou family's estate, favored by Zhou Quan, Zhou Yi's father. He was an orphan taken in by the estate due to his agility and sharp wit, which set him apart from the other servants. Zhou Quan had brought him to the town, where he assisted in managing the family's businesses, making him one of the few trusted stewards of the Zhou family.

With the whereabouts of the Zhou family members in the town unknown, Zhou Chen's solitary presence in this location greatly infuriated Zhou Yi. If not for Zhou Yi's extraordinary innate talents and remarkable auditory perception, it would have been unlikely for him to uncover the secret hidden beneath the artificial mountain.

Zhou Chen was initially taken aback, but upon hearing Zhou Yi's voice, his eyes immediately lit up, and even his trembling ceased.

"Young Master Yi, you are Young Master Yi?" he exclaimed.

"Yes," Zhou Yi confirmed.

"It is truly Young Master Yi!" Zhou Chen promptly leaped out of the opening in the ground, though his appearance was disheveled from the flying debris. Nonetheless, his face was filled with unadulterated joy.

Observing Zhou Chen's expression, Zhou Yi's demeanor softened slightly, and he inquired, "Why are you here? Where are my parents?"

"Young Master Yi, it was Master and Madam who instructed me to stay here," Zhou Chen replied with a bitter smile. "This secret chamber was constructed in secrecy by Master after he took control of this estate. Some valuables, such as precious fabrics and silverware from the town, are stored inside. Before they left, Master and Madam instructed me to remain here. However..."

Zhou Chen gazed at the now dilapidated artificial mountain in the distance, his expression filled with bitterness. "Now, I'm afraid this secret cannot be preserved."

Zhou Yi's mouth fell open in astonishment. He had never expected such circumstances.

However, at this moment, no amount of wealth stored within mattered more than his parents.

"Zhou Chen, what exactly has happened in the town?" Zhou Yi asked.

"Regarding that, Young Master, that day we were conducting our business as usual when suddenly, messengers from the Cheng family arrived and informed us that the bandits from Taia County were about to raid our premises. They urged us to swiftly pack up and leave the town," Zhou Chen explained, pausing briefly before continuing. "Upon hearing the news, Master immediately ordered the closure of our shops. All valuable items were stored in this secret chamber. He commanded me to take provisions and seek refuge in the chamber, strictly forbidding us from leaving under any circumstances, unless it was when the provisions were depleted or someone from the Zhou family came to retrieve us."

Zhou Yi felt a pang of worry. It seemed that Zhou Chen didn't know much beyond this. He casually inquired, "Zhou Chen, do you know where my parents went?"

Zhou Chen bowed slightly and replied, "Young Master Yi, before I entered this secret chamber, I recall Master mentioning that they were heading to the Cheng family."

As Zhou Yi recalled the tragic scene at the Cheng family, his head buzzed with a deafening noise. He felt as if all the blood in his body was rushing towards his head, threatening to burst it open.

Surprised, Zhou Chen reached out to support him, but as soon as his hand made contact with Zhou Yi's body, he was jolted away. Fortunately, even in such a state, Zhou Yi could distinguish friend from foe and had refrained from using his true energy; otherwise, the consequences might not have been so simple.

Upon seeing Zhou Chen lying on the ground in pain, Zhou Yi regained his senses. Taking a swift step, he approached Zhou Chen, pulled him up, and circulated a surge of wood-based true energy within his body, instantly healing his minor injuries.

"Zhou Chen, continue to follow my father's instructions," Zhou Yi instructed.

With that, Zhou Yi swiftly departed, moving like a flying arrow.

Zhou Chen responded with a nod, but when he turned back, he was dumbfounded.

The artificial mountain had been sent flying, leaving behind a dark and gaping hole. Anyone who laid eyes upon it would surely be tempted to explore its depths, making it nearly impossible for him to protect this secret.

Zhou Yi rushed toward the exit as if he were flying. He had already heard the neighing of his Hongling stallion from outside the gate. In addition, there were more than ten voices mixed with both excitement and anger.

"Such a fine horse! Capture it quickly..."

"Oh no, it ran over there! Block it..."

"It's coming this way, what a fierce horse..."

At this moment, besides the audacious bandits, who else would have the mind to chase after horses?

Zhou Yi silently flipped over the wall and stood in the corner, instantly catching the attention of his crimson stallion, which swiftly turned around and galloped toward him.

Behind the stallion, more than ten fierce-looking men followed. However, these men were undoubtedly horse lovers; they would rather be knocked down by a horse than wield their weapons.

But when the crimson stallion came to a stop, and they saw Zhou Yi, they realized something was amiss.

Without hesitation, one of them raised his large blade and swung it down, aiming for Zhou Yi's head. The malicious gleam in his eyes revealed his addiction to killing, his inability to restrain himself.

Zhou Yi's eyes widened, his upper body unmoving. Suddenly, he launched a powerful kick.

This kick was as fast as lightning, as heavy as a massive hammer, thundering out even faster than the man's blade.

Although the man watched as Zhou Yi executed the kick, his reaction couldn't keep up. He barely had the thought of stepping back or dodging before the kick struck his chest.

Despite the kick being just a light tap with the toe, the man was sent flying as if struck by a thousand-pound hammer. He soared through the air, his blade falling from his hand. With a resounding crash, the horse thief flew more than ten meters before crashing heavily to the ground.

The remaining horse thieves turned pale with fear. The leader threw his sleeves up, instantly shooting an arrow that soared into the sky, emitting a piercing whistle that reverberated throughout the county town.

Zhou Yi sneered repeatedly. He had been worried about how to gather the horse thieves in the town, but now someone had done the work for him.

Unaware of Zhou Yi's thoughts, the leader focused on buying time and courteously said, "I am red scarf(hongjin) thief Zong Kui. May I know who you are and why you killed my comrades?"

Zhou Yi knew exactly what Zong Kui was trying to do—buy time for his comrades to gather. However, their thoughts aligned, and Zhou Yi sneered in response, saying, "You don't need to know who I am. I simply want to know why the red scarf thieves, who have always operated in Taia County, decided to launch a violent attack on Taicang County."

Zong Kui raised an eyebrow and replied, "Our third-in-command, Guan Wei, and fourth-in-command, Liao, both died at the hands of the Cheng and Zhou families in Taicang County. That's why our leader brought our forces here to avenge our brothers."

Zhou Yi's expression turned colder as he said, "Avenge your brothers, huh? Killing people is acceptable, but if someone kills you, you demand revenge and hold grudges. Truly befitting of a group of horse thieves."

Zong Kui coldly stated, "Indeed, we can kill others, but others cannot offend us."

Zhou Yi lowered his head and suddenly asked, "I understand about Guan Wei, but what about Liao? And how did you confirm that it was the Zhou family in Taicang County?"

Zong Kui glanced toward the distance and faintly saw torches rapidly approaching. His heart filled with joy, but he continued to speak nonstop, "Those idiots from the Zhou family thought that by leaving Taicang County, they would remain unrecognized. Little did they know that the horses they rode bore the marks of the Zhou family in Taicang County. A few of our surviving brothers followed them discreetly and discovered the truth. Hehe, at first, our leader hesitated about whether to launch a hundred-mile assault and cleanse Taicang County with blood. But after receiving news of Liao's death, he made up his mind and presented his beloved steeds to the second-in-command of the Blue Sea Pirate Group. That's how the four major thief groups united."

Zong Kui's words gradually slowed down, and the joy in his eyes grew more intense. At this moment, the clamor of voices filled the air as dozens of people rushed in from various directions, totaling over a hundred individuals.

A voice rang out loudly, "Zong Kui, what's happening? Why did you shoot the signal arrow?"

Zong Kui quickly replied with deference, "Sir Li, there's something interesting here, and it involves a magnificent steed."

Sir Li's eyes immediately lit up, fixed upon the fiery-red stallion without blinking. As a member of the horse thieves, he could discern the quality of a horse at a glance.

He turned his head and noticed an intriguing young man standing beside the horse, a long, conspicuous cloth strip hanging from his back. However, at this moment, his eyes were solely captivated by that majestic red steed, oblivious to the mysterious figure beside it.

"Indeed, it's an exceptional horse. I'll have it for myself. Boys, take care of this fellow for me."

The band of horse thieves responded in unison, and several eager ones drew their blades, ready to charge.

Yet, right at that moment, the seemingly expressionless young man suddenly lifted his head.

In that instant, his eyes shimmered like stars.

The horse thieves were taken aback, unsure why, but as they gazed into those eyes, an indescribable chill crept into their hearts.

A faint smile appeared on Zhou Yi's lips, a smile pregnant with unimaginable remorse and indignation.

He slowly opened his mouth and uttered softly, "Uncle, I was wrong. It turns out that to eradicate evil is the only righteous path."

Though his words were not weighty, they resonated clearly among the hundred-plus people present. The numerous horse thieves exchanged puzzled glances, wondering if this man had lost his wits. Nevertheless, an unsettling coldness filled their bewildered hearts.

In a sudden blur, the young man's figure vanished before their eyes.

"Ah..."

A piercing scream tore through the night sky, and in a flash, it seemed as if someone had been thrown high up, disappearing into the night without a trace. Within moments, the chorus of agonized screams echoed one after another, as if contagious.

The enraged horse thieves shouted furiously, attempting to surround and strike down the mysterious figure. However, they soon realized that they couldn't keep up with his pace. In just a brief moment, more than half of the hundred-plus men fell, leaving only a dozen or so perceptive individuals. Sensing the dire situation, they promptly fled.

Sir Li was filled with terror and tried to distance himself, but he felt a weight on his body, causing his legs to buckle, and he knelt down, powerless.

One of Zhou Yi's hands rested on his shoulder, his voice as icy as an eternal glacier, "After you breached the city, where did the Cheng family members go?"

Sir Li's heart trembled, and he instinctively replied, "Spare me, my lord. After breaching the city, the Cheng family members joined forces with the Zhou family and fled to Xujiabao（Xu Family Fortress）."

"Xujiabao? Are the Zhou family members there as well?"

"Indeed, the news came from our leader. The core heirs of the three major families in Taicang County are gathered and holding their ground in Xujiabao."

Images of the towering walls of Xujiabao flashed through Zhou Yi's mind, bringing a sense of reassurance.

"How many members are there in your four major horse thief groups?"

Sir Li hesitated for a moment, feeling a tremendous force surge into his shoulder, causing excruciating pain that penetrated his very marrow. The overwhelming presence of his opponent seemed solid, shattering his resistance in an instant. In the face of a Innate expert, not just anyone could withstand such a formidable mental pressure.

"Combined, they exceed five thousand," Sir Li reluctantly replied.

"What is their strength like?" Zhou Yi inquired.

"We have five experts at the tenth level of inner strength, dozens at the eighth and ninth levels..."

Zhou Yi's heart grew colder and colder. It was inconceivable that the horse thieves possessed such formidable power, surpassing even a thousand-year-old prestigious family.

"How is the situation at Xujiabao?"

"Our leader sent a message tonight. They have been besieged for five days, creating several breaches. Tomorrow morning, they plan to launch a final assault, and they are confident they can take it..."

"Hahaha, confident they can take it?" Zhou Yi burst into laughter, a laughter filled with a thick aura of slaughter.

Sir Li, realizing the gravity of the situation, desperately pleaded, "My lord, spare me. I will never dare to be a horse thief again."

Zhou Yi's gaze turned cold and stern as he declared, "I have missed an opportunity once, and I will never miss a second chance."

With a swift leap, he soared into the air, not even bothering to mount the Hongling horse. Like a cloud or mist, he swiftly and gracefully dashed towards Xujiabao.

In his wake, Sir Li's body swayed twice before collapsing, unable to rise again, just like the countless lives he had taken before.

Chapter 137

The breath of the night was dark and peculiar, with a silence that carried its own unique sound. The mountains transformed into the shadows of mighty beasts, lurking and restless all around us.

After five days of relentless defense, Xu Family Fortress, renowned for its impregnability, had finally reached its limits. Though the ancestors of the Xu family had poured their hearts and souls into constructing the fortress, they never anticipated that their descendants would face such dire circumstances.

Under the combined might of the four infamous bandit groups from Tai'a County, there were over five thousand men, including five peak-level experts with tenth-layer internal energy and more than ten experts at the ninth-layer. Such a massive force was beyond any single family within Taicang County's ability to withstand.

Five days, a full five days. Led by Zhou Wude and Xu Yinjie, the core disciples of the Zhou, Xu, and Cheng families took turns to battle, each one bearing wounds and appearing utterly disheveled. They had fended off countless assaults by the bandits, and now, beneath the Xu Family Fortress, the corpses of the marauders numbered close to a staggering thousand. Among these near thousand bandits, there were even several experts with seventh and eighth-layer internal energy, and astonishingly, two grandmasters at the ninth-layer. Such heavy losses stirred both fear and rage among the many bandit leaders but only strengthened their resolve to annihilate Xu Family Fortress.

At this moment, everyone within the fortress knew that if the bandits breached the defenses, not a single soul would escape with their life.

"Ah..."

A shrill and desperate scream echoed from the city walls, reverberating through the silent night sky, yet the surrounding people seemed oblivious, as if they hadn't heard it at all. They didn't even bother to cast a glance in that direction.

Xu Yinjie lightly clapped his hands, his gaunt face deeply sunken. In the darkness, he resembled a ghostly figure, haunting and eerie. Wherever he went, the disciples of the three families stood tall, their chests puffed out, gazing at this frail old man with admiration and gratitude in their eyes.

On this night, the seventh bandit who had stealthily infiltrated the city walls was discovered and slain by the venerable elder. If it weren't for his tireless efforts patrolling the walls, their defenses would have likely been breached already.

However, as Xu Yinjie looked upon these disciples of the three families, who fought their way through bloodshed, his heart grew heavy. His gaze fell upon the city walls, where several breaches had formed, and even with the combined strength of the three families, they couldn't repair those gaps.

The bandits had come too suddenly, and their strength was overwhelmingly formidable.

"Xu brother, you've killed another one. You've surpassed my achievements from yesterday," an aged voice came from another direction. Zhou Wude strode forward with swift and steady steps, accompanied by the smiling figure of Elder Cheng Ningsheng.

It seemed that wherever he walked, it wasn't a city wall stained with days of bloodshed, but the magnificent and splendid gardens of his Cheng family. The young disciples and servants of the three families, upon seeing his smile, couldn't help but feel a surge of energy, as if the fatigue of the past few days had been somewhat lifted.

Xu Yinjie nodded to them, and the three men instinctively walked to a certain section of the city wall. Xu Yinjie waved his hand, and the few individuals who were guarding the area immediately bowed deeply and swiftly departed.

Though there were only three elderly men present, there was no doubt that they possessed the greatest martial prowess within Taicang County.

If any bandits were foolish enough to attempt an intrusion from this direction, they would undoubtedly be seeking their own demise.

As people in the distance gazed toward them, a massive torch illuminated their surroundings, casting its radiance upon Cheng Ningsheng's face, where his gentle smile was evident to all.

However, although Cheng Ningsheng's smile remained, his voice grew low, devoid of any humor. "Xu brother, tonight the situation seems somewhat amiss."

"You're right, I sense it too. They have begun assembling their forces below," Xu Yinjie said coldly. The old man's face remained expressionless, as expected of someone who practiced the Withered Wood Technique. A lack of facial expressions was natural, for if he were to adopt Cheng Ningsheng's smiling countenance, it would signal imminent catastrophe.

Zhou Wude let out a sigh. His back remained straight and sturdy, unaffected by the eighty-plus years of wind and rain. His vitality appeared no different from that of some young men.

"If we're not mistaken, they will launch a full-scale attack tomorrow morning," his gaze settled on the collapsed sections of the wall. "I'm afraid this time, we won't be able to hold them back."

Though Xu Yinjie and Cheng Ningsheng did not speak, their eyes expressed unanimous agreement.

Suddenly, Cheng Ningsheng spoke up, "Brother Zhou, Brother Xu, I have a suggestion. What do you think?"

"Go ahead," Zhou Wude replied solemnly.

"This time, it seems that the three major families of Taicang County are facing inevitable doom. However, we cannot simply allow ourselves to be annihilated. If you don't object, I propose gathering the most outstanding third-generation members of our respective families. At dawn, when the bandits launch their attack, let Zhou Quanyi, Xu Xiangci, and my granddaughter, Jiayun, lead them in breaking through the encirclement, taking the path through the mountains, and striving to escape with their lives."

Even as Cheng Ningsheng spoke these words, his smile remained unwavering, bringing a sense of tranquility to those who observed him.

"Why choose them?" Xu Yinjie objected unhappily. "Let Xu Xiangci be replaced by Xu Xiangqian."

"No," Cheng Ningsheng said firmly. "I understand your sentiment, and I know Xu Xiangqian is the foremost among the second generation of the Xu family. However, precisely because of that, if you were to assign Xu Xiangqian this task, it would undoubtedly attract attention and close off the only possible avenue of escape for the third-generation members."

"Cheng brother is right. If we want to send out the most promising and talented individuals from the third generation, not only can we not leave, but Xu Xiangqian must also stay," Zhou Wude sighed deeply.

Cheng Ningsheng smiled contentedly. "It's a pity. If your Xu family's ancestor could return, even if it were not just four groups of bandits, but ten, we wouldn't have to worry."

A certain glint flickered in Xu Yinjie's eyes, an indescribable mix of regret and frustration.

"Cheng brother, why talk about this now?" he paused and asked, "Have you selected the candidates?"

"Yes," Cheng Ningsheng replied. "I have chosen seven individuals. They have all shed blood in this battle, and their mentality is admirable. They should have promising futures. Entrusting the future of the Cheng family to them, I feel relatively at ease."

Zhou Wude shrugged his shoulders slightly and said, "Our Zhou family has few members, so as soon as we received the news, those with internal energy below the sixth layer were already instructed to hide in the mountains. Those who came with me are only Zhou QuanMing, Zhou Quanyi, Yi Hai, and Yi Xuan. After discussing among ourselves, Zhou QuanMing will lead Yi Hai and Yi Xuan in an attempt to break out, while I and Zhou Quanyi will stay behind."

Xu Yinjie's expression changed slightly, and he suddenly said, "Your suggestion is good, but I think it's better to make some changes."

Zhou Wude and Cheng Ningsheng exchanged a puzzled glance, wondering if this old man had some unusual idea. It seemed to deviate greatly from his usual character.

Xu Yinjie's voice grew even deeper, and even the two men who were close by had to focus their attention to hear him clearly.

"Tomorrow, I will stay behind alone, and all of you will go."

Both Zhou Wude and Cheng Ningsheng rolled their eyes simultaneously. Cheng Ningsheng objected, "Don't joke around. If we leave you alone here and make a grand exit, I guarantee that not a single one of us will escape."

A peculiar look flashed in Xu Yinjie's eyes as he said, "Gentlemen, there is something you don't know. Within our Xu Family Fortress, there is a secret passage that leads directly to the back mountains. This passage has existed since the day the fortress was built, but it has never been used in the past hundred years."

Zhou Wude and Cheng Ningsheng's eyes instantly lit up with a mixture of surprise and delight.

Since such a secret passage existed, while it may not be possible to evacuate all the people within the fortress, there would be no problem in sending out the core members.

Xu Yinjie continued, "Tomorrow morning, these thieves are likely to launch a full-scale assault. Hurry and take the time to count the number of people and leave."

Cheng Ningsheng hesitated for a moment and asked, "And what about you? Aren't you going to leave with us?"

Xu Yinjie smiled wryly but didn't answer the question directly. He sighed and said, "The three families, as we claim to be the three major clans of Taicang County, are actually nothing compared to others. Heh heh, Taicang County, Taicang County, it's truly too small and too weak."

Indeed, with the alliance of the three families, they had managed to gather over half of the martial forces within Taicang County. However, not to mention the entirety of Tai'a County, even when compared to the four largest bandit groups within Tai'a County, their strength appeared inferior.

This bitter reality was difficult for them to accept, hence their unfavorable expressions.

"Let's not dwell on this any longer," Xu Yinjie sighed lightly. "Let's go back and send away the promising young disciples from our respective families. Don't hold back. Let's leave them with the hope of survival, far better than sending them to their deaths here. Moreover, I believe that after this catastrophe, those young ones will surely rise again and make our three families' name resound throughout Taicang County, and perhaps even Linglang County."

"What about you? Are you really not planning to leave?" Cheng Ningsheng suddenly asked.

Xu Yinjie's gaze swept across the fortress, and there was a profound reluctance in his eyes. "This is my home. I was born here, and even in death, I want to be buried here. Besides, I must give an account to everyone who depends on the Xu family." He lowered his gaze and continued, "Regarding the secret passage, Xiangqian knows about it. After you've chosen the candidates, go find Xiangqian. He will guide you to safety."

Zhou Wude glanced deeply at Xu Yinjie and then turned and walked away without a word. Cheng Ningsheng took a few steps back but suddenly stopped. He said, "Yinjie, you don't blame me for leading those people here, do you?"

Xu Yinjie smiled faintly and replied, "Brother-in-law, do you think the four major bandit groups from Tai'a County joined forces just to target the county town? Even if you and Zhou Wude didn't come, they would still have razed Zhou Family and Xu Family Fortress to the ground. Otherwise, why would they have made such a trip for nothing?"

Cheng Ningsheng smiled wryly, said nothing more, and slowly descended from the city walls. In the midst of his movement, a figure emerged from the shadows—it was Xu Xiangqian, the most outstanding among the second generation of the Xu family.

"Father, why did you tell them about the secret passage?" Xu Xiangqian asked.

Xu Yinjie shook his head slightly and said, "Xiangqian, you must remember that Taicang County is our foundation. The influence here must never be left in a vacuum. We can allow the Zhou and Cheng families to become the leading clans of Taicang County, and we can humbly attach ourselves to them. But you must remember that as long as there is a possibility, we should never allow outsiders to establish a foothold here."

Xu Xiangqian's expression twitched slightly, as if he wanted to say something, but Xu Yinjie shook his head and continued, "I understand your thoughts. If another Zhou Wude were to appear in the county, we must do everything possible to make him a true resident of Taicang County, to make him truly consider this place his homeland. Do you understand?"

Xu Xiangqian finally lowered his head and said, "Yes, I understand."

"Well, this time Xu Family Fortress is in great danger. After you lead everyone out, immediately seek help from our ancestor. Although Xu Family Fortress may be destroyed, if our ancestor is willing to intervene, then not only rebuilding one fortress, but even two or three fortresses would be a piece of cake," Xu Yinjie's voice was deep and powerful. "This is a good opportunity, perhaps the only opportunity. You must seize it."

Xu Xiangqian responded heavily and suddenly asked, "Father, are you really not planning to leave?"

"Nonsense." Xu Yinjie raised an eyebrow. "This is my home. I will make anyone who tries to invade pay a sufficient price."

Although his words were plain, they carried an undeniable determination.

Xu Xiangqian clenched his fists tightly. He knew that countless pairs of eyes were closely watching him, and he absolutely couldn't show any signs. If the core members of the three families' intentions to abandon the fortress were discovered, it would surely extinguish any fighting spirit within the fortress. A single charge from the bandits outside would be enough to slaughter everyone.

Taking a deep breath, Xu Xiangqian turned and left. With each step, he felt a deep sadness, knowing that this would be his last meeting with his father.

Underneath the city walls, a kilometer away, a group of bandits patrolled cautiously. Anyone who dared to attempt leaving the fortress would be intercepted and ruthlessly killed by them.

A tall and stern-faced middle-aged man with a gaze as sharp as a snake locked his eyes onto Xu Family Fortress beneath the night sky. This man was Zhong Wei, the head leader of the Wolf Fang Bandits, one of the four major bandit groups in Tai'a County. Although he appeared to be in his forties, his actual age had long surpassed sixty.

The heads of the four major bandit groups in Tai'a County were all seasoned warriors over sixty years old, renowned ten-layer Internal Strength experts. However, within the Red Scarf Bandits, there were two ten-layer experts who, in terms of strength alone, had a slight edge over the other bandit groups.

After considering the invitation from the Red Scarf Bandits, Zhong Wei weighed the pros and cons and finally agreed. Besides wanting to gain some benefits from this opportunity, he also didn't want to offend the Red Scarf Bandits. After all, even among the ten-layer Internal Strength experts, there were varying levels of strength, and Zhong Wei was undoubtedly the weakest among the five.

Initially, everything went smoothly during their journey to Taicang County. But no one could have anticipated that after easily capturing the county town, they would encounter this tough nut, Xu Family Fortress.

The county town was like a wall made of mud, easily collapsing with a single push.

However, facing the towering walls of Xu Family Fortress, even with the abundance of skilled bandits, it took them a full five days and the sacrifice of nearly a thousand men and horses to breach the walls, leaving only a few openings.

Nevertheless, those few openings were already sufficient.

Zhong Wei licked his slightly dry lips, his eyes shimmering with ferocity. He clenched his hands and slowly released them, allowing his Internal Strength to circulate through his meridians. However, when it passed through his right shoulder, a faint pain still lingered.

His facial muscles twitched faintly, and the aura of killing emanating from him grew even stronger, causing his subordinates to shudder, knowing that their ruthless leader was about to unleash his fury once again.

During their initial assault on the city, Zhong Wei had encountered Xu Yinjae in combat. They exchanged several strikes, and Zhong Wei was struck by Xu Yinjae's palm on his right shoulder. While it wasn't a life-threatening blow, it caused him great pain.

Now, he had made up his mind. Once they breached the city at dawn, he was determined to capture Xu Yinjae alive. Before his very eyes, he would execute all the male members of the Xu family and distribute the women to his brothers for humiliation. He wanted to make the old man regret why he had injured him.

Suddenly, a cry of agony resounded from the darkness, followed by the thud of a heavy object hitting the ground.

Zhong Wei frowned. "Is the ambush still being set up?"

One of his men immediately responded, "Zhong Boss, the ambush has been ongoing, personally arranged by Hai Boss."

Zhong Wei snorted lightly. In his view, since the final assault was scheduled for tomorrow morning, it wouldn't matter if there were no more ambushes tonight. However, since it was arranged by Hai Huiqiao, he immediately dismissed the idea of interfering.

Hai Huiqiao was the wife of Lan Hanyang, the head leader of the Blue Sea Bandits, and they were both experts, with Lan at the ten-layer Internal Strength and Hai at the ninth-layer Internal Strength. They were skilled in coordination and their Internal Strength techniques complemented each other. When they joined forces, their combined power was nearly unmatched among the two ten-layer experts.

Moreover, Hai Huiqiao was known for her remarkable wit and was often called the "Wise Star."

The band of five thousand horse bandits had initially planned to attack the city of Taicang, with Hai Huiqiao strongly advocating for a preemptive strike on the Xu family fortress before moving on to the city. However, besides Lan Hanyang, no one else responded, perhaps due to their unwillingness to be commanded by a woman.

However, the reality proved Hai Huiqiao's foresight. The city of Taicang fell easily in a single battle, but the Xu family fortress, fortified and prepared, became a thorn in their side. It took the sacrifice of nearly a thousand bandit brothers before they glimpsed a glimmer of victory. Although they believed they would capture the Xu family fortress in the final assault the next day, they knew that many more of their comrades would perish.

Not far away, groups of people and horses began to gather. Over the past five days, these people had taken turns residing in the Xu family town, while the town's inhabitants either sought refuge in the fortress or fell at the hands of the bandits. They had occupied the entire town, making it their headquarters where thousands of them resided.

Although the sky was still dim, all the people from the town had gathered here. Despite being bandits, they possessed qualities no less than that of an army. Thousands of them arrived in the darkness, filling the space with a strong and intense aura of bloodlust.

While the horse bandits lacked sophisticated siege tools, they were no ordinary individuals. Each of them was a practitioner of internal energy cultivation. For them, the city walls posed a great obstacle, but not an insurmountable one. This had been demonstrated in the previous days' battles.

Of course, if it weren't for the city walls, allowing thousands of horse bandits to rampage freely within the fortress, the people inside the Xu family stronghold would have long collapsed and perished.

At this moment, several breaches had appeared in the Xu family fortress walls, thanks to the coordinated efforts of several formidable experts. As long as they organized enough manpower for a final charge, victory would be within reach.

By Zhong Wei's side were five additional individuals. Among them were the leader of the Red Scarves, Guan Qing, the second-in-command, Guo Shaofeng, the ferocious tiger Xu Hanbai, Lan Hanyang from the Blue Sea faction, and Hai Huiqiao.

Although the four men had different appearances, even the youngest among them, Lan Hanyang, was over sixty years old. However, in terms of cultivation, he was undoubtedly the most powerful among them.

"Is everyone here?" Guan Qing's voice resonated like muffled thunder.

"We're all here."

An unrefined voice came from Hai Huiqiao, but none of the men present dared to underestimate her.

This wasn't solely because of her husband but also due to her own accomplishments and status.

The gazes of the group converged on their target—the menacing black walls that appeared even more ominous in the darkness.

The sky grew darker, reaching its dimmest point just before dawn. No one spoke; they were all waiting. Even the continuous ambushes that had occurred over the past five days had ceased. It was as if they were united in spirit, for even the walls fell silent. Both sides seemed to be awaiting the moment when the first rays of sunlight would appear.

As the sky began to lighten, a faint milky band stretched across, seemingly binding all the peaks together. It was followed by a drunken crimson halo, which was soon shrouded by a heavy gray cloud.

The sky remained a light blue, and then, on the horizon, a streak of vermilion appeared, gradually expanding its reach and intensifying its brightness. Finally, the first ray of morning light emerged...

Hai Huiqiao nodded slowly, and Guan Qing raised his hand high. The hands of all the bandits tightly gripped their weapons, their eyes shimmering with a frenzied light.

However, at that very moment, an earth-shattering, colossal roar echoed in their ears, as if the mountains were crumbling and the seas were surging...

※※※※

On the city wall, Xu Yinjie kicked a bandit who had just climbed up, sending him flying. His face remained calm, without a hint of emotion, as if he had kicked away a withered leaf rather than a person.

Suddenly, he turned his head and saw a familiar face, one he had fought against for decades. His eyes held a trace of inquiry, as if wondering why this old man had appeared on the city wall.

Zhou Wude stood with his hands behind his back, calmly approaching Xu Yinqie. He looked down into the darkness below.

"Why haven't you left yet?"

"I want to leave too, but if I do, one of my lifelong wishes will remain unfulfilled."

"What wish is that?"

"I want to see whether it's your extraordinary martial arts skills or my invincible Daguandao (great guan dao) that will prevail," Zhou Wude pointed ahead into the darkness of the night and said, "There are plenty of bandits up ahead, enough for us to test ourselves."

Xu Yinjie finally opened his eyes slightly wider, and his sunken eyeballs seemed to regain a bit of vitality.

"What about your Daguandao?" Xu Yinjie asked.

Zhou Wude paused, a bitter smile on his face. "I gave it away," he said.

Xu Yinjie lowered his head again, his voice tinged with envy. "You have a great grandson."

Zhou Wude burst into laughter. "Yes, as long as Yi is here, there is hope for the revival of our Zhou family." He clapped his hands and suddenly declared, "But rest assured, even without the Daguandao, my hands won't be inferior."

"Tsk tsk, such a skillful hand technique. I must witness it," Cheng Ningsheng walked over with a jovial smile.

Both Xu Yinjie and Zhou Wude turned their heads simultaneously, their eyes filled with incredulity, as if they had suddenly seen the sun rise from the west.

Although Cheng Ningsheng had a thick skin, at that moment, a sense of annoyance and embarrassment appeared on his face.

"What kind of gaze is that?" Cheng Ningsheng exclaimed angrily.

Zhou Wude, surprised, said, "Brother Cheng, aren't you being confused? Are you, the cunning old fox from Taicang, really not afraid of death?"

A slight twitch appeared at the corner of Xu Yinjie's mouth, silently expressing his thoughts. Though he didn't say a word, his reaction clearly conveyed his meaning.

In his younger days, Cheng Ningsheng was known as the fox of Taicang. As he grew older, he naturally became the old fox of Taicang. Throughout his life, this old fox had dealt with countless people. It was precisely because of his cunning that the Cheng family maintained a dominant position, even when their martial prowess was lacking, never truly being suppressed by the Xu and Zhou families.

Furthermore, Cheng Ningsheng's greatest weakness in his life was his fear of death. Perhaps it was due to his sharp wit like a fox that he was always suspicious and indecisive, and his martial cultivation had stagnated.

This had become his nature, ingrained in his character, and could no longer be changed. Neither Zhou Wude nor Xu Yinjie had ever imagined that he would ascend the city wall at this moment. Even in their wildest dreams, they had not dared to hope for such a thing.

Cheng Ningsheng approached them, imitating Zhou Wude's posture, and said with folded hands, "I originally didn't intend to come, but suddenly there was something I couldn't let go of, so I came back to join the fun."

"What happened that you couldn't let go of?" Zhou Wude asked in astonishment.

Cheng Ningsheng replied indignantly, "We three have been fighting all our lives, and the thing I've always wanted to know is who between you two is the true number one expert of Taicang."

Zhou Wude and Xu Yinjie looked at each other, then glanced at the visibly angry Cheng Ningsheng. Finally, they burst into unabashed laughter. Even Xu Yinjie, who had cultivated the withered wood technique, showed a rare, ghastly grin, as if a starved ghost.

The sky seemed to have darkened to its utmost, and their laughter subsided as they gazed into the city below. Cheng Ningsheng spoke slowly, "With you two as my opponents, my life hasn't been in vain."

Zhou and Xu remained silent, but their hearts resonated with the same sentiment. The dawn's glow gradually emerged, and the sun hid behind the peaks, casting a hazy light that enveloped their surroundings. The light slowly permeated the pale blue sky, and the sky revealed a golden dawn.

Under the watchful eyes of the crowd, the first ray of light appeared...

The gazes of the three elderly men simultaneously grew intense, and their internal energy surged, their formidable momentum suddenly boiling.

However, at that moment, they heard a earth-shattering, monumental roar that reverberated like an avalanche...

※※※※

In a courtyard near the rear mountains of the Xu Family Manor, Xu Xiangqian, Zhou Quanming, and Cheng Jiahui, along with nearly fifty people, stood before a massive artificial mountain.

Xu Xiangqian summoned the power of his ninth-level internal energy, slowly shifting a corner of the artificial mountain, revealing a pitch-black passage leading to an unknown destination, spacious enough for three people to pass through.

Inside the passage, countless steps could be seen, a testament to the immense effort and dedication put forth by Xu's ancestors who had constructed it.

The night had grown dark, and only the torches held by the group emitted light and warmth, bringing a sense of solace to the endless darkness.

"Let's go," Xu Xiangqian said in a deep voice. "Yucai, lead the way. Zhou brothers, follow closely behind. Cheng brothers, stay in the middle. Xu family juniors, take the rear."

Yucai responded with a voice that faintly carried a trace of sorrow. Yet, at this moment, no one had any intention of mocking him. The individuals leaving from the Xu family were all true elites.

"Wait," Zhou Quanming whispered.

Xu Xiangqian and Cheng Jiahui turned their gaze simultaneously.

Zhou Quanming solemnly said, "Third brother, Yihai, Yixuan, let us kowtow to Father for the last time."

He turned and knelt toward the direction of the city wall. Zhou Quanming, Zhou Yihai, and Zhou Yixuan followed suit, vigorously kowtowing.

Xu Xiangqian and the others were slightly startled. Slowly, everyone voluntarily knelt down. Aside from the sound of foreheads hitting the ground, there remained only an overwhelming sense of sorrow and heaviness.

The morning mist still hung thickly, and a hint of blue haze appeared on the eastern horizon, floating gently like a wisp of smoke from a kitchen.

That first ray of light appeared before everyone's eyes.

Zhou Quanming rose to his feet, a trace of determination flashing in his eyes. He shouted, "Let's go!"

However, at that moment, they heard an earth-shattering, monumental roar that reverberated like an avalanche...

※※※※

In the distance, a figure appeared within the sight of the crowd.

The first ray of morning light, like a blade slicing through the darkness, illuminated him.

It was as if a dazzling, astonishing flash broke through the darkness, creating a rift in the sky, on the earth, in the eyes of people, and in their hearts.

He raised his head and let out a resounding howl that shook the ground.

Riding on clouds, carrying rain, exuding an overwhelming and tumultuous aura, Covering the heavens and earth, He approached, rolling and mighty...

Chapter 138

As the dawn broke, the pristine blue sky gradually unfurled a sheer veil of roseate hues. The tranquil azure dawn permeated through treacherous mountain passes, weaving through foliage and even sliding beneath fallen leaves, adorning every nook and cranny of the land in preparation for the arrival of the sun's radiant splendor.

Just before Xujiabao, a foreboding aura of impending battle lingered in every corner. Upon the city walls, it seemed as though everyone understood that today marked the final clash, silently awaiting the advent of this moment.

However, when daylight bathed the land, what they anticipated was not a bloody melee of carnage but a resounding thunderous roar that rent the sky. Within this ear-splitting howl, it appeared as though the very colors of the world changed, reverberating in the ears of each person, their gaze transformed, fixated on the direction from which the sound emanated, bearing a sense of impending calamity.

Suddenly, the thunderous roar, which seemed to fill every corner of the heavens and earth, ceased. The arrival of this howl was so abrupt, and its sudden halt equally unexpected. For a moment, the overwhelming noise that had inundated their ears dissipated, leaving a profound sense of unease. Anyone whose inner strength paled in comparison to the seventh level felt an involuntary weakness in their legs.

Amongst them, Hai Huiqiao was the first to regain her composure. Although her inner strength may not have been the most formidable among the bandits, undoubtedly, she remained the calmest and quickest to react. At this moment, her face had drained of all color, replaced by a profound fear in her eyes.

However, her expression lasted but a fleeting moment, and then she spoke as if nothing had happened: "This person is formidable; we cannot face him alone. Xu Hanbai, I request that you lead the Fierce Tiger 200 Suicide Squad as the first wave of resistance. Zhong Wei, I ask that you lead the Wolf Fang Reserve Team. If this person manages to break through the Fierce Tiger 200, you must step in and ensure he doesn't impede our overall assault. Guan Qing, the patriarch, and Guo Shaofeng, the second-in-command, I implore you to proceed with the original plan and commence the siege. As for the two of us, we will be in the middle, providing support at any given moment."

A moment of hesitation swept through the crowd, as a sense of foreboding began to rise within them, sensing that something was amiss. However, since their encounter with obstacles prior to Xujiabao(Xu Family Fortress), they had always entrusted Hai Huiqiao as their military strategist, and every action had been orchestrated by her. Now, with Xujiabao seemingly cornered by this chaotic band of bandits within five days, her achievements were undeniably remarkable.

Therefore, despite their uneasy premonitions, the group hesitated for a moment but ultimately chose to trust her judgment. With over four thousand formidable cultivators among the bandits, they couldn't possibly be frightened away by a single resounding roar.

Those whose names were called out were all mighty experts at the tenth level of inner strength, their reactions swift as they swiftly arrived at their prearranged positions.

As soon as the others departed, Hai Huiqiao immediately grabbed Lan Hanyang's hand and blended into the crowd, lowering her voice and saying, "Don't worry about anything else. Let's change our clothes quickly and leave..."

Lan Hanyang was taken aback and asked, "Why should we leave?"

"We won't have time if we don't leave now," Hai Huiqiao's face was filled with fear as she said, "The person who arrived is a innate powerhouse."

Lan Hanyang's expression remained relatively unchanged. Ever since he heard that earth-shattering howl moments ago, he had already had a vague sense of foreboding. After all, he himself was a pinnacle expert at the tenth level of inner strength, merely a step away from the legendary innate realm.

Since even he himself was taken aback by the resounding roar, it naturally means that the person who arrived is a innate powerhouse. Lan Hanyang lowered his head slightly and said, "Madam, we have four thousand people here. Can't we defeat a innate powerhouse?"

The name of a innate powerhouse had long been surrounded by countless legends among the prominent clans and top cultivators. However, those who had truly encountered a innate powerhouse were few and far between. Although the legends portrayed innate powerhouses as unbeatable and seemingly impossible to overcome with mere numbers, until one actually witnessed the strength of a innate powerhouse, it was inevitable for anyone to harbor a hint of fantasy in their hearts.

Not only Lan Hanyang, but even the others couldn't help but entertain such thoughts. Otherwise, they would have long dispersed and disappeared.

Hai Huiqiao's face turned deathly pale, and she solemnly said, "Patriarch, listen to me. Change your clothes and leave quickly!" She paused for a moment and continued, "Unless we have a swift cavalry of ten thousand elite soldiers ambushing and slaughtering them on the plains of Taia County, ordinary people simply cannot contend with a innate powerhouse."

In her heart, there was actually one more sentence left unspoken. Even in that kind of situation, they would only be able to deal with the lowest level of innate powerhouses.

Fortunately, from the sound of the howl, it could be deduced that the innate powerhouse who appeared this time was only of the lowest level. Otherwise, even if they changed their clothes, it would be difficult for them to escape.

Lan Hanyang's expression changed several times, and he hesitated before saying, "But...

"At this point, do we still need to talk about righteousness?" Hai Huiqiao exerted force in her grip and said, "We are here to assist, not to sacrifice ourselves. As much as treasures and wealth are desirable, they are meaningless without our lives."

Finally, Lan Hanyang no longer opposed and followed closely behind his wife, blending into the crowd. With the cover of trusted individuals, they changed into ordinary clothes.

※※※※

Guan Qing and Guo Shaofeng arrived at the front line. They brandished their large blades and shouted in a fierce tone, "Men, ahead lies Xujiabao, abundant with countless gold and beautiful women. As long as we can capture it, everything inside will be yours."

Guan Qing's voice was menacing, his words simple and direct. Yet, it was precisely because of this that it maximized the ferocity of the bandits.

With a roar, the bandits seemed to have forgotten the chilling howl that had sent shivers down everyone's spines just moments ago. Under the leadership of Guan Qing and Guo Shaofeng, they charged towards the several teams stationed at the gaps.

In just a moment, they reached the gaps. Before their eyes stood the last line of defense composed of servants, retainers, and guests from the three families. Even Guan Qing and Guo Shaofeng found the two old masters.

They all knew this was a matter of life and death. Each person tightly grasped their weapons as the distance between the two sides narrowed. Nervousness and excitement were evident in their eyes. At this critical juncture, no one had any room for retreat.

The individuals in the front row already saw the enemy's figures reflected in their eyes. They could even hear the heavy breaths emanating from their own and their comrades' mouths and noses, as well as those of the enemy ahead. The imminent battle was about to begin.

Suddenly, they heard a thunderous sound, a fierce shout that seemed beyond what a human could produce. Even in the midst of such tension and anticipation, even the bandits in the front row trembled, as the intense and hair-raising atmosphere seemed diluted by this powerful shout.

Everyone turned or looked up, their gazes surpassing the thousands of bandits, fixed on the final direction.

Then, a burst of light, an endless radiance flooded into the eyes of everyone...

※※※※

"Form ranks, draw your swords..."

With a thunderous roar, Xu Hanbai, the leader of the Fierce Tiger Suicide Squad, raised his Nine-Ring Great Blade and stood proudly at the entrance of the official road.

Behind him stood 200 elite members whom he personally trained and instructed. Even in the entire Taia County, they were a squad that could make any force tremble in fear.

Even the weakest among them possessed seventh-level inner strength cultivation. Moreover, these people revered Xu Hanbai like a deity and would never disobey his orders.

It was with this team that the Fierce Tiger had gained immense fame, daring to confront the Red Scarves Gang or the Blue Sea couple head-on.

At this moment, with Xu Hanbai's thunderous shout, the 200 soldiers behind him drew their swords simultaneously.

Their movements were precise and synchronized, as if they were one entity. A fierce and formidable aura converged at this moment. Even the tenth-level experts felt the intensity of this aura and hesitated to charge directly into the formation.

Before the Suicide Squad, the approaching figure rushed forward as if flying. As they looked at this man who emanated such immense power, their faces twisted in a ferocious expression, gnashing their teeth, fully releasing their own ferocious aura.

They firmly believed that under the head of the patriarch and the 200 Suicide Squad, they would be invincible, capable of overcoming any assault.

No matter who came, they couldn't break through their defense line. They would face severe injuries and even lose their lives in front of them.

This was not blind arrogance but the result of decades of battle experience, a deep-rooted confidence built up like the mightiest of mountains, indomitable.

Suddenly, the man approached, throwing something into the air. It seemed like an object soaring into the sky. Then, he leaped high into the air. As everyone looked up, they saw...

A burst of light!

※※※※

Zhou Yi moved swiftly, his figure resembling a cloud, a shower. He had pushed his Cloud and Rain Soaring Technique to its utmost limit in an instant.

Traveling from the county town to Xujiabao was not considered a short distance, but it wasn't too far either. However, when he set off, it was already too late.

Fortunately, as he faintly sensed the imposing black walls of the fortress, the first ray of sunlight had just emerged, casting a faint glow.

Before him appeared a formation of two hundred people. The formation didn't seem particularly thick, but once these two hundred individuals drew their swords, a powerful aura of battle-tested experience and unwavering confidence surged to the sky.

In Zhou Yi's perception, this aura seemed to faintly transform into a towering mountain, an unyielding and colossal mountain that couldn't be destroyed.

His gaze fell upon the advancing bandits in the forefront, nearing the city walls. Yet, there were several collapsed gaps on the walls, as if indicating the extreme brutality and intensity of the fierce battles of the past few days.

Zhou Yi's heart began to beat fiercely, as if an extraordinary force had burst forth from his heart, surging through every cell in his body in an instant.

His eyes widened, and he let out a thunderous shout, once again releasing a brief but earth-shattering roar that shook the soul.

Facing this Suicide Squad that resembled a towering mountain, a peculiar scene suddenly emerged in Zhou Yi's mind. It seemed as though he wasn't on this perilous battlefield but had returned to the peak of the mountain where he had gained enlightenment.

The towering mountain stood majestically, with a continuous drizzle of mountain rain. Although the fine mountain rain didn't possess the force of a raging storm, it seemed gentle and powerless. Even if it fell on a person, it would only leave a slight dampness.

However, beneath the mountain rain, the entire mountain peak was enveloped. Whether it was the towering ancient trees or the newly sprouting tender buds, none were left untouched by the mountain rain.

In that moment, Zhou Yi suddenly felt a certain sensation in his heart. He seemed to have comprehended the essence of mountain rain, which appeared seemingly weak but was pervasive...

His muscles on his back trembled, and the massive Great Guan Dao, weighing 360 catties, was unexpectedly lifted high by the muscles on his back.

Zhou Yi exerted force beneath his feet, suspending himself in mid-air. With a swift motion of his hands, the scabbard was suddenly released, and the three sections of the Great Guan Dao seamlessly assembled in an instant.

Facing the gradually spreading sunlight, a dazzling light gleamed on the immense and ferocious blade.

In a mere moment, just a moment...

That beam of light transformed...

One became two, two became three, and continued endlessly.

Countless beams of light, reflecting like the gentle mountain rain, softly showered down.

The entire Suicide Squad of two hundred people was enveloped in this radiance!

There was no overwhelming aura like a force swallowing mountains and rivers. After Zhou Yi's earth-shattering roar, his aura unexpectedly underwent an instant transformation, from unyielding and mighty to yin and gentle.

"Countless beams of light, like numerous raindrops, permeated every inch of the space below, transforming the official road into a scene resembling the mountain peak of that early morning. drenched under the invasion of mountain rain.

※※※※

Beneath the mountain rain, there was fresh air. But beneath the gleam of blades, there was bloody slaughter.

Suddenly, all the light disappeared.

Zhou Yi's body floated over the official road as if weightless, continuing to dash forward at a rapid speed.

The Suicide Squad of two hundred Lethal Tigers, led personally by Xu Hanbai, couldn't even delay him for a moment. He swept through them with a single slash, instantly breaking through their formation.

The terrain of Xujiabao was not flat. It descended from high to low, with the elevation increasing the closer it was to the castle.

On the city walls and beyond, all eyes turned to that direction. After the light disappeared, the entire battlefield seemed to freeze for an instant.

There, the original two hundred and one members of the Suicide Squad had vanished. They were gone, all gone.

In their place was a mixture of flesh and blood, a gruesome mishmash. All that met the eyes were vivid red blood.

The two hundred and one individuals were no longer recognizable as humans. Including Xu Hanbai, the tenth-level expert in internal energy, everyone had turned into chunks of flesh, mixed together without distinction.

With a single slash, the two hundred and one people had been completely dismembered, transformed into a pool of blood and piles of meat by the countless blade lights unleashed by the Great Guan Dao.

No one knew how many slashes this person had made within that burst of light, but everyone witnessed it clearly.

After that instant, the Lethal Tigers, renowned in Tai'a County, had vanished completely, ceasing to exist.

A cold and chilling sensation filled everyone's bodies.

Not only did all the bandits turn pale and lose their courage in an instant, even the three groups of servants and guests stationed on the city walls felt the same.

The aura of invincibility emanating from that figure dancing in the air instantly swelled in the eyes and hearts of the onlookers. In that moment, he seemed to transform into an otherworldly demon king from the depths of the abyss, eternally engraved in the deepest recesses of everyone's hearts.

A black figure suddenly soared from within the crowd behind him. With a stern face, he swiftly fled towards the side like a sly fox. His speed was unparalleled, as he had already darted more than ten meters away in the blink of an eye.

In the quiet and deathly still battlefield, among the motionless crowd, this person's actions immediately attracted the attention of countless people. In almost a single breath, everyone saw clearly that this person was none other than Zhong Wei, the leader of the Wolf Fang.

Zhong Wei was cautious and cunning. When Hai Huiqiao instructed him to intercept in the second round, he was filled with astonishment and uncertainty. Although he had never encountered a innate expert, he had heard rumors about such powerful individuals. Regardless of whether he believed in them or not, he would never be as arrogant and overconfident as Xu Hanbai.

So, while gathering the bandits, he had been carefully observing the front, wanting to see if the so-called innate expert was truly as exaggerated as the rumors claimed.

However, the subsequent events greatly exceeded his expectations. The overwhelming might of that single slash had completely shattered his courage and made it impossible for any resistance to arise in his heart.

Seeing Zhou Yi soaring through the air along the official road, rushing towards his direction like a flying bird, his heart immediately leapt with fear. At this moment, his only thought was to get as far away from this calamitous star as possible. He was willing to pay any price as long as he could distance himself from Zhou Yi.

Zhong Wei, without hesitation, turned and fled to the side, not daring to hesitate even for a moment. However, Zhou Yi, suspended in mid-air, had long taken in the entire situation on the battlefield. While everyone was frozen, either unable to move or still recovering from the impact of that previous slash, this sudden escapee seemed so conspicuous.

After the rain-like ferocious strike just now, Zhou Yi's momentum had soared to its peak. Even when he had defeated Lv Xinwen before, he had never surged to such heights. With a flick of his wrist, the giant guandao trembled, and the immense innate true energy within his body flowed like a river into the blade, reaching the edge of the weapon.

The tremendous power condensed into a single point, and a fluctuating blue radiance shimmered at the edge of the blade. Unlike the previous time, this blade aura wasn't metallic in color but rather a deep, oceanic blue.

After three consecutive fluctuations, Zhou Yi swung his arm, and the blade's edge was aimed directly at Zhong Wei, who was still fleeing. As if suddenly endowed with wisdom, the blade aura attached to the edge of the weapon flew out abruptly.

In an instant, a streak of azure brilliance tore through the sky. This slash seemed to tear through the void and traverse endless space.

Almost the moment the blade aura left the edge of the blade, it left behind a clearly visible trail of azure light in the air and swiftly reached Zhong Wei's position.

As a peak expert with internal energy at the tenth level of the acquired realm, although far inferior to a innate-level expert, he still had some perception when faced with the threat of death.

Almost instinctively, Zhong Wei's hand swept to his waist, drawing out a rapier. In an instant, his internal energy surged into the weapon, causing the rapier to straighten and emit a hissing sound, reminiscent of a venomous snake.

Without looking back, he thrust the rapier behind him. As a seasoned bandit, Zhong Wei had reached the pinnacle of skill with this rapier. Supported by his formidable internal energy, a dense and impenetrable web of swords formed behind him, impervious to the countless hidden weapons that filled the air. No projectile could break through his sword web.

With one person suspended in mid-air, wielding a blade, and the other on the ground, wielding a sword, it took only half a breath for the clash between the blade aura and the sword web to occur. A loud crack erupted, as if a massive stone had shattered a glass wall. The seemingly dense and intricate sword web instantly shattered into pieces. The blade aura effortlessly sliced through the sturdy barrier, akin to a sharp knife cutting through straightened paper, and continued its trajectory towards Zhong Wei, who was swiftly moving forward.

Unaware of the danger, Zhong Wei continued his sprint. Suddenly, before the eyes of everyone, his upper body tilted backward, and he flew into the air, creating a rain of blood. His lower body, however, continued sprinting forward at lightning speed, his legs propelling him relentlessly.

As he ran, an endless spray of blood filled the air, painting the surroundings in a gruesome scene. Even those watching from the city walls could seemingly smell the scent of the tragic and horrifying bloodshed.

As Zhong Wei's lower half collapsed onto the ground, nearly a hundred meters away from the initial clash, he convulsed, spilling the last of his fresh blood onto the earth. The sight of such a copious amount of blood flowing from a single person's body was unimaginable. Anyone witnessing this scene would feel a bone-chilling terror deep within their hearts.

A piercing scream suddenly erupted from Zhong Wei's severed torso, emitting a sound of unimaginable agony, as if it were the most tragic cry in the world. The pain, akin to weeping blood and shattered organs, unleashed its intensity through this mournful wail.

This agonizing scream acted as a signal, instantly shattering the current stalemate. "Escape!" someone shouted, though it was unclear who exactly. The four thousand bandits immediately turned around, fleeing like dogs with their tails between their legs, scattering to both sides of the road.

They swiftly turned their bodies and sprinted towards the distance, moving several times faster than when they had arrived.

Some high-level experts with internal energy at the eighth or ninth level, finding their path blocked by their own comrades, ruthlessly swung their weapons forward without hesitation. A cacophony of wailing cries echoed, as the four thousand thieves trampled over each other. Although they all possessed some level of cultivation, it was precisely because of their cultivation that their destructive power became even more formidable.

In just a moment, over a hundred people had been killed or injured at the hands of their own allies.

Zhou Yi's landing, his gaze fell upon the chaotic scene before him. He couldn't help but question how the Butcher of Blood, Lv Xinwen, had managed to slaughter every member of a thousand-year-old clan.

Were those people all fools? How could they not know to escape after witnessing the overwhelming power of a innate expert? These thoughts surged in his mind.

In that moment, he heard a thunderous shout, "Yi, Guan Qing and Guo Shaofeng are here. Don't let them escape!"

Turning around, Zhou Yi caught sight of four figures entangled near the city walls. His footsteps halted momentarily before propelling him forward like a shooting star. As his speed reached its peak and his cloud-like footwork was pushed to its limit, he transformed into a wisp of light smoke, arriving outside the city walls within a few breaths.

Guan Qing and Guo Shaofeng had already noticed Zhou Wude and Xu Yinjie, but likewise, the two elders had their attention fixed on them. As the sharp blades glimmered, Zhou Wude and Xu Yinjie recognized the terrifying weapon. Although they didn't understand how Zhou Yi had suddenly become so incredibly powerful, the two elders made the right decision—they tightly engaged Guan Qing and Guo Shaofeng.

If these two scourges were allowed to escape today, Tai Cang County would never know peace.

Zhou Yi's ghostly and elusive footwork reached its extreme speed. He arrived at the city gates in a manner that surpassed everyone's imagination. With the towering Great Blade raised high, he became like a scorching sun, blazing above their heads...

Chapter 139

With a dazzling brilliance akin to the scorching sun, the massive guandao descended in a swift motion. The surging blade light instantly spread out, enveloping the four formidable experts, each with ten layers of internal energy.

In the midst of their entangled battle, a peculiar sensation suddenly arose among the four individuals. The great blade in Zhou Yi's hand, illuminated by the sunlight, emitted a dazzling radiance. However, this intense glow bestowed upon them a sense of serene tranquility, as if a gentle breeze brushed against their faces.

The power and ferocity of this strike seemed far less formidable than anticipated. In their perception, this single strike transformed into an expanse of clouds—a layer upon layer of billowing clouds, interweaving, embracing, and converging into a sea of clouds nestled amidst towering mountains.

Cloud and Rain Soaring Technique, an innate cultivation method developed by Zhou Yi through observing the clouds and mist swirling around mountaintops and drawing inspiration from the enigmatic and elusive movement of clouds exhibited by the Xiao brothers.

Initially, when he first grasped this technique, it merely manifested as a set of light-footwork. However, after this arduous journey, when confronted with the formidable death squad of two hundred unwavering warriors, possessing a mighty and resolute aura, he unexpectedly experienced a sensation reminiscent of standing atop a mountain peak.

In that moment, it was as if he had once again entered a state of enlightenment, rediscovering the omnipresent mountain rain and boundless sea of clouds. It was under these circumstances that he finally succeeded in incorporating this feeling into his own blade technique. The execution of the terrifying guandao resembled clouds, mist, and rain. After sweeping through the formidable combination of the two hundred individuals, it once again surged towards the two pinnacle experts with ten layers of internal energy.

In the initial plan, the two elderly men sought to entangle Guan Qing and Guo Shaofeng. However, with Zhou Yi's appearance, the situation underwent a complete reversal. The two bandits now exerted every ounce of their strength to counter-entangle the two elderly men. Their moves became desperate, disregarding their own safety, as they firmly ensnared the old men within their grasp.

Having witnessed the might of Zhou Yi's blade, they no longer dared to face him directly. Even if it meant staying by the side of their fellow experts, they would not dare to experience the taste of being dismembered or beheaded by a chaotic blade.

However, as Zhou Yi executed that strike, the four individuals engaged in combat suddenly froze simultaneously. They realized that their opponents had disappeared, not only their opponents but even their comrades-in-arms fighting side by side with them were missing.

Around them, there was nothing but patches of clouds and mist, forming a labyrinth that seemed impossible to escape from, completely bewildering them. Zhou Wude and Xu Yinjie suddenly felt a subtle force gently touching their bodies, and they involuntarily took three steps backward. In just those brief three steps, their vision returned to normal.

Flashes of blade light shimmered before their eyes, and the sensation of clouds and mist from before seemed like a fleeting dream, instantly vanishing, leaving behind only a peculiar feeling etched in their memories, seemingly indelible.

All of a sudden, the blade light before them completely disappeared, and Zhou Yi stood with his feet apart, brandishing his blade horizontally. Several steps away from him, Guan Qing and Guo Shaofeng, the two prominent leaders of the Red Scarf bandits who organized the assault on Taicang County, stumbled and swayed, as if intoxicated, before finally collapsing to the ground, unable to hold themselves up any longer.

Their gazes did not harbor deep-seated hatred or resentment, but were filled with confusion and disbelief. It seemed they had never anticipated meeting their end in such a manner.

"Kill...kill them! Go out and kill!" Three thunderous shouts erupted from the mouth of an elderly man on the city wall. Cheng Ningsheng, the old master, no longer displayed his usual calm demeanor. With a crazed expression, he opened his mouth wide, and his ninth-layer internal energy surged to its limit.

Pointing at the bandits fleeing throughout the mountains and valleys, his voice resonated throughout every nook and cranny of the Xu family's stronghold, even reaching the ears of those hiding in caves: "Guan Qing, Guo Shaofeng, Zhong Wei, Xu Hanbai are dead, the bandits are in chaos. Everyone, bravely fight the enemy, behead one person, and receive a reward of thirty taels of silver!"

In an instant, everyone on the city walls turned red-faced, their eyes gleaming. No further mobilization was needed; as long as they could move, they rushed out without hesitation. They vied with each other, afraid of falling behind, as if their comrades would snatch away their chance for great achievements.

Zhou Wude and Xu Yinjie exchanged glances, initially taken aback but soon a glimmer of understanding flashed in their eyes. They couldn't help but be deeply impressed and sigh in their hearts. Indeed, Old Fox Taicang was still Old Fox Taicang. Even in such a situation, he remained so composed, with a mind as cunning and adaptable as ever.

With a shift in their gaze, they turned their attention towards Zhou Yi, who stood there calmly with blades in hand. Under the gradually rising sunlight, this young man exuded a majestic aura, reminiscent of the grandeur of towering mountains and vast rivers.

Recalling the overwhelming power he had displayed just moments ago, a rare sense of awe flickered in the hearts of the two elderly men. They couldn't help but feel a tinge of reverence, witnessing his ability to control life and death with such command.

※※※※

Within the backyard of the Xu family's compound, dozens of people stood before the artificial mountain, their expressions bewildered. Upon hearing the resounding long howl that filled the air, everyone sensed that something unexpected seemed to have occurred outside. However, no matter how they speculated, they could never have imagined that Zhou Yi, the sixth son of the Zhou family, had arrived under the cover of night and instantaneously altered the course of the battle.

Nevertheless, the hearts of these individuals were filled with hope for some miracle. Their actions paused momentarily, and the gaze of every young person focused on those from the second generation of their respective families. Meanwhile, Zhou Quanming, Cheng Jiahui, and Xu Xiangqian hesitated. Although they also anticipated the occurrence of a miracle, they didn't dare to risk the last hope of their respective families' resurgence.

Zhou Quanming stamped his foot abruptly and said, "I'll go and take a look ahead. Jiahui, Xiangqian, please lead them to leave quickly."

"No, I'll go. " Xu Xiangqian decisively replied.

Zhou Quanming furrowed his brows and said, "Xiangqian, our Zhou family still has our eldest brother Quanxin. Even if I'm absent, it won't matter much. But can the Xu family and Cheng family afford to lose both of you?"

Cheng Jiahui and Xu Xiangqian fell silent immediately. They were not fools and naturally understood each other's meaning. Although the three major prestigious families had suffered a loss of credibility, in relative terms, the Zhou family had the smallest estate and wasn't as extensive as the other two families. Thus, their losses were comparatively minimal and hadn't dealt a severe blow. Moreover, Zhou Quanxin, Zhou Yitian, and Zhou Yi had already left beforehand, preserving the hope of the family's revival.

However, the losses suffered by the Xu and Cheng families were incredibly immense. Although these two families had deep foundations and external reinforcements, ensuring their potential resurgence, the absence of Cheng Jiahui and Xu Xiangqian as core figures would undoubtedly introduce countless obstacles on the path to revival in the future.

"Second brother, let me go instead," Zhou Quanyi suddenly chuckled and said, "Have you forgotten what father instructed you? You must ensure the safety of Yi Hai and Yi Xuan. I entrust my younger siblings and two nieces to you in the future."

Before his words could settle, he swiftly darted out like a gust of wind.

Zhou Quanming reached out to grab him but failed to hold on, his expression turning exceedingly grim.

This departure was undoubtedly extremely perilous, and they all knew that if they reached the outside and saw breached city walls with enemy forces pouring in, their only choice would be to fight where they stood or lure the enemy elsewhere. Returning the same way would only lead the enemy back to their location.

Cheng Jiahui let out a sigh and said, "Let's go."

He gave a gentle push to Xu Yucai, one of the most outstanding individuals among the third generation of the Xu family. Xu Yucai's face was equally grim, but he turned around without uttering a word. With a pre-prepared torch in hand, he stepped into the pitch-black cave.

However, just as his first foot touched the staircase, a deafening roar erupted, sounding like the wailing of ghosts and the howling of wolves: "Guan Qing, Guo Shaofeng, Zhong Wei, Xu Hanbai are dead, the bandits are in chaos. Everyone, bravely fight the enemy, behead one person, and receive a reward of thirty taels of silver."

His feet suddenly felt as if they were locked by unbreakable chains, refusing to take another step downward. Simultaneously, he turned around, his gaze filled with boundless hope, looking up at the people above.

Every person's face wore an expression of disbelief, but the one common factor was the undeniable ecstasy etched on each face.

"It's my father's voice, there can be no mistake," Cheng Jiahui said excitedly.

The person in power of the Cheng family at this moment no longer possessed an ounce of composure. His eyes faintly shimmered, resembling the stars in the sky, radiating a bright brilliance.

"How is this possible?" Zhou Quanming murmured.

Xu Xiangqian's body trembled suddenly. Even with his ninth-layer internal energy, he couldn't conceal his excited expression.

"Our ancestor, it must be our ancestor who has come," he said with a trembling voice. The words seemed to drain all his strength, making his body almost collapse.

Both Zhou Quanming and Cheng Jiahui were momentarily startled, then asked in a mix of surprise and joy, "Is it that old man?"

Xu Xiangqian took a deep breath and said, "Besides that old man, who else could emit such a howl? Besides that old man, who else could swiftly behead four major leaders? He must have known about the dire straits faced by our Xu family, which is why he personally rushed here."

Zhou Quanxin and Cheng Jiahui simultaneously recalled the resounding and overwhelmingly powerful long howl. Instantly, they believed it to be true.

Among their three families, only the legendary ancestor of the Xu family could possibly possess such extraordinary power.

Cheng Jiahui's face suddenly changed, and he said, "This is not good." Zhou Quanming and Xu Xiangqian were taken aback by his unexpected reaction. They couldn't understand why he, who usually maintained a composed demeanor, would suddenly say that things were not good.

While Zhou Quanming was still puzzled, Xu Xiangqian's expression darkened involuntarily. He couldn't help but feel resentful in his heart, thinking, "We're at least relatives. Must you wait until Xujiapu is destroyed before you are willing to act?"

However, before this thought fully formed in his mind, Cheng Jiahui turned around and said, "Listen carefully, there is a secret passage in the back mountain of the Xu family. No matter what happens, it must not be leaked out. Tonight, even if you want to escape, you absolutely cannot let the secret be exposed. Now, all of you go out and kill the enemies. Kill as many as you can, but do not tarnish the reputation of the Three Great Families."

The expressions of Zhou Quanming and Xu Xiangqian suddenly changed, and they both realized something at the same time. No wonder Old Master Cheng had shouted without caring about his image. It turned out that he was trying to inform them...

The enemies are dead, and you must not escape. Quickly come out and fight the enemy, ensuring that no one knows of your intention to flee.

As the castle was on the verge of being breached, leaving behind all the servants and guests while the masters escaped wasn't a significant matter. However, if word of it got out, it would have disastrous consequences for the future revival of the three major families.

At the very least, the servants and guests who fought alongside them today would be deeply disappointed by their actions.

That's why, once Cheng Ningsheng realized, he immediately used his voice to convey the message. Cheng Jiahui, being Cheng Ningsheng's son, quickly understood the reasoning behind it and promptly devised a plan to remedy the situation.

The disciples let out a resounding roar before scattering and rushing outside, each eager to be the first. They were in the prime of their youth and would not willingly become deserters. Since they had the opportunity to fight back, they were filled with excitement and competitiveness. At the very least, they didn't want to be seen as cowards in the eyes of their young peers in Taicang County.

Cheng Jiahui clasped his fists towards Xu Xiangqian and Zhou Quanming, saying, "Please seal off the entrance to the secret passage. I'll go ahead." With that, he made his move, unexpectedly surpassing many of the younger generation and charging out of the courtyard.

Xu Xiangqian and Zhou Quanming could only smile wryly and helplessly seal the entrance to the secret passage. They exchanged a glance, silently acknowledging that Cheng Jiahui, this cunning middle-aged fox, truly lived up to his status as the legitimate son of the old fox of Taicang, carrying on the lineage of the fox family.

After they dealt with these matters in a hurry, they hurriedly arrived at the city walls. They had a perfect view of the bandits, but contrary to their expectations, they didn't see any old men with flowing white hair and an immortal aura. Instead, they saw their fathers and Zhou Yi, who had arrived at the Xu family stronghold with his great guan dao.

The two of them looked around for a while but found nothing.

Suddenly, Xu Xiangqian asked, "Why did the bandits flee towards the sides? The main road in the middle was completely empty. Did they all lose their minds?"

Unintentional words, but meaningful to the listeners.

The gazes of the three elderly men simultaneously turned towards the front, where they saw a river of dismembered bodies, a horrifying sight.

They realized that among the thousands of bandits, they had all chosen to flee towards the treacherous mountain paths on the sides. However, not a single person dared to look back and step over the sea of blood, escaping from the path they had taken when they arrived.

The three men exchanged glances once again, and their gaze towards Zhou Yi changed slightly.

※※※※

The bandits scattered in all directions, fleeing in a disorderly manner. Their fighting spirit was completely gone, and no one had the courage to turn back and fight.

Even though the pursuers were not powerful internal energy experts but ordinary servants and guards of the families, who were inferior in internal energy, the bandits dared not entertain any thoughts. They simply wanted to escape.

Escape, escape, escape...

The defeat was like a collapsing mountain. At this moment, even if immortals descended, it would be difficult to reverse the situation and prevent their chaotic retreat.

The treacherous mountain paths on the sides were filled with chaos, with only a narrow trail. The bandits trampled over each other, resulting in countless casualties.

However, at this moment, no one cared about these casualties. Their only thought was to avoid being left behind and let their former companions block the pursuers for them.

This sentiment echoed in the hearts of everyone and was acted upon by almost everyone.

Among the fleeing bandits, there was a group who managed to maintain some semblance of formation. They were perhaps the only group among all the bandits that could maintain a bit of cohesion.

The size of this group was not large, consisting of only about thirty people. Among the four thousand bandits, they were inconspicuous. However, the internal energy cultivation of the thirty-plus individuals was at least at the seventh level, and the two people they protected in the middle were none other than the only remaining couple from the Five Great Ten-Level Internal Energy Experts, Lan Hanyang and his wife.

Initially, their speed wasn't particularly fast, just following the fleeing bandits, going with the flow. However, once they left the most treacherous mountain path and escaped the sight of the city walls, their speed suddenly increased. In an instant, they left all the other bandits far behind, refusing to rest for even a moment, like startled birds, until they had escaped far beyond the boundaries of Taicang County.

"Lady, fortunately, it was your shout that allowed us to escape smoothly. Otherwise, we might not have been able to get away so easily," Lan Hanyang sighed and said with a bitter smile after they reached a safe place.

It turned out that the voice that awakened countless people with the cry of "Run!" came from Hai Huiqiao's mouth. She had intentionally changed her accent at that time, so no one could recognize her voice.

As one of the foremost figures among the bandits, they would have been targeted if it weren't for the sudden chaos. Once that terrifying young man set his sights on them, the chances of escaping unscathed would have been slim.

Looking at the ordinary clothes they were wearing, Lan Hanyang felt grateful. If it weren't for his wife's foresight, they might have truly lost their lives this time.

Thinking about the fate of the other four individuals who were on par with him, a chilling feeling gripped Lan Hanyang's heart, making it difficult to bear.

Hai Huiqiao let out a soft sigh. She glanced back in the direction they had come from and suddenly said, "For us, this may not necessarily be a bad thing."

Lan Hanyang's curiosity was piqued, and he asked, "What do you mean?"

Hai Huiqiao nodded slightly and continued, "The life of a bandit, although filled with thrills and grudges, is not a long-term solution. This major defeat, although unexpected, might also be a great opportunity for us to break free."

Lan Hanyang's lips twitched slightly, seemingly hesitant.

Hai Huiqiao said angrily, "Husband, you've seen the fate of Guan Qing and the others. If this person is not willing to let it go and comes to Tai'a County to find us, then what?"

Lan Hanyang trembled and hurriedly replied, "Alright, let's follow your suggestion, and we won't go back."

Hai Huiqiao then softened her tone and said, "Over the years, we have accumulated enough wealth. Let's leave."

Lan Hanyang nodded slightly, but as he looked back at the path they had taken, a sudden chill surged through him, extinguishing the last flicker of luck in his heart.

Chapter 140

For several days and nights, the pursuit of these bandits continued relentlessly. When Zhou Quanming and the others returned to Zhou Family Manor with the gold, this sensational event that had shaken the entire Taicang County was essentially coming to an end.

Zhou Yitian had repeatedly urged his father to return swiftly to Taicang County and gather information about the situation. However, these suggestions were consistently rejected by the wise and prudent Zhou Quanxin. Though Zhou Quanxin did not typically involve himself in the affairs of the family, at this moment, he displayed unwavering determination.

According to his words, the marauding bandits had besieged Taicang County for several days already, and even if they rushed there at the fastest speed, they would undoubtedly be too late. Moreover, since Zhou Yi had already gone, if they couldn't resolve the matter even with his presence, then their father-son duo would undoubtedly be heading towards certain death.

Rather than taking risks, it was better to proceed with the escort of the gold. Regardless of the circumstances, this batch of gold must not be lost. Even if the Zhou Family had been ravaged by the flames of war, with this gold, they could rebuild the Zhou Family from the ruins.

However, upon their return, they learned of the events that had unfolded, particularly the legends surrounding Zhou Yi. There were at least ten different versions circulating, and even some of the Zhou Family's retainers had varying accounts. Nevertheless, regardless of which version was told, one thing was certain—Zhou Yi, in their descriptions, had transformed into a monstrous being.

※※※※

Amidst a clamor, ten large carriages swiftly entered the Zhou Family's premises. Under Zhou Yihai's arrangements, over a hundred people from the Yuan Family had found a place to stay.

After the battle at Xu Family Fort, Zhou Yihai had also grown significantly. At this moment, he had begun assisting Zhou Quanyi in managing the estate, shouldering more responsibilities.

In fact, the third-generation descendants of the three major clans seemed to have matured overnight after experiencing the bloody battles on the battlefield. They gradually began to engage with the core of their respective families and systematically prepared to inherit the legacies.

Zhou Quanxin, accompanied by his son Zhou Yitian, arrived first at the Zhou Family's main courtyard. Patriarch Zhou had returned from Xu Family Fort and was residing in the ancestral estate once again. The Zhou family members who had sought refuge in the mountains to avoid the turmoil had also returned, reuniting as a joyful and harmonious family.

Beneath the looming threat of the bandits, the patriarchs of the three major clans set aside their personal interests and united against the common enemy. However, once the bandits retreated, their thoughts immediately turned inward. However, it was certain that at this moment, as long as Xu Yinjie and Cheng Ningsheng didn't lose their minds, they would never actively seek conflict with the Zhou Family again.

Upon entering the Zhou Family's main courtyard, Zhou Quanxin and his son immediately laid eyes on Zhou Wude, who was seated in the main hall. Zhou Wude appeared somewhat fatigued, for he was already advanced in age and lacked the vitality of a young man.

"Father, you must have been alarmed by recent events," Zhou Quanxin respectfully approached and bowed.

Zhou Yitian also paid his respects and then stood up, moving directly behind the elderly man and gently massaging his back.

Zhou Wude nodded in satisfaction, pleased with his grandson's attitude and skillful technique.

"Fortunately, we had Yi this time," the patriarch sighed. "If he hadn't returned unexpectedly and single-handedly killed four bandit leaders at the peak of the Internal Energy realm, those fellows might not have dispersed so easily."

Zhou Quanxin's brow slightly furrowed as he spoke, "Father, our visit to the Yuan Family this time was also fortunate because Yi was present. Otherwise, the two of us might not have been able to return smoothly."

Zhou Wude felt a twinge of alarm. Although he could see his son and grandson before him and knew that since they were here, they should be safe, his heart couldn't help but be filled with concern upon hearing those words.

"What happened? Tell me everything in detail."

"Yes."

Without hesitation, Zhou Quanxin recounted everything he had seen and heard, including the mention of Lv Xinwen. Even his own emotions fluctuated slightly as he spoke. Zhou Yi's impact on him at that time had been immense.

Zhou Wude nodded slightly, inwardly relieved. It was a good thing he had allowed Zhou Yi to go along initially; otherwise, this rescue mission would not only have been futile but might have cost him his eldest son and grandson.

However, no one could have imagined that such a small clan like the Fan Family would have connections with a innate expert.

Yet, simultaneously, a peculiar thought crossed their minds. Perhaps no one would have expected that within the Zhou Family of Taicang County, there would suddenly emerge a innate realm expert.

If news of such a formidable expert's existence had truly been known, even the boldest of bandits would think twice before daring to provoke them.

Soon after, when Zhou Quanxin mentioned the gift presented by the Yuan Family, Zhou Wude's brow furrowed involuntarily.

After a brief moment, he said, "Quanxin, you've made a mistake this time. Accepting the fifty thousand taels of gold is one thing, but acquiring a 20% stake in the Yuan Family's business is unacceptable." He spoke with a serious tone, "The Yuan Family resides outside Zhengtong County, where the major clans hold deep roots. They are not comparable to us who engage in minor activities. The Yuan Family's intention in involving you is merely to tie Yi to their own agenda."

Zhou Quanxin forced a bitter smile and said, "Father, I understand that. But since Yi made the decision, I couldn't really refute it."

Zhou Wude snorted lightly and said, "You are Yi's uncle, why couldn't you..."

As he spoke, an image suddenly flashed in his mind—the scene where Zhou Yi soared through the air with a long howl, his imposing presence terrifying four thousand people.

At this moment, he questioned himself deep within. If Zhou Yi were present and had made a decision about something, would he still have the courage to refuse or decline?

With this thought, a bitter smile appeared on his face. The might of a innate expert was beyond words to describe. Although Zhou Yi was his grandson, he could no longer view him with the eyes of an ordinary person.

"Yitian, go find Yi now. After he returned, he went into seclusion again. Sigh... He has already reached the innate realm, yet he still works so diligently."

Zhou Yitian nodded, lowered his hands slightly, and respectfully exited the room.

However, in his heart, he secretly thought that although the patriarch's words seemed like complaints, his expression and attitude showed no hint of blame. The patriarch did indeed hold a different regard for his sixth brother.

Zhou Wude's expression turned grave as he replied, "You mentioned earlier that the Yuan family also bestowed two women upon Yitian and Yi. What is the meaning behind this?"

A wry expression appeared on Zhou Quanxin's face as he replied, "Father, these two women are pure maidens from the Yuan family.

One of them is even the legitimate child of Yuan Chengzhi. That's why I allowed them to accept."Zhou Wude's face hardened, and he snorted lightly.Zhou Quanxin hurriedly continued, "Father, Yi has already reached the innate realm.

Even if he takes multiple concubines, it won't pose any problems. For a innate-level powerhouse, the consumption of female companions is insignificant."Zhou Wude let out a sigh and said, "You understand nothing. I'm not talking about Yi, I'm talking about Yitian. Don't you even care about his future?"

Zhou Quanxin quickly took out a jade bottle from his pocket and said, "Father, take a look at this. With this item, Yitian having one more concubine is not a big deal."

Zhou Wude, half-believing, opened the jade bottle, and immediately a refreshing fragrance filled the air. His face instantly changed, recognizing the contents of the jade bottle. Then, he looked at Zhou Quanxin with an expression of disbelief and suspicion.

"Father, these are Energy-Boosting Golden Pills,all gifted by Yi," Zhou Quanxin hesitated for a moment and continued, "From what I gathered from Yi's words, it seems that he has similar pills on him."

Zhou Wude nodded heavily. Although there were only three pills in the jade bottle, he knew their value well. If used wisely, they could greatly enhance the strength of the family.

"That's right, with these pills, Yitian will be fine. But he got married just last year and now he wants to take concubines. It might not look good in the eyes of the Cheng Family."

Zhou Quanxin spoke confidently, "Father, you can explain the situation to our visit to the Cheng Family and our in-laws. I believe they will understand."

After contemplating for a moment, Zhou Wude finally nodded silently. If the roles were reversed, he would probably make the same choice.

"Quanxin, what about the woman who is with Yi?" Zhou Wude inquired.

"I don't know," Zhou Quanxin sighed. "I only know their background and names, but everything was confirmed by Yi himself."

"Yi again?" Zhou Wude exclaimed in surprise.

"Yes," Zhou Quanxin replied.

Zhou Wude fell into a long silence, finally letting out a deep sigh. "Yi has grown up and has started to assert his own voice."

Zhou Quanxin lowered his head, feeling deeply moved. He never expected that among the third-generation descendants of the Zhou Family, the first one to assert his own voice to the elders was not Zhou Yitian, the eldest grandson, but the youngest, Zhou Yi.

"Wait a moment. Summon Quanming, Quanyi, Yitian, and Yi to come here, along with those two women," Zhou Wude said in a deep voice. "Since Yi has taken that woman, it's only right to grant him some family inheritance as well."

"Brother Six, you're truly amazing," Zhou Er exclaimed with admiration in his face. "You are indeed a innate expert, not like an ordinary person."

Zhou Yi's eyes rolled, unsure whether this statement was praising him or mocking him.

Following closely behind Zhou Yitian was Zhou Er, the youngest of the third generation of the Zhou Family. After Zhou Yi became a innate expert and returned to Zhou Family Village with a strong scent of blood, Zhou Yi immediately used seclusion as an excuse to avoid the peculiar gazes of others.

Zhou Er had repeatedly tried to find his brother to learn about the battles that took place at Xu Family Fort, but under the watchful eyes of Zhou Quanyi, he was never able to fulfill his wish.

This time, when Zhou Yitian returned, Zhou Er seized the opportunity to follow along. Zhou Quanyi could only shake his head and sigh, lamenting that despite his own carefulness and caution throughout his life, his son turned out to be as mischievous as a monkey, difficult to control. It was truly helpless.

"Brother Six, tell me, how did you do it? With one slash, you killed two thousand people, and eighty percent of the four thousand were killed by you. None of them escaped," Zhou Er's eyes sparkled like stars. "Did they just stand there and wait for you to kill them?"

Zhou Yi was taken aback and asked, "Er, what are you talking about? Where did you hear all these nonsensical things?"

Zhou Er innocently said, "Brother Six, these are all things the household servants have been saying. They were the ones who accompanied Grandfather in that battle. They say that you killed two thousand bandits in the rear, then slashed down the remaining half, and the bandits all kneeled down and begged for mercy. They say you showed mercy and spared their lives."

Zhou Yi's mouth hung open. Although he was already a peak innate expert, he couldn't help but feel a tingling sensation on his scalp upon hearing this exaggerated account of his achievements, multiplied tenfold.

His gaze turned towards his eldest brother, Zhou Yitian, who had a curious expression, silently waiting for an explanation.

Letting out a long sigh, Zhou Yi said, "Big brother, Er is still young, and I have nothing to say. But do you believe it?"

Zhou Yitian hesitated for a moment and replied, "If it were rumors about someone else, I might not believe it, but when it comes to you,

I dare not say. I've witnessed too many miracles in you. After countless unexpected events, I've developed a peculiar feeling inside."

Indeed, in Zhou Yi, he had witnessed too many wonders. After countless surprises, he had developed a strange sensation in his heart.

It seemed that anything was possible when it came to Zhou Yi.

Including the feat of slaying two thousand people with a single slash. If it had happened to anyone else, Zhou Yitian would have scoffed at it. But if it was Zhou Yi...

Even though his rationality told him it was impossible, deep down, he was half-believing and half-doubting.

Feeling the two pairs of eyes filled with anticipation, Zhou Yi finally became completely speechless.

He shook his head, suddenly feeling a heavy burden on his shoulders. The people around him believed in him so much, treating him as an invincible deity. While it touched him in his heart, it also made him somewhat uneasy. What if one day he failed to live up to their expectations? How disappointed would they be?

This thought flashed through his mind but was immediately suppressed.

After enduring so many trials, his determination had become as solid as a rock. Momentary confusion was like a wave under the support of a towering pillar, disappearing in an instant and posing no threat to him.

"Big brother, Er, I can honestly tell you that this is just a rumor," Zhou Yi said in a deep voice. "No one can slay two thousand cultivators with a single slash because that is beyond human capability."

As he spoke those words, a question arose in Zhou Yi's mind.

When he unleashed that slash, he had given it his all.

If those two hundred people hadn't formed a neat formation, if they hadn't been densely packed together within a small area, his slash wouldn't have created such an incredible and unbelievable display of power.

Slaying two hundred with a single slash would be impossible in any other situation.

It could be said that the might of that single slash had already become a thing of the past.

However, in his heart, there was a hidden and terrifying thought.

If his movements were just a bit faster, if his true qi was a bit stronger, if his figure truly merged with the pouring rain, would he be able to envelop the entire mountains and fields within a single slash?

If he truly reached such a level, then even if it were twenty thousand people, they wouldn't stand a chance against the unrivaled power of that single slash.

Of course, this thought was too crazy. Even he could only imagine it momentarily.

How could the power of a human truly compare to the vastness of nature? Those who harbored such thoughts were likely nothing more than delusional madmen overestimating their abilities.

Zhou Yitian and Zhou Er exchanged glances, both noticing the sudden confusion in Zhou Yi's eyes. They couldn't help but be greatly surprised.

"Brother Six, what are you thinking about?" Zhou Yitian asked.

Zhou Yi snapped out of his daze and awkwardly smiled. "Oh, it's nothing. I was just pondering a question about a technique and got a bit carried away."

Both Zhou Yitian and Zhou Er couldn't help but marvel. Perhaps it was only with the mindset of prioritizing martial arts at every moment that such incredible individuals could be cultivated.

"Brother Six, so you didn't actually kill two thousand with a single slash," Zhou Er said with disappointment.

Zhou Yi retorted, "Er, be more realistic. Killing two thousand with a single slash? Even if it were wheat, you couldn't harvest two thousand with a single swing of your sickle."

As he spoke, a sudden thought flashed in his mind. He slapped his thigh and exclaimed, "I understand!"

Perplexed, Zhou Er asked, "What do you understand?"

Zhou Yi turned his head and affirmed, "Big brother, do you remember Lv Xinwen?"

"Of course."

"This person was once rumored to have slaughtered an ancient family, earning him the nickname 'Butcher of Blood.' But what kind of slaughter can there be when thousands of people scatter and flee? It's all just misleading words," Zhou Yi said with a bitter smile.

Zhou Yitian exclaimed in surprise, then sighed in relief.

Although it was merely speculative talk, just looking at the treatment Zhou Yi was receiving at the moment, one could deduce it to be quite accurate.

As formidable as a innate powerhouse might be, if people scattered in all directions, they would still only have their two hands and two feet to chase after them. How many people could they truly kill?

Suddenly, a gentle yet powerful voice came from outside the door, "Yi, Yitian, come with me. Your father has something to discuss."

Zhou Yitian and Zhou Yi immediately stood up, while Zhou Er instinctively shrunk his neck and slipped into Zhou Yi's inner chamber, not daring to show his face.

Zhou Yi and Zhou Yitian exchanged a smile. When facing their third uncle, Zhou Er truly feared him like a tiger.

Chapter 141

Within the grand courtyard of the Zhou family, the patriarch Zhou Wude and his three sons, sat silently in their chairs.

As the two brothers, Zhou Yitian and Zhou Yi, entered side by side, their eyes glanced to the side, and in an instant, they caught sight of Yuan Liwen and Yuan Lixun standing in the hall. Yuan Liwen resembled a young bride meeting her in-laws, while Yuan Lixun exuded a similar aura, as if they were both stepping into a new family.

Zhou Yitian's expression slightly changed, but he quickly regained his composure. However, a faint trace of concern lingered in his gaze. He couldn't be sure how his grandfather, Zhou Wude, would treat Yuan Liwen. Meanwhile, Zhou Yi's face turned slightly red. Although he was unquestionably the most skilled martial artist in Zhou Village, he lacked experience in certain matters, which made him feel unusually awkward in this situation.

Zhou Wude nodded slightly towards the two brothers and then spoke, "Yi, please take a seat as well." Zhou Yi was taken aback and glanced at his elder brother, but he did not sense any dissatisfaction from him. With a nod, he sat down on a chair at the back.

As for Zhou Yitian, without needing any instruction, he stood firmly by his father Zhou Quanxin's side.

At this moment, Zhou Yitian no longer harbored even a trace of jealousy when facing Yi. The gap between innate and acquired was not solely manifested in martial prowess; even one's demeanor underwent a profound transformation upon advancing to the innate realm, as if they had been purified. Moreover, having witnessed Zhou Yi's formidable martial prowess within the Yuan family village, it would not be easy for anyone to summon feelings of jealousy, even if they desired to do so.

Yuan Liwen and Yuan Lixun exchanged a quick glance, both deeply moved. In a prestigious family, for the sixth-ranked son to hold a higher position than the eldest grandson was anything but ordinary. Yet, not only had this happened in the Zhou family, but it seemed that everyone accepted it as a matter of course.

Yuan Liwen's eyebrows furrowed slightly, and her heart instantly tensed up as a thought of worry emerged. However, she concealed it well, and due to the downward tilt of her head, no one noticed.

The two women had different thoughts, but they stood side by side, facing the scrutiny of the senior figures. Despite their inner apprehension, they carried themselves with grace and composure, showing no signs of hesitation.

Zhou Wude and the others did not make things difficult for them, only asking a few questions and giving a few instructions.

Subsequently, the patriarch stroked his beard, exuding an aura of authority as he spoke, "You are both daughters of the Yuan family, and it is a compromise for you to enter the doors of our Zhou family as concubines. In fact, it is our Zhou family that should feel indebted to you. Let me make it clear: the Zhou family is not a prestigious clan, and we don't have many strict rules. You can stay here comfortably. In the future, when you are with Yitian and Yi, their daily lives will still rely on your care and attention. You have to take care of everything."

Yuan Liwen and Yuan Lixun both lowered their heads respectfully and said, "This is the duty of a granddaughter-in-law. Please rest assured, Grandfather."

When Zhou Wude expressed acceptance and admitted that the Zhou family didn't have as many rules as they had imagined, a slight sense of relief washed over them. However, they also understood that in order to fully integrate into this large family, they would need to make efforts in the future.

Zhou Wude waved his hand and said, "Yitian, take your wife to meet Yanli."

Zhou Yitian's face blushed slightly as he replied, "Yes, Grandfather." He stepped forward and gave a signal to the somewhat bewildered Yuan Liwen, who nodded slightly and followed him with small, hesitant steps, gracefully retreating from the scene.

After leaving the courtyard, Yuan Liwen suddenly stopped in her tracks. Zhou Yitian turned around and gently took hold of her hand, comforting her in a soft voice, "Liwen, are you worried about Yanli?"

Yuan Liwen hesitated for a moment, feeling the warmth in the palm of her hand, and instantly found a sense of reliance. Perhaps it wasn't love at first sight for her with Zhou Yitian, but she deeply understood that this man would be her support in the latter half of her life.

"Young Master, will Uncle Six inherit the position of the family head in the future?" she asked softly.

Zhou Yitian paused for a moment, then laughed somewhat helplessly. "Impossible."

"Why? Uncle Six is an innate powerhouse."

"It's precisely because he is an innate powerhouse that he cannot inherit the position of the family head," Zhou Yitian's gaze became complex, filled with both gratification and indescribable regret.

Yuan Liwen's beautiful eyebrows seemed to slightly furrow as she asked, "Why is that?"

"It's simple, because Zhou Village can't contain him."

After these words were spoken, not only Zhou Yitian but even Yuan Liwen felt a strange sense of relief.

The two walked in silence, occasionally exchanging glances, slowly developing a sense of unspoken understanding.

Finally, they arrived in front of the courtyard where Zhou Yitian lived alone. In unison, they both stopped in their tracks.

Yuan Liwen looked up and saw the beautiful scenery inside the courtyard, which had not suffered any damage from the recent widespread theft incident that almost affected the entire Taicang County. When she agreed to become a concubine to Zhou Yitian, she knew that this moment would come sooner or later. However, even though she anticipated it, it still pained her heart. But she knew that there was no escaping this fate.

As she listened to the young and melodious voice coming from inside, flashes of her parents, elder brothers, and sisters' eyes with a mix of guilt and relief seemed to pass before her. Her heart ached, but her gaze softened.

She took a step forward and entered the room within the courtyard.

"Younger sister Yuan Liwen, pay respects to Sister..." she said as she bowed down.

※※※※

After watching Yitian and Yuan Liwen leave, Zhou Wude's expression softened, and he said, "Yi."

Zhou Yi quickly bowed slightly in his seat and asked, "What instructions do you have, Grandfather?"

Zhou Wude smiled and said, "Yi, I never expected that you would also grow up and choose a wife for yourself."

Zhou Yi's facial muscles twitched slightly, and he noticed the strange gazes of the four elders, feeling extremely embarrassed. In this moment, facing the elders, he suddenly realized that being an innate powerhouse didn't seem to be of much use.

However, he had not considered that if he were not an innate powerhouse, even if he wanted to accept Yuan Lixun, it was not only Zhou Wude who would strongly oppose it, but even Zhou Quanxin and his brothers would likely not pass this test.

"Grandfather, you jest," Zhou Yi reluctantly said after a moment of silence.

Zhou Wude's heart was filled with great satisfaction as he laughed heartily and said, "Yi, regardless, now that you have a wife, you can no longer reside in your previous place."

Zhou Yi hesitated for a moment before nodding slightly.

Zhou Yitian, like his brothers, used to live in a small courtyard. However, after his marriage, he immediately moved to a separate, larger courtyard. The original small courtyard was preserved and became his dedicated practice room for cultivating martial arts.

It seemed that Zhou Wude had made a decision in advance, and upon seeing Zhou Yi's agreement, he immediately continued, "Quanyi, how is the West Wing room arranged?"

Zhou Quanyi smiled and replied, "Father, rest assured, we tidied it up three days ago. It's all prepared now."

"Good, from now on, the West Wing room will belong to Yi," Zhou Wude then turned and said, "Lixun, in the future, Yi's main focus will still be on cultivating martial arts. As for the chores and miscellaneous tasks in his living quarters, it will be your responsibility. I'll send a few people over, and you can learn more by working with them."

Yuan Lixun blushed on her face. She had also heard the playful remark from the patriarch just now. She quickly whispered, "Yes, Lixun will not disappoint your expectations."

Zhou Yi's gaze shifted and he noticed her blushing and delicate appearance. His heart had an inexplicable reaction, but he quickly suppressed those emotions. To shake his unwavering determination would not be an easy task.

Zhou Wude nodded in satisfaction and said, "Yi, from now on, 20% of the land in the estate will be registered under your name. Also, you can have half of the 50,000 taels of gold from this time. And in the future, you will receive half of the profits from the 20% share of the Jinlin Yuan family."

Zhou Quanxin and his brothers still had smiles on their faces, as if they had known about this plan in advance.

In their hearts, they knew that the tactics used by the patriarch were no different from those used by the Yuan family—they were binding Zhou Yi to their own interests.

Although Zhou Yi was born into the Zhou family and couldn't turn a blind eye to their difficulties, the patriarch delved deeper into his thoughts. He wondered if, when all the elder generation and Yi's brothers of the same generation had passed away, Yi would still selflessly support the Zhou family as he did now.

It was necessary to plan ahead and make preparations for the future, to be proactive rather than reactive.

Zhou Yi was slightly taken aback and said, "Grandfather, are you mistaken? Why would I need so many things?"

Zhou Wude waved his hand and said, "I've already made up my mind. Let it be."

Zhou Yi opened his mouth, blinked twice, and suddenly heard his grandfather speak with such boldness and determination. The words he was about to say were immediately swallowed back.

Zhou Wude smiled satisfactorily and said, "You've been on the road for so long, you must be tired. Yi, you can rest now."

Zhou Yi quickly stood up and, with Yuan Lixun, left under the curious gaze of the elders.

Once they were gone, Zhou Wude chuckled and said, "I thought he had really grown up, but it turns out he's still just a kid."

Zhou Quanxin and his brothers could only chuckle in response. However, Zhou Wude's words were merely a passing remark. No matter who it was, after witnessing Zhou Yi's arrival with a resounding roar on that early morning, it was impossible to associate him with an ordinary kid.

※※※※

The West Wing room was considered one of the best courtyards within the Zhou family. Whether it was the courtyard where Zhou Quanxin and his brothers resided or the one where Zhou Wude himself lived, they were all inferior to the West Wing room.

After deliberate and careful decoration, it appeared even more exquisite and beautiful.

Of course, in the eyes of Zhou Yi and Yuan Lixun, it was just as it was. Their knowledge and experience surpassed what the small Zhou Village, with its decades-old heritage, could compare to.

As they entered the courtyard, over a dozen servants immediately greeted them. These individuals were personally appointed by Zhou Wude, and each one was astute and capable, indicating the elderly patriarch's high regard for them.

Among these servants, the most surprising was the accountant. He managed all of Zhou Yi's assets, and he would only leave the West Wing room once Yuan Lixun became familiar with the procedures.

After meeting them, Zhou Yi waved his hand to dismiss the servants. These people were all long-time residents of the estate and knew it inside out. It was only natural for them to be assigned to this place, given Zhou Yi's current status.

When Yuan Lixun and Zhou Yi were alone in the room, the beautiful young woman became visibly nervous. The blush on her face seemed to deepen.

However, Zhou Yi had not noticed this concern. Instead, he gave detailed instructions, saying, "Lixun, even though Grandfather has given those things to me, I have no use for them. In the next few days, focus on learning bookkeeping and find a way to discreetly send those gold coins to Third Uncle. After all, our estate is newly established, and we have no need for such extravagance. As a martial cultivator, I only require enough silver and wealth to meet my needs. Having tens of thousands of gold coins in my possession may not necessarily be a good thing for me."

After finishing his words, Zhou Yi expected a response but heard nothing. Surprised, he turned around and saw Yuan Lixun staring at him with her beautiful eyes, her face flushed red.

Zhou Yi scratched his head, a gesture he hadn't done in a long time. But for some reason, at that moment, he felt a slight sense of restraint, so he did it again.

Yuan Lixun lowered her head slightly and in a soft, almost whisper-like voice, said, "Yes, Young Master, I will remember your words."

Zhou Yi suddenly felt a chill run down his spine. Although he knew that the customs of the Yuan family were likely much grander than those of the Zhou family, he felt somewhat uncomfortable with such a formal address.

Yuan Lixun shifted her gaze and couldn't help but sigh inwardly. In the Yuan family, a senior maidservant would have already offered fragrant tea and a warm towel to clean their hands. But in the Zhou family, no one seemed to know about such customs.

She went to the kitchen, fetched hot water, prepared the tea, and took a clean towel, readying warm water to personally serve Zhou Yi. She methodically directed everything, especially when she handed him the warm towel, her eyes sparkling with a charm that once again stirred his heart.

※※※※

Everything had returned to normal in Zhou Village. Except for Zhou Yi moving out of his small courtyard and into the West Wing room, becoming the only member of the third generation of the Zhou family, aside from Zhou Yitian, to have an independent living space, there were no other changes.

As night fell, Zhou Village grew quiet, and most people drifted into their dreams.

In a side room of the Scripture Repository, Zhou Laibao suddenly stood up. His slightly hunched figure straightened with the strength of a powerful aura emanating from him. His eyes opened slightly, and a sharp gleam flashed within them as he fixed his gaze on the tightly closed window.

Outside, a shadow had appeared without warning.

"Who...?" he shouted in a stern voice.

Since Zhou Quanxin had just returned from the Yuan family in Jinlin, he was not residing in this room but had gone back to his own quarters to rest for a few days. Thus, Zhou Laibao was the only person stationed in the Scripture Repository courtyard.

The shock in his heart could be imagined when he suddenly realized that there was an extra person outside the door, silent and unannounced. It took quite a bit of courage to enter the estate of a Innate Realm expert.

A familiar, light cough sounded from outside the door, and Zhou Laibao immediately relaxed.

His once straightened back, like a spear, suddenly hunched again. He opened the door and grumbled, "Old Master, why are you also following Yi's example and being so silent?"

Since Zhou Yi had reached the Innate Realm and entered the Scripture Repository, Zhou Laibao had never been able to detect his presence.

With a hearty laugh, Zhou Wude strode into the room, exuding an air of confidence. Taking his seat at the table, he casually flicked his wrist and placed a jade bottle upon the surface.

"Laibao, I have come this time to deliver the pill of Gold to you," Zhou Wude proclaimed, waving his hand without a hint of negotiation. "Refusal is not an option."

Zhou Laibao was taken aback, for it seemed ages since the old master had spoken to him in such a commanding tone.

He forced a bitter smile and confessed, "Lord, to be honest, it is not that I do not wish to partake in the pill of Gold, but rather, I fear."

"What do you fear?" Zhou Wude asked, genuinely surprised.

Zhou Laibao composed himself and replied, "Lord, if you possessed the innate Golden Pill, would you choose to consume it?"

Zhou Wude paused, uncertain. After a moment of contemplation, he responded, "I do not know."

Zhou Laibao sighed softly, "Lord, our years have grown extensive, and the vitality within our bodies gradually wanes. Should we consume the pill, it may not bring about a breakthrough, but rather pose a threat to our very lives."

A wry smile crept upon Zhou Wude's face as he said, "Laibao, prior to today, I had no words to convince you if you were unwilling to consume it. For I, too, cannot be certain if your body can withstand the potency of the pill. However, there is now a solution to this dilemma."

With a flick of his wrist, he performed another magical gesture and produced another jade bottle, placing it calmly on the table. He said, "This is the Energy-Boosting Golden Pill that Yi brought back from his recent journey. Take one pill first, nurture your vitality for one or two months, and you will undoubtedly experience boundless energy. At that time, you can then take the Limit-Breaking Golden Pill to break through the ninth level limit, greatly increasing the possibility of reaching the pinnacle of the tenth level."

Zhou Laibao's eyes shimmered with astonishment. "The Energy-Boosting Golden Pill? Can Sixth Young Master really obtain such a treasure?"

Zhou Wude chuckled wryly and replied, "When it comes to Yi, one cannot judge by conventional standards."

Zhou Laibao hesitated for a moment, then nodded slowly, acknowledging Zhou Wude's evaluation of Yi.

Zhou Wude spoke slowly, "Laibao, once you have taken the pill and advanced to the tenth level, we will bring Yi back to the mountains. I want them to see that even if we depart from Hengshan, we can still stand equal to anyone. Let them witness that our strength and abilities are not inferior, regardless of where we are."

Zhou Laibao responded firmly, his eyes shining with a radiance that did not belong to an elderly person.

Outside the Scripture Repository, a shadow rustled, but it vanished in an instant without either of them noticing the slightest disturbance.

A question lingered in Zhou Yi's mind— Hengshan? Does such a mountain truly exist...

Chapter 142

After a month, tranquility finally settled upon the entire Taicang County, and the statistics of the various losses shocked everyone.

This time, the bandits targeted the three major influential families in Taicang, with the Cheng family suffering the most devastating blow. Especially within the county, it was almost entirely the foundation of the Cheng family. Thirty percent of the businesses belonged to the Cheng family, indicating the immense scale of their assets.

With the marauders breaching the city, all the businesses fell victim to looting. Even those not plundered by the bandits were pillaged by the lawless commoners within the city.

Fortunately, the Cheng family possessed great power and resources, having accumulated wealth over the years. Furthermore, they had the support of the daughter from the Linlang County, and the day of rebuilding their empire was imminent.

As for the Xu family, although their situation wasn't as dire, half of their city wall was destroyed, and they suffered hundreds of casualties among their guards and retainers. They too were not faring well.

In comparison, the losses suffered by the Zhou family were minimal, almost negligible. This was the advantage of being a small family that had not yet branched out. When faced with the danger of a collapsing nest, self-preservation was much simpler and easier than for those large families.

Moreover, they received support of tens of thousands of gold, propelling the Zhou family onto a path of rapid development.

Simultaneously, news of a congenital expert appearing in the Zhou family had spread throughout Taicang County at an astonishing speed, swiftly reaching the entire Linlang County.

If Zhou Yi were merely an expert at the acquired level, or if he hadn't displayed such astonishing power when facing numerous bandits, his fame wouldn't have spread so rapidly. However, when these two factors combined, no one could contain the rumors anymore.

On this day, dozens of fast horses arrived in front of the Zhou family's village.

After a moment, Zhou Quanyi himself came out to greet them.

Among these knights, the leader was surprisingly Lin Tao Li, a member of the Linlang Lin family.

This young prodigy of the Lin family possessed an awe-inspiring presence that was difficult for ordinary people to imagine. He was also a postnatal expert at the ninth level of internal energy. Anyone standing beside him would subconsciously feel a heavy pressure.

However, this time, Zhou Quanyi did not sense any pressure from him. Instead, Lin Tao Li became courteous and addressed him as "Uncle ," constantly positioning himself as a junior. This was treatment that Zhou Quanyi could never have expected during their previous meeting.

As Zhou Quanyi led him into the inner hall, he couldn't help but feel moved. He knew that this change was entirely due to Yi's influence. It seemed that Yi's display of power that day had spread to Linlang

County. Otherwise, it would be impossible for this young man to arrive here in such a short time.

After they were seated, Zhou Quanyi smiled and asked, " Lin, may I inquire about the purpose of your visit from afar?"

Lin Tao Li smiled faintly and glanced around the hall before saying, "Uncle , I have come this time specifically to pay my respects to Master （Shi Fu） Zhou."

To be addressed as "Master （Shi Fu） " indicated that the person was an expert at the Innate Realm. Although Zhou Yi was more than ten years younger than Lin Tao Li, compared to his martial achievements, Lin Tao Li willingly called him "Master."

Zhou Quanyi hesitated for a moment and said, "Lin, I can inform Yi, but whether he wishes to meet or not is beyond my control."

Lin Tao Li nodded slightly. If anyone else were to speak those words, it might be seen as arrogance. But when facing a meeting with an expert at the Innate Realm, no one would have such a feeling.

"Everything is up to Uncle ," Lin Tao Li said respectfully.

In his heart, he also felt a mix of emotions. Just a little over a year ago, Zhou Yi, like him, was also a postnatal expert at the ninth level of internal energy. Although Zhou Yi had already displayed incredible talent at that time, even he had been tempted and wanted to recruit Zhou Yi into the Lin family.

But never did he expect that in just a little over a year, within a miraculous timeframe, Zhou Yi had advanced from a ninth level internal energy expert to an Innate Realm expert.

When he first heard the news, his initial thought was disbelief, followed by shock. It was only after the rumors of the battle that day were accurately conveyed by the servants and retainers from Taicang County that the elders in the family confirmed it.

Although rumors may not always be entirely reliable, Zhou Yi's promotion to the Innate Realm was all but certain.

Because of this understanding, Lin Tao Li's proactive decision to go to Taicang County was highly supported by the elders of the Lin family. They saw the opportunity of establishing a close relationship with Zhou Yi, a powerful innate expert, as beneficial for the future development of their family.

※※※※

Zhou Yi wasn't practicing alone in a secret room but rather cultivating in his own courtyard.

In truth, at his level of martial cultivation, daily practice was no longer as essential as it was for postnatal cultivators.

Innate Realm experts pursue a moment of enlightenment. If there is another moment of enlightenment, similar to the one on the mountaintop, the benefits for Zhou Yi would far exceed the gradual cultivation accumulated over time.

If not for that, a few months ago, he would not have been able to defeat Lv Xinwen, who had been at the Innate Realm for over twenty years.

Of course, the state of enlightenment is elusive and unpredictable. Even Zhou Yi himself cannot guarantee when or if he will encounter it again. Therefore, he continues with his daily practice, never slacking off.

He took a long breath, exhaling for a seemingly endless two minutes, causing even his stomach to visibly flatten.

Holding one's breath for two minutes may not be a big issue for most people, but exhaling steadily for two minutes without interruption is an extremely challenging task.

Slowly standing up, Zhou Yi felt neither joy nor sorrow; he was in a peculiar state.

After each cultivation session, he would feel as though he had touched a certain power between heaven and earth. But this feeling was always elusive, leaving him uncertain. He didn't know if other Innate Realm experts also faced similar difficulties, but he felt quite frustrated.

At this point, he finally began to understand why the records he had seen before, similar to travel logs, constantly emphasized the importance of traveling far and wide to encounter experts.

Breaking through in martial arts was not an easy task. The efficiency of secluded cultivation was far inferior to learning from the best.

Without his experience in the Fire Crow Kingdom and the reminder from Xie Zhi'en, he would probably still be searching the dense forest for mythical beasts over five hundred years old, unsure if they even existed, unable to advance to the Innate Realm.

If Zhou Yi had not discovered his grandfather's secret collection and learned that using the Innate Golden Pill could help practitioners break through their final limits, he would likely have stayed in Zhou Family Village, pondering his situation and missing out on subsequent encounters.

His heart stirred, could this mean that he should venture out on a journey?

Suddenly, the door was gently pushed open, and Yuan Lixun softly said, "Young Master, would you like to take a rest?"

At this time every day, it was Zhou Yi's time to finish his practice. After spending several days together, Yuan Lixun had already figured out his routine.

Zhou Yi nodded slightly, and Yuan Lixun immediately brought out the prepared tea and delicacies, placing them on the table without making a sound.

Sitting quietly in the chair, watching Yuan Lixun's movements, Zhou Yi seemed to feel that a life with someone taking care of him wasn't so bad. He also realized that he didn't resist this feeling.

"Lixun, your internal energy is quite good. You've already reached the fifth level of cultivation," Zhou Yi suddenly spoke.

Yuan Lixun's movements slightly stiffened, but she quickly returned to normal. She raised her head, smiling sweetly, and said, "Young Master, would you really pay attention to my modest level of internal energy?"

A smile crept onto Zhou Yi's lips. The fifth level of internal energy was a memory he could never forget.

Although he wasn't hungry, he still picked up a piece of layered cake and slowly savored it in his mouth.

Yuan Lixun hesitated for a moment and said, "Young Master, just now, Third Uncle sent a message that Lin Tao Li, the young master of the Linlang Lin family, has come to the residence and wishes to meet with you. Would you be willing to see him?"

Zhou Yi's eyes widened, immediately lighting up. He asked, "How long has he been here?"

"About half an hour," Yuan Lixun replied, feeling a sense of surprise. Could this person be his friend, and was Zhou Yi annoyed that she hadn't notified him earlier?

Zhou Yi chuckled and stood up, saying, "Lixun, I'll go meet him now. Hopefully, he hasn't left yet."

Yuan Lixun breathed a sigh of relief when she saw that Zhou Yi didn't show any signs of blame. After seeing him off, she tidied up the room herself. Although the maids could have taken care of everything, Yuan Lixun was extremely careful when it came to Zhou Yi's matters. She preferred to handle things personally rather than delegate them to others.

Zhou Yi strode purposefully toward the main hall, with one thought dominating his mind: how to obtain the Lin family's Innate Hand Imprint techniques. If he could get a glimpse of those secret manuals, he was confident that he could significantly improve his own strength.

His steps were swift, and in a few flashes, he had already arrived in the hall.

It had been half an hour since Zhou Quanxin's letter arrived, and Zhou Yi was already doubting whether Lin Tao Li had already left. But before he even reached the hall, he heard a familiar laughter.

At the sound of that laughter, Zhou Yi couldn't help but smile.

"Brother Lin, you have come from afar, and I apologize for not welcoming you earlier," Zhou Yi walked in with a big smile, imitating his father's past demeanor and offering a courteous gesture.

The voices in the hall immediately quieted down. Lin Tao Li's eyes brightened, and he quickly stood up, saying, "Master Zhou, it's been a year, and you have successfully advanced to the Innate Realm. Congratulations, truly remarkable."

"Brother Lin, I was cultivating just now and couldn't come out to greet you. Please forgive me."

"Master Zhou, you're too modest," Lin Tao Li sighed with emotion. "With your achievements today, you still diligently practice every day. It truly puts us to shame."

He couldn't help but feel a hint of admiration. Behind every successful person, there is unwavering effort. Even though Zhou Yi had extraordinary talent, without such arduous cultivation, he would not have achieved what he had today.

Both of them sat down again, and Lin Tao Li took out a red gift list from his sleeve, saying, "My father heard about the severe losses Taicang County suffered from the bandit attack. Those bandits were originally wandering thieves from Tai'a County in the prefecture, and we have been unsuccessful in suppressing them. However, in Taicang County, those bandits encountered a tough opponent. Several of their leaders have died or gone missing, and now Tai'a County is much more peaceful. So my father sent me with a gift as a token of gratitude. Please accept it, Master Zhou."

Zhou Yi didn't take the gift list but asked with interest, "Did those bandit leaders not return to Tai'a County?"

"No, the five bandit leaders at the tenth level of internal energy, along with Hai Huiqiao, who was on par with them, did not return," Lin Tao Li confirmed.

Zhou Yi felt skeptical. He did kill four of them, but Mr. and Mrs. Lan Han Yang never saw them. Could it be that they were ambushed and killed on their way back? Otherwise, they would have returned to Tai'a County long ago, given their strength.

However, he didn't doubt Lin Tao Li's words because it was impossible for him to deceive Zhou Yi about this matter.

Casually picking up the gift list, Zhou Yi glanced at it, and his expression subtly changed.

This gift list was truly extravagant.

Twenty thousand taels of gold, five hundred Tianluo Swift Horses, fifty rolls of Dashing Silk...

These were just the main items, and there were numerous other miscellaneous goods, totaling more than a hundred items.

Even Zhou Yi was slightly shocked after seeing this generous gift.

Closing the gift list, he said, "Brother Lin, as the saying goes, one should not receive rewards without meritorious deeds. I'm afraid I can't accept this gift."

Lin Tao Li smiled wryly and took out another thick book-like object, handing it over. He said, "I knew Master Zhou wouldn't accept it, so I prepared this. If you still refuse after seeing this, then I have nothing more to say."

Zhou Yi was slightly taken aback as he opened the object, revealing a series of data listed inside.

Twenty horses, fifty taels of gold, several weapons, and so on...

Although the records were somewhat scattered, when added together, it would undoubtedly be a staggering amount.

Lin Tao Li explained, "After we received the news of the bandits' defeat, we immediately dispatched troops to Tai'a County and completely eradicated the hideouts of these four bandits. The items listed here are the spoils of our victory." He paused for a moment and smiled, saying, "Master Zhou, you can be considered the one who contributed the most to this success. We have allocated twenty percent of all the spoils to you. I hope you find it satisfactory."

Zhou Yi and the others finally understood. No wonder the Lin family suddenly sent these things. They were all obtained from the bandits' lairs.

Zhou Quanxin suddenly spoke, "Brother Lin, from what I know, those bandits are unpredictable. Do they have fixed lairs?"

"Linglang County is the foundation of our Lin family. Although we were helpless against the bandit groups in Tai'a County for decades, it doesn't mean we turned a blind eye. We managed to infiltrate a few of our clan members into their ranks and gather some information. It's not surprising," Lin Tao Li smiled faintly. "Although the bandits come and go like the wind, they do have a few fixed lairs. Unfortunately, we only found the hidden gold caches of the Red Scarf Bandit and the Fierce Tiger Bandit. As for the Wolf Fang Bandit and Blue Sea Bandit, we couldn't find any clues to their hidden treasures."

Zhou Quanxin and Zhou Yi exchanged a glance, both feeling astonished. The depth of the Lin family's scheming far exceeded their imagination.

Zhou Yi returned the account book and said, "Very well, since Brother Lin is so generous, I would be disrespectful to refuse."

A hint of joy appeared on Lin Tao Li's face as he replied, "It is my honor that Master Zhou accepts it."

The two smiled at each other, and after a moment, Lin Tao Li tentatively asked, "Master Zhou, have you heard of the name Master Shui Xuan Jin Shui?"

Zhou Yi shook his head in confusion, while Zhou Quanxin took a deep breath and said, "Master Shui Xuan Jin? The Guardian Grandmaster of our Tianluo Kingdom?"

"Yes, exactly, the Guardian Grandmaster," Lin Tao Li chuckled bitterly. "Your remarkable feat of single-handedly killing two hundred bandits with a single strike has spread to the city of Tianluo. Even Master Shui Xuan Jin was moved by it. The Tianluo royal family wants our Lin family to inquire if you would be willing to visit the capital of Tianluo and meet with Master Shui. If you are not interested, they will not disturb you. However, if you have such a desire, the royal family will personally send an invitation and escort you to the capital."

He spoke cautiously, attentively observing Zhou Yi's expression. To his relief, Zhou Yi's eyes had already shown unmistakable excitement, indicating his eagerness for this proposal.

"Brother Lin, since it is the Guardian Grandmaster summoning me, I dare not decline," Zhou Yi added casually. "When do you plan to go to the capital?"

Lin Tao Li was overjoyed. He hadn't expected Zhou Yi to be so easy to persuade. "Master Zhou, within half a month, the royal emissaries will arrive."

"Very well, then half a month later it is," Zhou Yi stood up and said, "I haven't finished my training for today. Excuse me, Lin ."

After leaving the hall, Zhou Yi's eyes sparkled with excitement. The prospect of meeting a Innate master in the capital of Tianluo Kingdom was truly exhilarating.

Chapter 143

His hands raised, and strands of innate true qi formed a subtle, almost imperceptible vortex around his body. With a slight exertion of his toes, his body seemed weightless as it bounced up, suspended momentarily in mid-air before bursting into action.

His figure transformed into numerous phantoms, creating dozens of afterimages within the confined space of the room. His feet seemed to touch the ground simultaneously, as if the boundless rain of mountains had descended upon every corner of the room.

However, as a faint sound of wood cracking emerged, all of Zhou Yi's afterimages vanished without a trace. He gazed at the tiny fragment of crushed wood beneath his feet and let out a sigh filled with melancholy.

After a moment, the door was gently pushed open, and Yuan Lixun entered, as silent as a cat. Her gaze swept across the room, and she immediately fetched a broom to clean up the wood debris on the floor.

Noticing the furrowed brow of Zhou Yi, she hesitated for a moment before summoning the courage to ask, "Young master, is something troubling you?"

Zhou Yi glanced at her in surprise. Ever since he incorporated the insights of clouds and rain into his swordsmanship, his martial skills had undeniably reached a new level. However, when he attempted to integrate these insights into his fist techniques, there was always a subtle sense of disharmony.

He had prepared over a hundred small wooden blocks, scattered throughout this relatively small room, and practiced his martial skills using the Cloud Rain Soaring Technique and Hand Seal Method. Yet, he quickly discovered that if he trained as he had before, there would be no issues. But if he attempted to incorporate his comprehension of clouds and rain into his fist techniques, it became an incredibly difficult and seemingly impossible task.

While swordsmanship and fist techniques shared the same lineage, they were inherently distinct. With each practice session, several small wooden blocks under his feet would shatter, indicating a flaw in his control of true qi. Such a technique, no matter how powerful, could not be employed in actual combat.

In these past few days, he had set aside Lin Tao li, immersing himself wholeheartedly in the practice of martial arts. Yet, he had made no progress, and a sense of frustration began to creep in.

However, unbeknownst to him, Yuan Lixun had been silently guarding him from outside the room, although she couldn't grasp the purpose of his actions. She made sure hundreds of identical wooden blocks were prepared by the servants.

Once the sound of his fist techniques ceased, she would personally enter, clearing away the broken wood chips and replacing them with fresh blocks, sparing Zhou Yi any concerns. Though these were mere trivial tasks, they bestowed upon Zhou Yi's heart an indescribable warmth.

As she caught sight of his relaxed expression upon seeing her figure and hearing her concerned inquiry, his previously furrowed brow gradually smoothed out.

"It's nothing major. I've just been pondering a new technique, but unfortunately, I haven't made the slightest headway so far."

Yuan Lixun was taken aback, her gaze towards Zhou Yi now tinged with both gratitude and moved sentiment. Although she had mustered the courage to inquire, deep down, she had never expected to receive an answer.

She was acutely aware of her place and the vast gap between them, never daring to expect true equality in his presence. However, Zhou Yi's attitude caused her heart to pound intensely for a moment.

Yuan Lixun quickly lowered her head and softly said, "Young master, please don't be impatient. My mother used to say that with deep cultivation, even an iron rod can be ground into a needle. This time may not be successful, but there will come a day when it will be."

Zhou Yi's gaze suddenly focused, fully understanding the wisdom in her words. However, since his encounter at the bottom of the lake, his journey had been smooth sailing. Even when he broke through to the Innate Realm, it hadn't required much effort. As a result, his mindset became his weakest link.

Upon hearing Yuan Lixun's words, a thought surged in his mind. Creating an Innate technique was no easy task. He had only been exploring for a few days, and it would be ridiculous if he could easily integrate the newly gained insights of clouds and rain into his martial arts.

He gazed at Yuan Lixun with a myriad of emotions, a sense of gratitude seeming to melt into tenderness.

The two stood silently, but after a while, they both felt a shift in the atmosphere. A faint blush appeared on Yuan Lixun's face. Though she may not have been a beauty, in that moment, her radiant blush seemed to outshine everything, like a blooming flower in his heart, etched in his memory.

Suddenly, a loud meow came from outside the window, startling Yuan Lixun, who jumped up like a cat. Her face flushed, she said, "Young master, I'll leave first."

Zhou Yi instinctively responded and watched as she hurriedly left. A tinge of regret welled up within him. He turned to look out the window and grumbled, "Where did that old cat come from, making such a noise..."

Outside the door, Yuan Lixun's face gradually regained its composure, but her heart remained anything but calm. Two distinct faces appeared in her mind, both of whom were her closest family, but the feelings they evoked were entirely different.

"Lixun, your luck has finally turned. If you can win the favor of Master Zhou, you can have whatever you desire. Sigh... Father really neglected you and your sisters before. It was my fault. But rest assured, from now on, Lixiang will be by my side, and I will personally take care of him. I promise to treat him as the heir to the family, never showing him the slightest bit of unfairness."

"Sister, Father said you were going on a distant journey. When will you come back to see me?"

"Little brother, when your internal energy reaches the sixth level and you become one of the core members of the family, I will definitely come back to see you."

Her heart ached faintly. Father, it's not just us siblings you've let down. Before Mother passed away, she always said that with deep cultivation, even an iron rod can be ground into a needle. But despite a lifetime of effort, she couldn't earn his affection.

Mother, I just don't know how your daughter will fare...

Turning around to look at the door behind her, that thin wooden panel seemed to separate the room from the outside world, creating two distinct realms.

Suddenly, she felt a tinge of regret. If everything had already been decided, why did she try to escape just now?

If he doesn't win his favor, would Father still consider his younger brother as the heir to the family?

She stood silently, her eyes gradually growing vacant, lost in thought...

※※※※

Inside the room, Zhou Yi swiftly took out three sections of the Great Guan Dao. With a flick of his wrist, he assembled the weapon in an instant.

Although he had possessed the Great Guan Dao for just over a year, it felt as if he had been bonded to the weapon for a lifetime. He knew every inch of it as if it were an extension of his own body. It seemed that his life and heartbeat were intimately connected to this formidable blade.

This sensation had grown particularly intense since he advanced to the Innate Realm.

If Zhou Wude, were to learn of this, he would surely be consumed with jealousy. Despite their decades-long relationship, Zhou Wude's bond with the Great Guan Dao paled in comparison to Zhou Yi's accumulated connection in just a little over a year.

Wielding the Great Guan Dao casually, the entire room seemed to be enveloped in a cloud. The clouds shifted and transformed, morphing into a dense mist. Within the layers of mist, the sound of rushing water emerged—a representation of rain. Under the mesmerizing display of the Great Guan Dao, the two common meteorological phenomena, clouds and rain, came to life.

After a moment, Zhou Yi sheathed the massive blade, and calm returned to the room. The nearly four-meter-long Great Guan Dao appeared enormous within the space, too tall to be held upright. However, under Zhou Yi's terrifying level of control, the weapon effortlessly brought forth the spectacle of clouds and rain in the room.

The difficulty of incorporating clouds and rain into Swordsmanship techniques was many times greater than using bare hands.

However, Zhou Yi simply couldn't achieve it—integrating clouds and rain into his fist arts. He sighed softly, well aware that the successful integration of clouds and rain into the Great Guan Dao had been a result of the intense spirit he experienced when facing the 200-strong Tiger-Killing Squad. It was that intense moment, stirred by the fearless bandits' aura, that had ignited a sudden burst of energy within him, granting him a sense of enlightenment. It allowed him to successfully infuse clouds and rain into his swordsmanship.

Yet, that kind of feeling, that enlightenment, was something that appeared unconsciously. It couldn't be controlled by mere will.

He let out a gentle sigh as he sheathed the Great Guan Dao. Since he couldn't achieve enlightenment, he would explore and study diligently. Yuan Lixun's mother had once said that with deep cultivation, even an iron rod can be ground into a needle. That saying still held true.

Suddenly, he turned his head and smiled. "Grandfather, please come in."

※※※※

Yuan Lixun was standing outside the door when she suddenly heard sounds coming from the room, jolting her awake. She turned around, scanning her surroundings in a panic. Not only did she not see Zhou Wude's figure, but she also had no idea where the cat that had been meowing earlier had disappeared to.

Suddenly, her eyes brightened. An elderly man walked in from the main gate, and it was none other than Zhou Wude, the patriarch of the Zhou family.

It turned out that the distance between them wasn't as great as she had thought. Zhou Yi had already heard the old man's voice. However, it seemed that the old man knew Zhou Yi was practicing, so he merely lingered outside the courtyard and didn't enter.

She greeted him respectfully, bowing deeply. "Grandfather."

Zhou Wude gave a low grunt and said, "I have something to discuss with Yi. You may leave."

Yuan Lixun dared not defy his command and softly replied before turning away and leaving.

As the door opened, Zhou Yi welcomed his grandfather inside. Seeing the stern expression on the old man's face, he couldn't help but ask with suspicion, "Grandfather, who has angered you?"

Zhou Wude shook his head slightly and said, "Yi, I've observed that although Lixun may not possess the beauty of Liwen, she is quite sincere. Moreover she is still Zeyu's granddaughter. If you don't like her, why not let me take her as my granddaughter? I can find a good family for her in the future."

Zhou Yi was stunned for a moment, unsure of his own feelings. However, the only thing he was certain of was that this feeling was far from happiness.

"Grandfather, who spread rumors in front of you? When did I ever say that I don't like her?" Zhou Yi asked.

Zhou Wude was surprised. "Since you like her, why is she still a virgin?"

Zhou Yi's face turned red in an instant. In such a situation, it seemed that his innate true qi was of no use. "Grandfather, how did you know? Who told you?"

"Do I need someone to tell me? I may be old, but I'm not blind to such things," Zhou Wude replied impatiently.

Zhou Yi hurriedly cleared his throat. "Grandfather, I don't want to discuss this matter now. However, I don't want her to leave my side."

As Zhou Yi spoke the second sentence, his tone was unusually firm. Zhou Wude nodded slightly and said, "Since you like her, that's good. If it were otherwise and you wasted the girl's youth, I wouldn't be able to face your grandfather, Zeyu."

Zhou Yi nodded obediently, but only he knew what he truly thought.

After a moment of contemplation, Zhou Wude said, "Yi, now that you've advanced to the Innate Realm, there are some things I want to tell you."

Upon hearing the seriousness in the old man's voice, Zhou Yi immediately became attentive. "Grandfather, please go ahead."

"Forty years ago, I came to Taicang County. With the help of the Great Guan Dao in my hands and the assistance of your esteemed grandfather Laibao, I carved out a domain for myself in Taicang County," Zhou Wude said with excitement. "Those were unforgettable years, and who knows how many storms we weathered."

Zhou Yi nodded repeatedly, expressing his admiration through his eyes.

Zhou Wude glanced at him, feeling both amused and helpless. "Well, since you already know all of this, I won't say anymore." He stroked his beard and seemed lost in thought. After a while, his expression darkened, as if he remembered something that troubled him. "Over forty years ago, I was a disciple of the Hengshan Sect, and one of the three elders, the Medicine Dao's Alchemy Disciple."

Zhou Yi widened his eyes and said, "Grandfather, forty years ago, you must have been in your forties."

"Of course."

"At over forty years old, you're still a disciple?" Zhou Yi asked incredulously.

Zhou Wude glared at him, almost slapping him across the face. Fortunately, he remembered that this grandson was an Innate expert, so he refrained from doing so. However, when he saw the smile in Zhou Yi's eyes, he suddenly realized that the feeling of suffocation and urgency that came to him when he recalled the past seemed to have inexplicably dissipated.

He wordlessly tapped Zhou Yi on the head, feeling a sense of pride and satisfaction. This little brat had finally grown up.

"Listen to me, your ancestor, the Medicine Dao's Grandmaster, was already over a hundred years old. In front of him, I was indeed a disciple," Zhou Wude explained.

Zhou Yi's eyes widened in genuine surprise. "The Medicine Dao's Grandmaster was an Innate expert?"

"Yes," Zhou Wude nodded solemnly.

Zhou Yi finally understood. His grandfather had mentioned that he was a registered disciple of the Hengshan Sect. At that time, Lin

Taoli had shown a look of great astonishment, indicating the immense influence of the Hengshan Sect.

Now Zhou Yi knew that the Hengshan Sect had three elders, which meant that there were at least three Innate experts within the sect. Their power was indeed formidable, explaining why even Lin Taoli was taken aback.

"When I was an orphan wandering the streets, the Medicine Dao's Master took notice of me and accepted me as his disciple," Zhou Wude proudly said. "With the help of my master, I made rapid progress, especially in the field of alchemy. I was praised by my master all the time."

Zhou Yi playfully said, "Grandson knows that you later became a registered disciple of the Hengshan Sect."

"Yes," Zhou Wude sighed deeply and continued, "Unfortunately, in my thirty-ninth year, I caused a tremendous disaster."

Zhou Yi's expression changed, knowing that this was the crucial part of the story, and he didn't dare to be neglectful.

"That year, when my master and the others were traveling, they accidentally encountered a spirit beast that was over five hundred years old. Overjoyed, my master immediately made a move and killed it, extracting its inner core. Then, my master gathered many precious medicinal materials, intending to refine the Innate Golden Pill," Zhou Wude murmured.

Zhou Yi's heart skipped a beat. "Grandfather, did you ruin the Golden Pill during the refining process?"

Zhou Wude let out a long sigh. "Such an important Golden Pill, how could they let me refine it?"

"If it wasn't you who refined it, then what disaster did you cause?" Zhou Yi asked.

A tinge of guilt appeared on Zhou Wude's face as he said, "At that time, everyone in the Hengshan Sect knew that we were about to refine the Innate Golden Pill. Once the Golden Pill was completed, one person would have the chance to advance to the Innate realm."

"One person?" Zhou Yi asked.

Zhou Wude chuckled and looked at him, saying, "Do you think the Innate Golden Pill is the same as the Limit-Breaking Golden Pill? The inner core of a five-hundred-year-old spirit beast can, at most, refine one Innate Golden Pill. This is the true reason why Innate experts are so rare."

Zhou Yi nodded, absorbing the knowledge, and urged him, "What happened next?"

"Later..." Zhou Wude shook his head and said, "At that time, my emotions were in turmoil, and when I was selecting auxiliary medicinal materials, I accidentally mixed in an inferior herb that wasn't mature enough into the pill furnace."

Zhou Yi's eyes widened, understanding what had happened. If inferior herbs were mixed in, then the Golden Pill was essentially rendered useless.

As expected, Zhou Wude continued, "My master was also excited at the time and, strangely, didn't inspect it. Three days later, the pill was completed, but what came out was not the Innate Golden Pill, but several Limit-Breaking Golden Pill. The other two elders in the Hengshan Sect wanted to execute me, but my master stopped them. However, he couldn't protect me any longer and had to expel me from the sect. But my master also said that if I could find another inner core of a five-hundred-year-old spirit beast or if a descendant of the Zhou family could cultivate an Innate disciple, then I would be allowed to return to Hengshan."

Zhou Wude's words became faster and more excited as he spoke, and his eyes even started to shine. Clearly, this matter had lingered in his heart for many years, and now that his wish was coming true, he couldn't contain his excitement.

Chapter 144

At this point, Zhou Yi finally grasped the general idea. Although Grandfather Zhou's talent was not top-notch, being able to cultivate to the tenth level of inner strength and reach the pinnacle realm was a testament that he was not a foolish person. It was just a past negligence that led to an irreparable fact, which ultimately resulted in his expulsion from the sect.

However, in Grandfather Zhou's heart, there seemed to be an extreme stubbornness, a desire to return to the Hengshan Sect. Zhou Yi couldn't quite understand this sentiment and didn't hold much longing for the Hengshan Sect himself. To him, the importance of the Hengshan Sect was far less than that of the Yuan family. But in Grandfather Zhou's mind, Hengshan was the place where he had grown up, just like Zhou Yi's perception of Zhou Village.

As long as there was a glimmer of possibility, he would never give up. "When we made that big mistake back then and left, besides Senior Martial Brother Wu Jian, the fellow disciples on the mountain turned their backs on us one by one, mocking me and Lai Bao, saying that we would never have a chance to return to the sect." A slightly abnormal flush gradually appeared on his face as he continued, "It's been over forty years, and I thought there was no chance of returning to the sect anymore. But the heavens have opened their eyes and bestowed you upon Zhou Village. This is a gift from heaven." The old man sighed for a while and said, "Yi, Grandfather really wants to thank you for fulfilling this final wish of mine." Zhou Yi quickly stood up and said, "Grandfather, there's no need for you to thank me. Does your grandson still need your thanks?"

Although he said this, deep down in his heart, Zhou Yi couldn't help but wonder if Grandfather was right. The extraordinary encounter in the lake back then was indeed a gift from the heavens.

Could it be that the heavens truly heard Grandfather's thoughts and chose him, casting that mysterious and unfathomable object into the lake?

Zhou Wude stroked his beard and said, "Yi, back then, Lai Bao and I were driven down the mountain by our fellow disciples. We will never forget that humiliation. That's why I gave him a portion of the Limit-Breaking Golden Pill and the Energy-Boosting Golden Pill,. Within two months, he will surely advance to become a master of the tenth level of inner strength." As he spoke, Zhou Wude's eyes sparkled with determination. "

By then, the three of us will go to Hengshan together. I want everyone to know that not only has our Zhou family produced a cultivator at the Innate Realm, but both Lai Bao and I have also become masters of the tenth level of inner strength. I want those who humiliated us in the past to deeply regret their actions."

Zhou Yi took a sharp breath, surprised by his grandfather's concern for those who humiliated them. Suddenly, he seemed to understand something. Grandfather's strong attachment to the sect and his desperate efforts to return to Hengshan were not solely due to their master-disciple relationship. It was also about reclaiming their dignity in the eyes of those who had humiliated them.

With a thought in his mind, Zhou Yi asked, "Grandfather, you're already in your eighties, and so is Lai Bao. But do you think that after forty years, the people who humiliated you back then could still be alive?"

Zhou Wude raised his eyebrows and said, "Rest assured, within the realm of Hengshan, the qi of heaven and earth is abundant. People who live there have a lifespan at least 30% longer than those outside. Moreover, those who once insulted us were merely in their thirties at that time. Now that even I am still alive, they should pose no problem at all."

Zhou Yi could only smile wryly. He already sensed that his grandfather's determination was deeply rooted and not something he could change. The older people grew, the more stubborn they became in certain matters, and Zhou Wude was undoubtedly no exception.

In the face of his grandfather's instructions, Zhou Yi naturally had no objections. In fact, he was quite eager and not at all resistant to joining the Hengshan Sect. As his grandfather had mentioned, with his status as an Innate Realm cultivator, he would undoubtedly be able to become an elder in the Hengshan Sect.

The position of an elder in Hengshan surpassed even that of the sect leader, granting them the privilege of freely accessing the sect's library. This privilege was exclusive to elders who had reached the Innate Realm. The Hengshan Sect had a history spanning three thousand years, with at least two or more Innate Realm cultivators in almost every generation. The wealth of knowledge contained in the sect's library was beyond the imagination of ordinary people.

The library of the Zhou family and the secret chamber of Zhou Wude's room mainly contained books transcribed by Zhou Wude during his time in Hengshan. However, given his status as a mere junior disciple at the time, he only transcribed acquired manuals, lacking any Innate Realm techniques. The only thing related to the Innate Realm was a biographical account similar to a travelogue.

Furthermore, according to Zhou Wude, the Hengshan Sect even had a Grand Elder who surpassed the ordinary elders. When Zhou Yi heard these words, his eyes sparkled like his grandfather's.

If elders were Innate Realm cultivators, then what about the Grand Elder...

Could it be the legendary figure known as the "Divine Dao," who was even more formidable than an Innate Realm cultivator?

The thought instantly filled Zhou Yi with excitement. If he hadn't already promised to go to the capital of Tianluo Kingdom and wait for Uncle Bao's advancement to the tenth level of inner strength, he would almost want to set off immediately for Hengshan.

Zhou Wude continued speaking, but suddenly changed the topic, saying, "Yi, although the Hengshan Sect may not be a prestigious and renowned sect, its three thousand years of heritage is not to be underestimated."

He stood up and went to a corner of the room. There, three long weapons measuring over a meter in length were displayed—the three segments of the Great Guan Dao, a large broadsword.

Zhou Wude gently caressed the Great Guan Dao and said, "This old friend was secretly passed to me by my master before I left Hengshan."

Zhou Yi exclaimed in surprise, "Grandfather, Father said that you forged it yourself."

Zhou Wude burst into laughter and said, "At that time, I had already been expelled from Hengshan. How could I dare to use the Hengshan name to deceive others? So, I had to claim that I forged this Great Guan Dao myself." He then let out a long sigh and continued, "In truth, this Great Guan Dao is so long and heavy not only because of the precious materials used but also because of the unique forging techniques that are not easily learned by ordinary people."

"Grandfather, could this be a treasure?" Zhou Yi's heart stirred.

"It can't be considered a treasure," Zhou Wude said with a bitter smile. "If the Great Guan Dao were a treasure, then my master wouldn't have silently stolen it and let me take it away. However, while it may not be a treasure, it is indeed crafted from materials used for treasures and forged using special techniques for forging treasures."

Zhou Yi frowned slightly and asked, "If it's made from treasure-grade materials and forged using special techniques for treasures, why isn't it considered a treasure?"

Zhou Wude let out a sigh and said, "Although all the materials and procedures were correct, it is actually just a useless weapon."

"A useless weapon?" Zhou Yi's eyes widened, and his expression turned somewhat unpleasant. He asked, "Grandfather, is it because there was a mistake during the forging process, resulting in its failure?"

"Yes," Zhou Wude replied dejectedly. "It's similar to when we refine a Golden Pill. We clearly use top-grade medicinal ingredients and the inner core of a five-hundred-year-old spiritual beast. But after the refinement, when we open the furnace, it turns out to be a Limit-Breaking Golden Pill. It is truly a great pity."

Zhou Yi raised his eyebrows and took the Great Guan Dao from Zhou Wude's hand. He gently caressed the blade, and his true qi circulated, rippling across the surface of the blade.

Slowly, the entire Great Guan Dao emanated a strange metallic color and emitted a faint buzzing vibration.

A faintly proud smile appeared on Zhou Yi's lips as he looked at the Great Guan Dao, as if he were looking at his own pride.

Suddenly, he flicked his wrist, and the three segments of the Great Guan Dao instantly assembled, causing the vibrations throughout the entire blade to become even more pronounced.

Zhou Wude watched in astonishment as he sensed an inexplicable power within the Great Guan Dao. Gradually, as this power spread, he experienced a thrilling and peculiar sensation.

It was an aura of dominance, as well as a sense of arrogance, as if it looked down upon the world, invincible against all, yet indulging in its own self-appreciation.

In the face of this arrogance, it seemed that everything had to make way for it. Anything obstructing its path would be completely crushed.

Zhou Wude involuntarily took a step back. Although he was well aware that this was not an attack directed at him by Zhou Yi, he couldn't help but instinctively retreat. His instincts didn't want to clash with this overpowering force that had almost become substantial.

In a daze, a strange thought emerged in his mind. It seemed that the source of this arrogance was not just Zhou Yi himself but the Great Guan Dao in Zhou Yi's hand.

This blade was crafted entirely from materials used for treasures and using the techniques for forging treasures. However, it ultimately failed during the forging process due to certain reasons.

However, except for those Innate Realm cultivators, no one else knew about it. This treasure had actually been successful, but for some reason, it was considered a failure. It was because it was too heavy. This gigantic and terrifying weapon, weighing over three hundred and sixty kilograms, was not suitable for use by Innate Realm cultivators.

Among the postnatal experts, faced with the weight and length of this blade, there were also few who were willing to use it. So, since its creation, it had been stored in the weapon arsenal, seemingly forgotten and untouched.

Until one day, it fell into the hands of a postnatal expert with innate divine power and, over several decades, spread its reputation throughout the entire county.

However, its true power had not been fully unleashed. It was only when Zhou Yi reached the realm of an Innate Realm cultivator and fused refined steel magnetic ore into it, completing the final step, that the true mysterious power within the Great Guan Dao was successfully awakened, allowing this treasure to see the light of day once again.

If it weren't for that, how could the feat of Zhou Yi incorporating the insights of "Clouds and Rain" into his swordsmanship, single-handedly slaying two hundred bandits, be sustained by an ordinary iron blade...

Feeling the tremendous aura emanating from the Great Guan Dao, Zhou Wude's face changed drastically. He had never experienced a similar sensation from the Great Guan Dao before.

After a while, Zhou Yi once again separated the segments of the Great Guan Dao and sheathed the blade.

"Grandfather, I don't care whether this Great Guan Dao is considered a useless weapon, but to me, it is the best weapon," Zhou Yi said, patting the blade. With a tone of extreme reverence and almost like a solemn oath, he continued, "In my lifetime, the Great Guan Dao is my weapon. I won't part with the blade, and the blade won't part with me."

As he spoke, the previously calm blade trembled slightly again, and the buzzing sound served as an accompaniment, resonating with Zhou Yi's words.

Just as Zhou Yi's voice fell, the strange sound suddenly disappeared completely. The coordination between the two was perfect, as if they had rehearsed countless times beforehand.

Zhou Wude opened his mouth, silently watching Zhou Yi, then looking at the Great Guan Dao. Finally, he let out a long sigh and said, "Yi, I finally understand that passing the Great Guan Dao into your hands was the most correct decision I made in my life."

※※※※

"Yi, there's something I want to discuss with you."

"Grandfather, please go ahead."

"What do you think of Yuan Liling?"

Zhou Yi was taken aback. Yuan Liling was the legitimate son of Yuan Chengzhi and would likely become the future head of the Yuan family. However, he couldn't understand why his grandfather suddenly mentioned him.

After considering for a moment, Zhou Yi shook his head and said, "Grandfather, I have only met Yuan Liling a few times and am not familiar with him." Then, he casually asked in return, "Why do you mention him, Grandfather?"

Zhou Wude cleared his throat and said, "During the recent bandit raid on Taicang County, I asked Lai Bao to take the elderly, weak, and women from the village to hide in the mountains. When they returned, it seems that Yi Ling has developed some affection for him."

Zhou Yi's eyes widened. Such a thing...

He had initially wanted to say that within a mere ten days or so, how could they develop any affection? But as the words reached his lips, he suddenly remembered what happened with his eldest brother.

Ever since Zhou Yitian met Yuan Liwen, he had been infatuated and willing to do anything to marry her, even if it meant dragging Zhou Yi down with him.

Although at his age Zhou Yi already feels a vague attraction from women, he is not inherently rebellious. It is impossible for him to take the initiative in pursuing relationships. However, if someone willingly approaches him, he will not reject their advances.

So when Zhou Yitian brought up the matter, and after Zhou Yi met Yuan Lixun, he immediately agreed.

If Zhou Yitian could be infatuated at first sight, then it wasn't difficult to accept that Yuan Liling and Zhou Yiling might have developed a mutual liking.

After pondering for a moment, Zhou Yi asked, "Grandfather, what do you mean by this?"

After considering for a moment, Zhou Wude said, "Lai Bao mentioned that the child has good character, and his martial arts skills are respectable among his peers, so he doesn't oppose this matter. The only concern is that the Yuan family is quite far away."

Zhou Yi also felt relieved. Lai Bao treated them, the third generation of the Zhou family, as his own. Each one of them was like his own flesh and blood. If he was satisfied, then there shouldn't be any major problems.

"Grandfather, I finally understand now," Zhou Yi said with a smile, "When Yuan Lixuan and the others returned to the Yuan family, Yuan Liling adamantly refused to go back, saying that he wanted to learn some martial arts because he got along well with Eldest Brother. It turns out that learning martial arts was just an excuse, and his real intention was to win the heart of Fourth Sister."

Zhou Wude's lips curved slightly. It was evident that his little scheme hadn't escaped the old man's keen eyes.

"Alright, let's see how things turn out for that kid. If he can truly impress Yiling, then let's support them," Zhou Wude said, laughing heartily, before leaving the room.

After watching the old man leave, Zhou Yi let out a sigh. In reality, the reason why his grandfather accepted this matter was because the Yuan family was one of the prestigious families, and they were a suitable match for the Zhou family. Moreover, Yuan Zeyu had a deep friendship with his grandfather, so naturally his grandfather leaned towards him.

If Yuan Liling were a powerless and insignificant boy without strong martial prowess, his grandfather might have opposed the matter.

With lingering concerns in his heart, Zhou Yi walked out. In another room in the courtyard, Yuan Lixun was sitting in a chair, embroidering something.

Zhou Yi cleared his throat, and Yuan Lixun immediately startled. She tidied up her things and approached him, asking, "Young Master, has Grandfather left?"

"Indeed," Zhou Yi nodded slightly and continued, "I want to ask you something." "Young Master, please go ahead," Yuan Lixun replied. "Yuan Liling is your older brother, right? What kind of person is he?"

Zhou Yi asked. Yuan Lixun hesitated for a moment, glanced at the corner of her eye, but couldn't find any clues from Zhou Yi's expression. She bit her lip lightly and said, "Young Master, Liling is the eldest son of Father's lawful wife. He has been clever and intelligent since childhood and is deeply favored by Father. Although he is only a few years older than me, he has already reached the sixth level of internal energy.

In the Yuan family, he is considered a core figure of the new generation." As she spoke these words, she felt a myriad of emotions in her heart. Being children of the same father, Yuan Liling enjoyed far better treatment than the two of them, siblings. Zhou Yi listened without any expression and said, "What about his character? Has he done anything questionable?" Yuan Lixun's heart chilled, unsure why Zhou Yi was asking such questions.

However, she didn't dare to hide anything and replied, "Liling is approachable, gentle, and has good character. He has no questionable behavior." This was her evaluation of her half-brother from the same father, and her words were sincere, without any hesitation. Finally, Zhou Yi smiled and said, "I understand." Summoning her courage, Yuan Lixun asked, "Young Master, may I know why you asked about Brother Liling's character?"

Zhou Yi didn't hide anything either and replied, "My grandfather told me that there seems to be a mutual liking between our Fourth Sister and your older brother. I am concerned about Liling's character, so I wanted to inquire with you. Since he has shown good behavior, let them spend some time together and see how it goes." Zhou Yi chuckled, "Marrying a daughter of our Zhou family is not an easy task, you know." Yuan Lixun's thoughts raced, unsure of how to feel about it all...

Chapter 145

Upon the grand avenue, the rhythmic sound of hooves reverberated in the air. A convoy of horses emerged from the imperial capital of Tianluo City, galloping without pause until they reached the county town. After establishing contact with the Cheng family, they swiftly continued their journey towards the Zhou ancestral village.

The horses in this convoy were all magnificent, renowned Northwestern black horses. With their tall frames, slender ankles, and broad chests adorned with well-defined muscles, they shimmered like black satin under the sunlight. While they couldn't compare to Zhou Yi's prized Hongling Horse, they were indeed an exceptional breed, handpicked from the finest stock.

Obtaining one or two of such fine horses in the Northwestern region would not be a challenging feat, but acquiring over a hundred and forming a complete horse convoy was no easy task. Within the boundaries of Tianluo Kingdom, there were hardly more than ten entities with such lavish resources, and this particular batch undoubtedly hailed from the royal Yu family.

Half a day later, when the horse carriage came to a halt before the Zhou ancestral village, it immediately caused a commotion. Not only did Zhou Quanyi step forward to welcome the guests, but even Lin Taoli also emerged alongside him. Meanwhile, news of the arrival of the royal Yu family's envoys finally reached Zhou Yi, who had been engrossed in his courtyard, pondering on how to integrate the principles of clouds and rain into his martial arts.

As he entered the main hall, Zhou Yi was astonished to find Zhou Wude and all his three younger brothers, along with their eldest brother, gathered there. To receive the royal entourage, even Zhou Quanming had returned from the county town. The only one absent from the Zhou family was Zhou Laibao, who remained secluded, fully dedicated to his pursuit of breaking through the tenth layer of internal energy.

As his gaze swept across the hall, apart from the Zhou family members, he noticed Cheng Ningsheng and his son Cheng Jiahui sitting nearby. What surprised him even more was the presence of the elderly Xu Yinjie and Xu Xiangqian from Xujia Village, as well as Lin Taoli from the Lin family 。

He inwardly chuckled with a bitter smile. The name of the royal Yu family of Tianluo Kingdom indeed held great allure even in a small place like Taicang County. The fact that the three major families had gathered under one roof for a representative of the royal family was a clear display of their lack of confidence.

In the Fire Crow Kingdom, with the influence of the Xie family, even if the ruler of the Fire Crow Kingdom personally visited, they wouldn't mobilize their entire family.

He couldn't help but sigh in his heart, but his gaze fell upon the two unfamiliar individuals in the hall. One of them seemed to be an old man, with tightly closed lips as if afraid to utter a word. Yet, within his eyes, there flickered a glint that an ordinary person would never detect.

With just one glance, Zhou Yi deduced that the old man's internal energy cultivation was not inferior to his grandfather's; he had reached the pinnacle of the tenth layer of internal energy. It seemed that with a single step, he could break through that barrier and advance to the innate realm.

Of course, although this step appeared simple, actually crossing it was incredibly difficult. There were many who reached the peak of the tenth layer of internal energy, but only a rare few could truly take that step. It required exceptional determination and an extraordinary stroke of luck. Clearly, this old man seemed unlikely to possess such good fortune.

Beside this old man, standing shoulder to shoulder, was a young man. This youth had a handsome face, with a green silk ribbon adorning his forehead and two large golden earrings dangling from his ears. His broad cuffs and collar, the robust lines and wrinkles on his face and hands symbolizing hard work, the straight bridge of his nose, and the gentle, slightly melancholic gaze — even Zhou Yi had to admit that he was remarkably handsome to an excessive degree.

Upon seeing Zhou Yi, both individuals revealed a hint of surprise in their eyes, though they quickly concealed it. However, how could they hide it from the people in the hall?

In truth, they had known of Zhou Yi's young age long before, but seeing him in person still evoked an involuntary sigh of astonishment. How could someone so young already possess innate strength? Especially the elderly man, who felt a tinge of melancholy and a hint of envy.

"Yi, come over here. Let me introduce you," Zhou Wude said with a hearty smile. It was evident that his conversation with the two had been quite enjoyable. "This is His Royal Highness Yu Xiaoyi, the eldest son of the current ruler."

Yu Xiaoyi slightly bowed and said, "Greetings, Master Zhou."

Zhou Yi cupped his hands and replied, "No need to be so formal, Your Highness. Your personal visit is an honor beyond our expectations."

Yu Xiaoyi was puzzled. Master Zhou's attitude was exceptionally amicable. Although he was the crown prince of Tianluo Kingdom, he was aware of the status of innate powerhouses within the country. Even the Guardian Grandmaster, Shui Xuanjin, showed no pleasant expression when facing the royal family, apart from the reigning monarch.

"And this is Mr. Xue Lie," Zhou Wude paused before continuing, "Mr. Xue Lie is the chief disciple of Master Shui Xuanjin, renowned throughout Tianluo Kingdom, hailed as the foremost practitioner among the tenth-layer masters of internal energy."

Zhou Yi's lips curled into a slight smile, but he wasn't surprised by the title. Being a disciple of an innate powerhouse naturally granted him access to innate cultivation techniques and precious artifacts.

If one could master an innate cultivation method and possess a precious artifact, it wouldn't be difficult to dominate peers at the same level. Let's not forget that the Xiao brothers, with their ninth-layer internal energy, could contend against their uncle. In the eyes of ordinary people, it was an incredible feat.

Xue Lie's attitude became noticeably more respectful. He stepped forward with large strides, disregarding the age difference, and deeply bowed before Zhou Yi. "Xue Lie pays his respects to Master Zhou."

Zhou Yi furrowed his eyebrows slightly, raising his hand to help Xue Lie up. He said, "Mr. Xue, no need for such formalities."

Although Zhou Yi's gesture was subtle, the slight lift of his hand was enough to astonish Xue Lie. He realized that he had no resistance whatsoever in the presence of Zhou Yi. This feeling was something he had only experienced with his own teacher.

At this moment, he finally believed completely that the young man before him was truly an innate powerhouse.

Zhou Yi glanced at the people from the Cheng and Xu families, nodding and smiling at them. Cheng Ningsheng and the others naturally returned the gesture with respectful salutations.

They had been sitting and chatting, but as soon as Zhou Yi entered, everyone stood up automatically, including the members of the Zhou family.

"Yi, His Highness's personal visit this time has brought us many good things," Zhou Wude's voice contained an unmistakable delight that he couldn't hide.

Despite Taicang County suffering from an unprecedented attack by bandits, the Zhou family not only remained unharmed but also obtained abundant rewards. Zhou Yi brought tens of thousands of taels of gold, and the gifts sent by Lin Tao Li were equally valuable. The multitude of gifts brought by the royal family from Tianluo City this time exceeded his expectations.

However, he understood that the reason these people generously offered gold and goods was purely due to the respect they held for

Zhou Yi. If it weren't for his grandson's innate realm, the Zhou family would not have gained such benefits. Not to mention, Zhou Wude himself would have suffered losses.

Cheng Ningsheng chimed in with a smile, "Master Zhou, this time the royal family has exempted Taicang County from ten years of taxes and provided a large sum of money and supplies to repair the damaged city walls. Upon inspection, I found that we not only have enough resources to restore the city walls but also to construct a larger wall ahead of Zhou Manor."

Zhou Yi's heart stirred. He was well aware of the expenses involved in building city walls. Otherwise, his grandfather wouldn't have invested significant amounts of money into it every year. Cheng Ningsheng's words clearly indicated that he had received approval from Yu Xiaoyi and the others, or perhaps it was even their own instruction.

He sighed inwardly, truly worthy of being people from the royal family, their generosity knew no bounds.

Zhou Wude laughed heartily and said, "Brother Cheng, in the face of the bandit invasion, the greatest credit goes to Xujia Village, and both your Cheng family mansion and Xujia Village's outpost have suffered significant damage. I will entrust this money and supplies to both of you as funds for the reconstruction of Cheng Manor and Xujia Village's outpost."

Zhou Yi was slightly taken aback, wondering when his grandfather had become so kind-hearted. Before he could react, Yu Xiaoyi chuckled and said, "Master Zhou, you jest. This time, the three major families of Taicang County bravely fought against the bandits, wiping out the troublesome thieves that had plagued the county. This is a tremendous achievement and a great service to the nation. How can we allow our heroes to shed blood and tears? The reconstruction of Xujia Village and the Cheng mansion will be undertaken by our royal family, ensuring fairness for both your families."

Xu Yinjie and Cheng Ningsheng couldn't contain their joy and hope. They immediately stepped forward, deeply bowing in gratitude.

Despite their respective strengths, the cost of rebuilding their homes was astronomical. Once rebuilt, it would undoubtedly deplete their resources. Now, a huge windfall had unexpectedly dropped from the sky, and they were naturally overwhelmed with happiness.

After expressing their gratitude, they looked at Zhou Wude with a hint of appreciation in their eyes. Of course, these three old men, who had engaged in hidden struggles for decades, could never be as intimate as true brothers. Their relationship could only gradually ease over time.

Once their conversation concluded, Xue Lie bowed deeply once again and said, "Master Zhou, my master, Shui Xuanjin, has heard of the emergence of another innate master in Taicang County and is overjoyed. He wishes for Master Zhou to come to the capital to discuss an important matter."

His voice brimmed with utmost sincerity, carrying an irresistible earnestness.

Yu Xiaoyi also bowed deeply and said, "Please grant my request, Master Zhou."

Zhou Yi pondered for a moment and replied, "It has been my long-standing wish to visit Master Shui in the capital. However, may I ask, Mr. Xue, what does Master Shui require my assistance with?"

Both Xue Lie and Yu Xiaoyi's expressions changed slightly. They exchanged a glance, and eventually, Yu Xiaoyi gritted his teeth and said, "Master Zhou, although our Tianluo Kingdom may not be on par with the three major powers in the Northwestern region, we are still among the top-tier second-rate countries. However, within the three counties, there is only one Guardian Grandmaster, Master Shui. So..."

Zhou Yi furrowed his brow. He was about to express his lack of interest in becoming a Guardian Grandmaster when he saw his grandfather beside him making exaggerated gestures and winking at him. This caused his words to shift, and he said, "I will need to consider this matter. I will give you both a reply in a few days."

Upon hearing that he did not outright refuse, Yu Xiaoyi and Xue Lie couldn't help but reveal expressions of joy. As long as there was no immediate rejection, it meant there was still room for negotiation. In particular, Yu Xiaoyi had already made up his mind. He was determined to achieve this goal no matter what. If he could obtain a commitment from Master Zhou to serve as the Guardian Grandmaster for Tianluo Kingdom, his position on the throne would be as stable as Mount Tai.

Zhou Wude chuckled and said, "Your Highness, Mr. Xue, you have traveled a long way. Please rest for the night. Even if you plan to return to the capital, it will be fine to depart tomorrow."

Zhou Yi nodded and added, "Indeed, please rest.

With that, he nodded to several family members and turned to leave.

Though his behavior was considered extremely rude, neither the members of the Zhou family nor the others harbored any feelings of anger.

For a Innate powerhouse , if they couldn't even enjoy such privileges, how could they demonstrate their power and esteemed status?

Upon returning to his room, Zhou Yi had Yuan Lixun prepare a cup of tea, a beloved beverage of his grandfather, sourced all the way from the distant land of Da Shen.

These tea cakes were originally meant to be smuggled goods, but this time, the Yuan family presented them as a gift to the old master.

Overjoyed, the old master shared one-fifth of the tea cakes with Zhou Yi. However, for Zhou Yi, the quality of tea mattered little once it reached his palate, so he decided to preserve this gift specifically for a few respected elders.

Sure enough, not long after, the old master arrived in his room. He took a seat across from Zhou Yi, picked up a tea cup, and took a sip, exhaling a contented breath, seemingly at ease.

"Grandfather, you gave me a meaningful glance earlier. What does it mean?" Zhou Yi straightforwardly asked, "Do you want me to take up the position of the Guardian Grandmaster or not?"

"Of course, you should take it up," Zhou Wude replied without hesitation, "Yi, if your grandfather hadn't wandered to Taicang County and settled here, building a prosperous legacy, I wouldn't have asked you to do this. Tianluo Kingdom is not the most powerful among the Northwestern countries. Above it, there are the Three Great Powers. Among them, the closest one to us is Kairong Kingdom. You could easily become the Guardian Grandmaster of Kairong Kingdom and enjoy the best treatment there. However, since our Zhou family has already established itself in Taicang County and branched out from this base, I hope you can become the Guardian Grandmaster of Tianluo Kingdom."

Zhou Yi nodded slightly, understanding his grandfather's intention. If he became the Guardian Grandmaster of Tianluo Kingdom, the Zhou family would undoubtedly thrive within the kingdom, and no one would dare to offend them again.

After considering for a moment, Zhou Yi earnestly spoke, "Grandfather, I understand your point, but my aspiration lies in the world. I want to pursue the highest level of martial arts and not be confined by any single country."

Zhou Wude chuckled and said, "Yi, do you think that becoming a Guardian Grandmaster would confine you? Hehe, being a Guardian Grandmaster is just a title. Unless the nation faces a major crisis or a Guardian Grandmaster from another country challenges you, you won't have to take action at all."

Zhou Yi raised an eyebrow and said, "But once I become the Guardian Grandmaster, won't I have to reside within the capital city? How can I explore the outside world?"

Zhou Wude's smile froze for a moment, and after a while, he sighed and said, "That is indeed a big problem."

In fact, for most innate experts, they usually reach the Innate Realm when they are over sixty years old, or even older. These individuals possess rich experiences and have little interest in traveling the world, which is why they accept the offerings from a particular country and become its Guardian Grandmaster.

For a young prodigy like Zhou Yi, who reached the Innate Realm at such a young age, he was truly unique. Therefore, when faced with this problem, Zhou Wude couldn't help but feel troubled.

Suddenly, Zhou Yi smiled and said, "Grandfather, you don't need to worry."

Zhou Wude's eyes brightened as he asked, "Do you have a solution?"

Zhou Yi shook his head and said, "It's not that I have a solution, but they have a solution."

Zhou Wude was utterly perplexed, looking at his beloved grandson with confusion.

Zhou Yi pointed in the direction of the capital city of Tianluo Kingdom and said, "Once I arrive there, I will discuss my aspirations with Master Shui. If he can resolve it, I will agree to take up the position of Guardian Grandmaster of Tianluo Kingdom. If even he is unable to help, then I'll just leave."

Seeing Zhou Wude's bemused expression, Zhou Yi quickly added, "Rest assured, as long as I'm alive, not many would dare to provoke the Zhou family. Whether I become the Guardian Grandmaster of Tianluo Kingdom or not, that won't change."

After contemplating for a while, Zhou Wude finally nodded slowly. However, there was still a hint of regret in his heart. If Zhou Yi could become the Guardian Grandmaster, the Zhou family would undoubtedly receive many corresponding benefits. But when he thought about his grandson's aspirations, his own thoughts faded away.

As long as he could make this grandson happy and help him achieve greater accomplishments in martial arts, the status of the Zhou family would undoubtedly rise. This was beyond doubt.

The next day, there was a bustling scene in front of the Zhou family's gate.

A massive cavalry departed from the Zhou family estate and headed towards the capital city of Tianluo Kingdom.

In addition to the two guests from the capital city, Lin Tao Li, unexpectedly accompanied the group.

Within the Zhou family, apart from Zhou Yi and Yuan Lixun, Zhou Quanxin and Zhou Yitian, father and son, also joined the journey. According to the words of the elder Zhou, they would inevitably travel the world in the future. Therefore, Zhou Quanxin and his son, who were destined to take over the Zhou family estate, had to follow and broaden their horizons.

As he watched the convoy slowly embark on the road, disappearing from his sight, Zhou Wude let out a long sigh, unsure of the mixed emotions in his heart.

However, from that moment on, the Zhou family stepped out of the small land of Taicang County and formally entered the sight of the Northwestern countries.

As for Zhou Yi, the pride of the Zhou family, would he be able to truly establish himself in the Northwestern region...

Chapter 146

In the vast northwest of the continent lies a place where mountains coexist with grasslands. Within the same country, there are sprawling mountain ranges and expansive plains. Tianluo Kingdom undoubtedly stands as one of these exemplary nations.

However, the capital of Tianluo Kingdom is built in a strategically accessible location. Not far from the capital, there are small undulating mountains that, after centuries of expansion, have gradually formed the current network of interconnected paths.

After a month-long journey, Zhou Yi and his companions finally arrived beneath the towering walls of this vital city within Tianluo Kingdom. As Zhou Yi stepped out of the carriage and gazed upon the imposing city walls, a wave of emotions surged within him.

If someone had told him three years ago that during this time, such tremendous changes would occur, even to the extent of the Tianluo royal family extending a respectful invitation, he would have never believed it. Yet, everything that had transpired in these three years had propelled him to heights unimaginable in the past.

Suddenly, an intense desire to see Shui Xuanjin as soon as possible welled up in his heart.

"Mr. Xue," Zhou Yi called out loudly.

Xue Lie, who was at the forefront of the group, immediately rushed over as if flying and exclaimed, "Master Zhou, what are your orders?"

"I wish to see Master Shui," Zhou Yi declared.

Xue Lie was taken aback. Wasn't Zhou Yi's trip to the capital precisely for this purpose?

He respectfully bowed while on horseback and replied, "Rest assured, Master Zhou. We will enter the city and spend a day in the royal estate. Tomorrow morning..."

"I wish to see Master Shui right away," Zhou Yi interrupted him calmly.

A hint of hesitation appeared on Xue Lie's face. Did Master Zhou have some unknown reason for wanting to meet his teacher so urgently?

Zhou Yi glanced at him, a smile playing at the corners of his lips. "So, Mr. Xue, are you reluctant to introduce me then?"

Xue Lie clenched his teeth and replied, "Since Master Zhou is insistent, Xue will comply."

At that moment, Yu Xiaoyi was also alerted and had arrived before them. Upon hearing Zhou Yi's request, he couldn't help but smile wryly. He had long known that these innate powerhouses were all unreasonable individuals. Initially, he thought Zhou Yi was an exception, but now it seemed that he was only better at concealing it.

He exchanged a glance with Xue Lie and said, "Master Zhou, if you wish to see Master Shui sooner, then allow Mr. Xue to accompany you. As for Mr. Zhou Quanxin and the others, let me take care of them, how about that?"

Zhou Yi pondered for a moment, then nodded slightly, shifting his gaze to Xue Lie.

With a touch of helplessness, Xue Lie left the caravan and rode toward the city gate. Zhou Yi whistled, and the fiery-red stallion immediately emerged from the procession. With a graceful leap, Zhou Yi landed perfectly on its back.

Without any urging, the fiery-red stallion closely followed behind Xue Lie's horse, setting off toward the inner city gate.

The longer Zhou Yi spent with the Hongling stallion, the more he grew fond of it. The horse was exceptionally intelligent, almost bordering on being telepathic, and their synergy became increasingly seamless.

However, the more Zhou Yi experienced this, the more grateful he felt towards Luo Xin. The gift of the horse was something he vowed to repay when the opportunity arose.

The bustling atmosphere of Tianluo City surpassed not only Taicang County but also the Fire Crow Kingdom Zhou Yi had previously visited. Every street was teeming with pedestrians, merchants, and people from all walks of life.

Yu Xiaoyi had once mentioned that although Tianluo Kingdom might not be on par with the three major powers, it was undoubtedly a significant nation in the entire northwest. Today, it seemed that his words held no exaggeration.

On the streets, pedestrians mostly walked along the sides, while the two middle lanes, intended for horse travel, remained surprisingly empty. Xue Lie rode his horse swiftly along these lanes, encountering no obstacles. Zhou Yi immediately understood that these two lanes were reserved for those with power and influence.

Of course, only on the main roads within the city could such lanes be maintained. In the narrow alleys, it would be impossible to create such dedicated paths.

Suddenly, a series of unbridled laughter echoed ahead, followed by the thunderous galloping of more than twenty spirited horses. While Xue Lie maintained a controlled pace due to being within the city, these oncoming riders showed no restraint, dashing recklessly as if they were in boundless wilderness rather than the capital.

As the opposing horse sped towards them, on the verge of colliding with Xue Lie's horse, the expert with ten layers of internal energy, a peak-level cultivator, had a slight change in his expression. A flash of anger flickered in his eyes, but before any visible action, he had already dismounted from his horse.

His feet touched the ground, and in an instant, his outstretched hands slapped forward. The galloping stallions swiftly approached, while his upraised palms landed precisely on their heads, unwavering and unyielding.

In that moment, the two horses in front seemed to have encountered an immovable object. They were blocked as if crashing into an impregnable wall, abruptly halted in their tracks.

Xue Lie's force was incredibly skillful, his palms infused with a subtle rotational strength. The two spirited horses immediately tumbled to the ground, still hissing and struggling, but they had not perished under his strike.

Zhou Yi watched with admiration. It would not have been difficult for a cultivator with ten layers of internal energy to strike down the horses with a single palm, but to intercept them without harming the animals' lives was an extraordinary challenge.

The two riders on horseback were clearly practitioners with accomplished internal energy cultivation. Although caught off guard, their reactions were swift as they pulled back on the reins, causing their horses to leap into the air.

The onlookers behind them were filled with shock and anger, reining in their horses and shouting curses.

Zhou Yi's brows slightly furrowed as he asked, "Mr. Xue, who are these people?"

Xue Lie quickly turned around, respectfully explaining, "Master Zhou, please forgive them. They are young masters and misses from several prestigious families in the capital. They may have acted arrogantly, but they did not intentionally collide with you."

At that moment, an enraged voice rang out, "Who the hell are you two? Where do you think you're from, daring to obstruct our path? Do you even know who we are?"

These young masters and misses were not fools. Upon witnessing Xue Lie's prowess, they immediately realized that his martial skills were profound and unfathomable, far beyond their capabilities. They didn't dare to approach and engage in a physical confrontation, resorting instead to shouting from a distance.

Xue Lie's face darkened, and his figure soared into the air, swiftly appearing before the individual who had spoken. He extended his hand, delivering a flurry of eight resounding slaps from different angles.

The person felt a surge of terror, shaking his head and attempting to dodge. However, he quickly realized that no matter how he evaded, it was futile. From the perspective of the onlookers, it even seemed as if he voluntarily presented his face for Xue Lie to strike, appearing thoroughly disheveled.

After the eight slaps landed, Xue Lie immediately retreated to his original position. His movement was as elusive as a ghost, as fast as lightning. By the time those individuals reacted, the eight slaps had already been delivered, and Xue Lie had returned to his original spot, as if he had never moved at all.

The beaten young noble let out a miserable groan, his mouth opening wide as he expelled a mouthful of blood, accompanied by more than ten bloodstained teeth.

Xue Lie's eight slaps had actually knocked out all of his teeth, leaving his mouth dripping with blood.

Instantly, the faces of these young nobles turned pale one by one, and no one dared to utter curses anymore.

At this moment, anyone with a little bit of wit knew for sure that they absolutely couldn't afford to suffer any more losses.

The reason Xue Lie resorted to such harsh actions, scaring these young masters and misses, was to prevent their ignorance from causing offense to Zhou Yi with their words. If Zhou Yi were to truly get angry and slay them all, it would undoubtedly stir up a major controversy, making numerous enemies within the city.

Of course, as an innate powerhouse, Zhou Yi had nothing to fear from provocation. However, since these young masters and misses dared to gallop freely on the main road, it indicated their influential backgrounds. If a feud were to arise between them, their plans to invite Zhou Yi to the capital as the Guardian Grandmaster of the country would be completely ruined.

After a moment of silence in the scene, Zhou Yi felt bored and said, "Mr. Xue, let's go."

Xue Lie was instantly overjoyed and eagerly replied, "Yes."

He didn't even mount his horse but strode forward, leading the horse by his side. Wherever he went, the young masters and misses immediately scrambled to drive their horses away, leaving a clear path. Even the young master with the missing teeth, holding his swollen cheek, retreated to the side. However, in his eyes, there was an intense look of resentment, staring fiercely at Xue Lie.

Zhou Yi rode his horse and followed closely behind Xue Lie, passing through the cleared path.

After they had passed, finally, one person stepped forward and respectfully cupped his hands, saying, "I am Zi Ruiwen. May I ask for your esteemed name?"

Xue Lie didn't even turn his head, proclaiming loudly, "I am Xue Lie. Ask your elders if they deserve a beating."

The young masters and misses in the vicinity were initially taken aback, then their expressions changed dramatically. The resentment and hatred in their eyes vanished completely, replaced by a hint of fear.

Trembling, Zi Ruiwen asked, "Is it Senior Xue Lie from Shao Mingju?"

Xue Lie burst into laughter and paid no further attention, continuing on his way without a care.

Only after the two of them had distanced themselves did the young masters and misses collectively breathe a sigh of relief. When their gaze once again fell upon the young man who had been beaten, a hint of relief could be seen in their eyes.

The injured young man held his swollen cheek, his eyes filled with fear. At this moment, even if he were given two extra doses of courage, there would be no trace of revenge left in his heart.

Suddenly, several shouts echoed from ahead, and dozens of city guards swiftly arrived at the scene. Upon seeing the young masters and misses on their horses, they came to a halt. The person leading them seemed to recognize Zi Ruiwen and immediately approached, trying to please him, saying, "Young Master Zi, we heard that there was a conflict involving your group. I don't know where this person is, but rest assured, I will apprehend him and ensure strict punishment."

Zi Ruiwen and the others looked at the captain of the guards with peculiar expressions. Although they were well aware that this person was just flattering them and seizing an opportunity to gain favor with the young masters, they couldn't expect him to capture Xue Lie...

Zi Ruiwen smiled lightly and replied, "Captain, your enthusiasm is truly appreciated. May I ask for your distinguished name?"

A few more obsequious expressions appeared on the captain's face as he said, "I am Zhang San, serving the young masters is my honor."

Zi Ruiwen pointed forward and said, "The person involved in the conflict is over there."

Zhang San's eyes immediately flickered with a sinister light. He waved his hand and declared, "Brothers, come with me and capture the culprit."

The soldiers behind Zhang San responded with an acknowledgment and prepared to follow him.

Suddenly, Zi Ruiwen spoke up, "Captain Zhang San, I also happen to know the name of this person."

Zhang San quickly halted his steps and asked, "Young Master Zi, who is this culprit?"

"This person's name is Xue Lie."

"Xue Lie, huh? Rest assured, Young Master, I guarantee that once he falls into my hands, no matter how fierce he may be... Wait, Xue Lie? That name sounds familiar."

Zi Ruiwen kindly reminded him, "You should be familiar with this person. He is associated with Shao Mingju."

Zhang San's face immediately turned pale, and he said bitterly, "Young Master, my apologies, but I must take my leave."

He turned around and walked away, no longer mentioning anything about capturing the culprit. The soldiers behind him exchanged glances and followed closely behind.

Seeing Zhang San's disheveled departure, the onlookers felt a slight relief.

Suddenly, someone asked, "Brother Zi, who is the person accompanying Xue Lie?"

Another person chimed in, "Perhaps he is a younger relative."

"It doesn't seem like it," the first person said. "I noticed that Xue Lie showed an unusual amount of respect towards that young man, as if he were bowing to an elder. How could he be a younger relative?"

The latter person was initially at a loss for words but then argued, "With Xue Lie's status, how could he bow like a young man? You must have seen it wrong."

The previous person hesitated for a moment. To be honest, the chaos just now, coupled with being questioned, made them suddenly doubtful. Perhaps they had indeed misinterpreted the situation.

However, Zi Ruiwen's complexion slightly changed, and he said, "This is disastrous."

Everyone looked at him inquisitively, and Zi Ruiwen sighed bitterly, saying, "I heard that about a month and a half ago, Xue Lie accompanied the Crown Prince to Taicang County."

At first, everyone was taken aback, but then their faces paled one by one. If this was true, then the person following behind Xue Lie must be that legendary figure who was not even twenty years old yet.

The thought of possibly having a conflict with that person just now filled everyone with remorse.

Zi Ruiwen shook his head slightly and sighed, "Everyone, we can no longer hide what happened today. When we return home, we should be honest with our elders and prepare to restrict our movements.

Each young master and miss had faces ashen. However, they silently blamed their misfortune, wondering why they had encountered such an untouchable figure today. Yet, none of them had considered whether they should have galloped freely on the main road.

※※※※

"Mr. Xue, your reputation in Tianluo City is still quite prestigious," Zhou Yi said with a smile, teasingly.

The incident just now did not provoke his anger, and a few casual remarks wouldn't cause any harm.

Xue Lie's face revealed a hint of embarrassment as he carefully said, "Master Zhou, it's not Xue Lie's reputation, but rather the reputation of my master."

Zhou Yi chuckled and said, "Since those people are young masters and misses from various influential families, why don't they recognize you?"

Xue Lie smiled bitterly and replied, "Master Zhou, since I became a disciple of my master, I have mostly focused on diligent cultivation. I don't enjoy attending social gatherings and banquets, so over time, there are few who know me."

Zhou Yi nodded slightly and said, "You're right. Without wholeheartedly cultivating the martial path, it would be impossible to achieve anything."

Upon hearing these words, Xue Lie couldn't help but feel a strong sense of agreement. Although his talent was decent, his achievements today and the reputation of being the number one below the innate realm in Tianluo Kingdom were primarily attributed to his diligent cultivation . He had never allowed himself to slack off even for a single day.

After traversing several streets, the number of pedestrians gradually decreased, and the terrain became higher, leading to a small elevated mound.

Finally, Xue Lie came to a stop, and Zhou Yi looked up. On the massive castle-like structure, three prominent characters were clearly written: Shao Ming ju .

The doors opened, inviting them inside. Zhou Yi focused his gaze and observed the entire castle. Wherever his eyes landed, he saw corridors, pavilions, towers, and terraces intricately built along the mountainside. The undulating walls surrounded a gently rippling pond, exuding a natural, harmonious, and yet elegant atmosphere.

He took a deep breath, and a sense of tranquility and delight suddenly surged within Zhou Yi's heart.

If he could live in a place like this for an extended period, it would truly cleanse the heart and make one reluctant to be tainted by the mundane world. Moreover, he faintly felt that the cultivation effects in this place should be far superior to those in the Zhou family village. He pondered whether he should find a scenic place in the future and build a castle like this. If it were really built, his parents, siblings, and relatives would surely be delighted.

Though he hadn't officially met Shui Xuanjin yet, his anticipation for her seemed to have deepened.

Suddenly, Zhou Yi felt a sensation in his heart. He turned his head to look and saw a person sitting in one of the pavilions. From a distance, that person gave him an exceptionally desolate feeling. However, just as this feeling arose, Zhou Yi's expression changed.

Because he had realized that although the person was sitting there, they gave off a sense of complete integration with the surrounding environment. It was as if they no longer existed and had become part of the surrounding scenery. The unity of heaven and earth had reached such a degree.

Xue Lie was about to guide Zhou Yi inside when he suddenly noticed that Master Zhou was quietly staring in one direction, seemingly forgetting about him. He felt puzzled and turned his head to look. A familiar figure immediately caught his eye, and he immediately understood the reason.

Letting out a soft sigh, he knew that such a realm was something he could never hope to achieve in his lifetime.

Silently retreating, Xue Lie dismissed all the attendants. When innate experts met, it was certainly not their place to interfere. In that case, it was better for them to stay away from this place.

Chapter 147

After stepping into the realm of Innate, Zhou Yi had encountered two formidable experts at the innate level, and the person before him was undoubtedly the third. As he leisurely approached the pavilion, he couldn't help but be slightly taken aback.

Whether it was Ting Shiguang from the Fire Crow Nation or Lv Xinwen, the Blood Butcher from the Golden Forest Nation, both possessed dignified appearances. However, the countenance of this Guardian Grandmaster of Tianluo Nation was somewhat amusing.

In truth, Master Shuixuan Jin's face was rather plump, and his eyes shone brightly. However, atop his head sprouted a pair of enormous ears. These unusually large ears resembled palm fans, gently swaying with the breeze within the pavilion.

Yet, in just a brief moment of surprise, Zhou Yi quickly composed himself and respectfully greeted, "Greetings, Brother Shui."

After his encounters with Ting Shiguang and Lv Xinwen, Zhou Yi had come to understand that the interactions between innate experts were not based on seniority, but rather on individual strength. As long as one had stepped into the realm of the innate, they could engage with their peers on an equal footing.

Shuixuan Jin stood up and cast a deep glance at Zhou Yi, suddenly sighing, "Brother Zhou, you truly are young."

Zhou Yi discerned the underlying sentiment within that sigh, sensing a tinge of emotion. Surprised, he lifted his head, carefully observing for a few moments, and his expression couldn't help but slightly change.

Shuixuan Jin, astonished, asked, "Brother Zhou, you actually noticed?"

Zhou Yi hesitated for a moment, shook his head, and replied, "I haven't noticed anything, Brother Shui. You're overthinking."

As Zhou Yi spoke those words, he seemed somewhat insincere. In truth, as Zhou Yi carefully observed, he noticed that the vitality within

Shuixuan Jin appeared to be slowly diminishing at an incredibly gradual pace.

When encountering the two innate experts before, Zhou Yi could sense a strong life force emanating from them, akin to the sensation of all things growing in spring. He knew that it was the aura generated by the immense vitality of innate experts, something only peers of the same level could clearly perceive.

However, in the case of Shuixuan Jin, this powerful vitality seemed to be gradually wilting, as if spring had receded, summer had passed, autumn leaves were falling, and winter was approaching.

Shuixuan Jin chuckled heartily and said, "Brother Zhou, your discerning eyes truly caught me off guard. But there's no need for you to hide. I am already 212 years old this year, and there aren't many good years left for me."

A tinge of embarrassment appeared on Zhou Yi's face, but deep down, he couldn't help but admire Shuixuan Jin. Despite knowing that his remaining time was limited, he maintained such a cheerful demeanor. This rare quality was evident in his clear gaze, and it truly impressed Zhou Yi.

Shuixuan Jin extended his hand and pointed, saying, "Please, have a seat, Brother Zhou."

Zhou Yi sat down before him, now harboring a great fondness for this elderly man of over two hundred years. However, his gaze still fell upon Shuixuan Jin's large ears.

Noticing his gaze, Shuixuan Jin smiled faintly, and in an instant, his ears miraculously shrank back to the size of an ordinary person's.

Zhou Yi's eyes widened in astonishment, immediately realizing what had happened. He asked, "Such a marvelous technique! I must inquire, Brother Shui, what kind of technique is this?"

"This technique is called Shunfeng Er, a innate technique collected by the Tianluo Imperial Family," Shuixuan Jin explained with a smile. "It's an extremely rare innate auxiliary technique, but not everyone can master it."

"Why is that?" Zhou Yi asked.

"Because this technique doesn't belong to any of the Five Elements techniques. To practice it, one must possess the innate talent for cultivating wind-based techniques," Shuixuan Jin calmly replied.

Zhou Yi's eyes brightened as he asked, "Are there other techniques besides the Five Elements?"

"Of course," Shuixuan Jin took a deep breath, seemingly wanting to absorb all the fresh air around him into his abdomen. He continued, "In the vastness of nature, there are endless variations, just like the myriad of the Dao. In this world, there are as many powers as there are attributes. The Five Elements power is the foundation of all powers, but it cannot represent all powers. The power of wind is merely one of the myriad aspects of the Dao."

Zhou Yi's eyes sparkled with excitement. Even his grandfather, Zhou Wude, had never spoken such words to him before. But this conversation gave him a sudden sense of enlightenment. In just that moment, he seemed to have gained a deeper understanding of the ways of nature.

Especially with the winds and rains he had previously comprehended, this feeling became even more pronounced.

He even had the sensation that he could burst through the membrane before his eyes at any moment, almost standing up to begin practicing his martial arts.

However, he restrained his thoughts and respectfully bowed to Shuixuan Jin.

Coming to the capital this time, it seems that he made the right decision. Just from this conversation, he had already gained a lot. Seeing Zhou Yi's attitude, Shuixuan Jin was somewhat taken aback and asked, "Brother Zhou, did your teacher never speak of these principles?"

Indeed, although these principles were not applicable to postnatal experts, they were the most fundamental teachings for innate experts. As long as there was a lineage, these basic principles would be passed down to disciples when they stepped into the realm of innate.

Zhou Yi's face turned slightly red as he replied, "Brother Shui, I have no lineage."

"No lineage?" Shuixuan Jin pondered for a moment and said, "But from what I know, it seems that your family has a deep connection with the Hengshan Sect."

Zhou Yi immediately knew that this must be information leaked by Lintao Li. He smiled faintly and said, "Our ancestor was once a registered disciple of the Hengshan Sect, but he left the sect and traveled outside the mountains forty years ago. He has yet to return to Hengshan, so I am not currently affiliated with the sect."

Shuixuan Jin's expression changed for a few moments, and he murmured, "If that's the case, how did Brother Zhou step into the realm of innate?"

Zhou Yi shrugged and said, "I used the principle of cultivating complementary techniques to enhance my internal strength, ultimately breaking through my limits and stepping into the realm of innate."

Finally, a look of astonishment appeared in Shuixuan Jin's eyes, and he asked, "So, Brother Zhou entered innate on his own, without consuming a innate Pill?"

"Yeah," Zhou Yi chuckled in a sincere manner. After pondering for a moment, he continued, "I've heard of the name innate Pill, but unfortunately, I have never seen one. But to be honest, ascending to innate is indeed much more difficult than advancing internal strength."

Muscles twitched slightly on Shuixuan Jin's face. After a long sigh, he finally said, "Brother Zhou, I initially thought you were like those young talents in the super sects, relying on innate Pills to advance. But now I realize that I have greatly underestimated you."

Zhou Yi was slightly taken aback and cautiously asked, "Brother Shui, when you mention the super sects, are you referring to secluded sects similar to Hengshan?"

Shuixuan Jin chuckled wryly and replied, "Hengshan can indeed be considered one of the secluded sects, but it has no connection with the super sects." Seeing Zhou Yi's apparent interest, he waved his hand and said, "Brother Zhou, it is said that you will belong to the Hengshan Sect in the future, and then you will naturally learn the inside story. It's better not to hear it from me."

Zhou Yi let go of his inquisitive thoughts, but after a moment of contemplation, he continued, "Brother Shui, do you say that those super sects also have young cultivators who have reached the realm of Innate Grandmasters?"

Shuixuan Jin hesitated for a moment, then solemnly said, "Yes, although those individuals are also exceptionally talented, compared to you, Brother Zhou, the difference is like heaven and earth."

His words were firm and unwavering.

Indeed, given Zhou Yi's age and the fact that he hadn't consumed a innate Pill, he had advanced to innate solely through his own abilities. While it couldn't be said that there were no others like him, he was undoubtedly a rare phenomenon.

Zhou Yi sighed bitterly in his heart. He had no exceptional talent to speak of. If it weren't for the inexplicable changes in his physique during that fateful encounter at the bottom of the lake, how could he have achieved what he had today?

Shuixuan Jin sighed a few times and then became solemn. He said, "Brother Zhou, since you have already realized that my remaining years are few, then you should also understand the purpose of my inviting you here."

Zhou Yi's gaze shifted, surprised that Shuixuan Jin had straightforwardly brought up this request. But upon further thought, it was in line with his character.

After considering for a moment, Zhou Yi said, "Brother Shui, there is something I don't understand. I hope you can enlighten me."

"Please, go ahead."

"Why did you agree to become the Guardian Grandmaster of Tianluo Nation?"

"Because I had a deep friendship with the previous monarch of Tianluo Nation," Shuixuan Jin replied without hesitation. "I have held the position of Guardian Grandmaster for Tianluo Nation for over a hundred and thirty years, witnessing its prosperity and development. From a small county-sized territory, it has expanded more than fourfold. Now, I am old, and my body has become fragile.

He let out a long sigh and continued, "I originally thought that once I passed away, Tianluo Nation would gradually decline like many other small kingdoms in the northwest. But unexpectedly, a talented master like you has emerged at this time." As he spoke, Shuixuan Jin's eyes gradually brightened, and he spoke with a hint of excitement, "That's why I invited you here, hoping that you can inherit my position and continue to safeguard Tianluo

Zhou Yi's gaze flickered slightly. In this moment, the old man before him evoked a strange feeling within Zhou Yi. Like his grandfather, Zhou Wude, this Master Shui also carried a burden in his heart. For the sake of this burden, they wouldn't find peace even in death. Though their goals might differ, their intentions were no different.

Seeing Zhou Yi silent, Shuixuan Jin spoke in a gentle tone, "Brother Zhou, I know that you have a promising future ahead of you, but Zhou Family Village is still a part of Tianluo Nation. Please consider my request, even if it poses a bit of a challenge for you."

Zhou Yi instantly recalled the conversation with his grandfather on that day, wasn't this exactly what he meant?

Seeing that Zhou Yi was somewhat intrigued, Shuixuan Jin's face lit up with joy. He said, "Zhou, over the past hundred years, I have collected quite a number of treasures. If you are interested, you might as well come and take a look."

Zhou Yi's expression stirred slightly as he asked, "Brother Shui, does the treasury of Tianluo Nation contain any innate manuals?"

Shuixuan Jin was taken aback and replied, "Yes."

"I would like to borrow a manual for reference. Could Brother Shui assist in arranging this?"

Shuixuan Jin burst into laughter and said, "Brother Zhou, this is a trivial matter. Just a word from you is enough." He paused for a moment and added, "In fact, if you agree to become the Guardian Grandmaster, not only will you have access to the innate manuals in the treasury of Tianluo Nation, but you will also have a share of one-tenth of the entire national treasury."

Zhou Yi was taken aback by the immense cost that Tianluo Nation had paid to win over a innate expert. It was an unexpected revelation, and he couldn't help but feel surprised.

After a few laughs, Shuixuan Jin said, "Brother Zhou, there are some things I shouldn't say, but since you don't have a lineage, allow me to speak beyond my bounds."

Zhou Yi nodded and said, "Please, go ahead, Brother Shui."

"Our innate experts possess the True Qi of heaven and earth, far surpassing the cultivators of the Postnatal realm. However, our energy is also limited. When choosing innate manuals, it's best not to be greedy for too many but rather to focus on a few that you can truly recognize." He sighed softly and continued, "The Hengshan Sect, after all, is one of the sects that has been passed down for thousands of years. Their collection is bound to be far greater than that of the Tianluo Royal Family. Moreover, under the guidance of the elders in the sect, it will be easier for you to find the right direction for your development. So, even if you come across those innate manuals, it's best to just take them as references and not try to grasp everything."

Zhou Yi remained silent for a while before bowing respectfully. "Yes, I have learned from your advice."

Shuixuan Jin waved his hand repeatedly and said, "Brother Zhou, there's no need to be so polite. It's just a bit of experience I've gained over the years."

He stood up and said, "Brother Zhou, I will enter the palace now and bring three manuals for you to peruse.

Unexpectedly, Zhou Yi hesitated. After a moment of contemplation, he said, "Brother Shui, you make a valid point. I have made up my mind. I only need the technique of the Shunfeng Er."

A sense of relief flickered across Shuixuan Jin's face. Zhou Yi had become a innate powerhouse at such a young age. Moreover, he wasn't arrogant or complacent but instead receptive to advice from others.

The future of this young man seemed truly boundless. At this moment, Shuixuan Jin was determined to make whatever sacrifices necessary to ensure that Zhou Yi became the Guardian Grandmaster.

※※※※

In a picturesque courtyard, Zhou Yi held a thin book in his hands, flipping through its pages one by one. Upon Shuixuan Jin's insistence, Zhou Yi had chosen to reside in his Shao Ming Ju Residence. This courtyard had been personally selected by the old man for Zhou Yi's accommodation.

However, apart from Zhou Yi himself, Zhou Quanxin and Zhou Yitian resided in the royal estate. Countless people visited the estate every day to build relationships with them, but Zhou Yi, living in the Shao Ming Residence, enjoyed rare tranquility. It wasn't that there were no people who wanted to meet the new generation's innate expert, but rather, no one dared to enter the Shao Ming Ju Residence.

True to his word, Shuixuan Jin retrieved the Shunfeng Er manual from the palace and handed it over to Zhou Yi on the same day. Now, holding this peculiar innate technique in his hands, Zhou Yi was carefully reading through it. He murmured to himself, seemingly gaining insights.

After a moment of contemplation, he approached the central desk and began transcribing the contents of the manual. Suddenly, a faint sound came from the door. The houses here were specially designed and well-maintained, and even the sound of opening a door was barely audible. However, for innate experts, no matter how slight the sound, it couldn't escape their perception.

Without raising his head, Zhou Yi casually asked, 'Is there something you want?'"

Yuan Lixun was the only woman from the Zhou family who accompanied them on their journey, and the only woman Zhou Yi allowed into the Shao Ming Residence. Even the maids and servants personally instructed by Shuixuan Jin had been asked to leave this courtyard. Having spent some time together, Zhou Yi and Yuan Lixun had developed a certain understanding. Zhou Yi knew that unless there was something important, Yuan Lixun wouldn't disturb him while he was reading.

A pleasant and soft voice sounded, "Husband, Lin Taoli is in the courtyard's outer hall and wishes to meet with you."

Zhou Yi nodded slightly, setting down his pen. He said, "He came quickly. I will go and see him. Hopefully, he brings good news."

Before coming to the capital, Zhou Yi had expressed his interest to Lin Taoli in seeing the hand-seal manuals stored in the Lin family's collection. Although Shuixuan Jin had advised against being greedy for too many techniques, Zhou Yi had a particular affinity for the hand-seal techniques, as one of his strongest martial arts techniques was based on hand seals. Therefore, even if he learned a little more, it wouldn't be excessive.

Entering the main hall, Zhou Yi saw Lin Taoli respectfully paying his respects. When they first met, the Lin family held the superior position, but now their status had completely reversed.

Lin Taoli felt a myriad of emotions in his heart, but his expression remained even more respectful. After Yuan Lixun served them tea, she bowed slightly and returned to Zhou Yi's study. She would not eavesdrop on their conversation.

Lin Taoli took out two thick books from his body and placed them on the table. He said, "Master Zhou, these are the authentic version and the hand-copied version of our Lin family's treasured Hand Seal technique, which has been collected for many years."

Zhou Yi's eyes brightened, and he asked in surprise, "What is the difference between these two books?" Lin Taoli shook his head and replied, "The hand-copied version was transcribed by my father himself, so theoretically, there should be no mistakes. However, since this is a crucial innate manual, it cannot afford to have any errors.

So, my father instructed me to bring both the original and the hand-copied versions, allowing Master Zhou to peruse them and then return them." Upon hearing this, Zhou Yi smiled. He understood their intention. If it were just the hand-copied version, he might have suspected that they were withholding something. But since they brought both the original and the hand-copied versions, there was nothing more to be said. After expressing his gratitude to Lin Taoli, who left satisfied, Zhou Yi couldn't help but sigh inwardly. Since reaching the Innate realm, he had encountered numerous obligations, and it seemed that in the future, repaying those debts would require a lot of effort and running around.

Chapter 148

Beneath his feet, as if treading on cotton, not a single sound was made. Before taking a few steps, Zhou Yi had already returned from outside the study. The study's door was left ajar, and before Zhou Yi entered, he saw Yuan Lixun standing at the desk, holding a pen and sketching something. Intrigued, he didn't speak to startle her but instead swiftly approached from behind.

On the table, a book lay open, displaying exercises for cultivating true qi. Besides that, there were vivid illustrations. Yuan Lixun, with pen in hand, was transcribing everything from the book onto another sheet of paper.

Her calligraphy was graceful and alluring, but what truly astonished Zhou Yi were the drawings. They were practically identical to the original illustrations, with no discernible differences, even in the minutest details. In just one glance, Zhou Yi knew that Yuan Lixun's artistic skills far surpassed his own, and her keen observation set her apart.

Compared to her, Zhou Yi's calligraphy and drawings were truly lacking.

Suddenly, Zhou Yi's gaze veered slightly and landed on Yuan Lixun's neck. The exposed snowy white neck, as if carved from marble, tempted one to caress it. Her well-proportioned shoulders swayed rhythmically in tandem with the movements of her pen.

She was completely engrossed in her current task, oblivious to the fact that someone was peering at her. And precisely because of her unwavering concentration, an inexplicable aura of intellect radiated from her, causing even Zhou Yi, standing beside her, to become slightly absent-minded.

Yuan Lixun's movements became slightly more pronounced as she unfolded a completed transcription paper and delicately placed it in a corner of the desk. She tiptoed ever so slightly, her waist gracefully arched, forming a marvelous curve before Zhou Yi's eyes.

As her elbow was about to touch her body, Zhou Yi instinctively lowered his waist and chest. For some reason, he suddenly relished this moment, hesitant to disturb the woman who was wholeheartedly transcribing the secret manual.

Abruptly, Zhou Yi realized that he had unconsciously activated the Breath-holding Technique. With his skill, once he employed this technique, even if he stood behind Yuan Lixun, she would have no chance of detecting his presence.

His face blushed slightly, and Zhou Yi inwardly wondered, could it be that he had developed a penchant for voyeurism?

Yuan Lixun lowered her head once again, flipping to the next page of the ShunFeng Er manual on the table and resuming her transcription. Meanwhile, Zhou Yi silently stood behind her, observing her every move.

He didn't quite understand why he was doing this, but he vaguely felt that something within his heart had been gently stirred.

Finally, Yuan Lixun set down her pen, and her cheeks were tinged with a faint blush as she wore a satisfied smile.

Zhou Yi suddenly snapped back to reality. His figure moved once again, and he silently and ghost-like left the room.

Yuan Lixun seemed to have noticed something. Surprised, she lifted her head and glanced to the side but failed to capture any trace of Zhou Yi's figure.

Zhou Yi arrived in the corridor outside the study and deliberately exerted a bit of force, creating a faint sound of footsteps.

Indeed, when Zhou Yi returned to the study's entrance, Yuan Lixun had already finished organizing everything and was smiling, awaiting his arrival.

"What were you doing?" Zhou Yi asked, feigning ignorance.

"Young master, I saw you transcribing this book, but you had only completed half of it before going to meet Master Lin. So, I took the liberty to finish it for you," Yuan Lixun lowered her head slightly and said softly.

After spending some time together, both sides had gained a certain understanding of each other. Yuan Lixun knew that although Zhou Yi was an innate powerhouse , he didn't have any peculiar temperaments and was always easy to talk to. That's why she took the initiative to transcribe the manual for him.

Zhou Yi nodded slightly and pretended to approach the desk. However, when he saw the papers in front and behind, his face involuntarily flushed.

The first half was naturally the portion he transcribed, and compared to the latter half, it seemed rather inadequate.

Yuan Lixun's gaze also fell upon the two sets of content, and her complexion changed slightly, feeling anxious in her heart.

After a moment, Zhou Yi picked up the first half that he transcribed, gently rubbed his hands together, and a wisp of smoke emerged. The paper instantly incinerated in his hands.

Then, Zhou Yi pursed his lips and blew softly, a gentle breath flowing out, effortlessly carrying the ash of the paper, which drifted lightly into the paper basket in the corner of the room.

Yuan Lixun widened her beautiful eyes in astonishment, filled with envy.

To cultivate martial skills to such a level was truly awe-inspiring.

Zhou Yi picked up the papers that Yuan Lixun transcribed, causing her heart to tense, unsure of how he would handle them.

"Your handwriting is excellent, and your drawings are also very good. Who did you learn from?" Zhou Yi inquired.

Yuan Lixun felt a wave of relief and hurriedly responded, "I learned my calligraphy and drawings from the elders in our clan, together with my younger brother."

"Your younger brother?" Zhou Yi was slightly taken aback. He inwardly berated himself for not knowing that she had a younger brother after several months of being together.

"Yes, my own younger brother," Yuan Lixun's expression dimmed quickly, indicating that her younger brother held a significant place in her heart.

Zhou Yi felt an inexplicable disturbance in his heart but promptly suppressed it. He asked, "What is your brother's name, and how is his life in the clan?"

A touch of nostalgia flickered in Yuan Lixun's eyes, and her soft voice carried a hint of etherealness. "My brother is a lovely child named Yuan Lixiang, and in the clan..." She paused, hesitated for a moment, and finally said, "His current life should be good, I believe."

Although Zhou Yi didn't possess much knowledge about worldly affairs, he understood the meaning behind her words.

"Doesn't he have a good life?" he asked.

Yuan Lixun hesitated and replied, "Perhaps he didn't have a good life before, but now, it must be very good." She lifted her head, finally displaying a hint of determination in her eyes, and said, "As long as I can continue to serve by your side, then his life will definitely be good."

Zhou Yi nodded slightly and glanced at the secret manual on the table. He said, "Transcribe this book again." He turned around and walked towards the room's entrance but stopped suddenly. "Your calligraphy and drawings are so good. From now on, any manuals I acquire will be transcribed and organized by you. Make sure not to make any mistakes."

Yuan Lixun was initially startled, but then it seemed like she understood something. She immediately lowered her head and responded with a murmured voice, "Yes... Young Master."

In the past, when she addressed him as "Young Master," she didn't feel much because she had already resigned herself to her fate. However, today, for some reason, she suddenly experienced a peculiar sensation in her heart.

A faint blush quickly flashed across her face. When she lifted her head, she realized that Zhou Yi had already disappeared without a trace.

Staring blankly ahead for a while, she eventually turned around and returned to the desk. She transcribed the first half of the ShunFeng Er manual once again. However, this time, it took her twice as long, and she made three mistakes along the way. When she finally completed the transcription and finished proofreading, her face was slightly flushed.

Her mind lingered on Zhou Yi's words from earlier. Could this be considered a promise?

Suddenly, she covered her reddened face, feeling surprised at herself. What had come over her?

※※※※

In his own room, Zhou Yi took out the manual that Lin TaoLI had sent.

His gaze fell upon the manual, and he suddenly realized that his mind was wandering. His heart skipped a beat, and he took a deep breath. In that moment, his powerful will swiftly took effect. Within the span of a single breath, he managed to completely gather his focus.

Zhou Yi placed the two books on the table and began flipping through them one by one. His first task was to check for any differences between the two books, although the possibility was unlikely, he couldn't afford to be careless.

His movements were swift, fully immersing himself in the task. With just a quick glance, he could discern if a page had any discrepancies. After half an hour, he had finished proofreading, and the two manuals were identical, without a single error. Even the illustrations were an exact match, revealing the meticulousness of the transcriber.

Putting away the original copies, he slowly perused the transcribed version in his hands. This time, he examined it carefully. The manual contained a total of five hand seal techniques.

Three of them belonged to the Earth element: Earth Seal, Overturning Heaven Seal, and Raising Heaven Seal. The Water element had two: Flowing Water Seal and Cloud Rain Seal.

Upon seeing the names of these five techniques, a hint of excitement flickered in Zhou Yi's eyes. He had secretly learned a portion of the Earth Seal and Cloud Rain Seal from Lin Taoli. Combining them with his own characteristics, he had created the Hidden Needle Seal, a hand seal technique that encompassed both offense and defense.

However, after his breakthrough to the innate realm and multiple uses, he always felt that something was missing from the technique. Especially after the revelation on the mountaintop, where he created the Cloud and Rain Soaring Technique, this feeling intensified.

Thus, he had long been eager to find an opportunity to examine the authentic versions of these two hand seal techniques. Finally, his long-cherished wish had come true.

Having found the two hand seal techniques in the manual, Zhou Yi examined them meticulously, constantly comparing them with the imagined changes in his true qi.

After a long while, Zhou Yi suddenly stood up. He planted his feet firmly in place and raised his hands flat in front of him. These hands before his eyes underwent a sudden transformation.

Initially, the speed was incredibly fast, even leaving a faint afterimage that was difficult to grasp. However, as Zhou Yi's movements became more skilled, his speed unexpectedly slowed down.

If the initial speed was eight or even sixteen times faster, then at this moment, it was eight or even sixteen times slower. Each movement seemed to require careful consideration before execution, giving off an eerie sensation, as if an old ox was pulling a broken cart.

However, simultaneously, an inexplicable sense of solidity, akin to the earth itself, emanated from him. Though his movements were slow, they appeared exceptionally condensed and profound. His hands were like enormous battlements, forming a moving, immortal Great Wall before him.

If the Lin family members were to witness Zhou Yi's current movements, they would surely be astounded. Because what Zhou Yi was performing at this moment was the Earth Seal, and not just any Earth Seal, but the genuine innate version.

This seal technique was originally a profound skill that could only unleash its true power in the hands of an innate expert. In Lin Taoli's hands and now in Zhou Yi's, the difference in realm and power was stark.

Suddenly, Zhou Yi's wrist trembled, and a hand seal paused abruptly.

In an instant, the invisible and mighty wall before him vanished into thin air.

Letting out a soft sigh, Zhou Yi gave a bitter smile. He realized that he hadn't truly mastered this technique. Learning an innate technique required more than just the utilization of innate true qi; it also involved the practitioner's comprehension of the essence of the technique. Without grasping the true meaning contained within the technique, even with powerful true qi, one would be unable to unleash its true potential.

Although Zhou Yi had a unique constitution, it hadn't been fully developed, so he still made some mistakes while practicing the Earth Seal. He furrowed his brows, deep in thought, and vaguely felt that this seal technique was profound and not any easier to comprehend than the Cloud and Rain Soaring Technique he had been studying.

With a sigh in his heart, he finally understood why Shui Xuanjin repeatedly warned against being greedy and biting off more than one could chew. It seemed that he was right.

However, Zhou Yi was unaware that if news of his speed of learning the Earth Seal were to spread, it would surely shock numerous innate experts. The ability to create a solid wall of qi in the first attempt at utilizing an innate seal was beyond the imagination of ordinary innate experts. Even the geniuses specializing in earth-based techniques would be unable to achieve such a feat.

Letting out another sigh, his hands once again began to move, but this time, he didn't form the Earth Seal. Instead, he performed the elusive, ethereal Cloud Rain Seal, which appeared and disappeared without a trace.

Hand seals formed in Zhou Yi's hands, flowing like running water. There was no hesitation or obstacle in the execution. His eyes glimmered faintly, as if he had poured all of his spirit into this set of hand seals.

Slowly, his feet started to move, executing a mystical dance within the narrow confines of the room. With the coordination of his footwork and hand seals, he seemed to vanish in that moment. The entire room was filled with a constantly shifting cloud of mist.

At this moment, Zhou Yi felt a surge of realization in his heart. He seemed to have faintly found the key to breaking through in his martial arts.

During this period of time, he had tried every means to incorporate his understanding of clouds and rain into his martial arts. However, no matter how hard he tried, he couldn't achieve perfection in doing so. Even though he could accomplish it when using the Great Guan Dao, he had failed to integrate it seamlessly into his fist techniques.

But after thoroughly reading the manual of the Cloud Rain Seal today, he had a sudden epiphany. He faintly felt that he had touched the edge of enlightenment he had experienced that day. With a little more effort, he could reenter that state of enlightenment.

If he could perform his fist techniques in that state, he would surely be able to smoothly integrate the sense of clouds and rain into his martial arts, just like how he had fused it with the Great Guan Dao.

However, just as his hand seals were forming in a continuous sequence and reaching the pinnacle of this technique, his movements suddenly came to a halt. He felt a slight conflict between the Cloud and Rain Soaring Technique he had created and the footwork that was meant to complement the Cloud Rain Seal.

One was light and agile, executed with lightning speed, like the patter of raindrops, vast and boundless, falling like a torrential rain, seemingly gentle but able to traverse every corner in an instant, just like a mountain breeze and drizzle.

The other was mysterious and unpredictable, like the ever-changing clouds in the sky, lacking a definite form. However, it was precisely because of this nature that when combined with the Cloud Rain Seal, it could unleash the full potential of the hand seals.

Zhou Yi realized that he needed to harmonize the footwork of the Cloud and Rain Soaring Technique with the Cloud Rain Seal, allowing the power of the hand seals to be maximized.

Zhou Yi could clearly sense that if these two cultivation techniques could be fused into one, their power would undoubtedly experience a transcendental enhancement. However, merging two distinct innate arts into a unified whole was far from an easy task. Moreover, these two techniques seemed to have the potential to blend, but they lacked an important catalyst.

With a gentle sigh, Zhou Yi collected the manual from the table. Countless thoughts churned in his mind. The more he cultivated, the more troubles seemed to arise. He pushed open the door and stepped out of the room, when suddenly his ears twitched, and his figure flickered, appearing outside the door in an instant.

At that moment, a familiar figure paced anxiously outside his door. Upon seeing Zhou Yi suddenly appear before him, the person couldn't help but be overjoyed and exclaimed, "Master Zhou, you have finally emerged!"

Zhou Yi smiled lightly and asked, "Mr. Xue, do you have an urgent matter to discuss with me?"

Mr. Xue nodded eagerly and said, "Master Zhou, envoys from the Kingdom of Kairong have arrived in Tianluo City. After an audience with our emperor, they seek an audience with our country's Guardian Master. His Majesty has agreed and will host a state banquet tomorrow at noon, requesting the presence of the esteemed master."

Zhou Yi was surprised and asked, "Are these individuals of special status?"

"Yes, among them are the third prince, Zhan Zhichao, and the fifth princess, Zhan Zhiyan, of the Kingdom of Kairong," Mr. Xue paused and cautiously continued, "and there is also a Guardian Grandmaster accompanying them from Kairong."

Zhou Yi's eyes instantly lit up, and he inquired, "Who is that person?"

"Cheng Fu. He has reached the Innate Realm for over twenty years, and he is one of the most outstanding figures among the new generation of innate experts," Mr. Xue said with concern, "Master Zhou, you have seen our master and should be aware of the changes in his health. Now, with Cheng Fu's sudden visit, I'm afraid..."

Zhou Yi waved his hand and said, "I understand. Please relay to our master that I also wish to meet the Guardian Grandmaster from the Kingdom of Kairong and request permission to accompany them tomorrow."

Mr. Xue took a step back, bowed deeply, and remained silent.

Chapter 149

At noon, the sun curled up the leaves with its scorching rays, while cicadas incessantly chirped, adding an extra layer of annoyance to the sweltering weather.

Sitting opposite Shui Xuanjin in the spacious carriage, Zhou Yi stole a glance outside. It was the time of the New Year when he was tasked to accompany his uncle to the Yuan family in Jinlin. Back then, it was still the depths of winter, with snowflakes dancing in the air. But now, within a few months, the weather had turned hot.

Half a year had passed as if in a blink of an eye, almost like a dream.

He turned his head to look at Shui Xuanjin, the old man who was well aware that his time was limited. However, there was no trace of desolation emanating from him. If not for Zhou Yi's perception as a congenital powerhouse, he would find it hard to believe that the vivacious and cheerful old man before him was rapidly succumbing to the passage of time.

As if sensing Zhou Yi's gaze, Shui Xuanjin opened his eyes, which he had closed to rest, and smiled. "Brother Zhou, I'm just an old man on the verge of entering the earth. I'm not some young maiden as beautiful as a flower. Why are you looking at me like that?" With these words, the old man even blinked twice, mischief twinkling in his eyes.

Although they had only met a few times and barely known each other for three days, for some unknown reason, they had developed a strong affinity for each other. Perhaps it was because Shui Xuanjin, being aware of his limited time, had let go of all pretenses, while Zhou Yi's emotions had become much more complex. However, one thing was certain—Zhou Yi held a genuine fondness for this old man.

At this moment, upon hearing the old man's teasing, Zhou Yi suddenly remembered the scene in the study from yesterday. His face flushed slightly as he asked, "Brother Shui, how did you know?" Surprised filled him because with his cultivation and strength, it seemed unlikely that he had failed to detect the old man's true condition.

Shui Xuanjin burst into laughter, and his nimble ears suddenly twitched.

Those ears seemed to come alive, slowly lengthening until they reached the same size as when Zhou Yi first saw them. If an ordinary person witnessed this scene, their immediate reaction would undoubtedly be that they had encountered a monster. If someone from the 21st century had traveled to this time, they would surely think that the old man before them had transformed into some kind of pig demon.

However, Zhou Yi knew that the reason the old man could achieve such an astonishing feat was simply because he had perfected the innate technique of Shunfeng Er to its peak. Even ordinary people experience subtle changes in the size of their ears when they are gaping in anger or scratching their heads. But for congenital powerhouses, these changes are even more exaggerated. They have complete control over every part of their bodies. Just like when Zhou Yi practiced the Bone Transformation Technique, in the acquired realm, he could only elongate or shrink his ears, but in the congenital realm, not only one head, but even two heads would be no problem at all.

Shunfeng Er itself is an Innate technique, so when it reaches its peak, the slight exaggeration of the ear's enlargement is not an overstatement.

As Zhou Yi looked at those ears, moving on their own without any wind, sudden realization dawned upon him, and he said, "Shunfeng Er?"

Shui Xuanjin burst into laughter, a joyous sound that couldn't be put into words. He said, "Brother Zhou, although Shunfeng Er may not have much practical use in combat, it is, after all, an Innate technique.

If you can't even perceive these slight movements, can it still be considered an Innate technique?"

Zhou Yi's expression slightly darkened as he asked, "Are you monitoring me?"

Shui Xuanjin waved his hands repeatedly and said, "I just happened to hear a faint sound during my daily practice. How could I be specifically monitoring you?"

His tone was open and selfless, and his gaze was as clear as water, devoid of the muddled ambiguity often found in ordinary old men.

Zhou Yi nodded slightly, inexplicably believing the words of the old man. Although there was no evidence, he simply chose to trust.

However, as he looked at those ears, envy welled up within Zhou Yi's heart. He made up his mind that after returning today, he would definitely learn this technique.

Seemingly sensing Zhou Yi's thoughts, Shui Xuanjin let out a soft sigh and said, "Brother Zhou, I know you want to learn this technique, but it's not an elemental power like the Five Elements. Without a natural affinity for wind-based techniques, no matter how hard you try, it will be difficult for you to grasp its essence."

A mysterious smile played at the corners of Zhou Yi's mouth as he replied, "I understand. Thank you for your guidance, Brother Shui."

Shui Xuanjin shook his head. He could naturally see that Zhou Yi hadn't truly given up, but it was good to let him encounter a setback. It's only after experiencing a setback that one truly learns a lesson.

Finally, the carriage came to a stop. They had arrived at the imperial realm of the Tianluo Kingdom, having left Shaoming Residence.

After getting off the carriage, Zhou Yi's gaze shifted, and he couldn't help but feel amazed in his heart. The power and influence of the Tianluo Kingdom indeed surpassed that of the Fire Crow Kingdom.

Before their eyes stood a grand palace made of red bricks, with white stone steps dividing into two sides. In the middle, there was a massive dragon sculpture with steps, exuding an aura of solemnity and majesty.

To their surprise, it was Crown Prince Yu Xiaoyi himself who personally came to greet them before the carriage. In front of Shui Xuanjin, Yu Xiaoyi didn't display any airs of a crown prince, instead showing utmost respect as if Shui Xuanjin were his own teacher. As soon as the old man alighted from the carriage, Yu Xiaoyi immediately approached, gently supporting the old man's arm with a smoothness that indicated this was not their first encounter.

Shui Xuanjin nodded slightly toward him, his gaze filled with the doting affection of an elder toward a younger generation.

Upon catching this gaze, Zhou Yi unexpectedly thought of grandfather Bao , who was currently exerting his full force to break through the tenth layer of internal energy in Zhou Family Village. He wondered if the grandfather Bao had successfully achieved his goal.

Ascending the steps, they quickly arrived at the front of the Dragon Pavilion. Looking up, they saw four ferocious dragons Statue perched on the rooftop. In the middle of the two dragons, there was a shining pearl. The two dragons turned their heads, greedily eyeing the pearl that was within reach, extending their enormous claws towards it...

The sculpture of the two dragons playing with the pearl was so lifelike that it could easily deceive the eye.

Zhou Yi's gaze lingered on it for a moment before he withdrew his gaze.

Inside the grand hall, the purple-red pillars depicted flying dragons and dancing phoenixes, intricately carved and vivid, almost coming to life. The walls of the hall were adorned with colorful murals, a feast for the eyes.

Surprisingly, the seating arrangement in the hall followed ancient customs, with numerous seats spread throughout the entire space. With a quick glance, Zhou Yi immediately spotted his Uncle Zhou Quanxin and Zhou Yitian among the attendees. It was somewhat unexpected to see them here considering their status.

Zhou Quanxin and his son nodded slightly in greeting to Zhou Yi but remained seated at the back.

Zhou Yi also nodded in return, but his gaze did not linger on them for long because he had already spotted the presence of a congenital powerhouse sitting in one of the seats in the grand hall.

Each congenital powerhouse possessed a unique aura, and the one sitting in the hall emitted a strong presence.

He sat calmly in the corner of the hall, but upon entering, anyone's first sight and perception seemed to be drawn to this middle-aged man in that corner.

He wore a rare deep red robe that resembled a massive light bulb, emitting boundless radiance and heat, constantly reminding everyone to pay attention.

Zhou Yi had never seen someone who exuded their aura so fearlessly at such a level before.

However, upon sensing his aura, Zhou Yi had to admit that this person indeed had the qualifications to be arrogant. The immense power emanating from him was unparalleled, even surpassing the three congenital powerhouses Zhou Yi had encountered before.

Although this man appeared to be middle-aged in appearance, Zhou Yi had heard from Xue Lie that his actual age was close to a hundred years. However, for a congenital powerhouse, this age was not considered old. If nothing unexpected happened, he still had at least a lifespan of over a hundred years.

Shui Xuanjin and Zhou Yi entered the hall almost simultaneously. The moment they entered, the man immediately opened his eyes. His eyes suddenly lit up, filled with powerful congenital true qi, and his sharp gaze swept over like a blade.

Yu Xiaoyi, who was supporting the old man, inadvertently looked up and met that gaze. Immediately, his eyes felt a sharp pain, as if being pricked by needles, causing extreme discomfort. He realized it was a battle of congenital powerhouse level, and he was merely a hapless bystander caught in the vortex.

Though he quickly closed his eyes, the uncomfortable sensation did not immediately dissipate. Tears welled up in his handsome face and streamed down his cheeks.

Zhou Yi's expression darkened. Stepping forward, he unexpectedly acted before Shui Xuanjin, raising his hands and swiftly forming seals. His ten fingers intertwined, as if a mysterious vortex appeared on his hands. His palms trembled like drums, and an invisible true qi instantly shot out.

When dealing with Lv Xinwen, the true qi he had unleashed had not reached the level of being silent and invisible. However, after studying the true essence of the Earth Seal and Cloud and Rain Seal, he made subtle improvements to his seal technique. The needle-shaped true qi stimulated by the Hidden Needle Seal not only became three times more powerful but also became even more difficult to detect and evade.

Cheng Fu's face slightly changed. He had only been probing earlier and hadn't made a real move. But he never expected that the other party would immediately attack without hesitation. This showed a lack of grace expected of a congenital powerhouse.

He snorted coldly and waved his hand. The garments he wore were loose and voluminous, especially his sleeves, which extended far beyond the normal length. When he waved his hand, those sleeves transformed into a sea of red, colliding with Zhou Yi's needle-shaped true qi.

A crisp sound echoed through the grand hall, like the clash of metal and stone, clear and pleasing to the ears.

Zhou Yi's eyes slightly narrowed, and then he heard Shui Xuanjin's voice ringing out from behind him, "I've long heard that Brother Cheng's robe is made from a combination of Fire Silkworm Silk and Steel Wire obtained from an active volcano. Seeing it now, it truly lives up to its reputation."

Zhou Yi's heart stirred, understanding that Shui Xuanjin's words were meant for him to hear. If he were to engage in an unarmed battle with Cheng Fu, without knowing the details of this robe, he would undoubtedly suffer a great loss.

Cheng Fu stood up slowly, calmly observing Shui Xuanjin. After a moment, he said, "Brother Shui, you flatter me. This is merely a humble robe, far inferior to Brother Shui's discerning eyes."

Shui Xuanjin smiled faintly and gently rubbed Yu Xiaoyi's temple with his hand. Yu Xiaoyi took a breath and opened his eyes. Although his eyes were still slightly swollen, he was no longer in serious condition.

Yu Xiaoyi lowered his head and softly said, "Thank you, Uncle Shui."

Shui Xuanjin pressed his hand firmly, and then he and Zhou Yi took their seats that had been prepared in advance.

As they sat down, the old man chuckled and said, "Zhou brother, thank you for lending a hand."

Zhou Yi smiled awkwardly and replied, "He was the one who embarrassed me; it has nothing to do with you."

As soon as Shui Xuanjin entered the grand hall, Cheng Fu immediately provoked him without any hesitation, clearly trying to force Shui Xuanjin to make a move.

Zhou Yi knew that Shui Xuanjin's physical condition was not suitable for facing a Innate expert. So he took the initiative to act, but how could such intentions escape the perceptive eyes of the old and immortal Shui Xuanjin?

They exchanged a glance, understanding each other's thoughts. Both the old and the young felt as if they had met too late, especially Zhou Yi. Whenever he thought about the short remaining lifespan of the other party, perhaps only a few years, his heart couldn't help but feel a slight pang.

Some people, even if they meet just once, feel like old friends, while others, despite meeting day after day, remain as strangers.

The emotions between people are truly the most elusive and irrational thing in the world.

Even Zhou Yi himself found it somewhat strange that what he did was indeed somewhat irrational. But if one had to consider the consequences in every aspect of life, then living would become too boring.

On the seat next to Cheng Fu, there were two handsome men and women who appeared to be in their early twenties. They had a somewhat similar appearance and exuded an air of grace and nobility that made it hard to look directly at them.

When Zhou Yi's gaze fell upon them, the two of them simultaneously bowed slightly in their seats.

Although these two individuals held high status, in the presence of the congenital powerhouses, they were unwilling to be disrespectful or provoke the displeasure of the congenital powerhouses over trivial matters.

A crisp bell rang out, followed by an elderly man in exquisite attire walking into the hall under the escort of several people.

When he appeared in the grand hall, everyone in the hall stood up, including the two young men and women. However, unlike the others who knelt down in reverence, these two individuals only bowed slightly in greeting.

The old man didn't immediately take his seat but instead approached Shui Xuanjin first, expressing his apology, "Uncle Shui, these are Master Cheng Fu from Kai Rong, as well as the Third Prince and Fifth Princess. They all wished to meet you, so I had to trouble you. Please forgive me, Uncle Shui."

Shui Xuanjin smiled slightly and replied, "Your Majesty, it is my honor to meet the royal family of Kai Rong and the esteemed Master Cheng Fu. You worry too much."

Zhou Yi naturally knew that this was Yu Ruipei, the current king of Tian Luo Kingdom. However, he didn't expect that even with the status of a king, he would show such respect to Shui Xuanjin. But upon further thought, it became clear to him. Shui Xuanjin had close ties with the previous generations of kings and had practically resided in Tian Luo Kingdom for the latter half of his life. Shui Xuanjin had watched kings grow up, establishing a relationship that couldn't be compared to that of other monarchs and the royal protector.

After Yu Ruipei greeted Shui Xuanjin, his gaze fell upon Zhou Yi, and a genuine smile spread across his face. He said, "Master Zhou, it is truly fortunate for our country to have the honor of your presence."

Zhou Yi slightly bent forward and bowed, saying, "Your Majesty, you flatter me."

When facing the ruler of a kingdom, Zhou Yi couldn't be as confident and proud as Shui Xuanjin. After all, the fact that he was only sixteen years old compared to someone who was over two hundred years old made his confidence much weaker.

Yu Ruipei didn't dwell on Zhou Yi for too long. He proceeded to greet the three distinguished guests from Kai Rong and ordered the serving of food and drinks, accompanied by music and dance. The atmosphere in the hall immediately became lively.

The people present in the hall were all renowned figures in Tian Luo Kingdom, representing the pinnacle of the country.

Given Zhou Yi's status, he should have occupied a separate seat. However, when he insisted on sitting with Shui Xuanjin, no one dared to voice any objections.

During the banquet, Zhou Yi often felt a burning gaze directed towards their table. This gaze seemed to penetrate their very beings, as if trying to see through them completely. However, strangely enough, this intense gaze carried no hostility or provocation. It simply left him feeling deeply uncomfortable.

With a slight frown, Zhou Yi whispered, "Shui Xuanjin, what does Cheng Fu want?"

Shui Xuanjin smiled and replied, "He wants to see if I'm truly nearing the end, as the rumors suggest."

Zhou Yi was taken aback and asked, "Hasn't he realized it?"

Shui Xuanjin chuckled, "Of course, he hasn't. Unless he engages me in a real battle, I will remain seated here, and who would dare to underestimate me?"

Zhou Yi opened his mouth to speak but hesitated, unsure of what to say.

Shui Xuanjin smiled and said, "It's strange though, when we first met, I could sense that you had already noticed my physical condition. Could it be that you have cultivated some peculiar technique?"

Zhou Yi smiled wryly and replied, "Shui Xuanjin, to be honest, I haven't cultivated any peculiar techniques. But I could sense that your life seemed to be gradually fading away, which is why I showed that expression."

Shui Xuanjin's face showed surprise, shaking his head with a long sigh. He said, "So it's an innate talent. It's truly admirable."

Zhou Yi knew in his heart that this heightened sensitivity was definitely related to the extraordinary encounter at the bottom of the lake that day.

Suddenly, Shui Xuanjin's voice of resignation reached Zhou Yi's ears, "Cheng Fu didn't see through my true condition today, but I'm afraid there will be troubles in the future. It's truly a headache."

As Zhou Yi looked at Shui Xuanjin's troubled expression, a strong emotion surged within him. He had the urge to take up the mantle of the Guardian Grandmaster, but the words lingered at the tip of his tongue. He managed to hold them back, but a hidden sense of sentiment welled up in his heart, unknown to others.

Chapter 150

The palace banquet went smoothly, perhaps because the King of Cairo was present or because of Zhou Yi's sudden appearance, which made Cheng Fu wary and refrained from further provocation throughout the evening. After enduring the meaningless banquet, Zhou Yi naturally departed with Shui Xuanjin.

Before leaving, he had intended to exchange greetings with his uncle and elder brother, but he sadly discovered that the two had already been engulfed by the surging crowd. After listening intently for a moment, he could only helplessly turn and leave.

These people were all approaching to establish connections, their flattery never ceasing. He understood in his heart that these people feared his innate identity as a strong individual and his association with Shui Xuanjin, which was why they dared not approach. However, if he were to take the initiative and approach them, he could guarantee that there would be no peace in the future.

With this thought in mind, Zhou Yi, lacking any sympathy, departed with Shui Xuanjin. As for Zhou Quanxin and the others, they could leisurely enjoy their socializing. After all, in the future, if

Zhoujiazhuang wanted to prosper under their hands, such occasions would be inevitable.

As for himself, as long as he diligently cultivated and served as a strong support for Zhoujiazhuang, that would be enough.

The wheels of the carriage turned gently, like an unchanged song drifting lightly along the main road. Although he was seated inside the carriage and didn't witness it firsthand, Zhou Yi still sensed that wherever this carriage traveled, people would bow and even prostrate themselves.

These people were ordinary citizens of Tianluo Kingdom, and no one forced them to do so. They bowed before this carriage solely because it carried an old man who had guarded Tianluo Kingdom for over a hundred years.

As Zhou Yi witnessed the devout gestures of these people, he felt their thoughts. He sighed inwardly, realizing that if these people were to know that the old man before their eyes could no longer protect them for much longer, he wondered how saddened they would be.

Finally, the carriage stopped in front of Shao Ming Ju Residence. Shui Xuanjin stretched and yawned, saying, "Zhou brother, I'm going to rest now. You should rest too."

Zhou Yi was surprised. "Rest?"

"Yes," Shui Xuanjin's ears flickered like fans, and he continued, "I assure you, I won't eavesdrop on your activities anymore. You can do whatever you want without worrying about this old man."

An annoyed expression crossed Zhou Yi's face, but Shui Xuanjin immediately strode away, leaving behind only his hearty laughter echoing in the surroundings. The nearby attendants near the carriage looked on in astonishment. They couldn't possibly know why Master Shui suddenly laughed so joyfully, but they assumed it must have something to do with Master Zhou. The thoughts of innate powerhouses are truly unfathomable.

Shaking his head, Zhou Yi returned alone to the courtyard. Just as he entered, Yuan Lixun came out of the house, handing him a hot towel that had been prepared for him.

Zhou Yi took it and casually wiped his face. Yuan Lixun spoke in a soft voice, "Young Master, I have transcribed the secret manual for you."

Zhou Yi's eyes brightened, immediately recalling Shui Xuanjin's large ears and his terrifying, unparalleled sense of hearing. Even with the use of ShunFeng Er for eavesdropping, he hadn't detected the slightest hint. Such methods were truly extraordinary.

"Excellent, give me the handwritten copy. I want to cultivate."

Yuan Lixun turned and left, returning a moment later with both the handwritten copy and the original manuscript. Zhou Yi opened the handwritten copy and glanced through it, nodding in satisfaction. "You did a great job," he said, pausing for a moment before adding, "Much better than me."

Yuan Lixun's heart finally settled, and a look of relief and enchanting smile appeared on her face. Zhou Yi was slightly taken aback. He realized that although Yuan Lixun wasn't the most beautiful person he had ever seen, at this moment, she was undoubtedly the most captivating to him.

Clearing his throat, Zhou Yi stood up and said, "I'll go take a look at the manual. You should rest." As he uttered the word "rest," he suddenly remembered the teasing of Old Man Shui Xuanjin, causing his face to blush slightly. He swiftly turned and left.

Yuan Lixun was stunned for a moment, recalling Zhou Yi's tone just now, which resembled the way a husband would speak to his wife. A sweet feeling inexplicably arose within her, and her cheeks flushed slightly.

※※※※

In just a few ups and downs, Zhou Yi arrived at the small stream in the courtyard. This stream was a natural feature of the courtyard, partly created by nature and partly by human intervention. However, during its excavation, every effort was made to maintain its original appearance, leaving almost no trace of alteration.

Sitting on a stone bench beside the stream, Zhou Yi calmed his mind and opened the handwritten copy of the manual. He had already read through its contents once, but there was a vast difference between reading and actually practicing. Truly mastering the techniques outlined in the manual was far from easy.

He sat quietly, silently reciting and memorizing the contents of the manual. After a whole hour, he closed the manual and half-closed his eyes, contemplating its contents in deep concentration.

Gradually, his ears started to elongate, extending and unfurling. With the power of an innate powerhouse and the guidance of the manual, it wasn't particularly difficult to change certain physical features of the body. However, the challenge lay in simultaneously altering external characteristics while unleashing the miraculous effects of the techniques. ShunFeng Er truly were an extraordinary skill.

This technique emphasized a single word: listening. But this form of listening was not ordinary; it was a miraculous technique that pushed the limits of human hearing. In the past, before Zhou Yi had attained his innate power, he had experimented with gathering and focusing his inner energy within his ears at Xujiabao. This had heightened his hearing to the extent that he could almost visualize scenes in his mind that he hadn't seen with his own eyes.

The ShunFeng Er technique followed a similar principle but was more refined and systematic than the experiences Zhou Yi had previously explored on his own. Of course, in terms of effectiveness, the difference between the two was immense.

Zhou Yi gradually circulated his true qi, and his ears reached an exaggerated state. Though not as large as Shui Xuanjin's, they had grown nearly half their original size. A gentle breeze blew by the stream, causing Zhou Yi's ears to sway lightly. A faint smile appeared on his lips because he could now hear the sound of the wind.

The wind conveyed events happening in the distance through its wondrous sound. In Zhou Yi's mind, a marvelous picture instantly formed. Within the garden, vibrant flowers of various colors swayed in the fragments of light carried by the wind. The stream absorbed the fragrant essence of the earth, nurturing the flora that bathed in its waters and absorbed nutrients from nature, thriving and growing.

Amongst the flowers and plants, countless insects emitted extremely subtle sounds that would be impossible for ordinary people to hear. These sounds merged with the symphony of nature, creating a unique composition. It was a brand-new world that brought Zhou Yi an entirely different sensation.

He finally understood that his once proud hearing ability was nothing but rubbish in the face of this extraordinary skill. It was like someone who had seen a widescreen digital TV from the 21st century and then went back to watch a 12-inch black-and-white TV from the 1950s—a feeling of disdain would be inevitable.

In his mind, the picture gradually expanded, becoming more and more vivid and realistic. Zhou Yi had a peculiar feeling that he no longer needed his eyes because his ears had completely taken over their function.

Colors...

When the first trace of color appeared in this world, the dry, monotonous black-and-white imagery was instantly replaced by dazzling hues. In the wind, he seemed to have a vague illusion that everything in the world had its own sound.

Whether it was animals, plants, or even the towering ancient mountains, the boundless earth, or the meandering streams, they all had their own unique sounds. In this world, everything was alive.

However, not everyone could hear such wondrous sounds, as the majority of them were beyond the range of human ears.

When one reached the pinnacle of ShunFeng Er cultivation, they could hear these mysterious sounds and perceive a true world through them. Zhou Yi's heart pounded vigorously as his entire focus centered on this technique. He listened intently to every sound around him.

Unbeknownst to him, his ears continued to elongate and enlarge. Suddenly, his half-closed eyes trembled, and an ecstatic smile spread across his face. His ears, which had previously elongated and enlarged, instantly returned to their original state, without any trace of abnormality. The changes that had just occurred seemed like a strange dream that never happened.

Yuan Lixun finally emerged from the room. She stood at a distance, observing Zhou Yi without disturbing him. She knew that he was currently practicing the extraordinary technique she had transcribed, even though she couldn't comprehend or understand it herself. But it was evident that Zhou Yi was immersed in it.

However, Yuan Lixun suddenly had a feeling that Zhou Yi, the flowers, the grass, the water—everything before her seemed to have become still. Time appeared to freeze at this moment, turning into a painting, an eternal and unchanging picture before her eyes.

In an elegant room within Shao Ming Ju Residence, Shui Xuanjin, who had been resting with closed eyes, suddenly opened his eyes. After a brief hesitation, his ears trembled for a while before decisively enlarging once again.

He listened intently for the sound he wanted to hear from a particular direction, but to his astonishment, he couldn't hear it. His ShunFeng Er seemed to have lost their former power at this moment, an unprecedented occurrence. However, he understood in his heart that it wasn't because that person had left Shao Ming Ju Residence but rather because he had entered a rare and almost unimaginable realm.

He felt a deep envy in his heart. As an innate powerhouse, every time he entered this realm, he gained unexpected and tremendous benefits. In his over 200 years of life, he had never experienced a moment of enlightenment. But Zhou Yi, at just sixteen years old, had seemingly grasped the intricacies of the world, comprehended the ups and downs of human existence. Could it be that at this age, he had already seen through the complexities of life?

He let out a long sigh. Such a genius truly couldn't be judged by ordinary standards.

However, he didn't know that Zhou Yi had actually entered this state of enlightenment before.

※※※※

The wind, the qi of heaven and earth, flowed boundlessly without discrimination of status or superiority.

As the wondrous sound of the wind brought more and more sounds into Zhou Yi's ears, as the painting in his mind suddenly came to life, he felt the wind... It was the power of the wind, the power of the air.

In this world, as long as something existed, it had its own sound. Whether speaking or in motion, as long as it existed, it would influence the air and be captured by the power of the wind.

When ShunFeng Er reached its pinnacle, what one heard was the power of the wind, the power of the air.

Everything within the courtyard was under his control, and he himself had completely merged into this environment. Suddenly, his tightly closed eyes seemed to transcend countless times and spaces, allowing him to see the scene he had long yearned for.

He stood at the peak of a mountain, watching the gentle mountain rain falling from the sky, witnessing the ever-changing endless clouds enveloping the mountains. At this moment, the wind blew, passing through the mountains, the clouds, and the mist.

A clear understanding emerged in Zhou Yi's mind. He stood up, forming hand seals with both hands—a combination of the Cloud and Rain Seal, the Earth Seal, and the Hidden Needle Seal. He took a step forward and moved through the courtyard, his figure resembling the wind, the rain, and the clouds—ethereal and enshrouded in a mist that seemed to envelop the entire world.

In this mist, pouring rain fell incessantly, creating a space entirely his own. Under the guidance of the wind's power, he felt this opportunity and once again entered a state of enlightenment, this time about clouds and rain. He successfully fused the three hand seals with his Cloud and Rain Soaring Technique.

From then on, an intimate connection was formed, and there was no distinction between him and the elements. He could feel the vast and mysterious power between heaven and earth—the wind, the rain, the clouds, and the mist. These forces intertwined through the wind, becoming his unique power.

A vast amount of heavenly and earthly qi surged wildly around Zhou Yi's body. His body seemed like an abyss, absorbing all the innate true qi into his being. Gradually, his body emitted a radiant glow, and the white light became even more dazzling in the twilight.

Fortunately, this area had been designated as a restricted zone by Shui Xuanjin, and no one except Yuan Lixun had witnessed such a remarkable sight. The immense influx of innate true qi cleansed Zhou Yi's physique, making his body more resilient and powerful.

One by one, the over 300 acupoints on his body lit up. They resembled tiny vortexes, greedily absorbing the seemingly inexhaustible heavenly and earthly qi, just like Zhou Yi's body.

Zhou Yi faintly sensed that when all the acupoints on his body were filled with the power of heaven and earth, a new transformation would occur. Perhaps then he could achieve another breakthrough in martial arts and enter a new realm.

However, to completely fill all of them with innate true qi was no easy task. Even in this state of enlightenment, Zhou Yi had no certainty that he could accomplish it.

As the heavenly and earthly qi fluctuated significantly, Shui Xuanjin within Shao Ming Ju Residence couldn't help but wear a wry smile. In his lifetime, he had traveled far and wide, even encountering exceptional talents in the distant eastern kingdom with unparalleled potential. Yet, even those prodigies seemed dim compared to this moment.

Although he had no knowledge of what exactly was happening to Zhou Yi, how far his enlightenment had reached, the sight before him left Shui Xuanjin in awe.

But anyone who could stir up the power of heaven and earth to this extent would undoubtedly experience a profound transformation through this enlightenment. Shui Xuanjin was almost certain that after Zhou Yi completed this enlightenment, there would be a tremendous change as if he was reborn.

When Shui Xuanjin first met Zhou Yi, he could sense his extraordinary potential, but he still had confidence in his own strength. With over 200 years of cultivation, although he hadn't made further progress on the path of innateness, he had reached the pinnacle of this stage. His innate true qi far surpassed Zhou Yi's in terms of quantity.

However, at this moment, when the old man felt the powerful fluctuations of heavenly and earthly qi in the surroundings, his confidence began to waver. Perhaps, when they meet again, he would no longer be able to suppress the young man solely based on the total amount of true qi.

Zhou Yi's body finally disappeared right in front of Yuan Lixun's eyes. In her vision, the entire courtyard vanished, leaving only a mass of clouds and mist enveloping the surroundings.

However, inexplicably, she didn't feel panicked or lost. It seemed to be because she believed that Zhou Yi wouldn't harm her.

Suddenly, her vision blurred, and all the clouds and mist dissipated, as if the sky had cleared up. The buildings, gardens, and flowing water reappeared before her eyes. And there stood Zhou Yi next to the stream, with the peculiar manual placed on the stone table beside him.

It all felt like a dream, one she didn't want to wake up from. Zhou Yi turned his head, giving her a gentle smile. Yuan Lixun could clearly sense his joy. For some reason, her heart also filled with delight. At this moment, their hearts seemed to be connected, sharing this wonderful feeling.

Finally, as the sky darkened, the last ray of light vanished from the world. Yuan Lixun seemed to sense it. Zhou Yi nodded slightly towards her, and then his figure disappeared into the night.

Chapter 151

The night breeze slithered through, causing the grand flags atop the palace to flutter and unfurl chaotically.

A gentle gust of wind passed through, weaving its way past countless guards, drifting before their eyes, and entering the royal estate.

Unseen by anyone, and imperceptible to all, what had just swept by was not merely a breeze, but a person—a person made of wind.

Swift and agile in his movements, he seemed to transform into a gust of wind itself, drifting into this heavily guarded royal estate.

Suddenly, he came to a halt, in a secluded corner where a pristine stone bench sat, unblemished by dust, even in such a place. Inwardly sighing, Zhou Yi couldn't help but lament the stark difference in quality between the servants of the Zhou family estate and their counterparts within the royal grounds.

He gently seated himself on the stone bench, his two ears trembling ever so slightly.

This time, his ears did not undergo the exaggerated enlargement they had before. They merely quivered, akin to an ordinary person gently stretching and flexing their ears when pulling at their scalp.

When ShunFeng Er first began cultivating their abilities, under the saturation of true qi, their ears would elongate and stretch to maximize the effect.

However, once they comprehended the true essence of wind's power, everything returned to simplicity. Even if they circulated true qi to their ears, there would be no noticeable external changes.

And that, is the true pinnacle of mastering this technique.

Zhou Yi's sudden enlightenment not only allowed him to merge clouds and rain into a seamless whole but also granted him an understanding of the essence of wind's power. In terms of achieving mastery in this art, he had even surpassed Shui Xuanjin, who had immersed himself in it for hundreds of years.

This is the enlightenment effect that innate experts dream of and desire, but it is elusive and cannot be sought after.

Faint strands of sound entered his ears, the sound of the wind and the vibrations of the air. No sound could escape his detection.

Swiftly, a rich and vibrant virtual world appeared in his mind. He heard and "saw" everything within the royal estate.

The innate expert he encountered today at the royal banquet, Cheng Fu , stood quietly in a courtyard, gazing up at the sky as if contemplating something.

His expression was unusually grave, filled with deep confusion, as if he had encountered an unsolvable problem.

However, to Zhou Yi's relief, the innate expert did not notice his presence. Even though Zhou Yi could feed back every move and action of Cheng Fu in his mind, there was no sign that Cheng Fu had sensed anything.

At last, he understood why he had not noticed Shui Xuanjin's eavesdropping when he was secretly observing Yuan Lixun transcribing the secret manual. It was because the effect of the ShunFeng Er technique was incredibly powerful, reaching an unimaginable level. However, this technique could only be effective in this particular aspect and had limited practical value in formal combat.

Suddenly, two people walked side by side.

The security within the royal estate was extremely tight, so only those close to Cheng Fu could approach him so easily.

Although the two individuals had yet to speak, Zhou Yi had already "heard" their appearances from the sounds carried by the flowing air.

They were the Third Prince, Zhan Zhichao, and the Fifth Princess, Zhan Zhiyan, from the Kingdom of Kai Rong.

"Master Cheng..." A pleasant and melodious voice resonated from Zhan Zhiyan's lips.

Cheng Fu finally withdrew his gaze from the distance and focused on the beautiful face of the Fifth Princess. He asked, "Your Highness, is there something you need?"

Zhan Zhiyan respectfully bowed to him and said, "Master Cheng, the guards informed me that you have been standing here since evening, without even partaking in dinner."

Cheng Fu smiled wryly and replied, "Thank you for your concern, Your Highness, but I am fine."

The Zhan siblings exchanged a glance, and Zhan Zhichao took a step forward, showing a much more respectful demeanor. He even appeared to be somewhat like a disciple in the presence of his master.

"Master Cheng, were you contemplating the Dao just now?" Zhan Zhichao asked.

"No," Cheng Fu shook his head. "Entering the realm of contemplation is not an easy task. It's not something one can achieve easily." He sighed lightly, then raised his head and said, "Have you found out about that person's background?"

Zhou Yi grew suspicious, wondering who could have captured Cheng Fu's attention to such an extent. Just then, Zhan Zhichao spoke up confidently, "Master Cheng, I have already sent my subordinates to investigate. The person who accompanied Master Shui Xuanjin to the palace today is a newly recognized innate expert from Linlang County. It is said that this expert has only stepped into the innate realm for less than a year, and..." He paused, hesitated for a moment, and then said in a tone even he couldn't believe, "It seems that this expert is likely not yet twenty years old this year."

Cheng Fu's expression suddenly became quite intriguing. His cheeks twitched slightly as he said, "What kind of people did you send? While it's possible for innate experts in their twenties to exist in this world, they certainly wouldn't appear in Tian Luo Kingdom."

Zhan Zhichao's face was filled with shame as he replied, "Yes, I will send someone to investigate again."

Although Zhou Yi's appearance seemed very young, the appearance of an innate expert couldn't be judged based on surface appearances, as that would be the least reliable method. Moreover, Cheng Fu and the others would never believe that Zhou Yi had truly entered the innate realm before the age of twenty.

Cheng Fu waved his hand lightly and said, "Forget it, let's not make a fuss about it for now. If we attract their attention, it won't be good. Anyway, when we return, there will naturally be news."

Zhan Zhichao hesitated for a moment and said, "Master Cheng, speaking of this Master Zhou, it reminds me of someone."

"Who?"

"Do you remember the group of bandits we encountered at the border between Kai Rong Kingdom and Tian Luo Kingdom?"

Cheng Fu snorted lightly and said, "You mean those loyal dogs kept by the Second Prince?"

"Exactly," Zhan Zhichao respectfully replied. "Last month, we received intelligence that those bandits suddenly raided the county city of Tai Cang in Tian Luo Kingdom, hundreds of miles away. Somehow, they managed to provoke an innate expert, who single-handedly slaughtered two thousand of them. Even the five top-tier martial artists at the tenth layer of inner energy were among the casualties, all dead."

Cheng Fu was momentarily taken aback and exclaimed, "Slaughtering two thousand people with a single stroke? That's utter nonsense."

Zhan Zhichao forced a bitter smile and said, "Master Cheng, we also know that this is purely a rumor, but those bandits did indeed disappear. Moreover, according to the accounts of some who managed to escape, the appearance of that innate expert does match the description of Master Zhou today."

Zhou Yi, who was eavesdropping, could hardly believe his ears. He had always thought that the bandits in Tai Cang County were just bandits living in Tai A County. But according to Cheng Fu and Zhan Zhichao, they were somehow related to Kai Rong Kingdom and were dogs raised by the Second Prince.

For a moment, it felt as if the blood in Zhou Yi's body had frozen.

Finally, he understood one thing. Why the Linlang Lin family, with its strength, would allow those bandits to roam freely, why the Tian Luo Kingdom, with its control over four counties and military power, would be powerless against them, and why, despite the presence of Shui Xuanjin, an innate expert, they allowed those bandits to survive on the border.

Behind all of this, there was the shadow of Kai Rong Kingdom.

His breathing quickened slightly, and his skin seemed to radiate a faint heat.

He remembered the dilapidated county city and the tragic deaths of the people. Gradually, a strand of fierce and murderous intent surged uncontrollably from the depths of his heart.

"Hmph, even if Tian Luo Kingdom has gained a Guardian Grandmaster, what difference does it make? We, Kai Rong Kingdom, have a total of ten innate experts." A sneer escaped Zhan Zhiyan's lips, her beautiful eyes blinking with a different kind of charm. However, the words she spoke were chilling, "Brother, why don't we ask the Ancestor to intervene? We can accuse him of killing our Kai Rong Kingdom's troops and demand compensation."

"Nonsense," Zhan Zhichao said with a wry smile. "Those fools went to Tai Cang County on their own. Not only did they breach the county's defenses, but they also besieged the stronghold of one of the esteemed families. They committed a grave offense. Even if they died, it would be in vain. We're still trying to distance ourselves from them, so how could we possibly intervene on their behalf?"

Zhan Zhiyan chuckled and said, "Brother, that's just an excuse. From what I know, this Master Zhou has been in Tian Luo Kingdom for less than five days, and he is not even the Guardian Grandmaster of Tian Luo Kingdom." A proud smile appeared on her face as she continued, "Think about it. Master Zhou used to be unknown, so it's certain that he recently stepped into the innate realm. The Tian Luo Kingdom's royal family invited him from Tai Cang County with the clear intention of appointing him as the Guardian Grandmaster.

But if our Ancestor were to intervene and promise to open the royal treasury and bestow some divine treasures upon him if he joins our Kai Rong Kingdom, do you think he would be tempted?"

Zhan Zhichao fell silent. Neither the royal treasury nor the divine treasures were within his authority to decide. Whether or not to recruit a newly emerged innate expert at such a tremendous cost was also beyond his decision-making power.

Suddenly, Cheng Fu spoke up, saying, "It's worth it."

Both Zhan siblings looked up at him, their eyes filled with indescribable astonishment, even Zhan Zhiyan.

Her suggestion had been made mostly in jest, but she hadn't expected Cheng Fu to firmly conclude with a single word. It greatly exceeded her expectations.

Why do you say that, Master Cheng?" Zhan Zhichao asked.

Cheng Fu's expression became extremely solemn as he replied, "You sent someone to inquire, didn't you? He is not even twenty yet, and for a person under twenty to be an innate expert, it is worth recruiting him at any cost."

Zhan Zhichao couldn't help but smile wryly. "Master Cheng, didn't you also say that it is impossible for a person under twenty to be an innate expert in Tian Luo Kingdom?"

"It is indeed impossible, but this person's appearance is so young. Even if he is not under twenty, he certainly won't be over fifty," Cheng Fu affirmed. "To step into the innate realm before the age of fifty is already a remarkable achievement."

The Zhan siblings exchanged a glance, their hearts stirred simultaneously. In their minds, they believed that as long as the

Ancestor were to intervene, Zhou Yi would undoubtedly choose Kai Rong Kingdom without hesitation, abandoning Tian Luo Kingdom. After all, people strive for higher positions, and water flows to lower ground. Since he is an innate powerhouse, he would understand how to secure a better future.

However, they were unaware that it was precisely because of their conversation that Zhou Yi did not lose control on the spot.

From the words of Zhan ZhiYan, he learned that within the kingdom of Kai Rong, there are a total of ten guardian masters, and among them, one is undoubtedly far superior to the others. Otherwise, Zhan ZhiYan would not possess such a near-blind confidence in him.

The strength of Kai Rong Kingdom was so formidable that Zhou Yi, at this moment, was utterly incapable of handling it. Realizing this, he immediately restrained his thoughts and suppressed the overwhelming urge to kill.

However, in his heart, Zhou Yi had already engraved the Second Prince of Kai Rong Kingdom. He was not a righteous hero who would openly challenge an entire kingdom for the sake of the tragic deaths in Tai Cang County. But if there was an opportunity in the future, he would not hesitate to slay that Second Prince.

Taking a deep breath, Zhou Yi rose from the stone bench. The night grew deeper, and he was ready to leave. He had achieved a lot through tonight's enlightenment and the mastery of his techniques. Accidentally stumbling upon this conversation had provided him with valuable insights. It was unnecessary to listen any further.

However, just as he was about to leave, he heard Zhan Zhiyan ask once again, "Master Cheng, if you haven't achieved enlightenment, why did you spend an entire evening here?"

Zhou Yi's footsteps halted. In truth, he was also curious about this question. It seemed unreasonable for an innate expert to solemnly stay in the same place without any apparent reason.

Cheng Fu let out a soft sigh. It seemed that he favored Zhan Zhiyan more. After pondering for a moment, he finally said, "Did His Majesty mention the purpose of our journey before we came here?"

"Father, the Emperor, mentioned it before," Zhan Zhichao half-bowed and said, "The Emperor said that the Guardian Master of Tian Luo Kingdom, Shui Xuanjin, is of old age, and it is rumored that his lifespan is not long. He instructed us to come and investigate the truth. If it is indeed true, then the tribute of money and provisions from Tian Luo Kingdom will have to be doubled in the future. But if it turns out to be a rumor and Master Shui Xuanjin is in good health, then as compensation, the annual tribute from Tian Luo Kingdom can be reduced by ten percent."

"Correct," Cheng Fu nodded slightly. "When I met Shui Xuanjin today, I immediately provoked him, wanting to test him. I was hoping to spar with him and discern his true abilities. Unfortunately, that person intervened and disrupted my plans."

Zhan Zhichao's expression tightened as he asked, "Master Cheng, did you discern his true strength during today's banquet?"

Cheng Fu's face grew even more solemn. "Although I did not take action again today, based on my observations, there seems to be something amiss with Shui Xuanjin's body. That rumor was not unfounded."

Zhan Zhichao's eyes instantly lit up. "That's excellent! Over the past century, Tian Luo Kingdom has developed rapidly, expanding from a single county to four counties. If Shui Xuanjin were to pass away, it would undoubtedly be a significant decline in the country's power, and they would no longer pose a threat to us."

However, Cheng Fu shook his head slightly. "Third Prince, I used to think the same way, but..." His tone grew heavy. "This afternoon, there was a powerful fluctuation of aura coming from that direction. The intensity of that aura was earth-shattering. Even I cannot compare to it."

The Zhan siblings' faces changed drastically. Zhan Zhiyan exclaimed, "Master Cheng, then this rumor..."

Cheng Fu let out a bitter smile. "Since he still possesses such formidable power, that rumor naturally falls apart."

Zhan Zhiyan blinked twice and suddenly asked, "Why would Shui Xuanjin do this? Could he have already guessed our intentions?"

Cheng Fu responded coldly, "He hasn't guessed. However, this is Shui Xuanjin showcasing his own strength, his response to my provocation today."

In a corner of the estate, Zhou Yi stumbled, almost falling back onto the stone bench. This guy is really too sensitive...

The Zhan siblings exchanged glances, and Zhan Zhiyan whispered, "Master Cheng, are you sure that aura was emitted by Shui Xuanjin? Could it be another master at the Innate level?"

"Impossible," Cheng Fu said decisively. "I have sensed the power of the wind, a power that only a few individuals in the Northwestern countries can master, and Shui Xuanjin is one of them. As for the master you mentioned, just by looking at their appearance, it is evident that they have recently stepped into the Innate realm. To evoke such a powerful manifestation of cosmic energy, even with prior enlightenment experiences, it would require at least twenty years of arduous cultivation." He let out a cold snort and continued, "If the information you gathered suggests that this person has been an Innate master for twenty years, then there might be a slight possibility. However, if they have just recently attained Innate status, it is absolutely impossible."

Indeed, it would be impossible for an ordinary Innate master to harness such a powerful cosmic energy within one year of attaining that level. However, Zhou Yi had entered the state of enlightenment multiple times in this short year, and his achievements could not be measured by conventional standards.

Zhan Zhichao nodded slightly and asked, "Master Cheng, what should we do since Shui Xuanjin has issued this challenge?"

"What should we do?" Cheng Fu snorted coldly. "Since he has issued the challenge, I certainly won't back down. We will rest for seven days. After that, it will be the time for Tian Luo Kingdom's royal hunt. At that moment, we will demand a challenge against the Guardian Grandmaster of Tian Luo Kingdom. We will use the ten percent tribute granted by His Majesty as a wager. I want to test whether Shui Xuanjin's wind-based power, honed through a hundred years of diligent cultivation, can overpower my enlightened fire-based power." He extended his hands, and a faint red glow appeared, exuding a strong sense of confidence. "The Zhan siblings' eyes also gleamed with excitement. They clenched their fists, brimming with a sense of absolute victory.

Meanwhile, Zhou Yi in the distance looked up at the sky. He suddenly realized that there were some things he couldn't predict or control.

Chapter 152

Two majestic eagles soared through the sky, dancing amidst the billowing white clouds. They would dart towards the sun, circling around it, transforming into two tiny black dots, and then gracefully spread their wings, gliding downwards like creatures swimming in an ocean of air.

Suddenly, a piercing whistle echoed from the ground below, as if responding to a hidden command. The two eagles swiftly changed their course, diving steeply towards the earth. Their bodies brushed the ground, causing a spray of blood and the pitiful cries of a hapless mountain chicken.

In an instant, the vibrant and colorful mountain chickens were caught in their grasp, and the eagles swiftly carried their prey to the vast open field outside the woods. A triumphant laughter erupted, resonating through the air. Lord YuRuiPei, the ruler of Tianluo

Kingdom, laughed heartily, and with a wave of his hand, attendants promptly stepped forward to attend to the magnificent hunting falcons.

This was the Royal Garden, situated twenty miles away from the capital of Tianluo Kingdom. Within the garden, there lay an entrance that led to the depths of the mountains—a special hunting ground reserved for the royal family and nobles of high status. After years of hunting, it had become increasingly difficult to find formidable prey within the garden. To secure a bountiful harvest, one had to venture deeper into the mountains, far beyond the garden's boundaries.

Despite the season not being optimal for hunting, Lord YuRuiPei still ordered the gathering of warriors to accompany the prince and princess of Kairong Kingdom, along with the master protector of the kingdom, for a hunting expedition.

This decision was closely tied to the flourishing martial prowess of the northwestern nations.

Witnessing the eagles' remarkable performance, Lord YuRuiPei's joy knew no bounds. He exclaimed, "Gentlemen, the esteemed envoys of Kairong Kingdom have arrived. Our warriors of Tianluo Kingdom shall welcome them with utmost enthusiasm!" His voice carried far, resonating through the vast expanse for miles to hear.

Although his internal energy cultivation had yet to reach the pinnacle of the tenth level, Lord YuRuiPei possessed strength equivalent to around the eighth level. With the support of Shuixuan Jin, his position as the ruler of Tianluo Kingdom remained as unshakable as Mount Tai.

Beside him, a resounding roar erupted, igniting the excitement in the eyes of over a thousand individuals.

Lord YuRuiPei turned around and asked, "Your Highness, will your men not participate?"

The third prince, Zhan Zhichao, smiled faintly and replied, "Since His Majesty the King has extended an invitation, let our young warriors showcase their skills as well." Clearly, he had come prepared, taking confident strides forward with four attendants closely following behind.

Lord YuRuiPei's expression slightly changed as he said, "Does the third prince intend to hunt personally?"

Zhan Zhichao burst into laughter and declared, "Indeed! In Kairong Kingdom, we uphold martial traditions. As a prince, I must set an example. How could I miss such a grand event?"

Lord YuRuiPei's face stiffened. Suddenly, a figure dashed out from not far behind him and deeply bowed, saying, "Father, what the third prince said is true. Your child is not talented, but I also wish to join the hunting party."

Everyone raised their gazes and nodded inwardly. The one stepping forward at this moment was none other than Yu Xiaoyi, the Crown Prince of Tianluo Kingdom.

Lord YuRuiPei's face eased slightly as he gave him a deep look, his eyes filled with undisguised satisfaction and admiration.

"Very well. Since that's the case, let the hunt begin. Off you go."

With a command from the King, numerous figures dashed towards the nearby forest.

Outside the garden, one could see beautifully crafted tents scattered across the grounds. These tents were set up temporarily by Lord YuRuiPei and his companions for this hunting expedition.

The decision to refrain from constructing permanent structures here was purportedly to avoid excessive disturbance to the creatures within the garden.

At this moment, inside one of the tents, Zhou Yi held a steaming cup of milk tea handed to him by Yuan Lixun. He took a sip and watched the crowd rushing off, unable to help but shake his head slightly. It was hard to call this a hunting expedition; it felt more like a farce. While humans feared fierce beasts, the same could be said for the beasts fearing humans, especially when they gathered in such a grand manner.

With so many people swarming in, any intelligent beast would choose to temporarily avoid their presence. Unless they entered the deep mountain pass, there would be no fruitful results.

His gaze suddenly focused as he recognized two familiar figures among the crowd. It turned out his Uncle Zhou Quanxin and older brother Zhou Yitian were also mingling in the crowd. With their strength and Uncle's familiarity with the forest, as long as they didn't encounter spirit beasts, there should be no unexpected incidents. In such a bustling place, the existence of spirit beasts would be truly incredible.

Therefore, Zhou Yi merely glanced at them and quickly averted his gaze. He trusted them, father and son, without a doubt.

Retracting his gaze, Zhou Yi looked at the steam wafting from his teacup, his mind as hazy as the clouds. It had been seven days since he overheard Cheng Fu and others' conversation. In these seven days, Zhou Yi had been constantly hesitant and indecisive, but he hadn't revealed the content of those conversations to Shuixuan Jin.

Until now, the seven days had passed, and the hunting activities were officially commencing. Tomorrow at this time, when the hunting concluded, it would most likely be the moment Cheng Fu issued his challenge.

Zhou Yi knew he could no longer delay.

Yuan Lixun looked at Zhou Yi in surprise. In his eyes, there seemed to be a hint of confusion. It was a gaze she rarely witnessed during their time together.

Unexplainably, a strong desire surged within her to dispel that trace of confusion. Although her rationality told her that if even Young Master couldn't solve the problem, she would be powerless as well, she couldn't help but softly ask, "Young Master, is something bothering you?"

Zhou Yi was taken aback. He turned his head and saw the worry contained within her bright, big eyes. His heart warmed involuntarily, and he let out a gentle sigh. "Yes, there is something that I can't make a final decision about, and it's been causing me great distress."

Yuan Lixun hesitated before saying, "Can you tell me about it? Perhaps, after speaking about it, you'll feel better."

Zhou Yi's lips twitched slightly. He had intended to tell her, but for some reason, the words got stuck in his throat. He introspected and suddenly realized that he didn't want her to know about his eavesdropping in the royal garden.

If she were to discover that he had engaged in such behavior, would her image of him be greatly diminished?

Zhou Yi bitterly smiled, wondering when he had become so sensitive. He shook his head, and a trace of disappointment flashed across Yuan Lixun's face. However, before she could offer further consolation, Zhou Yi spoke again, "If someone unintentionally does something, and although it's not necessarily a bad thing, it leads another person to misunderstand, a misunderstanding that could have grave consequences. But this consequence wouldn't affect the first person at all. What do you think? Should the first person ignore it or..."

As he spoke, Zhou Yi lifted his head and gazed at Yuan Lixun, as if searching for the ultimate answer on her beautiful face.

Yuan Lixun was slightly taken aback. Although Zhou Yi's words were vague, she understood them. Their eyes met for a brief moment before hers quickly averted, like a startled deer. Her heart raced with excitement and a hint of secret joy. It was a feeling she couldn't fully comprehend.

After a few intense heartbeats, her pulse gradually settled. She lightly bit her lip, carefully pondered, and a rosy blush spread across her cheeks. Yet, the words that came out of her mouth carried a peculiar determination.

"Young Master, my mother always taught me and my younger brother. Every person in this world has their own responsibilities. Some are significant, some are small, and those capable of shouldering great responsibilities do so, while those with lesser abilities handle smaller ones. As long as you do what you can within your capacity, then... it's enough."

Zhou Yi sat calmly, quietly chewing on her words.

Yuan Lixun didn't interrupt him; she simply watched silently by his side. She observed Zhou Yi's eyes gradually brightening as he contemplated. Suddenly, she had a feeling as if she were being drawn into his thoughts.

This man, although a prodigious innate powerhouse, always gave off the impression of being a big boy based on his previous actions. But upon reflection, wasn't it natural? Regardless of his martial cultivation reaching what level, he was still just a sixteen-year-old young man. At this age, isn't one still considered a big boy?

However, at this moment, there seemed to be a subtle transformation in Zhou Yi. It was as if the big boy had shed his youthful awkwardness, exuding the maturity and charm of an adult man.

Yuan Lixun's gaze softened, and this scene seemed to eternally reside in her heart.

Finally, Zhou Yi placed his tea cup down and nodded earnestly towards Yuan Lixun. Sincerely, he said, "Thank you."

"Uh..." Yuan Lixun was momentarily stunned, then quickly regained her senses, feeling quite flustered. It was as if someone had seen through the deepest secret in her heart. The blush on her face appeared even more vibrant, spreading to her ears and neck, as if a tender and sweet aroma was evaporating.

Zhou Yi's eyes brightened. However, at this moment, he had already made a decision in his heart and immediately composed himself, shifting his gaze away.

He softly said, "You're right. No matter what, I am still a person of Tianluo Kingdom." Then, he spoke loudly, "Shuixuan Jin, please come over for a moment."

Although the volume of his words wasn't loud, they resounded incessantly as if whispering in everyone's ears, making it clear to all.

Yuan Lixun opened her mouth in surprise. She never expected Zhou Yi to abruptly invite Shuixuan Jin like this.

In the distance, within the tent area of Kairong Kingdom, Cheng Fu's eyebrows furrowed slightly. A sense of unease seemed to loom over him. However, he immediately dismissed these thoughts, for he couldn't afford any distractions before the upcoming challenge. At this moment, his mind had no room for anything else.

In a flicker, Shuixuan Jin's figure appeared outside the tent and walked in with a smile, sitting down in front of Zhou Yi. Without needing to be told, Yuan Lixun immediately offered another cup of milk tea. Shuixuan Jin took it and drank it all, praising, "This is brewed very well."

Yuan Lixun lowered her head and smiled, saying, "Thank you for the compliment, Master Shuixuan."

Shuixuan Jin glanced outside and sighed, saying, "In the past hundred years, I used to personally participate in every hunting expedition. But now, my temperament has mellowed, and I no longer wish to exert myself."

Zhou Yi was slightly startled and said, "Brother Shuixuan, if you participate, who can compete with you? You would always secure the first place."

Shuixuan Jin chuckled softly and replied, "Who said that? Although I participate every time, I have never boasted about it. I only do it for the enjoyment."

Zhou Yi finally understood. Allowing innate powerhouses to participate in such hunting activities would indeed be considered cheating.

"Alright, you called me here. What's the matter?" Shuixuan Jin set down his cup and casually asked.

Zhou Yi also placed his cup down and looked up, speaking solemnly, "I want to know if Tianluo Kingdom needs to pay tribute to Kairong Kingdom every year."

Shuixuan Jin let out a light sigh and said, "That's right. It's not just our Tianluo Kingdom, but actually one-third of the smaller countries in the northwestern region have to pay a substantial amount of tribute to Kairong Kingdom each year."

"One-third?" Zhou Yi exclaimed, "The three major powers in the northwest?"

Shuixuan Jin nodded slightly and said, "Brother Zhou, as your focus has been on cultivation, you may not be aware of the underlying reasons. In fact, among the northwestern countries, the three major powers are the true rulers, while the rest are subordinate states. To prevent these smaller countries from achieving significant development, the three major powers established tribute requirements, compelling us to send a certain proportion of our tax revenues and resources."

Zhou Yi frowned deeply and asked, "Can't we resist?"

Shuixuan Jin gave a bitter smile and replied, "It's difficult when we're a scattered group..."

With just those four words, he expressed his helplessness entirely.

Indeed, in the northwestern region, apart from the three major powers, there are many countries ranging from four or five counties to just one county in size. The territories of these small countries are constantly shifting. Often, within a few decades, a country changes hands.

However, while changes of power occur, most of them happen through peaceful transitions. When a family loses control over the entire country, a new family naturally rises to replace the old royal family. The old royal family then steps down and becomes a prominent clan within the country.

It is precisely because of this peculiar system of inheritance that the northwest region has so many ancient and prestigious families that have endured for centuries.

Of course, this peculiar system only exists in the northwest. In the eastern Great Shen or the lands governed by the legendary Papal regime in the far west, the situations are much bloodier and more brutal.

Zhou Yi pondered for a moment. He was no longer the clueless young boy he once was. Over the past year, he had come to understand the situation. At the same time, he had a faint sense that there was an even greater force above the three major powers. It was this force that suppressed any discordant voices and gave rise to such peculiar systems of inheritance.

However, all of this seemed too distant and unattainable for the current Zhou Yi.

He took the filled cup in his hand once again and drank it all in one gulp. Then, as if making a decision, he said, "Brother Shuixuan, you should know my true age."

Shuixuan Jin nodded slightly and said, "Indeed, Brother Zhou, you have just turned sixteen this year. It is unprecedented and unparalleled for someone of your age to become an innate master. It is truly extraordinary."

Zhou Yi's face blushed slightly. He said, "Let's not dwell on that. Let's get to the point." He calmly looked into Shuixuan Jin's eyes and continued, "I know that you want me to take on the position of the Guardian Grandmaster of Tianluo Kingdom."

Shuixuan Jin's eyes instantly lit up. He said, "That's right. I know that this request is extremely difficult for a genius like you. However, I am nearing the end of my life and I cannot bear to see the rising Tianluo Kingdom fall into decline again. So, I implore you, Brother Zhou, to reluctantly accept."

As the old man spoke, he stood up from his seated position and deeply bowed to Zhou Yi. Despite his old age, his back remained straight and he bent down without hesitation.

Zhou Yi quickly reached out to support him and said, "Brother Shuixuan, if you can agree to one thing, then I will promise."

Shuixuan Jin suddenly looked up, his eyes revealing a mixture of surprise and joy.

Shuixuan Jin took a deep breath and replied, "As long as your request doesn't involve Yu family's abdication, I promise to fulfill it, regardless of the conditions."

With his status and authority in Tianluo Kingdom, Shuixuan Jin had the power to make such decisions on behalf of the Yu family.

Zhou Yi nodded slightly and said, "Brother Shuixuan, I am still young, and I want to travel the world and pursue higher levels of martial arts. I cannot confine myself to Tianluo Kingdom like you. Therefore, my request is to become the Guardian Grandmaster of Tianluo Kingdom but with the freedom to travel."

Shui Xuanjin was taken aback for a moment, then nodded deeply. "Brother Zhou, you're absolutely right. With your talent and young age, you're destined for even greater achievements. It wouldn't be wise to stay in one place for too long." After a brief pause, he continued, "Brother Zhou, I have a compromise in mind. What do you think?"

"Please, go ahead," Zhou replied.

"Our Tianluo Kingdom is a vassal state to the Kairong Kingdom. As long as the Guardian Grandmaster of our country can gain their recognition or, I should say, their fear, then Tianluo Kingdom can continue to develop peacefully," Shui Xuanjin said with a solemn expression. "If Brother Zhou can personally visit the Kairong Kingdom and defeat any of their experts in the Great Masters Hall, it will ensure ten years of tranquility for our Tianluo Kingdom. From then on, as long as Brother Zhou appears once every ten years and challenges and triumphs over any opponent in the Great Masters Hall, our Tianluo Kingdom will be free from any unwarranted provocation."

Zhou Yi's face showed an intriguing expression. "Shui Xuanjin, are you saying that as long as I can defeat any of the Kairong Kingdom's Great Masters, we can secure ten years of peace for Tianluo?"

"Exactly," Shui Xuanjin's eyes gleamed with anticipation. "The enlightenment you had seven days ago must have significantly advanced your cultivation. Even I can't fathom your true strength. So, if Brother Zhou is willing to take action, I believe you can emerge victorious."

Zhou Yi's gaze shifted in a particular direction, his face forming a sly smile. "Why go through so much trouble when there's a Guardian Grandmaster from the Kairong Kingdom right here?"

Shui Xuanjin's expression changed abruptly, and he quickly cautioned, "Brother Zhou, please don't act rashly. Challenging the Great Masters in the Hall is our privilege as representatives of the smaller kingdoms. It is through these challenges that the distribution of tributes and resources is determined. But if you were to challenge the Kairong Kingdom's experts elsewhere, it would be seen as a deliberate provocation, which could bring danger to our country." He paused for a moment and continued, "Moreover, Cheng Fu, despite being young, possesses a formidable reputation within the Kairong Kingdom. He once traveled to the Southern Isles and experienced a moment of enlightenment in the mouth of a volcano. His strength is unfathomable. It would be better for Brother Zhou to find a different opponent when you visit the Great Masters Hall in the future."

"He's young?" Zhou Yi chuckled and then said, "What if we haven't challenged them, but they, in their capacity as Guardian Grandmasters, challenge us instead?"

Shui Xuanjin was taken aback and replied, "If that's the case, then the outcome would be no different from the challenges in the Great Masters Hall."

Zhou Yi nodded, a mysterious smile crossing his face, and then fell silent.

After a moment of hesitation, Shui Xuanjin glanced in a certain direction, as if he had come to a realization.

※※※※

A day's time flew by like a fleeting moment.

At noon on the following day, a resounding horn echoed through the air above the garden.

The sound of the horn was long and far-reaching, with hundreds of horns sounding simultaneously. Even when deep in the mountains, the sound remained clear.

A gigantic hourglass appeared before everyone's eyes. After the horn ceased, a burly man removed the stopper at the bottom, and the sand began to trickle down, creating a "shua shua" sound.

Moments later, people started returning from the garden one after another.

Once the horn sounded, everyone who entered the garden had to return within an hour. If they failed to reach this place before all the sand in the hourglass ran out, they would lose their eligibility for evaluation.

Entering the depths of the mountains might yield better rewards, but without sufficient strength, there would be no chance of returning within the allotted time. The first group to emerge were naturally the weakest, the group of young nobles who could only wander within the garden. They lacked the ability to venture into the deep mountains. Although they managed to catch some small animals, none of them caught anyone's attention.

As time passed, more and more powerful individuals returned, their prey more dazzling than the previous ones. While there were no spiritual beasts, there were plenty of ordinary ferocious animals.

Zhou Yi sighed inwardly. Hunting these ferocious beasts required not only strong combat skills but also a deep understanding of the jungle. Of course, luck played a crucial role. With so many people entering the mountains simultaneously, it was difficult even to encounter a rabbit, let alone a ferocious beast.

Suddenly, the crowd stirred as the Third Prince of the Kairong Kingdom and his group returned successfully. They were a party of five and had captured three fierce leopards and two fox bears.

This achievement immediately drew everyone's attention. Being able to discover ferocious beasts ahead of so many experts showcased their formidable strength.

After a while, Yu Xiaoyi, Zhou Quanxin, and others returned one after another. Although they had also made fruitful gains, their achievements paled slightly in comparison to Zhan Zhichao. The citizens of Tianluo Kingdom couldn't help but wear slightly gloomy expressions.

Yu Ruipei, however, seemed oblivious and said, "Prince Third, you truly stand out among men. This hunting expedition, you deserve to be in the first place."

A loud cheer erupted from the Kairong Kingdom's tent, while the faces of Yu Xiaoyi and the others grew even more sour.

Suddenly, Zhan Zhichao waved his hand, silencing the cheers. Then, a tall figure stepped out from one of the tents.

The moment this person appeared, all eyes were immediately drawn to him. He was like a colossal sun, radiating brilliance wherever he went.

Zhou Yi's eyes narrowed slightly, and his heart instantly entered a wondrous state of tranquility, undisturbed like an ancient well.

Cheng Fu took slow steps forward, and with each footfall, the atmosphere in the entire garden seemed to freeze.

Yu Ruipei could no longer maintain his composure, a sense of unease creeping into his heart.

Finally, Cheng Fu arrived about thirty meters in front of Yu Ruipei. He lifted his head, his eyes gleaming like the blinding sunlight, firmly locking onto Shui Xuanjin.

"On behalf of His Majesty of the Kairong Kingdom, Cheng Fu requests a battle, wagering one-tenth of your nation's annual tribute for the next ten years. I invite the Guardian Grandmaster of your esteemed country to accept this challenge," Cheng Fu declared.

Outside the garden, a silence fell, where even the sound of a falling pin could be heard.

No one could have anticipated that Cheng Fu would issue such a challenge at this moment, and one that was impossible to refuse.

Everyone knew that if Shui Xuanjin were absent, the battle could be postponed. But now, facing this challenge, even if Shui Xuanjin were to die in the fight, he could not back down.

Shui Xuanjin smiled faintly, showing no signs of surprise, as if he had known all along.

Under the watchful gaze of countless people, he slowly stood up. Though he lacked the overwhelming presence of someone like Cheng Fu, the moment he rose, all the citizens of Tianluo Kingdom felt a sense of reassurance.

Shui Xuanjin had guarded Tianluo for a hundred years, and that intense, almost blind, confidence began to spread instantaneously.

However, only Yu Ruipei, the ruler of Tianluo Kingdom, and Shui Xuanjin's disciple, Xue Lie, still wore extremely grim expressions. Their fists clenched tightly, and there was a hint of undisclosed fear in their eyes.

Just at that moment, a clear and unrestricted voice, like a carefree cloud in the sky, resounded.

"If you seek battle, I shall fight..."

Chapter 153

A gentle breeze rustled through the forest, causing the leaves to softly collide, creating a delicate symphony of whispers. Though subtle, the sound held an undeniable sense of power.

Amidst the wafting tendrils of the gentle wind, a resolute and forceful voice rang out, piercing the serene ambiance like the clash of steel upon steel. It reverberated through the seemingly tranquil royal gardens, landing heavily upon the hearts of all who heard it.

"If you seek battle, I shall fight..."

A figure strode forth with swift and purposeful steps, leaving all in his wake instinctively stepping back. His lean frame, determined countenance, piercing gaze, and tightly closed lips exuded an unwavering resolve, akin to unyielding iron, sweeping over the hearts of those present like a tempestuous storm.

A hint of amusement gleamed in Shui Xuanjin's eyes. When Zhou Yi mentioned that particular matter, he had a moment of realization. And when Cheng Fu unexpectedly issued the challenge, he already understood why Zhou Yi seemed to have anticipated it.

Since Zhou Yi was willing to become the Guardian Grandmaster of Tianluo Kingdom at this moment, he would certainly seize the opportunity to take up the challenge ahead of Shui Xuanjin.

It was a feeling, a pure feeling. Although they hadn't communicated about it, an inexplicable understanding had formed between them.

The smile in Shui Xuanjin's eyes grew even more pronounced. He truly felt happy, not because someone would solve his dilemma, but because before he met his demise, he could form such a profound friendship with someone like Zhou Yi.

Zhou Yi's footsteps appeared slow but fast in reality. It seemed as if he had just emerged from a tent, taking only a few steps, yet he arrived before Cheng Fu.

With a respectful gesture, Zhou Yi exclaimed, "Master Cheng, please..."

Cheng Fu's expression grew extremely solemn as he looked at Zhou Yi, his gaze carrying a hint of complexity. He sighed softly and said, "Master Zhou, today I am representing the Kingdom of Kairong to challenge the Guardian Grandmaster of Tianluo Kingdom. You really shouldn't interfere in this matter."

Zhou Yi burst into laughter, his body suddenly exuding an overwhelming and intense aura. "Master Cheng, perhaps you are unaware, but just a moment ago, I accepted Master Shui's invitation and became the second Guardian Grandmaster of Tianluo Kingdom."

The once calm surroundings suddenly erupted like a boiling cauldron, as if the lid had been lifted off a pot of simmering water. The people present even forgot that there were two Innate Masters among them. They excitedly chattered, seemingly wanting to release their inner joy.

Among the northwestern countries, apart from the three major powers, the number of countries that could have two Guardian Grandmasters definitely did not exceed ten.

If Zhou Yi's words were to spread, it would undoubtedly shake the entire influence surrounding Tianluo Kingdom.

Cheng Fu's gaze instantly became piercing, while a trace of disappointment and annoyance appeared on the faces of the two princes and princesses from the Kingdom of Kairong.

They hadn't expected Zhou Yi to agree to Shui Xuanjin's invitation so quickly. For Innate Masters, such speed seemed a bit hasty.

Cheng Fu's gaze finally locked onto Zhou Yi, silently sensing the aura emanating from him. A peculiar smile suddenly appeared on his face.

Not only him, even Shui Xuanjin, not far away, revealed a trace of surprise in his eyes.

As both of them were Innate Masters, they could feel the potent power of the Metal element emanating from Zhou Yi's aura.

This was a power that had already acquired the essence of the Metal element, a sharp and seemingly indestructible force, akin to a sharp spear that could penetrate through anything in its path.

Shui Xuanjin felt an inexplicable shock in his heart. He had spent so much time with Zhou Yi, and he had even sensed his moments of enlightenment. He had believed that Zhou Yi was undoubtedly an

Innate Master who had mastered the Water element, but had accidentally triggered his hidden Wind element talent while cultivating the Whispering Wind(ShunFeng Er) technique.

However, he could never have imagined that such a powerful Metal element force would suddenly erupt from Zhou Yi. His eyes shimmered with excitement, filled with new anticipation for this seemingly bottomless young man.

Perhaps, in this very situation, he could defeat Cheng Fu, who had a renowned reputation and had also experienced moments of enlightenment.

Lowering his gaze slightly, Cheng Fu spoke with a smirk, "Master Shui, has Tianluo Kingdom decided that Master Zhou will accept our challenge?"

On this matter, he directly questioned Shui Xuanjin, without even asking the King of Tianluo Kingdom. However, Yu Ruipei showed no displeasure, but rather directed her nervous gaze towards Shui Xuanjin.

With a gentle wave of his elderly hand, Shui Xuanjin said, "Since Brother Zhou is the Guardian Grandmaster of Tianluo Kingdom, he naturally has the qualifications to fight. Does Master Cheng not understand this simple principle?"

Cheng Fu burst into a radiant smile, and his aura gradually became immense and abundant.

It was like a long-repressed volcano, gradually erupting at this very moment.

"Master Zhou, I cultivate the power of Fire. If you know you're no match, there's still time to replace yourself." His voice carried weight, but there was a hint of disdain in his tone.

If it were Shui Xuanjin's Wind element power, he would certainly be cautious. But since Zhou Yi cultivated the power of Metal, what was there for him to worry about? In his raging fire, any metal or stone would be reduced to ashes.

Zhou Yi smiled proudly. His hands extended flatly, gradually forming fists, and an eerie metallic hue shimmered on his fists.

Then, he took large strides forward, his fists swiftly moving and casting a barrage of shadows that blotted out the sky, resembling a massive boulder rolling towards Cheng Fu.

Finally, a hint of surprise flickered across Cheng Fu's face. This set of fist techniques was not considered impressive in his eyes. However, the aura emanating from Zhou Yi finally made him feel a touch of apprehension.

In Cheng Fu's eyes, Zhou Yi seemed to have truly transformed into a colossal boulder, rolling heavily towards him.

The power of the Metal element was sharp and unyielding, a pinnacle of impact that could devastate anything on the battlefield.

However, at this moment, Zhou Yi bestowed a different meaning upon his Metal element techniques. Though his fist wind was fierce, it lacked the terrifying sharpness of other Metal techniques. Instead, within this set of Metal techniques, there was a continuous and subtle artistic conception. In Cheng Fu's eyes, he even felt a sensation akin to a meandering stream.

Using Metal techniques, yet striking with the essence of Water techniques.

For a moment, Cheng Fu felt a throbbing headache...

As the intertwined fists drew near, Cheng Fu finally snorted in anger. His palms instantly turned as red as burning coals, and with a slight twist, even the air seemed to become scorching hot.

In an instant, before the onlookers' eyes, it seemed as though a wall of fire had appeared. Countless hands, leaving behind flame-like afterimages, formed a network of attacks in an instant.

Numerous dull sounds reverberated between the two of them, each explosion sounding like someone roaring at the top of their lungs next to their ears.

In just a few breaths' time, many people covered their ears and stumbled back. It wasn't until they retreated to a faraway place that they dared to stop, their gazes filled with fear.

The wall of fire suddenly dissipated, and Cheng Fu's feet danced lightly, akin to flames leaping and flickering at their highest point, making it impossible to predict his movements.

Wherever he went, the ground was instantly marked by clear footprints, surrounded by charred blackness. His footsteps were extremely fast, and in no time, the footprints on the ground became overlapped, densely packed, impossible to count. Within this range of his movements, it seemed as if the land had turned into a scorched black wasteland ravaged by raging flames.

Sparks flickered, flames raged.

The essence of Fire element power was similarly manifested perfectly in his fist techniques.

However, even with such immense power, even with the trapping effect of his true fire-like fist intent, he still could not overcome this peculiar set of Metal element techniques.

Zhou Yi's fists continued to wave without ceasing, his figure moving as if he were practicing his punches as usual.

Within him, the Ripple Qi flowed like water, combining the immense Qi of the Water element with the profound essence of the Metal element fist techniques, unleashing a unique set of Rolling Stone Fist.

He was like a stone rolling in a fiery pit, no matter how rampant the flames, unable to melt or forge this massive, foul-smelling, and unyielding boulder.

Zhou Yi's aura grew stronger and stronger, and the characteristic of Rolling Stone Fist, which could accumulate momentum, gradually emanated. Slowly, within the sea of fire, the size of the boulder seemed to grow larger and larger, reaching an incredible extent.

"Ha!"

Zhou Yi ignited his inner Qi, thunder rolled off his tongue, and he suddenly let out a thunderous roar that resounded like a bolt from the blue sky.

His hands were raised high, and the immense momentum accumulated by Rolling Stone Fist was instantly triggered, erupting completely.

The 16th move of the Thirty-Six Forms of Mountain-Crushing...

A tremendous and unavoidable force instantly shattered through the sea of fire, broke through the wall of flames, and arrived in front of Cheng Fu's chest.

At this moment, Zhou Yi's fists were no longer like a colossal boulder but rather like a massive guandao that had undergone the refining of intense flames, purging all impurities within the boulder, finally condensing into a powerful weapon capable of rending the heavens and splitting the earth.

With his palms raised high, resembling the edge of a blade, Zhou Yi, like a demon lord emerging from the depths of hell, tore through the endless void and returned once again, carrying an aura of madness, ferocity, and unstoppable might, enveloping the sky as he charged forward.

At this moment, the power of the Metal element finally revealed itself to its fullest extent.

Cheng Fu's eyes narrowed to a single point, finally understanding that the power of the Metal element could also be accumulated through this method and eventually erupt.

In that final eruption, surpassing his usual limit, it was indeed Zhou Yi's ultimate trump card that emboldened him to challenge his opponent face to face.

At that moment, he suddenly realized that under the overwhelming force emanating from his adversary, there was no escape for him.

Letting out a deep sigh, his palms intertwined, those hands resembling two blazing red iron rods in a charcoal fire, suddenly disappeared into his sleeves.

With a wave of his hands, accompanied by a whistling gust akin to a mighty gale, his sleeves fiercely met the oncoming attack.

A thunderous explosion erupted between the fists of the two, a sound that seemed to explode directly within one's heart, stirring the soul and leaving one spellbound.

The crowd once again retreated to the rear, even Zhou Quanxin and his son wore faces filled with astonishment, witnessing a duel that far exceeded the limits of human capability.

Within each of their punches lay not just physical strength but the utilization of the forces of nature itself.

The ferocity of fire, the sharpness of metal, perpetually entwined, seemingly engulfing the entire world within its grasp.

They had witnessed the battle between Zhou Yi and Lü Xinwen before, but it wasn't until this moment that they truly understood the immense disparity even among the innate powerhouses.

Compared to the current Zhou Yi and Cheng Fu, Lü Xinwen seemed like a toddler who had just learned to walk, unable to stand on the same stage.

Father and son exchanged glances, wondering when Yi had acquired such formidable strength. In just a few short months, he had transformed into an entirely different person, as if reborn. If this progress continued, one could only imagine the heights he would reach in the future.

Within a radius of two hundred meters, there was no other person apart from Zhou Yi. Even Shui Xuanjin, with his hands behind his back, had retreated to a distant place. Although he didn't fear the level of Qi and aura like others did, he didn't want to exert any influence on the two individuals engaged in combat in the field.

In the eyes of Yu Xiaoyi and the others, there was an expression of extreme astonishment. They all knew that innate powerhouses were incredibly strong, reaching a level beyond human comprehension. Even those who had just entered the realm of innate power were formidable enough to rival an army.

However, when they witnessed the clash between these innate powerhouses for the first time, they realized that humans could be so incredibly powerful. In their eyes, the two figures in the field were no longer mere humans; they were a blazing fire and a mighty sword.

One was a raging fire that consumed everything in its path, and the other was a sky-splitting blade that tore through the fabric of reality.

※※※※

After a thunderous explosion, Cheng Fu was sent flying into the air, seemingly unable to withstand the immense impact of Zhou Yi's formidable True Qi.

At this moment, joy was evident on the faces of Yu Ruipei and others, while the Third Prince and his entourage from the Kingdom of KaiRong had turned pale, devoid of the jubilation and triumph they had displayed earlier upon winning the hunt. Compared to their defeat in the contest against the Guardian Grandmaster, any number of captured ferocious beasts seemed insignificant.

However, Shui Xuanjin's expression slightly changed. In his heart, he sighed softly, lamenting the missed opportunity.

Although fire overcomes metal in the Five Elements, Zhou Yi had utilized an extremely peculiar method, accumulating his momentum to the extreme and erupting it in an instant. Not only did he shatter the opponent's fire power, but he also completely reversed and suppressed it.

In such a situation, even Cheng Fu could only retreat in defeat, injured and devoid of the ability to continue the fight. However, on his person, he wore a special-made long robe that, while not a treasure, was in no way inferior to one when it came to defense.

In mid-air, Cheng Fu's hands waved, causing the sleeves of his robe to flutter like butterflies. These sleeves, crafted from a combination of fire silkworm silk and steel wire extracted from an active volcano, were completely rendered useless under the assault of the innate True Qi from the two powerful experts.

Zhou Yi sighed inwardly. This was a bare-handed duel, and if he had wielded his Great GuanDao, even if Cheng Fu had two intact sleeves or even a turtle shell on him, Zhou Yi could easily sever him with a single strike.

He took a step forward, ready to pursue, but he witnessed the tattered sleeves floating through the air suddenly tear through the space, emitting a sharp whistling sound as they flew toward him.

His eyes narrowed slightly as Zhou Yi alternately struck with his fists, instantly deploying a mesh of Heavenly Nets in front of him. The fragments of the sleeves fell weakly, like nails meeting a hammer, no longer posing any threat.

However, in just that brief moment, Cheng Fu had already descended from mid-air to the ground.

At this moment, his appearance was extremely disheveled, especially with his bare arms exposed, looking indescribably comical.

However, not a single person in the entire garden dared to laugh. Their minds were still immersed in the fierce battle that had just taken place. They harbored a deep-rooted fear of these two monsters cloaked in human guise. They couldn't even think of mocking them.

Cheng Fu maintained an extreme calmness, devoid of any negative emotions such as shame, annoyance, or resentment due to his recent defeat. His spirit had reached an unprecedented level at this moment.

Within the Master Hall of KaiRong, there were ten Guardian Grandmaster in total.

Although Cheng Fu was not the most powerful among these ten Grand Masters, he could at least rank within the top five. He had only entered the realm of Innate for a mere twenty years. However, unlike other Innate powerhouses who underwent seclusion to cultivate and accumulate the power of heaven and earth, using Innate True Qi to cleanse their bodies, Cheng Fu chose a different and more arduous path of cultivation.

After being promoted to a Grand Master, the following year, he left his family and traveled barefoot throughout the world, arriving at the far-flung Nanjiang Islands. In those dangerous waters, he endured ten years of hardship, traversing countless inhabited and uninhabited islands. Finally, during a volcanic eruption, he comprehended the essence of fire's power and entered the realm of enlightenment coveted by all Innate powerhouses.

Enlightenment, a moment of enlightenment, instantly propels one to soar to great heights, transforming into a dragon from a fish.

In that moment, his Innate True Qi made significant progress, and the fire cultivation technique he practiced reached an astonishing level of power.

It was precisely because of this that he had the confidence to challenge Shui Xuanjin, who had already been in the realm of Innate for over a century.

To challenge a hundred-year Innate powerhouse with only twenty years of cultivation was not a privilege granted to everyone.

However, he did not anticipate that there would be an even more formidable opponent before him.

In that last exchange, he had already concluded that the Innate True Qi possessed by his opponent was even more powerful than his own.

In his mind, Cheng Fu's thoughts flashed with the information obtained by Zhan Zhichao.

Those fools, This person is definitely not under twenty years old, but rather has stepped into the realm of Innate for less than twenty years..."

Time seemed to freeze at that moment.

The two Innate powerhouses faced each other from a distance, their gazes meeting in mid-air. The intense aura they emanated seemed to ignite brilliant sparks, dispersing their power in all directions.

Unconsciously, a larger area was cleared around them as they stood as the focal point.

Although no one wanted to miss this rare encounter between Innate powerhouses, nobody dared to enter their sphere, fearing the inexplicable calamity that might befall them.

Cheng Fu slowly raised his hand, his voice deep and powerful, "Master Zhou, on the Nanjiang Islands, I witnessed a volcanic eruption and was inspired to create a set of Lava techniques. I request your guidance, Master Zhou."

Zhou Yi's heart skipped a beat, but he maintained a calm demeanor and replied, "I would be honored to offer my insights."

Cheng Fu nodded slightly, and in the next moment, his body moved.

Unlike before, his figure no longer resembled a flickering flame but suddenly transformed into a vast expanse of red.

With incredible speed, he left multiple afterimages in the space within a short span of time. The red garments fluttered, transforming into a dazzling radiance in an instant. He seemed to have become the rushing lava cascading down from the heights after a volcanic eruption, continuously scouring everything in the world.

The surrounding air temperature seemed to rise to an unbearable level in an instant. Although the actual effect was far less exaggerated than what everyone imagined at that moment, upon seeing the vast expanse of red, resembling splashing molten lava, a horrific scene of volcanic eruption involuntarily appeared in the minds of all present.

Even though they hadn't personally experienced it, Cheng Fu, in that moment, managed to vividly recreate the scene they had witnessed before in their hearts. His ability to convey his own sensations through the exchange of Qi and aura was undoubtedly a power that emerged after enlightenment.

At this moment, Zhou Yi's eyes narrowed slightly, and he immediately sensed the immense pressure surrounding him. It felt as though he had been transported not to the royal garden but to a colossal island.

The highest point on the island was a massive crater, a volcano in the midst of eruption.

The volcano roared like a gigantic beast, spewing forth scorching smoke and torrents of brown flames. The surrounding peaks seemed to be on fire, with dark red clouds of smoke, and lava flowing like rockets, weaving into an immensely vast kaleidoscope.

And he stood at the very center of this kaleidoscope, as if on the verge of plunging into the searing magma, to be reduced to ashes.

He suddenly realized that within this sea of fire, where the power of fire had been brought to its extreme, the power of gold was indeed under unimaginable suppression. He could no longer break through this sea of fire by accumulating his own momentum.

He let out a deep sigh, and in that moment, he felt as if he had returned to the mountaintop of the past.

The mountain rain that continuously fell from the sky, the clouds and mist that obscured the distant endless mountains.

A gust of wind blew, causing the pattern that resembled a painting to ripple gently, as if invisible hands were gently pushing from behind, bringing the picture in his mind to life.

Suddenly, everyone inexplicably felt that a fine drizzle had begun to fall before them. The raindrops were small, but it seemed to be everywhere, encompassing everything.

Then, a mass of clouds and mist dispersed, as if they had always been present in that place, as if they had existed for countless millennia.

They suddenly realized that the terrifying sea of fire had disappeared, and the magma that seemed capable of destroying the world had vanished. The previous red world had been replaced by white wind and rain clouds.

Gentle breeze, fine rain, boundless clouds and mist...

Everyone looked at each other, and few could understand what had happened.

Only Shui Xuanjin widened his eyes, even he was infected by the sudden appearance of this strange phenomenon. When Cheng Fu unleashed the power of fire to its most powerful extent, as if transforming into a mass of lava, he did indeed worry for Zhou Yi.

This kind of supreme technique derived from enlightenment was not something ordinary Grand Masters could easily withstand through long-term absorption of the power of heaven and earth.

Only by bringing a certain power to its utmost extreme could one resonate with the forces of heaven and earth, giving others a sense of shared experience.

Even Shui Xuanjin himself, when faced with such incredible supreme techniques, could only rely on a hundred years of arduous cultivation and unleash all of his refined Innate True Qi to barely defend himself.

However, Zhou Yi's performance once again shocked him. It turned out that this young man, who was not yet twenty, had truly mastered the power of wind, rain, clouds, and mist.

When these four powers, capable of coexisting, manifested and enveloped the sea of fire, he knew that the outcome of this battle had been determined.

Silently, the pervading clouds and mist suddenly dispersed.

Everything returned to normal, with no more sea of fire, no more clouds and rain, no more wind and mist. There was no flowing lava, no mountain rain, and no swirling clouds and mist.

In the center of the arena, only two people stood calmly, as if they hadn't moved at all from the beginning to the end.

They realized that everything they had experienced just now was nothing more than illusions. The cause of these illusory scenes, which seemed so real, were the two individuals before them.

However, even though everyone understood this, their awe and reverence for them only grew stronger, a fear that seemed to be etched into their bones.

Innate powerhouses were the true masters of this world. The power they wielded surpassed the limits of the human body. Faced with such tremendous power, even an army would likely crumble.

At this moment, all that remained in their hearts was the fear of power.

※※※※

Cheng Fu raised his hands, which had returned to normal, with no trace of the eerie fiery red color. He extended a respectful fist towards Zhou Yi and said, "I have lost."

Everyone's breath seemed to catch in their throats, and after a moment, they realized the significance behind his words.

Suddenly, an eruption of cheers broke out from the crowd. Even Yu Xiaoyi couldn't help but raise his fist and cheer. The cheers of the attendants of the third prince, Zhan Zhichao, when he claimed the top hunting spot paled in comparison to the overwhelming jubilation now.

In the battle between the two protectors of the nation, their protector had emerged as the ultimate victor.

For all the subjects of Tianluo Kingdom, this was an unparalleled source of immense pride. They lifted their heads high, and the despondency that had initially accompanied their failed hunt vanished in this moment.

In stark contrast, the envoys from the Kingdom of KaiRong wore exceptionally ugly expressions. However, when their gazes fell upon

Zhou Yi, there was an indescribable look in their eyes—a mixture of fear and reverence.

After witnessing the battle just now, even the most unruly individuals would no longer harbor any disrespectful thoughts. They knew that in the presence of this man, they were like ants, easily crushed at his whim, without any resistance.

This was the power of an Innate powerhouse, a power that surpassed what a practitioner of acquired Inner Strength could ever aspire to.

Unaware of the surrounding commotion, Cheng Fu suddenly asked, "Master Zhou, was it you who triggered the aura of heaven and earth that day?"

Although he did not specify the exact date, the three Innate powerhouses present were well aware.

"Yes, it was me who triggered it during my moment of enlightenment," Zhou Yi said without hesitation.

"Enlightenment," Cheng Fu chuckled bitterly. "Indeed, it was enlightenment." He let out a bitter laugh, regretting his impulsive challenge. If only he had known earlier, how could he have been so rash?

Unfortunately, the aura of heaven and earth that day was not the power of fire. So, without personally witnessing that scene, he could never have imagined that it would be an extremely rare experience of enlightenment.

He felt a tinge of bitterness in his heart. He had spent more than a decade, nearly brushing shoulders with death, before having his enlightenment in the Southern Islands. Meanwhile, the other party had a similar experience without even leaving this small corner of Tianluo Kingdom.

People truly couldn't be compared.

Letting out a soft sigh, Cheng Fu loudly congratulated Yu Ruipei in the distance, who dared not approach. Then, he turned around, his bare arms swaying as he strode away. Moments later, he disappeared from everyone's sight.

Zhan Zhichao and his sister did not call out to him; they knew that after his defeat, Cheng Fu wanted to find a secluded place to be alone. As long as they returned to the Kingdom of KaiRong, they would most likely meet again.

Water Xuanjin approached, gently patting Zhou Yi's shoulder and smiled, "How do you feel?"

Zhou Yi smiled softly and replied, "I have gained a lot."

"Join me for a drink," Water Xuanjin's voice carried an indescribable joy. "I haven't been this happy in a long time."

The two exchanged a smile and walked side by side, departing like the wind.

Only after the three Innate masters had left, the entire garden erupted once again with thunderous cheers...

Chapter 154

Within the courtyard of Shao Ming Ju Residence, there lay a modest bamboo grove. As the gentle breeze swept through, the bamboo swayed gracefully, producing a rhythmic melody that drifted in the air like enchanting music.

Ever since returning to this place, Yuan Lixun's smile had never faded. In her eyes, when she looked at Zhou Yi, there was a subtle yet undeniable sense of admiration.

Before this day, although she had heard many people discussing Zhou Yi's martial prowess, and even heard the legendary tale of him single-handedly slaying two thousand men with a single stroke, it had all been hearsay. As they say, seeing is believing, and only when she witnessed the awe-inspiring display of otherworldly innate power by Zhou Yi did she truly grasp the unfathomable strength possessed by this seemingly ordinary young man.

If, before this day, due to their growing acquaintance and several days spent together, she had developed a vague fondness for Zhou Yi, then after the battle today, that feeling became even more vivid.

Zhou Yi, with an air of maturity, held the steaming cup of tea she had offered. Puzzled, he asked, "What are you laughing at?"

A slight blush tinted Yuan Lixun's cheeks as she gently shook her head. "I'm not laughing," she replied.

Taking a sip, Zhou Yi thought to himself, "She's lying right to my face." However, he immediately followed that thought with another, "But her smile is actually quite beautiful."

A hearty laughter echoed, and Shui XuanJin's figure flashed at the entrance, already standing beside Zhou Yi.

Zhou Yi smiled and said, "Brother Shui, I spent the entire evening drinking with you yesterday. Aren't you satisfied yet?"

Shui XuanJin shook his head and said, "Brother, amidst the enjoyment of last night, there are a few matters I need to discuss with you."

Yuan LiXun quickly took a step back and said, "Master Shui, please have a seat. I will brew tea for you."

Her words were merely an excuse, a way for her to indicate to the two men that she wouldn't eavesdrop on their conversation.

Zhou Yi furrowed his brow slightly and said, "The tea here is already quite good. No need for any special preparations."

A sweet sensation filled Yuan LiXun's heart as she faintly sensed that Zhou Yi had no intentions of avoiding her. She lowered her head and softly replied, taking a new teacup and pouring a cup of rich milk tea from the pot onto the table in front of Shui XuanJin.

Shui XuanJin took a sip and smiled, "It's excellent. No wonder Zhou brother dotes on you."

Yuan LiXun's face grew even redder, but Zhou Yi cleared his throat and didn't respond directly. Instead, he said, "Brother, if you have something to discuss, please speak openly."

Shui XuanJin looked at Zhou Yi earnestly and said, "Before today, I had no idea that you not only mastered the Way of Wind, Rain, and Clouds but also possessed such profound attainment in the Way of metal. If I'm not mistaken, it seems that you crossed this barrier not by consuming the innate Golden Pill, but by integrating the internal energy of metal and water to ascend to the innate realm."

Zhou Yi nodded slightly and said, "You're right. I indeed have not consumed the innate Golden Pill."

When he said these words, he cleverly chose his phrasing. He merely stated that he had not consumed the innate Golden Pill, without admitting that he had broken through his limits using the fusion of metal and water internal energy.

If the old man before him were to find out that Zhou Yi had broken through not by using the fusion of metal and water internal energy but by using the fusion of wood and fire internal energy, he would be astounded beyond measure. Of course, Zhou Yi would never voluntarily reveal this troublesome matter. No matter how insightful Shui XuanJin was, he would never suspect that Zhou Yi not only grasped the essence of the metal and water dual systems but also had comparable attainment in the wood and fire dual systems' true qi cultivation.

Shui XuanJin sighed softly and said, "Brother, in fact, the opponent you fought against today, Cheng Fu, is also a master of dual-system techniques. Like you, he did not consume the innate Golden Pill but, through his own efforts, combined with two top-tier postnatal techniques, he broke through the barrier from fire to earth at the age of seventy-eight, entering the innate realm."

Zhou Yi was taken aback and asked, "Dual-system techniques? If he is also a innate expert in dual-system techniques, why didn't he use earth-based powers?"

Shui XuanJin couldn't help but smile bitterly and replied, "Brother, you jest. He has only been in the innate realm for twenty years, focusing all his energy on one system of techniques. Even so, he has only reached the high-tier of the Hundred Scattered Heavens. If he were to simultaneously cultivate true qi of two systems, let alone twenty years, even if he had fifty years, he might not possess such strength."

Zhou Yi blinked his eyes twice, thinking to himself, What is the Hundred Scattered Heavens?

Shui XuanJin noticed his reaction and suddenly remembered that before him stood an anomaly that could not be perceived through ordinary eyes. To have entered the innate realm before the age of twenty, cultivating the power of the metal and water systems to the high-tier of the Hundred Scattered Heavens, not to mention the secondary branches like the wind system—there was no need to mention those. He sighed inwardly, realizing that this gifted individual, with his extraordinary talent, would probably never understand the solitude and sorrow of his own cultivation journey.

However, Shui XuanJin pondered for a moment and realized that at least he had stepped into the innate realm, unlike those struggling in the postnatal realm. He sighed softly, feeling a hint of helplessness, as the old man said, "Brother Zhou, I'm not referring to you. You are different."

Zhou Yi forced a bitter smile, knowing that he truly was different.

The old man continued, "Masters like you, who break through the innate realm relying on their own power, possess a much deeper understanding of the qi of heaven and earth compared to those of us who ascended through consuming the innate Golden Pill. When you initially enter the innate realm, it is only the infusion of innate qi into your body, forming innate true qi. However, as your true qi accumulates to a certain degree, you can comprehend the heaven and earth, activate the qi within a certain range, and unleash formidable power that far surpasses the limits of the human body. Moreover, masters like you who have experienced enlightenment can release the insights gained in that moment of enlightenment through this method, thereby surpassing us in terms of power."

Zhou Yi silently nodded, recalling his battle with Lv XinWen in the past. Lv XinWen, like Cheng Fu, had been in the innate realm for over twenty years. However, Lv XinWen relied on the power of the innate Golden Pill. Although he possessed innate true qi, when compared to Zhou Yi's and Cheng Fu's ability to activate the qi of heaven and earth within a certain range, Lv XinWen was far behind.

If they were to meet again now, Zhou Yi estimated that with just one move, he could seriously injure Lv XinWen.

Suddenly, Shui XuanJin waved his hand. The hand swayed gently in the air, as if it could transform into the wind at any moment.

Zhou Yi's gaze abruptly focused as he keenly sensed that the power of the wind within a hundred meters of his body seemed to be drawn towards his hand. It was evident that he had reached the stage of attracting the qi of heaven and earth. However, what he attracted was not the power of fire but a kind of energy belonging to the wind.

The old man sighed deeply and said, "I spent a full 101 years in arduous cultivation before truly comprehending the Way of Wind and being able to borrow the power of the wind within a hundred meters. But Cheng Fu accomplished it in only twenty years, and you..." He paused, unable to bring himself to say it, sighed once more, and continued, "And not only do you master your own powers, but you also possess the virtualized power of enlightenment. If I were to face you, I'm afraid the odds would be heavily against me."

Zhou Yi awkwardly scratched his scalp, realizing that he had no response to this particular aspect.

Only Yuan LiXun, who was beside the two, looked at Zhou Yi with a peculiar affection in her eyes, and it seemed to be gradually expanding without restraint.

After a moment of reflection, Shui XuanJin finally said, "Brother Zhou, today, seeing that you excel in so many systems of techniques, I am delighted but also somewhat concerned."

"What are you worried about?" Zhou Yi asked, surprised.

Shui XuanJin spoke earnestly, "I know you have exceptional talent, being able to grasp so many forces of heaven and earth simultaneously. It is truly an incredible feat. However, everyone has limited energy. It would be best for you to find the power you are most adept at and enjoy the most, and focus on its development. In doing so, your chances of breaking through the Hundred Scattered Heavens and entering the One-Line Heaven will be much greater."

Zhou Yi's eyes lit up, and he asked, "Shui brother, what are the Hundred Scattered Heavens and the One-Line Heaven?"

With a face full of doubt, Shui Xuanjin asked, "You don't know?"

"Indeed, I don't," came the response.

Shui Xuanjin smiled wryly and said, "My friend, it's better to ask about this after you join the Hengshan Sect. I can only tell you that those who have just reached the Innate realm are called 'Bai San Tian'— the Hundred Scattered Heavens. If one can break through this realm, they will enter the realm of 'Yi Xian Tian'—the One-line Heaven." He let out a bitter laugh and continued, "Given my aptitude, it's impossible for me to ever break through to the One-line Heaven in this lifetime." Zhou Yi responded with a hint of disappointment, but the thought of soon joining his grandfather on their journey to Hengshan filled his heart with anticipation. He didn't pay much attention to Shui Xuanjin's persuasion. With his constitution as a practitioner of the Five Elements, Zhou Yi had no concerns about a matter that troubled others. Seemingly sensing the disappointment on Zhou Yi's face, Shui Xuanjin quickly consoled him, saying, "Zhou, my friend, at your age, you have already comprehended the true essence of water elemental power and reached the advanced stage of Bai San Tian, capable of channeling the Qi of the heavens and earth within your body. With that, your chances of breaking through to the One-line Heaven in the future are still very high."

Zhou Yi nodded slightly at the old man, brimming with confidence in himself. Slapping his forehead, Shui Xuanjin exclaimed, "I'm getting old and forgetful, going off on tangents again." He chuckled and continued, "My friend, today I went to the palace and discussed it with the emperor.

This time, you represent Tianluo Kingdom, wagering one-tenth of our annual tribute to Kairong Kingdom. Since you've won, starting from this year, the tribute we offer will be reduced by one-tenth. And the emperor's intention is to bestow this one-tenth upon you."

Zhou Yi was taken aback and said, "Your Majesty is truly too generous. This reward seems a bit excessive." Shui Xuanjin chuckled and said, "You won it with your own strength. If it's not given to you, then who else? Even if you don't want it, it can be bestowed upon your family." After a moment of consideration, he added, "If the Zhou family in Taicang County wants to thrive and expand, they will likely need a significant amount of wealth, and this is a great opportunity." Zhou Yi immediately stopped refusing.

The old man's last words had truly touched him. Of course, he also understood that the royal family's generosity came with the intention of using him as a shield. And if he were to lose in a future martial arts contest against the masters of Kairong Kingdom, this generous gift would probably come to an end. However, the fact that the Tianluo royal family was willing to offer such a grand reward was truly unexpected for Zhou Yi. If the royal family were to face any danger in the future, he would find it difficult to stand by and do nothing.

※※※※

After seeing off the old man Shui Xuanjin, Zhou Yi returned to his own room. Although Yuan Lixun was officially his concubine, they had never shared a bed until now. This surprised not only Zhou Wude but also Shui Xuanjin, who secretly wondered about it. If it weren't for Zhou Yi's clear trust in Yuan Lixun, they would have thought that Zhou Yi didn't like her at all. After all, as an Innate expert, there weren't many concerns when it came to intimate matters between men and women. As for the notion of it affecting one's cultivation, it was even more absurd. However, Zhou Yi and Yuan Lixun seemed to have not noticed anything amiss. They had gotten through these days of companionship just like that.

As Zhou Yi closed his eyes on the bed, he resumed his daily routine of practice. Although epiphanies could lead to a rapid and substantial improvement in one's abilities, they still required long-term and unwavering efforts to solidify the gains.

Otherwise, it would be extremely difficult to have another epiphany in the future. After an unknown period of time, Zhou Yi snapped out of the hazy state. He opened his eyes and asked, "Lixun, is there something you need?" Outside the room, there was a faint sound, but just by hearing that familiar breath, he knew it was Yuan Lixun. Normally, she would never come near this place at this time. So if she had come now, there must be something important to communicate.

Yuan Lixun's gentle voice immediately sounded, "Young Master, the Third Prince and Fifth Princess of the KaiRong Kingdom have arrived. They wish to see you."

"The prince and princess of Kairong Kingdom?" Zhou Yi pondered with surprise for a moment, but he couldn't figure out why they would visit him. It couldn't be that they came to challenge him because of Cheng Fu's defeat, right? "Young Master, do you intend to see them?" urged Yuan Lixun. "If you don't want to, I can go back and inform them that you are in seclusion for cultivation and cannot be disturbed." A faint smile appeared on Zhou Yi's lips. Regardless of their intentions, he would never be afraid. If that's the case, why should he have any reservations? He reached out and opened the door, saying, "Where are they?"

"They are waiting in the living room," Yuan Lixun whispered. "Young Master, it seems they are not here to cause trouble." Zhou Yi waved his hand slightly and said, "Of course not. Have you ever seen anyone come to a Grandmaster of the Innate realm to cause trouble?" Yuan Lixun giggled softly, covering her mouth. Coming to cause trouble in front of an Innate expert would be seeking death.

With the intelligence of Zhan Zhichao and his sister, they surely wouldn't make such foolish moves.

After a moment, the siblings entered the living room one after the other. This courtyard was one of the best in Shao Ming Ju Residence, and even the living room was quite spacious. Zhou Yi's gaze swept across the room, and he was surprised to see that behind Zhan Zhichao and his sister, there were only two veiled women. But it wasn't strange to think about it. After all, this was Shao Ming Ju Residence, with two Grandmasters of the Innate realm from Tianluo Kingdom present. If anything untoward were to happen to them here, Zhou Yi and Shui Xuanjin might as well find a big tree to hang themselves from. Zhou Yi's ears twitched slightly, and the distant air felt normal. He didn't detect any signs of eavesdropping.

Presumably, Shui Xuanjin knew that he had mastered the extraordinary Wind Ear Qi technique and realized that he couldn't hide his eavesdropping anymore. And since he didn't want to anger Zhou Yi, he chose to ignore the presence of these two princes and princess. When Zhou Yi entered, Zhan Zhichao and his sister quickly stood up. They both bowed and said, "Greetings, Master Zhou." Zhan Zhichao's gesture was expected, but Zhou Yi was surprised to see Zhan Zhiyan imitating a man's fist-clenching posture.

However, Zhou Yi maintained his composure and said, "Please have a seat." After both sides took their seats, Zhou Yi straightforwardly asked, "May I know the purpose of your visit?" Zhan Zhichao smiled faintly and said, "We heard that Master Zhou has stepped into the Innate realm, so we came to pay our respects." A hint of skepticism flashed in Zhou Yi's eyes, and he asked incredulously, "You came just for that?" With his status, he no longer cared to speculate about the intentions of others by any means necessary.

That was the advantage of having superlative strength—sometimes the most direct approach was the best. Of course, to be able to do so, one's own strength had to be outstanding; otherwise, it would be like drawing a tiger that ended up resembling a dog. Zhan Zhichao waved his hand lightly, and the two women behind them slowly approached. A fragrance reached Zhou Yi's nose, though he couldn't identify the perfume. Nonetheless, his nose didn't reject it. The two women knelt a few meters in front of Zhou Yi, holding up a list of gifts in their hands. With his keen eyesight, Zhou Yi had already read the contents of the list at a glance. His heart skipped a beat as he noticed that the items on the list were of considerable value.

Furthermore, there were a few items he had never heard of before, but they were listed in the first few rows, indicating their exceptional value among the gifts. Zhou Yi wasn't a haughty person, and after seeing the contents of the list, it would be false to say that his heart was unaffected. Suddenly, Zhan Zhiyan chuckled lightly, her laughter carrying a unique charm. "Master Zhou, I've noticed that you lack personnel to care for this residence. Why not let these two maids stay and serve you?" As soon as she finished speaking, the veils that had covered the faces of the maids fell off inexplicably.

What lay hidden behind the veils were two stunningly beautiful faces.

Chapter 155

As the veil slipped away, revealing cascading locks of lustrous, jet-black hair, they gracefully bowed. Their heads rose with a perfect poise, cheeks blushing like delicate blossoms, glowing akin to the dawn's embrace of the setting sun, an exquisite juxtaposition.

In the midst of Zhou Yi's momentary bewilderment, they reached up and delicately pulled at the straps around their necks, allowing their billowing robes to slide down their bodies. Clad in sheer black gowns, their alluring figures partially exposed, showcasing their graceful curves, slender waistlines, ample bosoms, rounded derrieres, slender snowy legs—such a sight that captivated souls and turned heads.

Zhou Yi's ears twitched slightly, and he immediately caught the slightly heavier breaths of Yuan Li Xun behind him, along with the hastened rhythm of their heartbeats. Though Yuan Li Xun concealed it well, even to the point of not arousing suspicion from others, how could he possibly deceive Zhou Yi?

It brought an inexplicable sense of joy to the depths of his heart. This feeling was so odd that even Zhou Yi himself found it inexplicable.

Zhan Zhichao and his sister intently observed Zhou Yi, only to find his gaze merely fleeting over the alluring bodies of the two women, seemingly lost in thought, as if he hadn't truly noticed them.

Exchanging a glance, a hint of disappointment and regret appeared in their eyes. Yet, they weren't surprised. Given Zhou Yi's status and power, the Tianluo Imperial Family would go to great lengths to win him over. It would be strange if they didn't employ a multitude of captivating beauties to accompany him.

However, little did they know that the desires of the Tianluo Imperial Family had been thwarted by Shui Xuanjin.

With the personal reception of this Grand Master, the feeling of respect it evoked was not something a few women could compare to.

"Dear sirs, Zhou Yi's path of cultivation does not require the attendance of others. I appreciate your kindness," Zhou Yi casually remarked, but his words carried a powerful force that dared not be disobeyed.

Zhan Zhichao smiled gracefully, seemingly unaffected by the situation. He spoke softly, "Since it is Master Zhou's wish, please excuse yourselves."

The two women obediently placed the gifts on the ground, picked up their veils and outer robes, and bowed before retreating.

Zhan Zhichao once again bowed and said, "Master Zhou, please do not be upset by this disturbance. Consider this gift as our token of apology."

Although Zhou Yi held no favorable impression of the emissaries from KaiRong Kingdom, he couldn't deny that this prince had a rather extraordinary way of winning people over. At the very least, this respectful and seemingly heartfelt attitude would not arouse resentment in others.

However, Zhou Yi waved his hand and said, "There's no need. As a humble mortal, I have little need for such worldly possessions. It would be better for the prince to take them back."

Zhan Zhichao chuckled helplessly and said, "Master Zhou, we offer these gifts as a token of apology, and nothing more." He paused for a moment and continued, "Master Zhou, now that you have reached the advanced stage of the Hundred Scattered Heavens realm, may I inquire when you plan to strive for the One-Line Heaven realm?"

Zhou Yi raised an eyebrow, his gaze slightly focused, and replied, "You are a cultivator of the acquired realm, so how would you know about the innate realm?"

Zhan Zhichao smiled calmly and said, "Although I am a practitioner of the acquired realm, within our KaiRong Kingdom's imperial family, there is a revered ancestor who is a powerful One-Line Heaven expert."

Zhou Yi's gaze underwent a subtle change as he recalled the words he had heard that night, and suddenly everything became clear to him. Sensing the apparent interest of the innate expert before him, Zhan Zhichao hurriedly spoke, "Master Zhou, our ancestral founder once said that the difficulty of breaking through from the Hundred

Scattered Heavens realm to the One-Line Heaven realm within the innate realm is even greater than the difficulty of breaking through from the acquired realm to the innate realm. If not for this, with the talent of Master Shui Xuanjin from your esteemed country, I'm afraid she would have already surpassed her current realm."

Zhou Yi let out a disdainful snort and said, "Your Highness, if you have something to say, just say it directly. This beating around the bush won't do us any good and who knows how long it will drag on."

Zhan Zhichao was momentarily taken aback. Among the ten innate Grand Masters in KaiRong Kingdom's Great Master Hall, he had yet to come across anyone who displayed such straightforwardness and frankness in their dealings.

He thought to himself that perhaps it was precisely because of this unique personality that Zhou Yi had been able to achieve such great heights in the martial path.

However, he was unaware that Zhou Yi had long understood his intentions from their conversation. Since that was the case, he naturally had no intention of wasting any more time.

Zhan Zhichao's expression immediately turned solemn, and he spoke loudly, "Master Zhou, if you don't mind, on behalf of our ancestral founder, I invite you to come to KaiRong. There, we are willing to open the doors of the royal martial repository to you. Furthermore, when you are ready to strive for the One-Line Heaven realm, our ancestral founder can provide you with protection and blessings. With this, the possibility of your breakthrough will be much greater."

Zhou Yi half-closed his eyes, seemingly contemplating the pros and cons, but deep inside, he sneered. Just based on the fact that they harbored bandits and allowed them to plunder and wreak havoc within Tianluo Territory, he could never cooperate with them.

Of course, Zhou Yi would never speak those words aloud.

Finally, he shook his head and said, "Thank you for Your Highness's kind offer, but I am ultimately the Guardian Grandmasterr of Tianluo Kingdom and it would be inappropriate for me to go to your esteemed country." With that, he stood up and said, "Li Xun, see our guests off." He turned around and walked away, not giving the two princes and princess any opportunity to detain him.

Yuan Li Xun respectfully replied, "Your Highnesses, our young master is currently in seclusion for cultivation. If there has been any negligence, please forgive us."

Although she apologized, she subtly positioned herself to block the sight of Zhou Yi's departing figure, as if unwilling to let anyone call out to him.

Zhan Zhichao sighed, while Zhan ZhiYan chuckled and said, "I've heard that Master Zhou has a beautiful concubine who serves him exclusively. You must be her, right?"

A sense of desolation flashed through Yuan Li Xun's heart. After all, her status was merely that of a concubine, seemingly forever unable to stand by Zhou Yi's side as an equal. However, ever since she had followed Zhou Yi, not even Zhou Wude himself had mentioned her specific status. So, she deliberately avoided thinking about it.

But now, Zhan ZhiYan's words shattered the last remnants of her illusion. She inwardly sighed, realizing that her thoughts had indeed been too extravagant.

Her mind raced through countless thoughts, but these fleeting musings were quickly brushed aside. Without hesitation, she respectfully replied, "In response to Your Highness's words, I am indeed the one who serves the young master."

Zhan ZhiYan looked deeply into her eyes and suddenly smiled, saying, "Master Zhou is truly an interesting person. I hope we will have the opportunity to meet again in the future."

The two siblings, even though they had addressed Yuan Li Xun, nodded slightly in courtesy before leaving. They displayed flawless etiquette, leaving no room for criticism.

After they left Shao Ming Ju Residence and traveled several miles in their carriage, Zhan Zhichao suddenly spoke, "Sister, I've said before that this is not a good idea. I'm afraid it might cause his aversion." He sighed softly and continued, "Look at that woman who serves him exclusively. On paper, she's his concubine, but from what I can see, she's clearly a virgin..."

Zhan ZhiYan huffed, "If he hasn't even touched his own concubine, can he really be considered a man?"

Zhan Zhichao's expression changed slightly and he said, "Be careful with your words, sister. This statement absolutely cannot be spread."

Zhan ZhiYan seemed to understand the weight of those words. She stuck out her tongue playfully, displaying a somewhat adorable expression.

Zhan Zhichao pondered for a moment and said, "From what I can see, Master Zhou seems to be someone with strong willpower, completely devoted to pursuing the martial path. Perhaps he chooses not to be burdened by emotional attachments, which is why he acts this way."

Zhan ZhiYan hesitated for a moment and said, "That's right. When you mentioned our ancestor earlier, he was also tempted, but for some reason, he eventually gave up. It's a pity..." She sighed deeply and continued, "Now that he has refused, what should we do?"

Zhan Zhichao contemplated for a moment and said, "Let's return and truthfully report everything to our father, the king. As for how he chooses to handle it, it's beyond our imagination." A hint of indescribable meaning crossed his lips as he added, "Even the emperor himself, I'm afraid, would have a headache dealing with such a genius."

Zhan ZhiYan pursed her lips and smiled slightly, as if she had encountered something that delighted her greatly.

After Zhou Yi entered the room, instead of immediately beginning his cultivation, he took out a book and quietly read. Whether he truly absorbed the contents of the book, only heaven knew.

Zhan Zhichao's proposal had undeniably sparked some interest in Zhou Yi, but he absolutely refused to accept any benefits from KaiRong Kingdom.

After a while, Yuan Li Xun walked in. Her face was slightly flushed, but Zhou Yi could sense that there was a sense of joy in her heart, a stark contrast to her earlier mood.

Unexplainably, Zhou Yi also felt a hint of delight. He put down the book in his hand and asked, "Li Xun, have they left?"

"Master, the two princes have already left," Yuan Li Xun smiled and said, "They were very polite and even brought you such beautiful maids."

Zhou Yi blinked twice and said, "Are they beautiful? I didn't look carefully just now."

He said this sentence naturally, but it was definitely a lie.When he glanced at the two women earlier, their appearance and figure were firmly imprinted in his mind. If judging solely based on looks and physique, they even surpassed Yuan Li Xun. However, for some reason, when Zhou Yi looked at them, he didn't feel the same warmth he felt when he was with Yuan Li Xun.

Perhaps it was because of his preconceptions, or perhaps it was because they were people from the KaiRong Kingdom. Regardless, Zhou Yi truly didn't pay much attention to them. Instead, he was more focused on Yuan Li Xun, who stood behind him at the time.

Upon hearing Zhou Yi's words, Yuan Li Xun grew visibly happier. A faint smile appeared on the corner of her lips, subtle but carrying a touch of sweetness on her face.

Zhou Yi was taken aback, hesitated for a moment, and murmured, "Li Xun, what I mean is... actually, I mean..."

Yuan Li Xun tilted her head, a hint of confusion in her eyes. In her impression, Zhou Yi didn't usually hesitate or stutter when he spoke.

Finally, Zhou Yi took a deep breath and said, "What I mean is, actually, having you by my side is enough."

Yuan Li Xun let out a soft gasp, her face turning beet red. She lowered her head and lightly acknowledged, even a blush spreading to her neck.

Although Zhou Yi was an innate Grand Master, first and foremost, he was a person—a sixteen-year-old youth at that. Even with unexpected achievements in certain aspects, it was still difficult for him to talk nonchalantly as if nothing had happened in moments like these.

With a light cough, Zhou Yi said, "I'll go see Uncle and the others. I'll be back later today." After speaking, he swiftly departed like a shooting star.

Seeing Zhou Yi flee as if he were escaping for his life, Yuan Li Xun couldn't help but burst into laughter. It was strange, but once she laughed out loud, that fiery feeling instantly diminished by half.

She watched the direction Zhou Yi disappeared in and suddenly realized that leaving the Yuan family might not be such a bad thing after all. Perhaps the happiness her mother often spoke of had already been found by her.

Her eyes gradually grew misty, and eventually, she became somewhat infatuated...

Without stopping, Zhou Yi's figure transformed into a gust of wind as he floated away from Shao Ming Ju Residence. He didn't even alarm a single person as he headed towards the Royal Manor in the imperial estate.

The Royal Manor where Zhou Quanxin and his son resided was not the top-tier estate designated for hosting the KaiRong Kingdom. Instead, it was a small garden located ten li away from that estate.

Although it was comparatively smaller, the actual area of this garden was in no way inferior to the entire Zhou family estate.

Zhou Quanxin and his son had thrived in the capital city of Tianluo, constantly entertaining guests from all over. These guests held significant positions, and in the past, it would have been impossible for them to even spare a glance at a small aristocratic family from Taicang County.

If Zhou Quanxin sought to join these powerful families as an individual, he would undoubtedly receive top-level treatment. After all, a top-notch martial artist at the tenth level of Internal Energy was not something every family could casually possess.

However, when Zhou Quanxin arrived in Tianluo as a member of the Zhou family from Taicang County, they were completely ignored. If it weren't for the Crown Prince publicizing the relationship between Zhou Quanxin and the newly promoted innate Grand Master, Zhou Yi, it was certain that the father and son would have been neglected in the capital city of Tianluo.

However, at this moment, especially after Zhou Yi's powerful battle and defeating the enemy, the number of people coming to pay their respects at Zhou Quanxin's manor increased dramatically. It was like a swarm of bees, starting from the early morning until the moon rose high in the sky, without any interruption.

When Zhou Yi arrived at the scene, he was slightly surprised to witness such a massive gathering. Could it be that he had come to the wrong place?

After pondering for a moment, he swiftly made his way inside. In the blink of an eye, he had passed through countless carriages and entered through the main gate.

The carriage drivers and the guards in front of the carriages looked at each other, as if something had just passed by their eyes. However, when they began searching, they couldn't even spot a fly. They couldn't help but feel suspicious, but no one dared to call out casually.

After entering through the main gate, Zhou Yi's ears trembled slightly, instantly capturing all the sounds in the courtyard. He immediately pinpointed the location of Zhou Quanxin and his son.

He lifted his foot and continued speeding towards them, his speed even faster than before. It was as if he had become an invisible and intangible gust of wind.

In this manor, the strength of the attendants far exceeded that of ordinary places. Even Zhou Yi didn't dare to be careless.

Finally, he evaded the gazes of dozens of people and arrived in the main hall of the manor.

In the room, there were already three unfamiliar men sitting opposite Zhou Quanxin and his son, engaged in a deep conversation. It seemed that they had established a good rapport.

Zhou Yi's footsteps didn't falter as he strode inside. His entrance was not subtle, immediately drawing the attention of several people in the room. As soon as they saw him, including Zhou Quanxin, they all froze for a moment before standing up with expressions of joy.

"Yi, you're back," Zhou Quanxin said excitedly.

Zhou Yi nodded in response and glanced briefly at the three strangers' faces. He said, "Uncle, I have something to discuss with you."

Before Zhou Quanxin could speak, the three men immediately bowed repeatedly, as if they had been intending to leave. Naturally, Zhou Quanxin had no interest in keeping them, so he let Zhou Yitian see them off. After they left, he said, "Yi, if there's something you need to discuss, you don't have to make the trip yourself. We can come over. There's no need for you to run around."

Zhou Yi was stunned for a moment, completely speechless. He couldn't bring himself to make his elder relatives go through the trouble of coming to see him.

After the two sat down, Zhou Yi got straight to the point. "Uncle, Master Shui Xuanjin came to see me. He said he wants me to handle the one-tenth tax revenue I won."

Zhou Quanxin was taken aback, then his eyes gleamed brightly. It was as if he had just discovered a treasure. "Yi, are you telling the truth? All of that one-tenth belongs to us?"

Zhou Yi looked at his uncle strangely and nodded slightly. His uncle's reaction seemed overly excited.

Zhou Yi couldn't help but sigh inwardly, realizing that the allure of money was truly remarkable, even his uncle had fallen into its clutches and couldn't extricate himself.

Chapter 156

Zhou Yi didn't stay long in the estate. After informing his uncle of the news, he departed gracefully. The news of his appearance spread throughout the entire estate like a gust of wind, and the crowds waiting outside the gates were eager to catch a glimpse of this young master.

Although only a few days had passed since his battle with Cheng Fu, the entire Tianluo Kingdom was already well aware of it. Whether acquainted or not, the people of Tianluo Kingdom felt excitement and joy at Zhou Yi's victory over the innate master from the Kai Rong Kingdom.

The people outside the gates were no exception. However, despite their excitement, none of them dared to enter recklessly. It was only when Zhou Yi finally emerged after a long wait that they realized he had quietly left.

No one discovered how he had departed, but aside from their regret, these people had no reason to suspect anything. If even an innate powerhouse could be discovered by them, that would be truly strange.

However, since Zhou Yi's visit, the area outside the estate had become bustling, devoid of any moments of tranquility. Zhou Quanxin and his son, Zhou Quanxin, lived in a mix of pain and joy. While they were delighted that the reputation of Zhou Family Manor had spread throughout Tianluo City, they were also overwhelmed by the various attentions that clashed with their cultivation practices.

※※※※

As if transformed into a gust of wind, Zhou Yi had returned to Shao Ming Ju Residence. As soon as he entered his courtyard, he saw Yuan Lixun sitting on a wide chair in the courtyard. She supported her chin, quietly gazing at the pavilions in the yard. There seemed to be an indescribable sense of desolation emanating from her entire being.

Zhou Yi was slightly taken aback and hesitated for a moment. Unexplainably, he had this feeling that Yuan Lixun was homesick...

He tilted his head and pondered for a moment, then suddenly smiled. With a swift movement, he was already by Yuan Lixun's side. He coughed softly, causing Yuan Lixun's body to tremble as if startled, much like a frightened little rabbit. But once she saw that it was Zhou Yi standing beside her, the panic and wariness in her eyes instantly faded away, replaced by a hint of girlish shyness.

"Young Master, you're back," she said softly.

Zhou Yi nodded firmly and said, "Come, let's go out."

"Go out?" Yuan Lixun asked, puzzled. "Where are we going?"

"We've been here for a while now, but we haven't gone out to explore yet. Today, let's go and see the bustling streets of this city," Zhou Yi chuckled and said, "What do you say? Are you unwilling?"

Yuan Lixun excitedly nodded, then suddenly paused and shook her head. It seemed that something wasn't quite right, and a blush bloomed on her face, resembling a rosy apple, tempting one to take a bite.

Seeing her excited expression, Zhou Yi's heart inexplicably lightened.

Side by side, they left Shao Ming Ju Residence. Along the way, even though there were servants who noticed them, they immediately bowed respectfully, not daring to obstruct them in the slightest.

※※※※

On the spacious streets, there were many towering taverns.

While not every tavern was packed with guests, even from the outside, one could see that at least sixty percent of the seats were occupied. Zhou Yi and Yuan Lixun strolled along the streets, savoring this rare leisurely time.

As Zhou Yi felt the lingering gazes of the woman beside him, captivated by the various shops, he couldn't help but feel a tinge of sentiment. Since he began his cultivation, the days he could spend on the streets had been few and far between. Especially in the past two years, apart from the time he accompanied his mother and siblings for a stroll in Taicang County, he had never truly relaxed like this.

And Yuan Lixun, who followed him, had always taken great care of his daily life, leaving no spare time for her to wander the streets. This time, the two of them had left Shao Ming Ju Residence on a whim.

If Zhou Yi hadn't unexpectedly sensed the loneliness in Yuan Lixun's heart, they would have had no reason to leave without cause.

After wandering on the streets for a while, Zhou Yi hadn't found anything useful. It wasn't that his standards were too high; it was simply because his focus was solely on cultivation, lacking any interest in the mundane items used by ordinary people.

On the other hand, Yuan Lixun had purchased some water-based makeup and wrapped it up in a small package. Without saying a word, Zhou Yi reached out and took it, carrying it in his hand. Yuan Lixun opened her mouth to speak but ultimately blushed and acquiesced.

They walked along the side of the street, not in the center of the main thoroughfare. It wasn't because their status was lacking, but rather because strolling this way created a more relaxed and carefree shopping atmosphere.

Suddenly, Zhou Yi's eyes brightened, and he pointed ahead, saying, "Lixun, you've been with me for nearly two months now, and I haven't given you anything. Let's go take a look over there."

Yuan Lixun looked up and saw a three-story building ahead, with the three words "Feng Lai Xiang" written on the signboard. Just by looking at the sign, she immediately knew what kind of place it was.

After a moment of hesitation, she whispered, "Young Master, Feng Lai Xiang is known for having the most exquisite jewelry. Perhaps we should try another store."

Indeed, when it came to jewelry in the northwest kingdoms, Feng Lai Xiang was undoubtedly the top choice, leaving its competitors far behind. It was said that Feng Lai Xiang not only had influence in the three major empires of the northwest but also seemed to have connections with the famous superpower, Da Shen, in the east.

Because of this, Feng Lai Xiang had branches in almost every country and important city in the northwest. Any person of status, when seeking to purchase jewelry, would undoubtedly choose Feng Lai Xiang as their first option.

Zhou Yi waved his hand slightly and said, "It's alright, go ahead and choose."

His voice was filled with confidence. At this moment, Zhou Yi, from any perspective, was an incredibly wealthy man. While it was impossible for him to buy all the Feng Lai Xiang stores, it was more than enough for him to purchase one of the branches.

Under Zhou Yi's insistence, Yuan Lixun reluctantly entered Feng Lai Xiang. Although she came from a prestigious family, as the daughter of a concubine and with her mother having passed away early, she had little experience in such settings.

The pitiful few pieces of jewelry at home were the belongings left by her own mother. Although Yuan Lixun had received several sets of exquisite, luxurious, and extravagant jewelry and clothing prepared by Yuan Chengzhi, she had never worn a single piece. Therefore, when she entered Feng Lai Xiang for the first time, her eyes couldn't help but light up, dazzled by the shimmering brilliance of the precious artifacts inside.

As Zhou Yi's gaze shifted, he took in the sight of these precious gemstones, but he didn't have much of a reaction. These gemstones and the like might have moved him in the past, but ever since he reached the Innate realm, his interest in such items had greatly diminished. He was almost indifferent to them.

Suddenly, a cold and contemptuous voice rang out, "Who is this country bumpkin, daring to show up in Feng Lai Xiang? Mr. Xu, the standards of Feng Lai Xiang are plummeting."

Zhou Yi furrowed his brows slightly, while Yuan Lixun's face had long turned red. She felt anxious, unsure if her actions had embarrassed Young Master.

Zhou Yi looked up and saw a tall and spirited young man standing at the staircase on the second floor. He appeared to be around twenty-five or twenty-six years old, with a rather handsome face. However, the arrogance on his face and the disdainful gaze greatly diminished his image.

"Young Master Zi, please be magnanimous and spare us ordinary people from your condescension," a middle-aged man in a harmonious colored silk robe walked over with a smile, bowing deeply and saying, "Please come upstairs. We have prepared special jewelry and gemstones for you, guaranteed to satisfy your desires."

Young Master Zi seemed to be quite satisfied with this person's attitude and no longer lingered. With a group of attendants surrounding him, he swaggered up to the second floor.

However, nobody noticed that behind this person, a servant discreetly and instinctively dodged, trying to hide from sight. The middle-aged man in the silk robe turned around and approached Zhou Yi and Yuan Lixun. He smiled wryly and said, "Please forgive me for my actions earlier. I had no choice. If the two of you make purchases in our humble store today, I will personally make the decision to reduce all costs by ten percent."

With Zhou Yi's current wealth, he naturally didn't care about that ten percent. However, the man's words were sincere, leaving him with a faint sense of goodwill.

"If you are able to make such decisions, may I ask..."

"I am Xu Shan, the shopkeeper of this jewelry store," Xu Shan said with a slight bow, "I hope you can forgive what happened just now."

"So, you're Shopkeeper Xu. I've heard about you for a long time."

Zhou Yi spoke, but his tone lacked the slightest hint of having heard about Xu Shan before.

Xu Shan chuckled, seemingly unconcerned. He had encountered countless people in his life and could tell that although this young girl lacked worldly experience, this young man was far from ordinary.

Zhou Yi's gaze swept across the first floor before suddenly asking, "Shopkeeper Xu, what do you have on the second floor?"

Xu Shan hesitated for a moment and replied, "On the second floor, we have some exquisite pieces of jewelry, surpassing the quality available on the first floor. However, the prices correspondingly reflect that."

"Very well, please take us up to see it," Zhou Yi said casually.

Xu Shan sighed and said, "Young sir, I know you must have a significant background. If I'm not mistaken, you must be from a distant land."

Zhou Yi asked in surprise, "How did you know?"

Xu Shan gave a bitter smile and replied, "Judging by your demeanor, it's clear that you are not an ordinary person. If you have resided in the Tianluo Kingdom, then you should have heard of the Zi family, one of the Five Great Aristocratic Families."

Zhou Yi's heart stirred, and he asked, "The young man who went upstairs, he is from the Zi family?"

"Yes, that young man is Zi Ruiguang, the legitimate heir of the Zi family and the third young master. Xu Shan hesitated for a moment and continued, "You are an outsider after all. It's not worth offending the Zi family for the sake of pride."

Zhou Yi smiled faintly and said, "What's so great about offending the Zi family?"

Xu Shan's gaze froze, and he suddenly looked at them with a gaze that seemed to be looking at fools. His lips twitched a few times as he looked at the young couple in front of him. He couldn't figure out which family this young man came from to ask such a question.

Although he wanted to ignore them, he couldn't bear to see them lose their lives for no reason.

With a light cough, Xu Shan spoke with a serious tone, "Young sir, the Zi family is one of the Five Great Aristocratic Families in the Tianluo Kingdom. Even the king himself would have to give the Zi family three parts face."

Zhou Yi suddenly showed a look of enlightenment, as if he had just realized the other party's power.

Xu Shan thought to himself that this young man was truly irresponsible. If I hadn't pointed it out today, he probably wouldn't even know how he would end up.

While Xu Shan was contemplating, Zhou Yi suddenly grabbed Yuan Lixun's hand and bypassed him, heading towards the staircase to the second floor.

Xu Shan was taken aback and quickly caught up, asking, "What are you two planning to do?"

"Of course, we're going upstairs to take a look," Zhou Yi blinked innocently and said, "Since there are good things up there, why waste time down here?"

A flush of redness surged on Xu Shan's face as he gave Zhou Yi a deep look and said, "Young sir, didn't you hear what I said just now?"

"I heard," Zhou Yi replied very honestly, "But there's one thing I forgot to tell you."

Xu Shan was puzzled and instinctively asked, "What is it?"

"When the king of the Tianluo Kingdom sees me, he should give me four parts face," Zhou Yi said, no longer paying attention to Xu Shan and directly walking upstairs.

Xu Shan's eyes widened. He had encountered arrogance before, but never such audacity. Giving the Zi family three parts face, but demanding four parts for himself from the king of the Tianluo Kingdom. Did that mean he had complete control over the Zi family?

Feeling a hint of anger, Xu Shan made up his mind to stop this person from going any further.

After all, this was the premises of "Feng Lai Xiang," and a fight here would certainly not be a good thing for the shop. With this in mind, Xu Shan's body moved, and his legs filled with strength as he dashed forward. He extended his arm, intending to grab Zhou Yi and forcefully stop him by pulling him back through Yuan Lixun.

However, as he reached out, his hand grasped nothing but air. Zhou Yi's arm was clearly in front of his eyes, but when his palm reached its supposed destination, it suddenly disappeared. It vanished right before his eyes.

This surprise was no small matter. Xu Shan felt a chill in his heart and was about to step back when he saw the two young people already entering the second floor. He was left dumbfounded. Their movements weren't particularly fast, yet their speed was unimaginable. Before he could react, they had already reached the second level.

Such skill sent shivers down his spine.

Although he hesitated for a moment, Xu Shan immediately extended his hand, and a person quickly approached him. He whispered, "Quickly go to the neighboring restaurant. Zi RuiWen should be there.

Tell him that the Third Young Master might be in trouble and ask him to come and handle it."

The person nodded and swiftly disappeared.

Finally, Xu Shan took a deep breath, straightened his attire, and walked steadily into the second floor.

※※※※

Inside the second floor, the decorations and furnishings were distinctly different from the first floor. If the first floor exuded simplicity and elegance, the second floor exuded a luxurious and noble atmosphere at every turn.

It was Zhou Yi's first time in such a place, and even he couldn't help but feel curious. However, his curiosity was just that—curiosity. It was highly unlikely that he would feel fear or apprehension.

On the second floor, there were over ten closed rooms, some open and some shut. There were several servants and beautiful maids outside the doors. When the attendant saw Zhou Yi and Yuan Lixun, he instinctively recoiled and his expression subtly changed. But then he straightened his posture, his gaze flickering as he pondered something.

As Zhou Yi ascended the stairs, he was able to "hear" the movements of everyone in the vicinity without even using his eyes. He naturally noticed this person's actions, but he didn't pay it much mind. During his battle with Cheng Fu at the Royal Manor, which took place in front of thousands of people, it wouldn't be surprising if this person had been among the crowd and caught a glimpse of his face.

After all, this person was Zi Ruiguang's attendant, and it was normal for the attendants of one of the Five Great Houses of Tianluo Kingdom to attend such a grand event.

Zhou Yi sneered coldly and pulled Yuan Lixun's hand, striding forward. In an instant, they arrived at the door guarded by these attendants.

Surprised expressions appeared on the faces of the guards, but their actions didn't show any dissatisfaction. They silently extended their hands, seemingly intending to subdue Zhou Yi without disturbing the person inside the room.

However, their expressions turned ugly and filled with disbelief in the next moment. Zhou Yi and Yuan Lixun inexplicably disappeared, as if they had vanished into thin air before their eyes.

Then, as if blown by the wind, the door they were guarding swung open. When they looked up, there was only a fleeting shadow.

The guards exchanged bewildered and terrified glances. What kind of person was this?

At that moment, a figure darted forward like lightning. This person had a sharp appearance but a displeased expression. It was Xu Shan, the manager of Feng Lai Xiang.

Upon seeing the guards' expressions, he felt a sense of unease. Casting a quick glance at the room, he swiftly walked inside.

His status was far beyond ordinary, and as the guards found themselves at a loss, they looked at him with eyes filled with pleas for help.

With a bitter smile, Xu Shan pushed open the door and entered, criticizing himself inwardly. He had no choice but to enter the room, despite the uneasy feeling.

Chapter 157

In each elegant room on the second floor, there was a distinction between the front and back halls. As Xu Shan pushed open the door and entered, half of the heavy burden that had been hanging over their hearts finally lifted. It turned out that Zhou Yi and the others didn't directly enter the inner room but silently admired the paintings and calligraphy hanging on the wall in the outer room.

The moment Zhou Yi stepped into the room, his eyes immediately fell upon a particular painting on the wall. It was a landscape painting, exquisitely lifelike and captivating. However, it was evident that this was not the work of a renowned artist, as the painting lacked any signatures or seals.

If it weren't for the fact that the painting was indeed a remarkable piece, it wouldn't have been displayed in this location.

But in Zhou Yi's eyes, this painting was more than just a decorative artwork; it was a depiction of profound cosmic principles and universal truths. He was certain that only a master of innate talent, one who had attained considerable enlightenment beyond the realm of clouds and rain, could have created such a masterpiece.

Although this painting might not have much immediate practical value to Zhou Yi, if he were to contemplate it for an extended period, grasping the profound cosmic principles it contained and allowing them to resonate with his own insights, it should offer some assistance.

He couldn't help but sigh inwardly, acknowledging his fortunate luck. If it weren't for that Ziruiguang insulting Yuan Lixun, he wouldn't have come up here and certainly wouldn't have laid eyes on this landscape painting.

This landscape painting, unless it fell into the hands of a master who comprehended the mysteries of the clouds and rain, would remain an enigma even if it hung here for a hundred years. Not even Cheng Fu or Shui Xuanjin would be able to fully grasp its profundity.

Faint footsteps sounded behind him, and as Zhou Yi turned around, a mischievous smile naturally graced his face. Xu Shan could only smile wryly, deeply bowing to Zhou Yi. Observing the pained expression on his face, Zhou Yi contemplated for a moment before pointing to the landscape painting on the wall, making his intention abundantly clear.

Xu Shan let out a long sigh, nodding his head like a pecking chick. As long as he could convince this inscrutable star of calamity to let go of his grievances, he would be willing to pay any price, no matter how great.

After all, he conducted business within the Tianluo Kingdom, and offending the five major clans would undoubtedly lead to unfavorable consequences. Even with the profound background of Feng Laixiang, he didn't wish to casually provoke the local powerhouses.

Of course, after witnessing Zhou Yi's skills, he also held a deep sense of fear within him. To achieve such prowess at such a young age, who knew what formidable support lay behind him?

As long as these two individuals didn't cause trouble within his Feng Laixiang, he would be grateful to the heavens.

Zhou Yi smiled faintly and nodded toward Yuan Lixun. Though the young girl's age was similar to Zhou Yi's, she possessed sharp wit and immediately understood his intention. While she felt relieved that he was no longer entangled in the matter concerning Ziruiguang, a hint of disappointment lingered in her heart.

However, as she stepped forward, preparing to remove the painting, a familiar voice, filled with familiarity, reached her ears, saying, "Lixun, leave this place, and I will settle the score for you."

Yuan Lixun was momentarily stunned, her heart suddenly filled with sweetness, and a dense feeling of happiness surged within her. It seemed as if even her movements became lighter and swifter.

The door to the inner hall suddenly emitted a soft sound, and Zi Ruiguang walked out with an unpleasant expression. His displeasure immediately turned into extreme dissatisfaction when he caught sight of Zhou Yi and the others.

Xu Shan was instantly struck with a splitting headache. He hadn't expected the young master to come out so soon. It seemed that he had no interest in the carefully prepared jewelry and the like in the building.

At that moment, Yuan Lixun happened to approach the landscape painting. She naturally ignored Zi Ruiguang, as if he didn't exist at all. Oblivious to his presence, she reached out her hand and attempted to take down the painting.

Zi Ruiguang snorted in anger, his gaze falling upon the painting. Suddenly, he froze. Seeing Yuan Lixun's fair jade hand about to touch the frame of the painting, he immediately exclaimed, "Wait!"

His voice carried no regard, his eyebrows slightly raised, as if everyone in the world should obey his command.

However, neither Zhou Yi nor Yuan Lixun would truly comply with his orders. Yuan Lixun, seemingly unaware, took down the painting, removed it from the frame, and nonchalantly rolled it up.

Zi Ruiguang's face turned iron blue. In his more than twenty years of life, he rarely encountered someone who wouldn't give him face like this.

When he angrily shouted, the attendants outside rushed in. Although they held deep fear for Zhou Yi, they wouldn't dare to show any negligence when their master summoned them.

Zhou Yi watched as Yuan Lixun returned to his side, carrying the rolled-up painting, and couldn't help but smile. He turned to Xu Shan and said, "Mr. Xu, how much for this painting? Name your price."

Xu Shan let out a long sigh and said with a bitter smile, "This painting serves as a decoration in this building. If the young master is interested, feel free to take it."

Zhou Yi shook his head slightly and replied, "That won't do. I don't have the habit of taking things by force."

Zi Ruiguang let out a cold snort and suddenly declared, "Mr. Xu, I want that painting."

Xu Shan's mouth fell open, and his face revealed an expression of great anguish, as if he had swallowed a fly and felt extremely uncomfortable.

Zhou Yi seemed to have not heard his words and continued to smile gently as he said, "Mr. Xu, not only do I want this painting, but I also want to know its origin and who painted it, and why it is hanging here."

Zi Ruiguang's anger grew more intense, and he suddenly exclaimed, "Are you two deaf? I said I want that painting."

Zhou Yi waved his hand slightly and said, "Where did this annoying fly buzzing around come from, disturbing our peace of mind?"

This time, the faces of Xu Shan and the others completely changed. If the conflict before had been minor, this statement could be seen as provocation.

Under normal circumstances, the attendants by Zi Ruiguang's side would have scolded or even resorted to violence. However, just a while ago, they had witnessed Zhou Yi's elusive and immeasurable skills. They knew that provoking him would lead to no good.

Yuan Lixun covered her mouth and chuckled softly, but her gaze unintentionally glanced at someone's face, causing her delicate eyebrows to slightly furrow. However, it was just a momentary lapse, and she quickly regained her composure because she couldn't recall the person's identity.

However, that person's gaze remained fixed on Zhou Yi, oblivious to Yuan Lixun's change in expression.

A trace of anger and embarrassment flickered in Zi Ruiguang's eyes, but he quickly suppressed his resentment and forced a smile. He said, "I am Zi Ruiguang of the Zi Mansion. How should I address you? It seems we are not acquainted."

Although Zi Ruiguang was annoyed, growing up in such a prestigious family didn't make him a useless fool. At the very least, he knew that he should inquire about his opponent's background beforehand. If the situation seemed too difficult, he couldn't touch matters that would cross the bottom line between noble families.

Zhou Yi smiled faintly and replied, "No need to establish any relationship with me. I don't need friends who are stuck in the mud, with dog-like eyes looking down on others."

As he spoke, he blinked at Yuan Lixun twice. A hint of a blush appeared on Yuan Lixun's beautiful face, and she quickly lowered her gaze, but there was a clear smile in her eyes.

When they first met, Zi Ruiguang had mocked Yuan Lixun as a country bumpkin. So now, when Zhou Yi referred to Zi Ruiguang's dog-like eyes, it was a clear tit-for-tat, indicating that he didn't consider Zi Ruiguang on the same level.

Zhou Yi's attitude was unexpectedly audacious and even overbearing, seemingly dismissing the entire Zi Mansion.

Zi Ruiguang's face finally turned dark and seemed as if it was about to drip water. He snorted angrily, no longer concerned about any reservations.

If he allowed himself to be spoken to in this manner and still remained patient, then the reputation of the five major noble families in the Tianluo Kingdom would truly be tarnished.

He waved his hand, coldly ordering, "Seize them."

He hadn't lost his senses completely and knew that this place wasn't suitable for killing. However, once these two individuals were captured, countless means of dealing with them would follow.

Since the master had given the order, the attendants and guests had no choice but to obey. They lamented inwardly but still rushed forward.

Zi Ruiguang had a total of twelve people by his side, nine of whom were trained attendants from the Zi family, while the other three were recruited from outside as guests.

The six attendants were the ones currently attacking. Judging by their approach, it was clear that they excelled in combined attacks, displaying a fierce aura that seemed to have been forged through battles on the battlefield.

Naturally, Zhou Yi couldn't regard these few individuals highly. He smiled faintly, preparing to take action when he heard a hurried sound of footsteps approaching from outside. Subsequently, the door to the room was pushed open, and someone swiftly stepped inside.

As this person entered the room, they happened to witness the attendants making their move. They also saw Zhou Yi and Yuan Lixun, seemingly relaxed and unaware of the looming shadowy fists and sharp gusts of wind.

The person's face immediately changed, filled with fear. Without thinking, he rushed forward and shouted, "Stop!"

His voice was filled with both fear and strength. The six attendants who had launched their attack were momentarily stunned because they were extremely familiar with that voice. However, for some reason, the tone seemed slightly different from what they remembered.

Zi Ruiguang's face suddenly filled with hope, but it quickly turned into speechlessness. After this person appeared, not only did he show no intention of helping Zi Ruiguang, but he swiftly rushed forward, arriving between the six attendants and Zhou Yi before anyone else.

With his back turned to Zhou Yi, he completely handed over his rear to the person without any defenses. At the same time, he extended his hands and launched a fierce attack.

The six attendants, upon realizing the person in front of them, had their faces change simultaneously. Faced with this palm strike coming out of thin air, they didn't dare to retaliate or even attempt to block. They stood like wooden stakes, perfectly straight and unmoving.

Without mercy, the person struck each of them with a palm, instantly sending them flying away. However, his strikes were imbued with hidden force, only causing the six to be sent flying without causing any real harm.

After completing this act, the person turned around and deeply bowed to the ground, respectfully saying, "Master Zhou, my younger brother acted foolishly and offended you. I implore your magnanimity to forgive his unintentional mistake. When we return, I will certainly punish him severely."

Xu Shan, Zi Ruiguang, and the others were initially stunned, but their eyes quickly widened. Although they didn't recognize Zhou Yi, when they heard the recent rumors spreading throughout the capital about the renowned "Master Zhou," they knew that they shouldn't provoke him if they wanted to continue thriving in the capital.

Excitement and fear filled the eyes of the crowd. Especially the attendants, who realized that they had dared to make a move against a master at the Innate Realm, their backs were instantly drenched in cold sweat.

Fear also appeared in Zi Ruiguang's eyes. His previous arrogance disappeared in an instant, replaced by deep dread.

Zhou Yi glanced at the person and said, "You are Zi RuiWen."

"Indeed," Zi RuiWen said excitedly, "I never expected that Master Zhou would remember my name. It is truly my honor."

Zhou Yi shook his head inwardly. Zi RuiWen had displayed a much stronger aura than Zi Ruiguang when they first met, riding through the center of the street with a group of young masters and misses. But now that Zi RuiWen recognized him, he became so restrained and obsequious.

A wave of annoyance surged within Zhou Yi. He had no desire to have any dealings with these people. He sneered and said, "Young Master Zi, you sure have quite the presence. I think Young Master Zi Ruiguang's mouth needs some proper discipline."

Zi RuiWen's expression changed slightly, and he immediately replied respectfully, "Yes, Master Zhou is correct."

Then, Zi RuiWen turned around and stood in front of Zi Ruiguang, saying, "Look up."

Zi Ruiguang looked up in confusion and suddenly felt a burning pain on his face. Zi RuiWen was slapping him one after another. After just a few slaps, his face had become swollen like a pig's head, with blood dripping from the corners of his mouth, a horrifying sight.

However, apart from instinctively dodging the first slap, Zi Ruiguang stood straight and endured the rest without begging for mercy.

Zhou Yi frowned and said, "That's enough. We'll call it quits for today."

Only then did Zi RuiWen stop and said, "Thank you, Master Zhou."

Zi Ruiguang bent down and said, "Thank you, Master Zhou," his face was already severely swollen, and he could barely speak clearly.

Zhou Yi paid no attention to him and said, "Mr. Xu, can you finally tell me the value and origin of this painting?"

Xu Shan finally woke up from his daze and quickly responded, giving a series of instructions.

After a moment, someone brought a ledger, and Xu Shan flipped through it. He smiled bitterly and said, "Master Zhou, I have found out. This painting was made two months ago by a destitute traveler who had a meal in our inn but couldn't pay. So he made this painting on the spot as payment. The innkeeper at that time found the painting quite good and decided to waive his food and drink expenses, and used this painting as decoration."

"Paying with a painting?" A wry smile appeared on Zhou Yi's face. He sighed deeply, realizing that the world was truly full of wonders. It was astonishing to think that a powerful Innate Realm expert could end up in such a destitute state and would negotiate with ordinary people like this. It was truly an extraordinary story.

Xu Shan respectfully said, "It is as Master Zhou said."

Zhou Yi pondered for a moment and asked, "Did Fenglaixiang also operate an inn here?"

"Yes, we have similar jewelry stores and inns in all major cities."

"If someone has a meal but cannot pay for the drinks, how do you usually handle it?"

After hesitating for a moment, Xu Shan finally said, "According to the inn's rules, if someone really tries to eat without paying, we have to force them to vomit out as much as they have eaten."

Zhou Yi's expression became even more strange, and he said, "The innkeeper of your establishment still has some foresight. Fortunately, he accepted this painting instead of resorting to violence. Otherwise, your inn would have had a hard time."

Xu Shan was slightly taken aback and asked tentatively, "Why is that?"

Zhou Yi took the painting from Yuan Lixun's hands, gently stroked it, and said, "The author of this painting is a master of the Innate Realm. His understanding of the laws of heaven and earth is not inferior to mine. Even if I were to encounter him, I wouldn't dare to claim victory easily. If the bodyguards or staff of your inn had tried to force him to vomit out the food he had eaten... hehe..." He playfully glanced at Xu Shan and continued, "Of course, perhaps your inn also has hidden masters of the Innate Realm, who knows?"

Xu Shan's face became extremely interesting, and his eyes widened like never before.

Zhou Yi laughed heartily and said, "How much is the value of that meal? Go back and report a sum to Shao Mingju, and they will settle with you. Lixun, let's go."

Yuan Lixun softly replied and followed Zhou Yi to the door. However, her footsteps suddenly halted, as if she had remembered something. But she forcefully suppressed her surprise and continued to follow Zhou Yi.

Zhou Yi didn't speak to the Zi brothers again, which relieved them both.

Although Zi Ruiguang had lost face and looked at Zhou Yi with a tinge of resentment, the dominant feelings in his heart were fear and regret.

Chapter 158

Leaving the Fenglaixiang Jewelry , they turned onto a side street. Zhou Yi sighed apologetically, "Li Xun, I had originally intended to pick out a few pieces of jewelry for you, but I didn't expect this turn of events. We ended up with nothing. I promise to make it up to you next time."

Yuan Lixun smiled faintly, pointing to the painting scroll inside Zhou Yi's package, saying, "But we do have this, don't we? How can we say we gained nothing?"

Zhou Yi raised an eyebrow, cracking a smile, feeling warmth fill his heart as well.

Suddenly, Yuan Lixun's smile faded, a hint of hesitation showing on her face. Concerned, Zhou Yi quickly asked, "What's wrong?"

He certainly didn't think Yuan Lixun was unhappy because there were no gifts. But her change in expression did worry him.

Unexplainably, every move, every smile of Yuan Lixun's could tug at his heartstrings. Though their initial meeting wasn't of Zhou Yi's choosing, at his age, being a young man who had barely interacted with anyone other than those involved in his cultivation, the first woman to stay by his side was naturally the easiest to find a place in his heart.

Yuan Lixun pursed her rosy lips and spoke softly, "Young Master, just now, I saw someone I know."

"Someone you know? You have acquaintances here?" Zhou Yi asked in surprise.

"Yes, the person you may not recognize, but I will never forget," Yuan Lixun said in a low voice.

Zhou Yi's gaze slightly hardened; he sensed a vague hint of fear. He gently asked, "Who is this person?"

"Young Master, do you remember the Jinlin Fan family?" Yuan Lixun asked softly.

"Of course I do," Zhou Yi replied with a sunny smile. "In this lifetime, I don't think I'll ever forget them."

It was precisely because of the conflict with the Jinlin Fan family that Zhou Yi had his first encounter with a preeminent cultivator.

"The current head of the Fan family, Fan Shuhe, has two sons. One is Fan Haori, and the other is Fan Haoyue," Yuan Lixun solemnly said. "The person I encountered earlier was Fan Haoyue."

In Zhou Yi's mind, a face flashed instantly. It was the young noble he had encountered when he returned home from the Fire Crow Kingdom and passed through Jinlin. At that time, the arrogant young man had tried to covet his Hongling Horse. However, Zhou Yi was in a good mood and didn't want to bother with him, so he simply taught him a small lesson and left.

It was only later that he learned the person he had encountered was the second young master who had returned home. From him, Zhou Yi obtained enough refined magnetic steel to refine his great guandao once again.

These memories flashed like lightning in his mind, and the once-fading figure became clearer and clearer.

"Lixun, how did you recognize him?" Zhou Yi asked.

Yuan Lixun's face slightly reddened as she said, "This person once visited my family. After seeing me, he sent someone to propose marriage to my father. However, my father rejected him outright." She lightly tapped her chest, seemingly still shaken by the experience.

Zhou Yi's eyes briefly glanced at her chest. Yuan Lixun was not much younger than him, just sixteen years old, and as a girl who matured early, her chest had slightly developed with two small budding curves, though they were still hidden under her clothes. It was different from a man's physique, and when his gaze swept over, he couldn't help but look a little longer.

Yuan Lixun, with her feminine intuition, noticed this and her face turned red, feeling embarrassed. She lightly reprimanded herself and wondered why she would make such a gesture.

She looked up, feeling nervous, and saw Zhou Yi's face full of embarrassment. His sincere smile flowed through her heart like a warm spring, causing her face to gradually flush with redness.

Zhou Yi cleared his throat and said, "Lixun, I'll escort you back home, and then I'll go take a look at that guy." He paused and added, "It's quite strange that he has joined the Zi family."

Yuan Lixun nodded slightly. One of her hands was already tightly held by Zhou Yi, and his other hand gently wrapped around her slender waist.

Her heart warmed, her body softened, and then she felt a sensation as if they were soaring through the clouds. The wind whistled in her ears, and the scenery in front of her flew by like a blur, heading towards the distance.

She nestled her head against a warm embrace, hoping that it would remain like this forever...

Zhou Yi's speed in using light-footwork had vastly improved after comprehending the power of the wind. It was incomparable to before.

Even with a person in his arms, they returned to Shao Ming Ju Residence in no time.

After gently setting down the reluctant Yuan Lixun, Zhou Yi surprisingly felt a twinge of reluctance himself. But when he thought of Fan Haoyue, a poisonous thorn seemed to pierce his heart, making it hard to let go.

Although this person didn't seem threatening, since he had involved himself with one of the five major families of Tianluo, caution was necessary.

After escorting Yuan Lixun back to her room, Zhou Yi left once again. However, this time he left cautiously, not alerting anyone, not even Shui Xuanjin, who didn't notice his disappearance.

Of course, that was because Shui Xuanjin no longer used his extraordinary eavesdropping skills. Once he learned that Zhou Yi also mastered the same techniques and seemed to surpass him in their application, the old man became very tactful and no longer tried to provoke him.

After leaving Shao Ming Ju Residence, Zhou Yi's appearance underwent a tremendous transformation as he sprinted through the city.

His body inexplicably grew by a whole size, his bones expanded, completely altering his physique. What was even more dramatic was that his facial features had truly and completely changed.

His appearance now resembled that of a weasel-faced monkey, a face that once seen would be hard to forget, and even harder to find any resemblance to Zhou Yi.

Of course, his clothing underwent a complete change as well. This was not difficult; in Shao Ming Ju Residence, he had dozens of sets of clothes, so he simply chose one at random to wear.

Although the clothes felt a bit tight, it gave him the appearance of a sleek night suit.

In a moment, Zhou Yi had returned to the second street outside Fenglaixiang Jewelry . With a quick listen, he could tell that the group of people was no longer there.

This was to be expected. After such an incident, it would be incredible if the Zi brothers were still hanging around.

Zhou Yi gently closed his eyes. He was standing in a dark corner of a small alleyway, a place that would not attract anyone's attention. He confidently activated his listening skill without any hesitation.

His ears immediately became sensitive, and the frequency gradually increased. Although his ears didn't physically enlarge, the speed was enough to astonish anyone.

Before long, a faint smile appeared on Zhou Yi's face. He silently waited in this spot.

Relying solely on his hearing, he quickly picked up the voice of Zi Ruiwen, the eldest son of the Zi family. He was chatting happily with someone in a nearby tavern, seemingly unaffected by the recent events they had encountered.

Once he located Zi Ruiwen, Zhou Yi effortlessly honed in on a hurried breathing sound.

In his mind, various sounds continued to flow, gradually forming a three-dimensional picture.

Inside a spacious carriage, Zi Ruiguang sat with a look of grievance on his face. His face was still swollen, but it appeared to be coated with ointment, giving it a glossy sheen. Zhou Yi could clearly sense from his breathing that he was indignant about the events of the day. Zhou Yi could even hear his inner thoughts in that voice.

Within a ten-meter radius of the carriage, there was no one in sight. However, dozens of cultivators with at least a seventh-layer inner strength surrounded the carriage, as if they were protecting and monitoring the people inside.

Zhou Yi immediately understood that Zi Ruiwen, the third young master of the Zi family, was definitely under house arrest.

He didn't expect Zi Ruiwen to wield such power within his own family, to the point where even his brothers didn't dare defy him. It seemed that he was specifically groomed within the prominent family. Otherwise, when Zi Ruiguang was slapped by Zi Ruiwen in Fenglaixiang, Zi Ruiguang wouldn't have been so afraid to resist.

Suddenly, a person approached the carriage, opened the door, and entered. They took out some things and said softly, "Third Young Master, please have your meal."

Zi Ruiguang snorted in anger and said, "I don't want it. Take it all away."

Upon hearing this voice, Zhou Yi's expression subtly changed. Since he remembered Fan Haoyue, it was only natural that he recognized his voice. So, as soon as he heard the voice, he immediately identified the person.

Fan Haoyue let out a long sigh, seemingly talking to himself. "Third Young Master, you have truly suffered today. That Zhou Yi is arrogant and egotistical, considering himself above everyone else. Not only did he not put you in his eyes, but he also didn't care about the entire Zi family."

Zi Ruiguang's breathing became agitated once again. However, he didn't drive away Fan Haoyue because his words had indeed hit the mark.

Fan Haoyue glanced at him and continued, "Third Young Master, rest assured, such an evil person will surely face retribution."

"Will he face retribution?" Zi Ruiguang's eyes flickered, and he said fiercely.

"Of course," Fan Haoyue's voice became sinister. He said, "I have heard that Zhou Yi is not only arrogant, but also ruthless and cruel. For the sake of a woman, he once slaughtered an entire family, who were heirs to a legacy that spanned several decades, including a postnatal master with a tenth-layer inner strength. He seized their family fortune." He paused and said, "In my opinion, today he had the same intention. If he becomes deeply offended by you, he can legitimately plunder your family's wealth. If it weren't for the Second Young Master arriving quickly, the consequences would be unimaginable..."

Zhou Yi's ears trembled slightly, thinking to himself how the situation had been twisted around. If it weren't for the Fan family coveting the Yuan family's wealth, none of these subsequent events would have unfolded. But in Fan Haoyue's mind, he was likely cast as a villainous character. If Fan Haoyue didn't take the opportunity to defame him, that would be strange.

Zi Ruiguang pondered for a moment and asked, "Fan Yue, where did you hear this? Why have I never heard of it?"

Zhou Yi inwardly sighed. The scions of prominent families indeed had some insight. Although Zi Ruiguang despised him to the core, he still had his own judgment in such matters. However, Fan Haoyue actually used the alias "Fan Yue," which naturally represented his unwillingness to forget the Fan family's legacy.

Fan Haoyue let out a light sigh and said, "Third Young Master, I also accidentally learned about this incident. It is said to have occurred in the Jinlin Kingdom. If you don't believe me, you can send someone to inquire, and then you will have a clear understanding."

Hearing Fan Haoyue's earnest assurance, Zi Ruiguang couldn't help but be somewhat convinced.

Fan Haoyue suddenly lowered his voice and said, "Third Young Master, with that person insulting you in such a manner, will you really swallow your pride?"

Zi Ruiguang's face twitched, intensifying the pain he felt there. After a moment of silence, he let out an angry snort and said, "After all, this person is a grandmaster at the Innate level, highly regarded by Master Shui Xuanjin, and respected by His Majesty. What can I do?"

Fan Haoyue's face grew dark and gloomy. He said, "Third Young Master, if you're really willing to swallow your pride, then I have nothing more to say. But if you can't bear this humiliation, then I have a way to help you vent your anger."

Zi Ruiguang's eyes immediately lit up, and he stared fixedly at Fan Haoyue. After a moment, he spoke in a low voice, "What do you have in mind? I don't want to walk into a death trap."

Fan Haoyue smiled faintly and said, "Third Young Master, you can rest assured that the plan I propose will not put you in danger. Once it succeeds, it will undoubtedly make Zhou Yi suffer heart-wrenching pain."

Zi Ruiguang hesitated and asked, "Tell me your plan."

"Third Young Master, as I mentioned earlier, Zhou Yi is infatuated with beauty. He once wiped out a prestigious family in the Jinlin Kingdom for the sake of a woman. Do you know who that woman is?"

Zi Ruiguang was taken aback and said, "Is it the woman from today?"

"Most likely," Fan Haoyue added fuel to the fire. "Although I haven't seen her myself, Zhou Yi's behavior today clearly shows that he values this woman greatly. He is willing to go against you and the Zi family for her. You can imagine the position she holds in his heart."

Zi Ruiguang's eyes flickered uncertainly. While he acknowledged Fan Haoyue's words, he also understood the dangers involved.

Fan Haoyue leaned in closer and said, "I've done some research. This woman is merely a fifth-layer inner strength practitioner. With our capabilities, we can easily capture her. Then, we can..." He made a slicing gesture with his hand and continued, "Of course, since this woman has captivated Zhou Yi to such an extent, perhaps she possesses unique skills in bed. If you're interested, you can have a taste." He chuckled and said, "After all, she is the forbidden fruit of an Innate grandmaster. If she were to submit to you..."

Zi Ruiguang's heart trembled, as the identity of the Innate Grandmaster weighed heavily on him like a towering mountain. Naturally, he didn't dare direct his intentions towards Zhou Yi.

However, when faced with a maid by Zhou Yi's side, there weren't as many scruples.

Moreover, the mere thought of playing with a woman who belonged to an Innate grandmaster caused an abnormal flush to rise on Zi Ruiguang's face. A strange sensation, like venom, spread through his heart.

"Fan Yue, are you confident?" he asked, his voice trembling.

"Of course," Fan Haoyue replied, patting his chest. "As long as that woman leaves Shao Ming Ju Residence, I am confident that I can capture her and deliver her to your bed."

Zi Ruiguang hesitated for a moment and said, "She is that person's woman. It won't be so easy to get her, right?"

Fan Haoyue sighed and said, "Third Young Master, precisely because she is that person's woman, think about it. Is there anyone in the capital who would dare to harm her?"

Zi Ruiguang nodded, surveying the entire capital of Tianluo Kingdom. Besides the man in front of him, who seemed somewhat deranged, there was likely no other person who would entertain such thoughts.

Fan Haoyue chuckled, "Since everyone thinks the same way, we can go in the opposite direction and easily capture her."

After considering for a long time, Zi Ruiguang suddenly asked, "Fan Yue, why are you helping me like this? What is your ulterior motive?"

Fan Haoyue maintained a composed demeanor as he knelt in the carriage, respectfully stating, "Since I arrived at the Zi Residence, I have been nothing more than a humble ordinary guest, never receiving any recognition from anyone. This time, I offer my counsel to you, hoping that you will consider promoting me, having witnessed my wholehearted dedication in serving you after this matter is resolved."

Zi Ruiguang watched as Fan Haoyue bowed his head and pressed closely against the luxurious carpet on the carriage. A strange and fleeting sense of murderous intent welled up in his eyes, but it quickly disappeared.

His determination was firm in his heart - if this matter couldn't be accomplished, he would rather die than admit to being responsible for it.. But if this plan of Fan Yue's were to succeed, his first action wouldn't be to promote this person; instead, he would swiftly eliminate them, for only by silencing them completely could he find peace of mind.

As for the captured woman, though she possessed a fair countenance, she was far from being extraordinary. Even among the courtesans in their household, there were several who rivaled her.

However, this woman happened to be the woman of an Innate Grandmaster, and the mere thought of this identity was enough to make him feel a burning sensation throughout his body. With his status, he had been with countless women, even married ones, whom he could have at his disposal. But the woman connected to an Innate Grandmaster was something he had never even dared to imagine.

"Very well, Fan Yue, focus on accomplishing this task. If it succeeds, I will make you the leader of my personal retinue and personally recommend you to my father, ensuring a bright future for you."

Fan Haoyue's expression instantly brightened with joy. He raised his head and reverently kowtowed, saying, "Thank you, Young Master, for your graciousness."

Yet, a hint of eerie color flashed in his eyes as he screamed madly in his heart, "Zhou Yi, I will have my revenge."

However, at that very moment, their ears were simultaneously assaulted by a piercing, crowing sound akin to a rooster's cry: "Fan Haoyue, the Jinlin Fan Clan, you slaughtered my entire family. Today, I've come for vengeance!"

Chapter 159

The sudden thunderous roar echoed through the air, shattering the calm like a massive stone plunging into still waters. Instantly, it stirred the shouts and chain reactions of countless onlookers.

Around the carriage, several dozen skilled attendants stood guard, among them, six were meticulously chosen by the Zi family, their prowess reaching the seventh layer of inner strength.

Only those attendants nurtured since childhood were willing to serve the family even at the seventh layer of inner strength. Of course, once they reached the eighth layer, they would no longer be mere attendants but true members of the family's inner circle.

However, for the majority of individuals, reaching the seventh layer through their own strength was already the limit, even within esteemed families like the Zi.

From any perspective, the defenses around the carriage were exceedingly tight. Yet, with one commanding shout, an inexplicable, off-balance sensation befell these guards.

The one at the forefront bellowed, "Be careful, everyone!" He swiftly unsheathed his sword, a vibrant green steel blade gleaming with faint traces of red light.

His skills were undoubtedly the most remarkable among them all. With a quick glance, he already spotted a figure descending from above. Reacting swiftly, he stomped his feet and instantly soared into the air, simultaneously extending his hand. The longsword in his grip transformed into a streak of light, thrusting forward with lightning speed.

However, just as his blade was about to strike, a blinding white light flooded his vision. Soon after, an excruciating pain shot through his eyes, causing his sword to deviate from its intended path.

Seizing the opportunity, the figure landed on the ground, raising his hand as a cloud of white powder billowed into the air.

"Watch out, it's lime!" someone suddenly cried out. The attendants were filled with anger at this turn of events.

As attendants of the Zi family, they had countless experiences in real combat. However, whether it was sparring with each other or clashing with attendants from other noble families, they had never encountered such underhanded tactics before.

Indeed, in the fiercely martial northwest kingdoms, using such methods to strike at the enemy was considered highly contemptible.

When the figure sprinkled the lime, he followed it with a powerful punch that struck the leader's nose. The leader, already teary-eyed, fell to the ground after taking the blow, while his precious sword was deftly snatched away.

The figure seized the sword and immediately charged toward the carriage.

Several attendants squinted their eyes, having clearly discerned the person's appearance. It was a burly man with a pointed nose, his eyes bloodshot, fixated on the carriage as if it held something that deeply enraged him.

These attendants had heard his furious shout earlier, and they couldn't help but feel astonished. However, a few of them knew that the guest who had entered the carriage to deliver food earlier was named Fan Yue. They immediately associated this name with Fan Haoyue.

However, at this moment, no one voiced their inquiries. Several attendants crossed their longswords, launching a coordinated series of strikes.

Yet, in mid-air, the figure executed a swift spin. His sword moved like a blur, either parrying the attacking swords or narrowly evading them.

Everyone was filled with astonishment. In just that brief moment, the figure had already rushed to the front of the carriage, extending his sword and cleaving open the door.

Inside the carriage, both individuals had tense expressions. Although their backgrounds were different, the only commonality between them was their relatively low level of inner strength, both having reached only the sixth layer.

Witnessing that so many attendants were unable to do anything against this person, fear naturally gripped their hearts.

Zi Ruiguang glared at Fan Yue with a gaze filled with hatred. He had already concluded that this was an enemy seeking revenge.

The intruder kicked open the carriage door and leaped inside, instantly appearing beside the two individuals. Just as they were about to defend themselves, they felt a sharp pain in their hands and realized they had been pierced through by the intruder.

They let out a horrifying scream, too terrified to make any further movements.

This person who descended from the sky was none other than Zhou Yi. After overhearing their secretive conversation, he was consumed by anger.

Glancing at his clothes and the large pile of lime in the corner, he swiftly came up with a plan to put on a show. Despite being an innate powerhouse, his age was still relatively young, and he had no psychological burden when it came to concealing his identity. Moreover, using lime was a deliberate choice on his part. Most likely, no one would suspect that a grandmaster at his level would resort to such methods.

Of course, he drew inspiration from Fan Haoyue's words just now. Since everyone assumed that was the case, he decided to go against the tide.

With his sword held high, and now inside the carriage, the attendants naturally dared not approach. If they were burdened with the accusation of causing harm to the Third Young Master, they wouldn't survive.

Zhou Yi's voice grew sharp as he said, "Fan Haoyue, I never expected you to end up like this."

His words were filled with intense anger, and even a deaf person could sense the deep-seated hatred contained within.

Fan Haoyue's face turned incredibly pale. He had never seen this person before, nor did he have any idea how he had drawn the attention of this ominous figure.

"E-e-elder, you've mistaken me..." Fan Haoyue pleaded with a sobbing tone, "I'm not... I'm not the one, I swear."

"Not you?" Zhou Yi burst into sharp laughter. "You are Fan Haoyue, the second son of the Fan family from Jinlin Kingdom. When your family invaded my home all those years ago, I engraved the faces of you and your father and brother in my memory. Even if you turned to ashes, I would recognize you."

Fan Haoyue's complexion turned exceedingly grim. Starting from a small family, the Fan family had risen to power, and they had eliminated numerous minor noble families. There was no telling which remnant of those families this sneering man belonged to. But at this point, he could no longer deny it.

"Who are you exactly? ..." Fan Haoyue spoke with a hoarse voice.

Upon hearing his admission, Zi Ruiguang inside the carriage and the group of attendants outside collectively breathed a sigh of relief. While this person was audacious, they hoped that he had a legitimate grievance and would only trouble Fan Haoyue.

Zhou Yi sneered, saying, "Fan Haoyue, after your family annihilated mine, I arrived in Tianluo City. So many years have passed, and I thought I would never have the opportunity for revenge. But it seems fate has finally opened its eyes and brought you before me."

Zi Ruiguang quickly interjected, " This person concealed his identity and sought refuge in our Zi family, clearly harboring ulterior motives. Please, hero, kill him."

Zhou Yi spat and said, "You rode in the same carriage with this guy, so you're definitely his friend. You deserve to die too."

With a wave of his hand, Zhou Yi's sword flashed, leaving a wound on Zi Ruiguang's neck. A spray of fresh blood suddenly spurted out.

Zi Ruiguang instinctively covered the wound on his neck, his face filled with bewilderment. Slowly, he collapsed, his gaze filled with confusion. He never imagined that he would meet such an inexplicable death.

Zhou Yi reached out and gripped the speechless Fan Haoyue under his arm. Then he leaped out of the carriage, slashing his sword through the crowd, cutting a path of bloodshed.

His movements were lightning fast, and he acted swiftly. Before the others could even react to Zi Ruiguang's death, he had already escaped.

Some attendants rushed into the carriage to check if the Third Young Master had any hope of survival, while the rest turned to pursue the intruder.

However, after a moment, they realized that the intruder was far more familiar with the environment than they were. He deliberately sought out hidden corners and alleys, and as they chased after him, he only grew more distant until he completely disappeared.

Although they were born and raised in the city, as attendants of the Zi, it was impossible for them to venture into these cramped alleys that were like dog dens, where commoners resided.

Thus, in their minds, they assumed that this person must have lived in such an environment for a long time to be so familiar with it.

Little did they know that in this world, there existed a unique skill called "Shun Feng Er," or "Wind Listener," which granted exceptional knowledge of the surroundings.

By the time Zi Ruiwen and his men arrived, all they saw was chaos and carnage. The Third Young Master lay lifeless in a pool of blood, his eyes still filled with disbelief.

The current head of the Zi family naturally erupted in furious anger. Anyone whose child had died would transform into a raging beast in an instant.

Under his orders, the history of the Fan family in Jinlin Kingdom was swiftly investigated, and Fan Haoyue's appearance was compared with the descriptions.

At this point, the truth behind the incident was revealed. The mysterious man was a member of a minor noble family that had been wiped out by the Fan family. After the destruction of his family, he had been hiding among the nearby commoners. On this day, when he suddenly encountered Fan Haoyue, he seized the opportunity to seek revenge at the cost of his own life.

As for Zi Ruiguang, he had merely fallen victim to unfortunate circumstances, killed on a whim by the avenger.

It was likely that Fan Haoyue had been abducted by this person, who planned to exact cruel revenge. However, even if Fan Haoyue hadn't been taken, the members of the Zi family harbored a deep hatred towards him. If Fan Haoyue were to appear alive in their presence, the Zi family would undoubtedly be the first to not spare him.

In pursuit of this matter, the Zi family launched a city-wide search. Even the royal family was alarmed and sent assistance to investigate. However, the intruder seemed to have vanished into thin air, never appearing again within the sight of others.

Zhou Yi swiftly maneuvered, leading the others through several narrow alleys. He increased his speed, leaving the pursuers far behind. Eventually, he took Fan Haoyue out of the city.

In a secluded location, Zhou Yi threw Fan Haoyue down heavily and spoke in a deep voice, "Fan Haoyue, you managed to escape with your life in Jinlin Kingdom. Instead of living in seclusion, you've come out to cause trouble. It's your own doing that you're on a path to self-destruction."

Fan Haoyue seemed resigned, letting out a long sigh and saying, "Falling into your hands is a result of my ill fortune.

Zhou Yi's heart stirred, and he asked, "I heard that when you escaped from Jinlin Kingdom, you had a batch of treasures in your possession."

Fan Haoyue finally understood why this person went to great lengths to capture him. It turned out that besides seeking revenge, he also coveted the wealth in Fan Haoyue's hands.

Letting out a bitter smile, Fan Haoyue regarded Zhou Yi with eyes filled with a mixture of pity and contempt. He said, "Are you referring to the gold and silver given to me by Yuan Chengzhi? Heh... Do you really think that old man was so kind-hearted?"

He took a deep breath and continued in a voice filled with resentment, "That old man gave me a large sum of gold and silver. But as soon as I left the city, a group of bandits followed me. They not only wanted to rob me of my money but also sought to take my life. Fortunately, I was lucky enough to survive after falling off a cliff. Otherwise, I would have died long ago." He paused for a moment and spoke with a hint of interest, "If I still had that gold and silver, perhaps I would have settled in a rural area. But my hands are empty, so what can I do..."

Zhou Yi was slightly taken aback, silently lamenting. So Yuan Chengzhi had left a contingency plan. However, he was unaware that Fan Haoyue hadn't died and had nearly put his daughter in grave danger.

If only Yuan Chengzhi had known, perhaps he wouldn't have made such a decision.

Zhou Yi pondered for a moment and asked, "I overheard your conversation earlier, and it seems you hold a deep hatred for Zhou Yi. Why is that?"

A grimace flashed across Fan Haoyue's face, and he replied, "They all say that I caused the downfall of the Fan family. It was me."

Zhou Yi was greatly puzzled and asked, "How could it be you who caused the downfall of the Fan family?"

Fan Haoyue's face twitched slightly, his eyes filled with fear as if he had recalled an unforgettable memory.

Furrowing his eyebrows, Zhou Yi gently patted Fan Haoyue's body, sending a chilling energy surging through him. Fan Haoyue shivered and instantly regained clarity.

He looked at Zhou Yi with lingering fear in his eyes, then cleared his throat and said, "The surviving servants who managed to escape said that Zhou Yi, the person who passed by our caravan before, was riding a red stallion. They claimed that it was because I had the intention to loot the valuable horse that he came to the Yuan family and assisted them in killing Grandmaster Lv Xinwen, my father, and my elder brother..." Fear resurfaced on his face as he continued, "But it wasn't me. I had nothing to do with it."

Zhou Yi remained silent, shaking his head slightly. As a party involved in the incident, he knew for certain that he had nothing to do with the downfall of the Fan family.

Regardless of whether he had coveted Zhou Yi's red stallion.

His journey to the Yuan family in Jinlin was inevitable.

He wondered what those fleeing servants and attendants had said to Fan Haoyue that had left him so terrified, even bordering on being neurotic.

"Because Zhou Yi killed Lv Xinwen, you seek revenge against those around him," Zhou Yi casually asked.

Fan Haoyue's face contorted with ferocity as he replied, "Not only do I want to seek revenge against Yuan Lixun, but also against Zhou Yi. I will spread the news of Zirui Guang's affair with Zhou Yi's woman. I want to create an irreconcilable conflict between the Zi family and Zhou Yi. I will make sure Zhou Yi suffers a miserable fate."

Zhou Yi couldn't help but shudder, looking at Fan Haoyue whose eyes seemed bloodshot, as if they were about to burst. A chill ran down his spine.

It was astonishing how a person, when pushed into a corner with no way out, could become utterly deranged.

At the same time, Zhou Yi had a realization. When a person becomes insane, their actions cannot be judged by conventional standards. Even a minor figure with only sixth-layer inner strength could unleash unimaginable destructive power.

If it weren't for Yuan Lixun recognizing this person and allowing him to overhear their conversation.

The subsequent events can be easily imagined. Not only would Yuan Lixun meet his demise, but it would also lead to animosity between him and the Zi family of Tianluo.

Even if the Zi family were to hand over Zi Ruiguang, it would be difficult to appease his anger. If the entire Zis were uprooted as a result, not only would Shui Xuanjin not stand idly by, but the entire Tianluo Kingdom might become their enemy. If the family were to be implicated in the end... Zhou Yi took a deep breath, his eyes filled with a chilling intent.

Zhou Yi took a deep breath, his eyes gleaming with a chilling resolve.

However, just as he heard the sigh, Fan Haoyue, who had been on the brink of madness, suddenly calmed down. It seemed he realized that his time was running out or recalled something significant. He spoke in a hoarse voice, "Sir, who exactly are you? Can you reveal your true identity and let me die with clarity?"

Zhou Yi was taken aback and asked, "What did you say?"

Fan Haoyue forced a bitter smile and said, "I suddenly remembered that every time my father went to exterminate rival families, he took my elder brother with him. He thought I had weak cultivation and would only be a hindrance, so the three of us never acted together. Yet you just claimed that the three of us invaded your family together, which is utterly impossible."

Zhou Yi was sweating profusely, realizing the flaw in his disguise. He contemplated for a moment, hesitated, and then his facial bones underwent a strange transformation.

Fan Haoyue's eyes grew wider and wider until they were round. He finally saw clearly the familiar face before him, a face that had left an indelible mark in his bones, a memory he could never forget.

"You... you..." his voice trembled, "Zhou Yi."

"Yes, as you said, it's your own fault," Zhou Yi said calmly.

A glimmer of realization flashed in Fan Haoyue's eyes. He finally understood why this person killed Zirui Guang along with Zirui Guang, eliminating any potential threats.

His teeth chattered, and only now did he begin to feel fear.

Zhou Yi reached out and with a powerful force, severed all signs of life within Fan Haoyue.

Then, Zhou Yi tossed him into a dense forest, not bothering to dig a grave or create any burial rituals. This person's malevolence had crossed his bottom line.

When it came to dealing with Lv Xinwen and Fan Haori, Zhou Yi didn't mind burying their bodies. But with this person, although Zhou Yi couldn't bring himself to torture him, he couldn't possibly dig a grave for him either.

After giving Fan Haoyue one last glance, Zhou Yi turned and walked away. His speed reached its peak, allowing him to enter and exit the city walls even in broad daylight without being noticed by anyone.

As for what happened to Fan Haoyue's corpse after Zhou Yi's departure—whether it was devoured by wild beasts or discovered and buried by someone else—Zhou Yi no longer cared.

However, this incident left Zhou Yi with a lingering sense of unease, a faint feeling of impending danger.

Chapter 160

Once back at Shao Ming Ju Residence, Zhou Yi didn't notice anything out of the ordinary. Although the third young master of the Zi family had been assassinated in the city, such an event wouldn't be enough to disturb the tranquil seclusion of Grandmaster Shui Xuanjin. Therefore, the residents of Shao Ming Ju Residence remained oblivious to the incident. Even if they were aware, given the status of Shao Ming Ju Residence, no one would pay it any mind, let alone associate Zhou Yi with the matter.

Zhou Yi's figure floated effortlessly as he entered Yuan Lixun's room. He saw her holding a piece of embroidered handkerchief, gazing at it with a dreamy expression. Her face would flush at times, and her delicate eyebrows would occasionally furrow, as if burdened with unspoken thoughts.

Gently shaking his head, he thought to himself, "Girls indeed tend to be sentimental creatures."

A soft cough brought Yuan Lixun back to her senses. She hastily stood up, tucking the handkerchief into her bosom.

Curiously, Zhou Yi asked, "What were you doing?"

Yuan Lixun's face displayed a hint of embarrassment as she replied in a voice barely audible, "I was looking at the memento left by my mother."

Zhou Yi instantly felt a surge of respect for her. If she considered her mother's belongings important, then her elders would naturally be his elders as well. However, he couldn't fathom why she would blush while looking at her mother's belongings. Shaking his head slightly, he realized that girls' thoughts were too mysterious for him to comprehend.

"Young Master, have you seen it?" As Yuan Lixun noticed that Zhou Yi didn't pursue the topic further, she secretly breathed a sigh of relief and quickly changed the subject.

After pondering for a moment, Zhou Yi replied, "Lixun, you must have seen it wrong. That person simply doesn't exist."

Yuan Lixun paused, about to explain herself, but stopped abruptly when she noticed Zhou Yi winking at her, wearing a peculiar smile on his face.

She hesitated for a moment, then seemed to understand and said, "I understand. Indeed, there is no such person. It was just my eyes playing tricks on me."

When Yuan Lixun first arrived at the Zhou family, she initially referred to herself as a concubine. However, as she spent more time with Zhou Yi, she couldn't remember when it started, but they began addressing each other as equals.

This change wasn't deliberately corrected by anyone; it simply evolved naturally, like water flowing into a canal.

Zhou Yi chuckled softly and said, "Lixun, you must have cultivated up to the fifth level of the water-based technique."

Yuan Lixun's face blushed slightly, and she nodded gently.

To reach the fifth level of the water-based technique at the age of sixteen was considered quite ordinary among the children of prominent families.

After contemplating for a moment, Zhou Yi said, "Lixun, I will ask Shui Brother for a few servants to assist us."

Yuan Lixun's expression immediately changed, the color draining from her face. She lightly bit her lip, lowered her head, and whispered, "Yes, Young Master, I... I will obey."

Zhou Yi hastily waved his hand and said, "Lixun, that's not what I meant." Countless thoughts swirled in his mind as he hurriedly continued, "What I meant was, when I cultivate, it would be best if you are by my side. That way, the progress of your inner energy cultivation should also accelerate. As for those menial tasks and attending to others, let the actual servants handle them. I hope your inner energy can break through to the sixth level or even higher as soon as possible."

Yuan Lixun looked at Zhou Yi in astonishment. At that moment, it seemed as if Zhou Yi had suddenly shed numerous halos.

He no longer appeared to be the innate grandmaster revered by countless people, but merely a sixteen-year-old youth. The kind of tender youthfulness that seemed to have long faded had once again returned to him.

As if understanding something, Yuan Lixun once again lowered her blushing head and emitted a nasal sound that could only be faintly heard, even with attentive ears, with a shy undertone.

However, unlike before, her face once again bloomed with an enchanting blush that left room for imagination.

The city had entered midsummer. The branches of the trees swayed gently, and the weather became scorching at noon. Men and women in the city had donned their summer attire, and throughout the entire Tianluo Kingdom, an air of vitality seemed to permeate.

On this day, several fast horses suddenly arrived at the front of Shao Ming Ju Residence. The servants at the gate initially paid no attention, but when they learned the identity of the visitors, they immediately dispelled their previous arrogance and became cautious.

Shortly after, Zhou Yi, who was practicing cultivation alongside Yuan Lixun, unusually went out to greet the guests. This treatment was even more distinguished than what the King of Tianluo Kingdom would receive.

Outside the estate, two elderly men with rosy complexions and vigorous appearances were accompanied by Zhou Quanxin and his son, all wearing cheerful smiles.

"Grandfather, Grandfather Bao, you're here," Zhou Yi joyfully welcomed them. His gaze shifted to Zhou Laibao, and his face immediately brightened as he said, "Congratulations, Grandfather Bao, congratulations, Grandfather."

Zhou Laibao laughed heartily, his face filled with joy.

Zhou Wude nodded, stroking his beard, and suddenly asked, "Laibao naturally deserves congratulations, but why are you congratulating me?"

Zhou Yi immediately replied respectfully, "Grandfather, your greatest wish was to develop our Zhou family's estate, right? Our Zhou family estate already has you and Uncle as experts at the tenth level of inner energy. Now, with the addition of Grandfather Bao, we have three such powerhouse."

Zhou Wude burst into laughter, saying, "Yi, I didn't expect you to have reached the innate realm already, yet your words are still so sweet."

Zhou Yitian took a step forward and said, "Brother Yi, in our Zhou family estate, we don't just have three experts at the tenth level of inner energy. We also have you, a Innate powerhouse."

Zhou Wude and the others nodded in agreement. Without Zhou Yi, it was likely that not only would they have been unable to obtain these limit-breaking Golden Pills, but even during the initial hunt for the Golden Crown Python, the elite members of the Zhou family estate would have suffered heavy casualties.

Zhou Yi led everyone into his courtyard, and the new maidservants immediately served the best tea as a gesture of hospitality. This was a duty originally assigned to Yuan Lixun, but since Zhou Yi's return, he forcefully took over her responsibilities, insisting that she accompany him in his cultivation.

These maidservants were naturally transferred from other courtyards within Shao Ming Ju Residence. Given Zhou Yi's current status, such a small request would be eagerly fulfilled by countless people if he asked for it.

Shortly after everyone settled down, Grandmaster Shui Xuanjin entered with a hearty laugh.

Upon learning the identity of Grandmaster Shui, Zhou Wude and the others immediately became more reserved. Although Zhou Yi was also an innate grandmaster, he was, after all, their junior.

But Grandmaster Shui was an elderly person over two hundred years old, and just his age alone was like a heavy mountain pressing on everyone's hearts.

Seemingly sensing the discomfort, Grandmaster Shui only stayed for a short while before bidding farewell and leaving, leaving the joy of a family reunion to Zhou Yi.

Zhou Yi naturally understood that for Grandmaster Shui to personally come here and meet his grandfather was a great show of respect. Just by seeing the excitement on his grandfather's and others' faces, he understood the significance of being valued by an innate powerhouse in their hearts.

Thus, he was genuinely grateful for Grandmaster Shui's actions.

After Grandmaster Shui left, everyone relaxed once again. Zhou Wude contemplated for a while and looked at the maidservants around them. He said, "Yi, there's something I want to discuss with you."

Zhou Yi understood and whispered, "You can all leave. There's no need for your service here."

The maidservants, who had received the best training, respectfully bowed and orderly retreated.

Zhou Wude and the others had expressions of satisfaction, realizing that the maidservants in a prominent family were indeed extraordinary. At least, the maidservants in Zhou family estate couldn't possess such qualities.

Yuan Lixun hesitated for a moment and was about to leave when she suddenly felt her wrist being pulled by Zhou Yi. He smiled and said, "Lixun, you're not an outsider. Why go outside?"

Yuan Lixun blushed slightly. Sensing the gazes of Zhou Wude and the others, she felt somewhat embarrassed and lowered her head, unable to look at them. But in her heart, she was filled with a wonderful feeling.

Zhou Wude smiled faintly. Although Yuan Lixun's current status couldn't be compared to Zhou Yi, she was, after all, the granddaughter of an old friend for many years. Seeing that she had gained Zhou Yi's sincere affection, he couldn't help but feel happy for them.

"Yi, Laibao and I have discussed it. Now that he has successfully advanced to the tenth level of inner energy, it's time for us to return to Hengshan."

Zhou Yi looked at his uncle and elder brother. His uncle had a smile on his face, but his elder brother wore an inexplicable expression. Obviously, Grandfather hadn't informed his elder brother.

With a slight smile, Zhou Yi said, "Brother, there's something I know about not long ago."

He explained Zhou Wude and Zhou Laibao's backgrounds but concealed the true reason why they were expelled from the sect. He only mentioned that they violated the rules, which led to their departure from Hengshan.

Zhou Yitian was taken aback, and even Yuan Lixun beside him was surprised. When she learned that Zhou Yi would soon accompany Zhou Wude and Zhou Laibao back to Hengshan, her facial expression couldn't help but change.

Zhou Yitian's eyes were filled with indignation as he said, "Brother Yi, when you go back to Hengshan with Grandfather this time, you must uphold his reputation. Teach a lesson to those who dare to underestimate him."

Zhou Wude smiled wryly and said, "Yitian, don't be silly."

The old man sighed deeply and said, "Before Yi achieved the innate realm, I also often thought about how to make those people regret the insults they made to us, the two brothers, decades ago. But..." He paused and continued, "Since the last time I had an open conversation with Yi and talked about this matter, the knot in my heart with Laibao has been untied. After all, we are all fellow disciples. It's time to let go of some things."

Zhou Yitian widened his eyes and said, "Grandfather, how can you say that?

A peculiar expression appeared on Zhou Wude's face, seeming somewhat ashamed and sorrowful.

"Yitian, before our departure, I had a heartfelt conversation with Lai Bao. If it weren't for my previous mistakes, they wouldn't have treated us so mercilessly. I shattered their only ray of hope, and if the roles were reversed, I'm afraid I wouldn't have treated them any better," the old man said with a bitter smile.

As soon as they heard these words, Zhou Quanxin and Zhou Yi exchanged glances and immediately understood the true meaning behind Zhou Wude's words. If the Innate Golden Pill was successfully refined, it would undoubtedly be chosen by someone among their fellow disciples to consume. Although it might not be themselves, it was still a glimmer of hope.

However, when the dream of the Innate Golden Pill was shattered, it meant that their dream of advancing to the Innate realm was completely crushed. In such a situation, it was understandable that these people couldn't control their emotions.

Zhou Laibao also nodded slightly and said, "For many years, the Old Master and I have held a grudge against our former fellow disciples' final reproach. But it wasn't until Yi stepped into the innate realm that our hearts truly let go. There were reasons behind what happened, and we can't really blame them."

A flicker of realization crossed Zhou Yitian's face. With the conversation reaching this point, he understood that the rules his grandfather and the others had violated in the past were probably not simple. However, as a junior, he felt awkward about directly asking about their mistakes. And judging from his father's expression, it was unlikely that he would mention it either.

Zhou Wude lightly stroked his beard and suddenly said, "Yi, Laibao and I have come to terms with it. While we hope you can join Hengshan and contribute to our sect in any way possible, the decision is ultimately in your hands. If you truly don't want to, then so be it."

Zhou Yi smiled bitterly and said, "Grandfather, you mentioned that the Hengshan lineage has been passed down for thousands of years, is that correct?"

"That's right, the Hengshan lineage has been around for three thousand years," Zhou Wude proudly declared. In his heart, Hengshan, where he had lived for forty years, was forever his pride. Even being expelled from the sect hadn't changed that.

"How is the collection of books in Hengshan?"

"It's extensive."

"If I were to join, would I have the freedom to peruse them at will?"

"You are already an innate grandmaster. Even within Hengshan, you would be among the top figures, so naturally, you would have that privilege."

Zhou Yi spread his hands and said, "Grandfather, since there are such abundant conditions, why would I refuse?"

A smile gradually spread across Zhou Wude's face. He knew very well that Zhou Yi, who hadn't even reached twenty, had achieved the innate realm without consuming any Golden Pills. Such conditions would make him a highly sought-after talent in any sect. No sect would refuse such a genius because everyone knew that Zhou Yi's progress in martial arts was far from stopping.

And of course, the reason he chose Hengshan was due to his own reasons.

"Good, Yi. Since you've made your decision, pack up and prepare to accompany me on the journey," Zhou Wude stood up and said, "We'll set off tomorrow morning."

The old man hurriedly left with Zhou Quanxin and the others. Although their identities were special, they didn't dare to live next to an innate grandmaster. It was more comfortable for them to stay in the royal estate.

After they left, Yuan Lixun suddenly spoke, "Young Master."

Zhou Yi turned around, his expression blank, and asked, "What is it?"

"I...," Yuan Lixun met his gaze and suddenly felt guilty. She lowered her voice and said, "Young Master, I also want to accompany you."

Zhou Yi furrowed his brows and said, "What should we do? It seems that Hengshan doesn't accept female disciples."

Seeing Zhou Yi looking troubled, Yuan Lixun's eyes welled up with tears. She said, "I won't be practicing martial arts. I'll be there to serve you. Can't I do that?"

Zhou Yi quickly said, "Of course, of course you can."

Yuan Lixun was taken aback, surprised by Zhou Yi's sudden change in attitude. She didn't understand why his stance had changed so drastically.

Zhou Yi blinked twice and said, "Lixun, even if you didn't say anything, I would still take you with me. I wouldn't feel comfortable without you."

Yuan Lixun paused for a moment, suddenly realizing the meaning behind his words. Her face turned bright red, and she gently scolded, "Young Master..."

Zhou Yi burst into laughter and quickly walked away, saying, "Lixun, I'll go and inform Master ShuixuanJin. I'll see you later."

Watching Zhou Yi flee as if escaping, Yuan Lixun suddenly found it amusing. After spending this time together, she had come to understand that only in front of his family would Zhou Yi reveal his carefree side, like a true sixteen-year-old child. But in front of others, he was the lofty innate grandmaster with limitless prospects.

In his heart, it seems that I have truly become his family. With this thought, Yuan Lixun felt a mixture of pride, contentment, and a hint of anxiety and a racing heart. Her eyes shimmered, cheeks flushed, as a feeling called happiness surged within her. It seemed that she finally understood what her mother had tirelessly pursued before...

"Zhou, my friend, since you wish to go to Hengshan, I naturally won't oppose it. However, after parting ways today, I'm afraid we may never see each other again," ShuixuanJin let out a long sigh and said.

Zhou Yi remained silent. He didn't know how long it would take to return this time, nor did he know how many more years ShuixuanJin had left.

ShuixuanJin shook his head and said, "Zhou, I hope you will always remember our ten-year agreement. With that, I can peacefully depart."

Zhou Yi nodded solemnly and said, "Elder brother, rest assured, I will never forget about it. But perhaps it won't even take ten years. Within two or three years, I will definitely come down the mountain for a visit."

A smile appeared on ShuixuanJin's face, and he said, "Good. Although my life span is short, I'll still be fine within the next two or three years. When we meet again, I'll treat you to a drink."

Zhou Yi looked at the rosy-faced old man, realizing that apart from him, there were only a few who knew that ShuixuanJin's life was as fleeting and fragile as a candle in the wind.

A tinge of sadness flickered in his eyes as a strange thought emerged in his mind. Human life is truly fleeting, even for the powerful cultivators of the Hundred Scattered Heavens, whose lifespan is merely a little over two hundred years. Compared to them, the spiritual beasts have lifespans that reach several hundred years. Zhou Yi couldn't help but wonder if, as humans continued to cultivate, there would come a day when they could surpass those powerful naturally nurtured spiritual beasts in terms of lifespan.

Printed in Great Britain
by Amazon

38909743R00407